# THE MONSOON WAR

## Also by Bina Shah

Before She Sleeps
A Season For Martyrs
Slum Child

# THE MONSOON WAR

a novel

BINA SHAH

Delphinium Books

THE MONSOON WAR



Printed in the United States of America


For information, address DELPHINIUM BOOKS, INC.,
16350 Ventura Boulevard, Suite D
PO Box 803
Encino, CA 91436

Library of Congress Cataloguing-in-Publication Data is
available on request.
ISBN 978-1-953002-23-5
23 24 25 26 27 LBC 5 4 3 2 1

*Jacket and interior design by Colin Dockrill, AIGA*

Girls are coming out of the woods,
wrapped in cloaks and hoods,
carrying iron bars and candles
and a multitude of scars

—Tishani Doshi, "Girls
Are Coming Out of the Woods"

Men invented war; women invented resistance.
—Yasmina Khadra

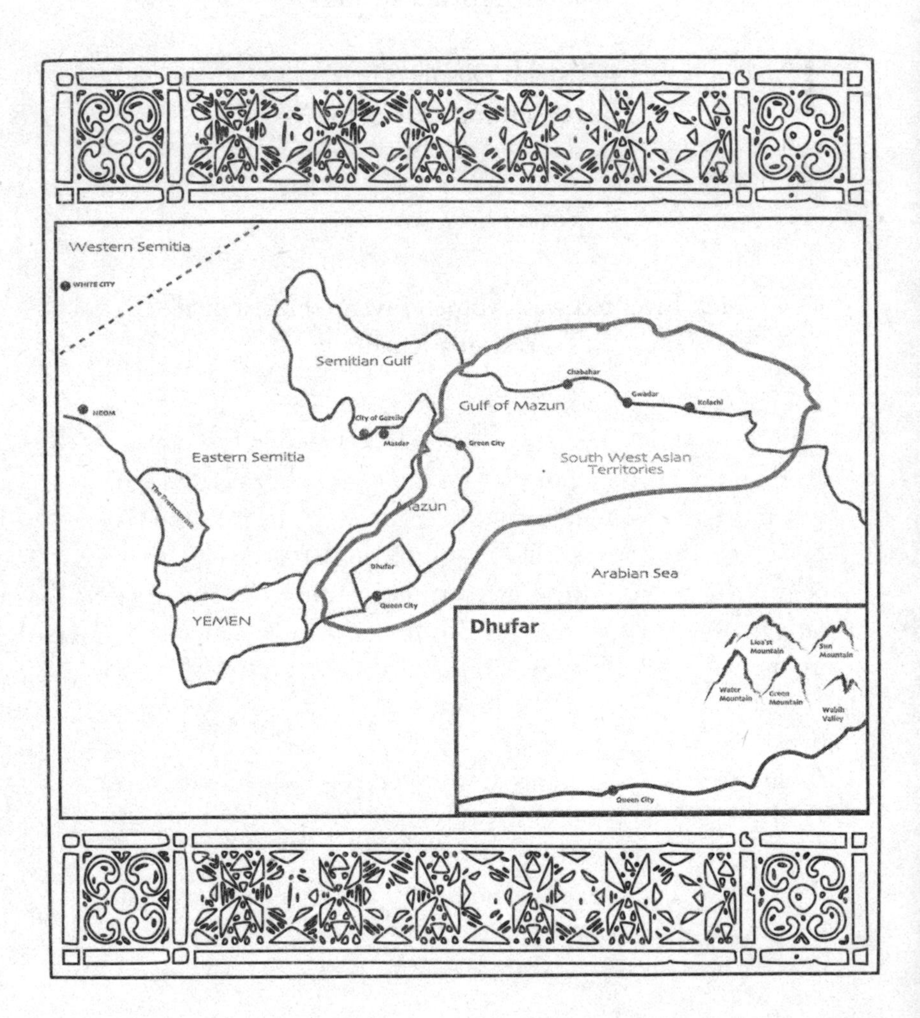
Western Semitia
WHITE CITY
NEOM
Semitian Gulf
City of Gazelle
Masdar
Eastern Semitia
The Protectorate
Gulf of Mazun
Chabahar
Gwadar
Kolachi
Green City
South West Asian Territories
Mazun
Dhufar
Queen City
YEMEN
Arabian Sea
Dhufar
Sun Mountain
Water Mountain
Green Mountain
Queen City

# PROLOGUE

## The Black Thread

In the public square of a small town in Dhofar, three days' drive away from Green City, a black veil hangs from the end of a lamppost. It flaps in the wind, a flock of crows, the sail of a pirate ship, rippling in the sky as twilight retreats and the black thread of night approaches.

The few passersby going home at sunset do a double-take; at first it looks like the body of a woman suspended in the air. Then they gawk as they realize that there is no woman there. It is as if she has simply climbed to the top of the pole, taken off her clothes, and flown away.

Within several hours, town officers come to cut it down and send it to the state lab for analysis. The owner of the veil must be DNA-identified so that she can be punished for her act of rebellion. Local officers overlook reporting the veil to the Agency, thinking it too minor a crime. So the image fails to appear on the Metro Bulletin, and officially, nobody knows what has happened in the Wabiha Valley. The Agency would never let it air anyway; it could provoke disturbances on the streets of Green City, Kolachi, Gwadar, Chabahar. The Agency wants nothing but silence about these kinds of petty crimes, symbolic, provocative, but ultimately meaningless as they are.

But someone snaps a photo, and the illicit image of the hanging black veil quickly circulates from one home to the next. It is passed along from device to device, seen by untold pairs of eyes. Witnessed in darkness, alone, or in front of others, the screen tilted away to shield the image from being discovered by someone who would inform the Agency of its existence.

The black veil does different things to different people: For some, it causes a rush of illicit excitement at the sight of the abandoned garment; for others, it causes the cold fingers of fear to wrap around their throats in the middle of the night. Teenage girls begin to talk to one another about what the veil means. Women have been known to strip themselves naked when they go insane, so perhaps this is just the action of a lone madwoman, another one of those lost souls whose reason has abandoned her under the pressure of caring for children and Husbands.

It's said that those women are sent for extensive treatment and rehabilitation to a pristine white building, next to the Girls' Markaz, pumped full of drugs, and sent back within months to continue their mission of pregnancy and childbirth, pregnancy and childbirth. The drugs don't harm the fetuses and they make the women calm, unafraid. A humane treatment for the genetically flawed.

Some say the black veil is a growing sign of the immorality that has been taking hold in Green City, producing women who no longer obey. It's been thirty years since the Perpetuation Bureau diktats ordained women to their natural roles. Women who refused to sleep with their Husbands or wouldn't eat in an attempt to be too weak to fall pregnant were dealt with according to the gravity of their crime. Reluctants fell into line, once "convinced" of their previous misconceptions about their role in Mazun's future. Some of them had even become trainers at the Markaz, the most enthusiastic cheerleaders for the new system. Nobody is more qualified to spread a new way of life than a recent convert, once she's been assured of forgiveness for all her past sins.

But life is a little more relaxed now. The Perpetuation Bureau has eased up on some of its regulations since infant girl birth rates have risen nicely in the last five years. The women have been working so hard at saving Mazun from catastrophe, they deserve a little leeway. Some argue that this is a mistake, that the country will lose its grip on the women, and that the authorities will soon regret their leniency. For the pessimists, the discarded black veil is a symbol of this laxity.

Of course, the officers can find no trace of DNA nestled in the veil's black threads. Whoever put the veil up on the lamppost is not that careless. Nor can it be traced to any store in Dhofar. What is clear is that its owner didn't buy that veil anywhere in Dhofar, nor did she ever intend to wear it. It's as if she pulled it out of the air, out of nowhere, a magician's trick with a scarf and sleight of hand. And then she climbed up to the top of the tallest structure in the town and strung it up to the extended metal branch that held the lamp over the Square, extinguishing its light.

Scores of kohl-rimmed eyes widen when they see it, sharp and clear on the screens that they hide from their Husbands and children. They know exactly what it is: A sign that something big is coming. A signal not to lose hope. And a warning to the authorities, the Collectors, the Agency, the Bureau, that something big is about to happen in Dhofar.

# PART ONE

## The Wife

# 1.

Alia surveys the items on her pantry shelves, her eyes taking in the bottles, cans, boxes arranged in careful symmetry, according to her meticulous likes and dislikes.

A strong smell comes from one of her large pickling jars. Tears prickle her eyes. She hates preparing torshi in her own home; the stench haunts the corners of the house for weeks, getting into their clothes and drapes, the cushions on the chairs. It's impossible to wash out of her hair or get it off her hands, no matter how many lemons she rubs over her skin until it stings.

But her children love the tart, sharp taste of any pickles: radishes, onions, or turnips, they crave them all. When she makes mango torshi with turmeric and saffron, the children dance around her and catch her legs in the tangle of their small arms, thanking her and smothering her with their kisses. Torshi laces the blandest meal with a kind of divine combustion that makes their eyes roll back into their heads with pleasure. Her torshi draws compliments from her Husbands, who fight over the leftovers. Making sour pickles is how she achieves peace between them; otherwise they would fight over her instead.

Ever since Alia gave birth to her second set of twins, her nose has become so sensitive that she nearly faints at the height of summer, with all the smells of the village—composting garbage, fertilizer, animal droppings—assaulting her from morning till night. She vomits nearly every week, pregnant or not. She deliberately keeps her own meals bland, saving all the herbs and spices for the family's meals. The smells that waft from her kitchen window attract the attention of the entire village.

All of them, small farmers living in terraced steps cut out of the north side of Sun Mountain, stock their cupboards and closets with government rations and whatever they can cultivate on their small plots of land. The other women are all envious of how Alia creates such wonders from the simple, meager ingredients they all have access to. "What's so special about her hands?" they gossip to one another. "I heard she uses spells to bewitch her Husbands. They eat shit and think it's roasted lamb!" But the truth is their household's land is more fertile than many of the other households. The yields are better, the crops more resilient in recent years.

Alia has no real secrets, except for a new device, made to look very old, its screen cracked, its buttons barely working. She swears to keep it forever because it houses all her most valuable recipes. The Frontier Office promised them all new devices three years ago, but no sign of them ever arrived in their village.

The real value of her device: It connects to the Spectrum, a network whose signal can sometimes be caught from the mountainside, if you stand in the right spot at the right time. On it, Alia sees video clips and news flashes talking about unfamiliar places, people, and events. She thinks they come from Eastern Semitia; she isn't sure. But she knows the broadcasts don't come from Green City.

Alia turns her mind back to the torshi; some is missing from her pantry. Her grandmother, who had come across the sea from Chabahar, was the source of the recipes for all the different types of torshi, none of which the Sun Mountain's people had ever tasted before.

The Wife is crafty and thrifty, stockpiling whatever surplus comes from the crops to barter them for little items of more exotic food brought into town by traders from other parts of the Territories. The cultivated meat, the laboratory-crafted vegetables, and the soy proteins are too expensive for the villagers. The rations come from warehouses filled with leftovers from the Wars and the abandoned space missions: processed, minimized, packed in tubes and pouches, irradiated, thermostabilized. The soldier rations were meant for young men at the peak of their health and energy, but the space food lacks salt or fat, keeping the explorers dissatisfied, even when full. Some of the meals have terrible chemical tastes; others just taste spoiled.

Alia's children once fed some of the rations to a wild goat that they wanted to tame and keep in the courtyard. It had eaten out of their hands for a week, then promptly died. Her children don't get sick from eating the rations, so they don't complain. None of them want to be charged for Refusal by the Collector who oversees the distribution of the rations once a month in the town square.

When the Wife prepares anything that was alive only a few hours ago, before being cut down or slaughtered or plucked from a tree, it's like a hit of the purest drug. She shares, but not too generously—she can tolerate the other Wives' snide remarks, and a little of her rice-vermicelli dessert shuts them up for at least a week. Her children need friends; they all roam their village in packs, commanding the back lanes and alleyways with the savagery of street cats. Every day a dozen children troop through her house and sometimes she can't tell her own from the rest. They've all grown alike over the years, tangled hair, patched clothes, dirty faces. She recognizes her children by their smell: sweeter, more innocent than the others—another benefit of fresh food and the alchemy of her cooking.

When she first noticed things going missing from her pantry, she suspected one of the village children. Any one of them could have been instructed by their mother to steal a jar of date jam or a tin of curry. Hunger binds them all together, robs them of their pride. She'd sent her own children to scavenge from others' garbage when the crops had failed or the monsoon rains had flooded them out.

She doubts she'll ever discover the thief's identity. All their houses were built in the years before the Agency installed low-cost cameras and heat sensors in all homes. The Works Department has been updating their houses, but they've forgotten this hamlet on the desolate north side of the mountain. The small, cramped huts dotting the mountains stay warm in the winter and cool in the summer, thanks to the rooftops' mix of white bio-concrete and limestone. They're lucky to have roofs over their heads, but fancy surveillance equipment is not meant for people like them.

As Alia counts her cans and tins for the fourth time, she thinks about how the farther away people lived from Green City, the less benefits and the more problems they see. Last year a monsoon caused a landslide that blocked one of the long tunnels under the Three Brides, a trio of mountain peaks named after the snowy veils they wear in the winter. Two months they left us to rot, Alia thinks as she shifts boxes and bottles back and forth, trying to see if something's fallen to the back of the cupboard. But no, there are still two rounds of soft goat's cheese and four parcels of flatbread missing. And where's the precious jar of olives that she's made last for almost a year now?

The government dropped extra rations by drone throughout the days of entrapment and the children of the village clambered up and down the mountain to see who could nab the most pouches and boxes. Her own children brought home no less than twenty-five of the wretched things, throwing them triumphantly at her feet like a cat bringing dead animals to its owner's doorstep. But who wanted to eat more of their rotten space food and soldier's meals? Each bite tasted like surrender to the ways of the city, instead of the life of the mountains. The mountains had birthed them, these hard, rocky people who survived only by the toil of their own hands.

Finally the South West Asia Army's Engineering Corps blasted through the rocks and reestablished road links between this side of the mountain and the lower villages. The villagers were desperate by the time the first Army trucks rolled into the village; their solar panels had nearly worn out with the strain of recharging their electric grids and their moto-bikes. Many of them had fallen sick, including Alia's children. They'd eaten the saffron and walnuts and juniper berries from the storage shelves. This meant no cash crop for at least another four months, until the next crops were ready for the harvest.

No, the people of far-off, prosperous Green City care little for the ones in all of Dhofar, let alone the outcasts on Sun Mountain. The Wife grows cold and hateful whenever she thinks of the rich Leaders, driving on smooth roads in cars that cost more money than she'll ever see in her lifetime. The wealthy, well-fed city Wives who receive the best of medical care for their pregnancies, and only get assigned two Husbands at the most.

Let them spend a winter here, she thinks. Let them try to feed the number of mouths they've foisted on us. The fertility workers they send to weigh the women in Wabiha and check on their menstrual cycles find it difficult to reach Sun Mountain. The only people who spit in their direction are the Collectors, who come to harass them and extract money in surplus of what they claim Green City's owed. But the people of Sun Mountain resist, all the same.

"Noor!" Alia calls out, suddenly losing her patience with the stench of the pickles, the claustrophobia, and her own resentful thoughts turning round and round in her head. Resistance be damned. She backs out of the pantry, gulping cleaner air. "Noor!"

Her youngest child tumbles into the kitchen, short dark hair standing straight up in bristles, two fists rubbing against a pair of sleep-encrusted bright blue eyes. She'll get the truth out of Noor; catlike, quick-footed, clear-hearted, he can never lie to her. The five older ones always band together, trying to fool her into mistaking one for the other. Only Noor is vulnerable, having no double to hide behind.

"Noor, has anyone been inside the pantry since yesterday?" Alia gestures with her jaw toward the pantry. "I think some of the torshi is missing."

"No, Ma, I haven't seen anyone," singsongs Noor. The Wife loves the soft, sweet voices of her children. The eldest is sixteen, the twins are already pubescent, the fourth and fifth nearly eight years old. Noor is the baby of the family. The Wife never wants this last, most special childhood to end.

How anyone could have sneaked into the pantry to steal food is beyond her; she's always in the kitchen during the day. At night, she and the Husband whose allotted night it is pull down the mattress leaning against the wall to fulfill the Bureau's reproductive requirements in ways either mechanical or dutiful, depending on her state of exhaustion. Everyone else shares the other room, which doubles as a day room and study area for the children—those of them who care to study anyway. Whoever doesn't want to be trapped among the snores and the stale warmth of night bodies creeps up to sleep on the roof.

Most of the children start the night with their fathers and end up on the roof, giggling and punching one another until they all fall asleep like puppies, arms and legs everywhere. Lately, Noor goes up with the others, where they lie awake late into the night and watch the constellations wheeling above them. They give the stars ridiculous names, like "Donkey" and "Broken Axle" and "Vomit," or spend hours imitating all the adults in the village, especially the schoolteacher, whom they hate more than anyone else in their lives.

Alia shouts at them when Noor appears in the mornings with dark circles cut into his soft cheeks just under his eyes: They should know better than to keep the youngest up so late, but what better did any of them know? It's her fault for being an ignorant woman, for not teaching them better.

"Think hard, Noor," says Alia. "See it in your mind, like a picture." Noor is smarter and sharper than the rest; he's often her eyes and ears against the others. Their rough-and-tumble ways, their never-ending tumult, exhausts her on the best of days.

A rapid succession of blinks, then a regretful shake of his head. "No. I haven't seen anyone." Noor sticks his thumb back into his mouth, no matter how often she tells him to give up the bad habit. The blue eyes, though, give her a different answer.

Alia is good at reading eyes. Eyes tell the truth when tongues and mouths lie. The widening of pupils, the small muscles that lift the eyebrows, the rapid blinking in a state of high tension, the darting back and forth of a glance trying to search out the closest means of escape. She reads Noor's eyes now, as clear and transparent as mountain pools, and sees the lie within them. She doesn't press the matter further, but she becomes more watchful over Noor's comings and goings, noting when her youngest whispers to one of the brothers, or distracts her with a cheerful greeting or sudden burst of tears for no apparent reason.

One morning, she makes Noor stay back in the house and help clear up the dishes. The older children are at a sports day at school, competing in the races. Her Husbands finish breakfast quickly and make their way to their small farm, where the saffron is ready to flower. They must weed and grub the land religiously in the month before the fields turn into glorious carpets of purple.

Fifty years earlier, the people grew roses in this area for perfumes and attars and pastries and soaps. Then the rivers dried up and plunged the villages into grim drought. The khareef, the monsoon, did not arrive properly for years, thought to be one of the late aftereffects of the Final War. The rose business died off; most people moved away from the villages. Sun Mountain became brown with death.

Saffron wasn't native to the mountain, but the Farm Assistance Program brought them free corms and taught the villagers how to plant and harvest them. They were given special vacuum tubes to remove the spice from the stigmas, a job that their forefathers would have had to do by hand. Less water was needed for saffron than for roses. Still, in some places they were able to rebuild the aflaj, the system of water channels their forefathers had etched into the mountainsides to bring water to arid land.

The saffron went to Green City, whose pharmaceutical companies extracted chemicals from the spice to produce all sorts of formulations for Alzheimer's, depression, arthritis—diseases that the villagers know and suffer from but cannot name.

The saffron brought in some money and some people began to trickle back into the mountains, to try their luck. Even the khareef eventually returned, and turned the mountains lush and fertile again.

Their villages are cursed still, though, because no girls are ever born here. They meet the quotas for cultivation but have failed, year after year, to meet the quota for this other crop, more precious than saffron, roses, or even gold.

Instead of punishing them, though, the authorities leave them alone. They're only a few villages on a forsaken mountainside, perhaps inbred with a genetic mutation that makes the women completely unable to bear girls. When they die out, this unwitting aberration, too, will come to an end.

"Can't I go with my Papas?" Noor's voice is a chirrup that peaks and dips like a swallow in flight.

"Son," says Alia's youngest Husband, the one with Noor's blue eyes, "stay with Mama and help her. Soon you'll be big enough to come with us, but right now, Mama needs you."

Noor grows tearful. The young Husband, quiet and bookish, unlike the other two, who are men of the earth as craggy and browned as the mountains, kneels down and clasps the child to his chest. "I'll bring you a pomegranate. They're beautiful right now, round and ripe. They're so heavy, they hang low to the ground and the goats try to nibble at them."

"Okay, Papa." Noor giggles. "But make sure it's the biggest."

"I will, my son. It'll be as big as your head." And then, to the Wife, "You look beautiful today." He's gone before she can remind him that she's not beautiful, she's weathered and beaten down, like all the women in this village, and in the world, as far as she knows. His tender falsehoods make her ache for his arms around her at night.

The Wife starts to run the water for the dishes. Then she turns from the sink and also kneels down in front of Noor. "Noor-darling."

Adoration is written all over his young, sweet face, his cheeks still rounded, milk teeth still intact. She carried this child beneath her ribs for nine months, every cell of her body had attended to his survival. She doesn't feel made for this business of mothering and Wiving, but her love for Noor is so strong, it consumes her until only her throbbing heart reminds her she's still alive and sentient.

"You can tell me the truth, that you've been taking the food. I understand. I won't get angry. There's not nearly enough to eat for all of us, nothing good anyway, and I know you get hungry. You're growing so fast. Look at you, so big already! So . . . tell Mama. It is you, isn't it?"

Noor's head dips. His round ears look like the handles of a small jug, slightly protruding from his finely knitted scalp. She could reach out and hold those ears in her hands and turn Noor's head this way and that, as if pouring a cup of tea. Or she could pull hard, to extract the truth out of her child.

But Noor's silence is an emphatic refusal to obey her, for the first time. Somewhere Noor has learned a new code, found new loyalties. Never before has the child refused to tell her something when she asks.

"Then who is it? Your brothers?"

Noor brings his upper teeth down on his bottom lip, chewing it worriedly, as if trying to stop the words from spilling out. "I can't . . ."

"I promise I won't let them do anything to you. You can tell me."

Suddenly the child bolts for the door, arms and legs flying.

"Noor! Stop! Come back here!" Alia runs after her child. She stops at the door, fingernails clutching the doorframe, breathing hard, looking at the tap running in the sink. She can't waste the precious rainwater that took weeks to collect and store. Cursing, she dashes back to the sink, pulls the tap shut, then goes after her child.

She sees Noor scrambling down the dirt path in front of the house, sure-footed as a mountain gazelle. All her children know every dip and drop of the way, but so does she, and her legs are longer. As she tears down the path, she decides, with animal-like instinct, not to stop Noor, but to give chase. He'll lead her to the thief, or thieves. He's fleeing the burden of her mistrust, too much for his childish heart to bear.

Noor will head for the east trail, wide and well worn, that leads to the terraced fields and the small dam on the watercourse that irrigates the crops. Husbands often give the children shelter against their mothers' anger, letting them play with a spade and chase butterflies in between the rows of newly tilled earth. All the village children trudge past the fields, taunting their elder brothers who toil with their fathers, in search of a mythical wadi on the far side of the farmland. They gambol through the sideways-growing date palms, pushing aside brush and scrubs until they stumble into the riches of the shallow waters, chasing after toads, beetles, dragonflies, worms. Alia did the same when she was a girl, dreaming of the wadi before womanhood claimed her as its prisoner.

Instead of going east, Noor cuts across the small copse of acacia trees where the trails merge, and flees down a steep narrow path that goes west, toward the rocky outcrops too barren to till, or to graze animals on. The path once connected to another village lower down the valley, but a flash flood destroyed that village about ten years ago. Over the years the path has become a thin straw of dirt, barely used.

Alia follows Noor at a distance. She doesn't want the child to spot her and stop, or worse, fall. The farther away from the copse, the bleaker the terrain: jagged rocks of charcoal gray and smoky slate wait to turn an ankle or break a foot, while steep mountain walls, brown and dry as snakeskin, watch them both with indifference.

The blue sky cups the edges of the mountains and domes away into heights as cold as space. If anything happens to either of them, if they die out here, their bones will become part of the mountains, and nobody would ever know.

The Wife's legs ache with the effort of walking down with her knees half bent and thighs flexed to balance herself against gravity's pull. The villagers climb up and down all day, their leg muscles powerful and their lungs conditioned to endure. Still, this is a long, difficult distance for her. Noor moves with confidence, as if he's spent many hours traversing up and down this abandoned path.

After a half hour, the sun travels higher in the sky and the colors of the rock walls begin to change from dark gray to dull red, spread in rippling strata. Clouds alternate with the sun; the valley is dappled with shadow and sharp sunlight, like the patches of a quilt. Alia is momentarily distracted by the magnificence of the vista, and sees something glinting several hundred meters below.

A black car lies in a wreck at the bottom of a cliff. Alia stops in her tracks, even as Noor keeps moving, feeling his way down with his hand touching the rock wall for balance. Is that where Noor is going, drawn to the mass of twisted metal and broken glass like an arrow finding its target? What if it exploded as Noor gets to it?

"Noor!" A fear beyond her control rips the scream from her throat. It flies down to the child's ears like an eagle with its claws out. From far away she sees the child start, then look up and around to see where she is. There's no mistaking his mother's voice, imprinted on his cells since the moment of his conception.

She remembers the hour of his birth, thick dark hair plastered wetly on the baby's scalp, head and face misshapen with the effort of pushing his way out of her body. She couldn't stop him then, can't stop him now even if he falls down the cliff to the twisted metal hulk below.

Alia's hand clutches at her collarbone as she watches Noor wobble, putting out his small hands to regain his balance on the slope. Soon, he steadies himself and continues to climb down. Alia follows, pebbles and stones dislodged by her own feet raining down the path in front of her. It becomes a moving slide. She falls heavily on her backside, spilling down the trail in a tumble of flailing arms and legs.

When she comes to a stop, the palms of her hands are bleeding. She wriggles her feet cautiously, then thanks the Warrior Queen that her ankles aren't turned or broken from the fall. Adrenaline forces her heart into a rapid drumbeat, accelerating once more when she realizes that Noor has disappeared again.

## 2.

Alia crawls the rest of the way on her hands and knees, stones graze her shins, but she won't stop until she finds Noor.

She pushes herself upright, wincing. The underside of her robe is ripped; one shoe has come off and gotten lost somewhere. She finds it underneath her and slips it back on. Tears gather at the corners of her eyes. She leans back against the rock wall, and casts her eyes out into the valley. A few dark birds wheel lazily against the ice-blue sky. Walking out a few paces to the edge of the trail, she spots the ribbon of road winding through the mountain curves that must have brought the car in this direction. She's only about fifty meters above the wreck now.

It was once an elegant machine, all smooth lines and polished surfaces: a large sedan, with blackened windshields and hologram markings. Light-sensitive paint still glows against the shadows cast on its hull by the tree that stopped it, a solid thirty-foot juniper at least one hundred years old. In time the harsh mountain wind and sharp sun will dry it out, fade its colors. It looks like a spider stepped on by a giant, its insides bursting out of the man-made exoskeleton.

Alia tries to see its license plate, but the bent bumper pushes the plate underneath the body. No one's ever seen a car like this around here; who would want to come to this godforsaken part of the mountain anyway? Has anyone else besides Noor discovered the car? The trail looks unused; the flowers are tangled at its edges, and weeds push through the path, ready to swallow it up from sight.

Noor. She curses the car for distracting her. "Noor? Noor? Where are you, Noor?"

The mountain muffles the sound of her voice. She steps carefully around a pile of rocks, turns a few feet, then calls out in a different direction. "Noor? Noor, answer me, child! Nooooor!" Why won't he call back to her?

"Noooooorr . . ."

Her voice is thrown back to her in an echo. An echo means a cavern; a cavern means that there is shelter somewhere. Is that where Noor's hiding?

Alia looks up and down, left and right, and spies it almost immediately, a small indentation behind a boulder. Stepping forward a few careful paces more, rounding the boulder, the indentation changes and becomes a hole, an opening into solid rock wall. She kneels down and puts a cautious hand in, feeling around for bats, snakes, a small warm body.

Her arm sinks all the way into open space, and she sees a bunch of small stones piled there. She kicks them away and the hole becomes a gaping mouth. It grows bigger and bigger. Her stomach jumps; is this the lair of a leopard or a wolf, hiding cubs from hungry foxes or eagles? Are there mountain snakes waiting to sink their fangs into her foot if she treads on their nests?

Her love for her child is bigger than her fear. Once the rocks are cast aside, she thrusts herself into the gap, wriggles in like a worm, and suddenly she finds herself inside the mountain. A small cave, where the gap widens out into a chamber barely four and a half feet high, perhaps ten feet long. And it isn't empty.

The darkened space is dank and sea-like, a briny-foamy-musty smell rises to her nostrils, making her gag with its powerful stench.

"Hello, Mama."

Forcing herself to breathe slowly instead of dragging the dust into her lungs in large gasps, Alia peers into the darkness, eyes slowly adjusting to the lack of light.

"Noor, where are you?"

"I'm right here."

Noor is not alone. There are other eyes watching her, other faces lined up against the cave wall, staring at her.

Alia stumbles and falls, hitting her forehead on the stone floor. Somehow she ends up on her back. The faces circle around her, looking down anxiously; Noor holds her hand, crying. "Wake up, Mama, wake up. I'm sorry I ran away. Please wake up now, Mama."

Alia blinks slowly. Dim light streams in from the cave's entrance. She's still in that weird place between the conscious and unconscious. She might still recognize this as a dream and wake up on the mattress in her own kitchen, next to one or the other of her Husbands.

"Give her some space . . . she needs air."

"Do we have any water?"

"Give her a blanket."

Alia tries to sit up and eight hands reach down to help her.

"Who are you?" she whispers. The faces register uncertainty at how to answer her. Women's faces: different skin tones, pale and dark, long hair and short, all looking slightly thin and fragile.

One of them nearly speaks, when Noor pipes up: "They came from Green City"

Alia is bewildered. "How did they get here? Why are they here?"

The woman with the nose ring speaks up. "I'm Rupa." Her voice reminds the Wife of an anklet that she wore when she was a girl: Its tiny bells, delicate and singsong, chimed when she moved. For a second, Alia sees herself as this woman, slim, with dark hair that falls beyond her waist. Young, before the marriages and the children. What she could have been, what she'd never had a chance to be. She shudders at this glimpse into a different life.

The others, emboldened by Rupa's overture, press forward: a pale woman with silver-gray eyes; an African woman with dozens of thin braids; a young girl, barely out of her teens. They hesitate, sensing Alia's fear.

Noor says, "This is Grace. Diyah. Mariya." He points to each one in turn, his voice echoing off the cave walls, the sibilance of consonants surrounding them like ghosts. These women seem to glow eerily in the darkness of the cave. Long silken hair, milky limbs, curved hips and breasts that make the Wife want to look away from them in shame and dislike.

They wait for her to introduce herself. Their eyes are fixated on the Wife. The weight of their stares is an unbearable tension on her body.

She gathers all her strength to whisper, "I'm . . . Alia." The word she hasn't spoken in years—decades. Her name. It's the tradition of the mountain not to use women's names, to replace them with their familial ties: Wife of. Mother of. Daughter of. She says her name again, trying it out in her mouth. "Alia. My name is Alia." It grows to nonsense in her mouth and she falls silent again.

"They're lost, Mama. They need our help." Noor reaches a hand out to the nearest woman, the one with the cloud of black hair and the small gold nose ring shining in her nostril. Rupa.

Noor brings Rupa's hand close to Alia's, then joins them together. "I want to help them. They're my friends."

Alia takes each of the women's hands in turn, remembering a picture on her screen of a black abaya flapping in the wind. Why are these women not wearing veils?

"Did you really come all the way from Green City?" she asks them.

"Yes, we really did," says Rupa. "Well, from the outskirts. We live—" She turns to the others, and Alia can see them nod, giving her permission to continue.

"Underground," adds the woman with the silvery eyes: Diyah. "In hiding."

"From who?" says Alia. "Your Husbands? Have you run away from them? I've never heard of anyone doing that." The air is heavy and cold, and in a far-off corner she hears a scratching, rustling noise. Bats, rats, or a snake? This isn't a welcoming place for anyone to hide in for long. The temperature at night drops down to zero outside; the women will freeze if they stay here much longer. "Are there more of you?"

Rupa looks to the others again, more hesitantly this time.

The woman with the braids, Grace, speaks then, her voice slow and warm. "We never had Husbands." She crosses her arms in front of her, her body now a closed door. They're shrouded in shadows and secrets, these women.

"But everyone has Husbands," says Noor. "My mama has three."

Grace moves a few steps away from the circle, facing the cave wall. The others slowly break away and join her, Rupa last, with an apologetic glance at Alia. They huddle together and whisper furiously among themselves. It isn't hard to guess what they're saying. We have to trust her. But we can't. But we have no one else. Without her, we'll die.

Noor's been stealing food to keep them alive, his new friends. And he's landed her in the middle of an unfolding catastrophe. Yes, even a child of six understands that every woman has Husbands, and those without are not normal, not proper. And if they're in hiding, someone is looking for them.

Alia looks at her feet twisting in their rubber sandals against the stone floor of the cave. She tries to control her breathing, to slow down the drumming of her heart.

She brushes her hand over Noor's head, feeling the shape of his fine skull underneath her fingers. What would these women say if they knew the secret Alia was really keeping, like all the other women of the village, of Sun Mountain? That Noor is actually not a boy, but a girl. That the mothers raise all their daughters as boys from birth in order to shield them from the Collectors, who comb the mountainside looking for girls to enter into Green City's cursed system of multiple marriages.

Alia had first become aware of the practice as a young girl herself, when one day a friend of hers, Salwa, had disappeared from the village. Apparently, Salwa and her mother had gone on a trip to visit relatives in another part of the mountain. Salwa's mother returned after several weeks, but Salwa did not; it was said that her uncle and aunt had asked to keep her on for the entire summer.

Then, a month after that, a boy appeared, whom Alia had not seen before, walking along the pathway that led to the far fields. The boy did not speak to Alia, and ran ahead of her before Alia could see his face properly. But there was something familiar in the way he moved: a flash of Salwa in the tilt of his head and the way his elbows flapped out. Salwa's mother said this was Salwa's cousin, Hisham. He had

had a bout of ill health and his parents thought the air of the higher peaks would do him some good.

Alia reported the appearance of Hisham to her mother later in the day, but her mother didn't pay much attention to the news. Alia felt let down, that night, when she woke up for a drink of water and overheard her mother talking to her father in the kitchen. "Sloppily done," said Alia's mother. "If you want to get it right, you have to hold the intention the day your daughter is born."

*Get what right?* thought Alia to herself, crouched in a corner, listening in the dark.

Her Husband grunted his agreement. "The Collectors don't pay much attention to us up here, she probably thought she could get away with it."

*Get away with what?* Alia thought.

"They'll notice, once the women here start to do it more. And they will, trust me. It's not the same for me, I'm too old, but the younger lot, they don't want to lose their daughters to the Collectors anymore."

"It might work," replied Alia's father. "If they're clever about it. Your women's ruses somehow always seem to work. Like you said, decide from the day the child's born. Or even before."

Alia didn't know about the Collectors—she'd never seen one, although she knew they were fearsome—but she began to notice, over the following weeks and months, that every once in a while, a girl vanished, and in her place, a boy came back. The girls were always younger than Alia. If an older girl vanished, that meant she'd been married to someone on another part of the mountain. And a boy never materialized in her stead.

As Alia grew older, she realized the boys who appeared looked like the girls who had gone. Alia probably had always known, unconsciously, that the lost girl and the found boy were one and the same, but it seemed to happen so seamlessly, so ordinarily, that everyone just easily accepted it as a part of their ordinary lives. Nobody spoke about it.

With the passing of another few years, it seemed that boys were everywhere, that girls weren't even being born anymore. The Husbands pretended not to notice that their daughters were disappearing, being replaced with sons.

As the practice spread, a rumor began to spread with it: that the Virus, which had killed so many women and girls in the Gender Emergency, had somehow made a resurgence on the mountain. Perhaps the Virus had found its way through winds that pushed nuclear fallout to the peaks of Dhofar, into their water supply, and the women were drinking contaminated snowmelt containing shreds of the Virus, thus affecting their fertility and their wombs. That was why so many boys were being born, alas, but perhaps it was a generational issue and in five years things would go back to normal. Except that things never did.

The authorities in Sheba City promised to send experts to the mountains of Dhofar to investigate the phenomenon. But the experts never showed up. Every once in a while, a Collector would come to the village and gather the village committee at the Collector House. "What's wrong with all of you, no girls again this year?"

The villagers remained mulishly silent. The Collector wanted to threaten to have all the boys taken for medical examination, but he knew he could never carry out the threat; it would be a step too far. The villagers would riot, overpower him, and throw him down a ravine. It was only one small village; who would really want a girl from such a desolate place anyway? She'd probably be more like a goat or a sheep than a human. The Collector rationalized his failure to bring back any girls in this way, telling his superiors that the people of the village were damaged from too much inbreeding.

When Alia was married for the first time and pregnant with her first child, she stayed home while her Husband went to toil in the fields. Normally Alia would have been helping him, but during pregnancy, women were excused from farmwork. The small house was quiet and still dark in the winter morning, Alia taking a break from chopping vegetables to sit for a few minutes with a cup of ginger tea. She hoped it would work against the horrible morning sickness that had afflicted her from the first month; her ninth month seemed very far away from today . . .

There was a sudden knocking on the window. Alia looked up to see Elham and Wadad, two women of the village who were close to her age. They had both been married and given birth within the last three years. "Sister Alia," said Elham, "let us in, we want to talk to you."

Alia hefted herself off her stool and went outside, pulling her shawl around her shoulders. She ushered the women into the house, made them sit, gave them cups of tea, and presented a plate of dates in front of them. It was meager fare, but all the households of the village entertained neighbors and friends like this. There might be rivalries and squabbles among the villagers, but when a visitor came to your home and called on your hospitality, your honor lay in how generous you could be despite your own penury.

"Sister Elham, Sister Wadad," said Alia, then stopped, put her hand to her mouth, and gagged.

"Don't talk," said Wadad. "We know you're struggling. It's like that in the first few months. Eh, Elham?"

"She's right," agreed Elham. "And it doesn't get any easier. Just listen and pay attention, Sister Alia."

The two women outlined to Alia the choice that lay before her. She might give birth to a girl or a boy. But if she gave birth to a girl, no doubt the Collector would descend on the village and, when she came of age, claim her for Sheba City. On the other hand, if she gave birth to a boy, the Collector wouldn't bother her.

Alia became agitated. All methods of determining a child's sex before birth had been banned for decades in Mazun, their country. Alia hadn't been thinking about her baby's gender on purpose, not wanting to confront the possibility that she might have a daughter who would be taken from her and sent to a Markaz for marriage training, then married multiple times. She gripped her stomach with both hands and her forehead grew clammy. "What do I do if it's a girl?"

"Drink your tea," said Elham kindly. "And keep listening."

They told her that she could protect her daughter from the Collectors and the Perpetuation Bureau through the method practiced in the village: raising her daughter as a boy from birth, never revealing the child's true sex, and keeping the secret from the Collector or any other government representatives Sheba City would send their way.

Alia said, "Is this what you did with your children?"

Wadad answered, "I had a boy, so it wasn't necessary."

Elham pursed her lips and looked out the window innocently. "So did I."

"But your Husbands . . . do they . . . know?"

"They're happy to have boys. More help for them in their work. Everyone needs an extra pair of hands on the farms, or in the store. They don't ask questions. Childbirth is women's business, they don't concern themselves with it too much," said Elham.

Wadad's eyes narrowed. "Not since Nayba, anyway."

Alia hadn't heard the name Nayba since she was nine or

ten years old, and hearing it now, she remembered the story. Nayba lived on Star Mountain and had a beautiful daughter, with eyes the color of the mountain lakes and hair like beaten copper. The Collector assigned to their village knew he'd be promoted for finding a girl like that. Instead of letting her stay on the mountain, he had the girl sent to the Girls' Markaz in Sheba City. Within a month she was married to four of the provincial capital's richest men, never seen on Star Mountain again.

Unable to bear the loss of her daughter, Nayaba committed suicide. Nayba's Husbands mourned for mother and daughter, but the entire village was devastated. One of them dying felt like the death of them all, when there were so few of them already.

"Ever since Nayba, any girl born in the village is announced as a boy, disguised as a boy, and the Husbands go along with it. They don't want more Naybas," said Wadad. She looked at Elham, who was shaking her head furiously. "What? She needs to know."

"It's bad luck to talk about suicide to a pregnant woman!"

Alia gaped at the two women, all of them hardly older than girls themselves. Her mind filled with a thousand questions, but she was unable to give voice to any of them. "What should . . . what should I do?"

"Don't make any decisions now. Think about it. You have three months . . . four? Yes, four months to decide," said Wadad.

"But surely you wouldn't want to be the first woman in the village to give birth to a girl in ten years, would you?" Elham gazed keenly at Alia, and Alia could feel the weight of the question as strongly as the pressure in her belly coming from the growing child.

She'd made up her mind before the women even left her

house. Four months later, when she'd given birth to her first child, she told everyone it was another boy. Her Husband nodded, seemingly pleased. "Good, I can do with the help in the field."

The Collectors have long stopped looking for female treasure on the mountains; the villages do not have to give up their daughters. Maybe the Collectors even know about the ruse, but can't be bothered to stop it; there are more girls down in the valleys and small towns of the coastal plains, easier to find, where compliance with the rules is less of an issue.

When they reach eighteen, Alia's children will decide whether they want to go back to living as girls or carry on as boys, or stay hidden in some twilight zone flitting back and forth between both. Alia sometimes wishes she herself had been raised as a boy, but it's only been the last twenty years or so that the mothers have been doing this with their daughters.

Alia wonders if the woman with the silver eyes, who looks as though she can see unseen things, can tell that Alia is not the mother of five boys, but five girls. She's not in the mood to tell them the truth. Although what's another risk compared to the battle of childbirth, the blood spilled during labor, the wounds her body has never healed from?

But her fidelity to the pact the women of the village have made to one another, and to their daughters, prevails. Alia has to make sure that none of them really get a good look at Noor. In the darkness of the cave, that's easy, but she hopes they'll be gone before long.

## 3.

"It was Fairuza who called our sanctuary the Panah," says Diyah. She sounds like she's about to tell Alia a story. Alia sinks down to the floor, legs folded underneath her, Noor's head in her lap. He's come crawling back to her, fearful at the sound of the invisible woman's voice.

Diyah explains to Alia that in Green City they lived in an underground shelter, made of reinforced concrete and radiation-proof materials, a remnant from the Final War, safe from the eyes of the men above ground.

The Virus. The Final War. Alia has only vaguely heard these terms, maybe in the village school where she spent a few years at a wooden desk, sharing a tablet with another giggling little girl. She'd hardly paid attention to the teacher telling them about the great conflict that had destroyed two countries—India and Pakistan—and engulfed many more in a nuclear fallout so dreadful that millions more died of starvation and radiation poisoning. She could hardly envision farmland turned into waste, animals dropping dead in fields, people dying of severe burns from a weapon that had fallen thousands of miles away from them. And yet it had happened, and ruined the world they'd all known.

The Virus followed: a swift mutation of a cancer that killed women only, and left the men alive. The few surviving females were seized, married off to multiple men, forced to bear children to repopulate. It was hard, too, to connect the demands of the Collectors and the Perpetuation Bureau to these far-off events—it's been nearly fifty years since the time of the Virus. And yet Noor, lying in her lap, his hair cropped like a boy's and his femaleness hidden underneath boy's clothing, is a direct result of all of this.

Alia stiffens when Diyah tells her that their method of survival was to make contact with rich men yearning for companionship: widowers who'd lost treasured wives, men who had no chance of finding spouses in the new regime. The exchange: their money and protection in exchange for companionship. Nights spent with these men, holding them, soothing them, being there with them.

Alia remains silent when Diyah has stopped speaking. The silence grows until it's almost another person among their number. Finally Mariya pleads, "Say something. Please."

"So you're whores?"

Grace laughs, a short burst of staccato chuckles.

"Of course not," says Rupa, indignant.

"At least that's what we told ourselves," murmurs Grace.

"But you went to their beds. Gave them your bodies." Alia can't explain why she feels so confused about these women and their secret. She and all the other women of the village are duping the Collectors, keeping girls out of their system through subterfuge. What these women were doing in the Panah, wasn't it the same kind of thing? But she is a mother, protecting her children. And she herself submitted to the system. She's got three Husbands to prove it. Are these women just being selfish, if they were only protecting themselves?

"No, we didn't," says Mariya.

"Not in the way you think," adds Diyah.

"It was our company," Rupa says. "Our time. Our attention. Our presence. That is what they wanted, more than our flesh."

"Are you trying to tell me they would spend the whole night with you and not touch you?" Alia is incredulous.

"Touch was allowed. Sex was not. That was the deal."

Alia snorts.

Diyah says, "They all wanted something more important than sex, Alia. They wanted time, exclusive time, with a woman they didn't have to share with anyone else."

Diyah's words unlock a guilty memory inside Alia: one night, not long after her third marriage, she lay next to her youngest Husband in the bedroom, after joining with him in silence so as not to awake the children or disturb the other men. That night, he intoned soft words under his breath while embracing her, and his throaty sighs aroused her curiosity while his body joined with hers.

"What were you saying . . . before?" she asked him, after they had pulled apart, in the drifting moments while she waited for him to fall asleep. He blushed hard, his eyes closed, as if he were a shy girl. She saw his face in the dim light and smiled to herself. Sometimes it felt as if he were another one of her children. "You can tell me."

He picked at the skin on his thumb, hemmed and hawed, until finally she teased it out of him. "It's poetry."

"Poetry?" She didn't know whether to laugh or take him seriously.

"My family liked poetry," he continued. "I heard it all the time from my mother. She used to sing it as she worked. She tried to teach me. I don't remember the verses, but I remember some words."

"But why . . ."

He moved his face close to her, whispered close in her ear, "My beloved, my moon, my country, my song . . . Do you want to know what I dream of sometimes?" She nodded her head, knowing that he could feel the movement against his shoulder.

"I dream that it's just the two of us. You and me. That we are the only lovers in the world."

His words evoked a torrent of feeling in her, more than his caresses. Her breath came in short sharp gasps, her stomach tightened, and a strange electricity made her limbs stiffen. She wanted to hear more, but at the same time, she wanted to stop him from speaking this blasphemy. No one was supposed to admit to wanting to keep a Wife all for himself. Yet here he was, voicing these illicit thoughts, and worse than that, she was quickening to them. They were going inside her, filling her with ideas taking seed in her mind and heart. Dangerous ideas that had to be rooted out before they could choke her and him both.

She shushed him and feigned sleep. In a few moments he, too, fell silent. She could not sleep in any of her Husbands' arms, even though they all reached for her to hold on to after sex, as if she were the log that would keep them afloat in the tumultuous rivers of their dreams. This new Husband was the one who let her go when he slept, only flinging an arm out in her direction to make sure she was still there.

She rarely spent the entire night with any one of her Husbands; she had to see to the children—one or the other was always sick, and there was always a chore waiting before everyone else had woken up. But that night, she stayed with him until the white thread of dawn separated the night sky from the earth. All night she remembered the words he whispered to her under the cover of darkness.

As the wind rustled through the qataf tree and the faint scent of pine wafted in through the windows, Alia wished she only had to spend her nights with this one, the one who was kindest, the one who treated her with consideration in bed and out of it. To the others, she was a workmate, the mother of their children, the center of their home. But this one had called her his country. He had given her a vision: of herself as a homeland. And for the first time, she saw herself as whole, not a land divided among three men and their children.

As he dreamed of his country beside her, she touched his hand lightly with her fingertips. Noor was conceived that night; nine months later, the child that was born had the same bright blue eyes.

Facing the women, she pushes the memory away, pushing it back into its place deep in her chest. Whores or not whores, it doesn't matter now. "That place you lived in. Panah. What does it mean?"

Rupa reaches for Alia's arm. "It means 'refuge.' It was a sanctuary. We were safe there."

"Safe from what?"

"From the Bureau. The Agency. Forcing us to do what they wanted. They thought it was wrong, Fairuza and Najwa. They didn't want to be prisoners to four or five Husbands, to be forced to take drugs that made them have a dozen children, or more, like animals."

Alia pulls her arm away and dusts herself off. "I am not an animal."

"I'm sorry," says Rupa. "I didn't mean to insult you."

"We're all under a great deal of strain," says Diyah, playing the diplomat. "We've been on the run. We're tired, hungry, and cold. And frightened."

"If it hadn't been for your son bringing us food, we would have starved," adds Grace.

Mariya says, "We're truly grateful." The others murmur their agreement. "Thank you. You saved us, you know."

Alia looks down while Noor hides his face in her side. They're truly fools, these women: so brazen, so open with their emotions, not just their bodies. The mountain people are different, don't give themselves away so easily. A stranger is an enemy until he's proved himself trustworthy. But never an ally until you have suffered together. And never a friend until her son has married your daughter and your families are joined in blood. This is the mountain way.

But it's also their way to help those who are lost, who throw themselves at your mercy to escape a wildcat's teeth, a broken leg at the foot of a cliff, or the threat of thirst and starvation. The mountain way is to always provide shelter. These women's Panah, their sanctuary, reminds Alia of that. The ancient codes are embedded in the rocks and cliffs, and the bones of the ancestors they've buried under heaps of stones and boulders because the soil isn't soft enough for their graves.

She squats on her haunches again, staring at Diyah with the frank, piercing look of the mountain people. Diyah's eyes are clear and unguarded. "Say it again, the names of those two women who started your shelter. . ."

"Najwa and Fairuza. They founded the Panah," says Diyah. "After them came Ilona."

Alia says, "And who is Lin? Tell me again."

"The last one," says Grace. "She died." Noor sucks harder on his thumb at the word *died*. It roils the women, like ocean waves whose current is disturbed deep below, while Grace stays calm.

"And this Lin," says Alia slowly. "Did she also sleep with the men, like you did?" She still can't understand the distinction the women are making between sleep and sex. Alia herself sleeps with three men, not because she wants to, but because she has to. Real rebellion, to Alia, would be to sleep with one man and one man alone. Or none at all. She doesn't understand these women; their explanations are making her head hurt.

"Not when she became our leader," says Grace. "She was busy making the whole thing work. We're the ones who slept with the men."

"The burden of responsibility was hers alone, and she bore it well," says Diyah. Her voice is softer, soothing. "She did her best for us."

"Until it all fell apart," adds Rupa. "And we had to run."

"You were found out?" They nod. "And you came here," says Alia. "In that car. Yours?"

The women don't speak for a while. "It wasn't ours," ventures Rupa at last. "It belonged to a man sent to find us, and take us back to the Agency."

"But we refused," says Diyah.

"You refused?" Alia is baffled. "But didn't they force you? There must have been more of them than you. How did you get away?"

"There were no others. He came alone," says Mariya. "He said Lin had called him, but we didn't believe him."

Grace says, "We surrounded him, and beat him senseless, and then took his car and escaped. All of us except one."

The women look at one another, but leave the missing one's name unsaid. Instead, they tell her how they took off across the desert, Grace at the wheel: she was a transport driver in the life she'd had before she came to the Panah. They headed south, following the sun and moon; they kept the car's navigation switched off in case they were being tracked. They wanted to put as much distance as possible between themselves and Green City. Maybe they'd reach the coast of Dhofar and be able to get on a boat, sail somewhere where they could disappear. They were improvising, trying to adapt to the chaos into which they'd been flung. They knew nothing except the aching, insistent need to survive.

After a night's driving, they climbed the path to the Wabiha Valley, the gateway to the mountains beyond. A leopard crossed the steep mountain road in front of them, and Grace swerved and sent the car crashing into a tree. Nobody was hurt. They pulled themselves out of the wreck and began to climb the mountain. That was how they found this cave, where they'd hidden themselves. Noor found them a few days later, in desperate need of food, having subsisted only on the water from a trickling stream near the cave.

Alia can't understand how, despite all the physical deprivations they've suffered, the women of the Panah still look so beautiful. Then again, she's only got the women of the village, aged before their time by years of physical labor and childbearing, to compare.

"A leopard?" Alia says doubtfully. It's been years since one has been seen on Sun Mountain.

"Yes," says Grace. "It was dark, but I could see its spots. And its eyes. They shone in the headlights. Like lasers. That's how we knew we were in Dhofar."

Alia sits back on her haunches, blankness crowding her head. The women glance at one another, waiting for her to respond. Noor crawls in and out of each woman's lap, winding himself around their legs and nestling in the crooks of their arms. By the end of the tale he is back at Alia's side, his thumb fixed in his mouth. He's never seen so many women gathered in one place before. Neither has she. Each woman in their village lives in the bowels of the household, directing what goes on inside, with little time to gather together in groups, or to socialize, apart from hurried conversations while bringing food to their Husbands in the fields. Some of the women gather together, to meet for talk or gossip, but Alia spends most of her time alone. She sends her children out, to find someone's missing brother, or ask another woman if she has buttons to spare for a shirt she's mending. Alia hides in the shadows, shrinks away from the eyes of others. She takes up as little space as possible.

But how has Noor found these women? He likes to explore, and nothing could be more tempting to him than a cave. His curiosity has led him straight to them; it's too late to undo this fact.

Alia still doesn't know whether or not to believe the women. Are they spies sent here by the Agency to draw out the villagers, to catch the rebels and insurgents fighting against the regime from the border areas of Mazun? Is Alia being led into a trap? She sees the women a little better now in a thin thread of light streaming weakly in from the roof of the cave. Limestone dust dances in the half-light. Rainwater has cut striated patterns into the walls at different angles; when the heavy rains come, the women will be drenched. This is no place for them to stay.

Then the sun shifts angles, the light disappears, and Alia wants to be back in the open air, out of the dankness. The air smells stuffy and fetid now, of too many bodies pressed close together, of their sweat and fear.

"I must go. It's late," Alia says. Noor lets out a disappointed little whine, but she ignores him. He still obeys her; soon he'll be as bold as his older siblings, doing the opposite of what she commands just because he can.

"Will you be able to find us again?" asks Rupa. Grace, too, looks anxious, but less willing to admit to it.

"I know where this cave is. You'll get more food tomorrow. Can you make do for now?"

The women will not go hungry tonight. Their supplies are meager, but the company and succor she and Noor had given them will make their bellies seem less empty. "At least we know we aren't alone anymore," says Diyah.

"Will you bring the food, or will Noor?" asks Grace, to the point.

"We'll see." As Alia turns to leave, she notices the alarm they transmit to one another with their eyes. They reach for Noor to hug him close to themselves and cling to him a little longer than necessary. He submits to their hugs and kisses gamely, snuggles with Diyah, presses his forehead to Mariya's.

Alia doesn't feel jealous, watching them bidding her child farewell. Noor's been everyone's child, even in the village, since the day he was born. And she, who had so many children, can spare him for a few moments longer to these women who have never really known love. In that way, she is far richer than them.

# 4.

"The first thing . . . we have . . . to do," huffs Alia, "is hide . . . the car."

She and Noor make their way slowly and carefully back up the mountain, Noor in front, Alia behind him in case he stumbles and falls backward. Every step along the rocky path makes her shudder; she holds her hand to her hip to steady herself as she climbs. In some places the incline is so steep, she has to crawl, putting her hands onto the ground.

Noor glances back at his mother open-mouthed. "What car?" Even his cheeks and ears are red with effort.

"You haven't seen it?" She pushes Noor's shoulders until he faces the right direction, then puts her hands on his head and pushes it down. "Look. That's how they got here."

The shock spreads on Noor's face like a stain, as though he can't connect the twisted remains of the car to the women in the cave. He looks at the car bewildered, then turns again to his mother. "You're hurt, Mama." He reaches out for her hand and lets out a hiss between his teeth at her palm, bloodied and torn. "Mama, there's blood."

"It doesn't hurt, Noor-child," she lies.

"Did you get hurt in that car? Were you there when it crashed?"

"No, Noor. It wasn't me in the car. It was—"

She hesitates. All her instincts tell her to protect her child, even though they're already in too deep . . .

They are in roughly the same spot where she'd first seen the wreck, but the chasm seems deeper and farther away now. Shadows on the walls of the limestone cliff are starting to lengthen; the sun travels incessantly across the sky. A chill in the air brings news that rain is coming; she smells it on the breeze. Far in the distance, a layer of dirty brown clouds are gathering. The khareef is overdue, like a woman waiting to give birth. When it comes, it will shroud the mountains and coastline in mist and fog. In a good year, the rains are gentle, carpeting the entire region a verdant green and swelling the waterfalls, reminding everyone of the gardens of Paradise. In a bad year, the monsoon brings mudslides and flash floods, rendering the roads impassible and turning the mountains into deathtraps.

Alia stares hard at Noor. Despite the panic on his face, his eyes reflect the part of the sky that is still cloudless, still clear. She has to calm her child before she can decide what to do next.

"So is that where my torshi went? Into those women's bellies?"

Noor nods. A smile tugs at the corners of his mouth, and his eyes sparkle. The tone of his mother's voice, the warmth and affection in it, tells him she isn't angry with him.

"What else did you take for them? Tell me everything."

"Some of the apricots. And the dried breads. Also a little soap, they wanted to wash."

"The honey, too?"

"No, I ate that."

"And how did you find them in the first place?"

He tells her he was trying to catch up to his brothers one morning as they went to the fields, but they left him behind, and he couldn't keep up with them. "So I went up the path instead of down, and then there was a cave I'd never seen before, and they were in there! Like magic, Mama. They told me not to tell anyone, but you found them, too." His face is bright; Alia knows he's thrilled to finally be able to share the secret with her.

Oh, how she loves this child. But when does she have the time to tell him how much? When he was born, she promised she would let him be free, to roam their mountain, to romp with the other children, not to burden him with her fears and anxieties. Son, daughter, these things don't exist: this is Noor, her beloved, her last-born child. She pulls him close to her, burying her face in his close-cropped hair, taking in his scent, feeling his arms encircle her neck and glorying in the feeling that he is still hers. As long as she has Noor, she has everything.

He squirms in her arms after a moment, pushing out of her embrace. "Mama, what are they doing here?"

"I wish I knew, Noor."

"But they told you. They're from Green City. They ran away from their home. They said they can't go back. Is anyone looking for them, Mama?"

"I don't know." The mudslides and avalanches, the floods that swell the irrigation channel and sometimes sweep away their crops, are a constant fear during the rainy months—the months of khatr. Their word for danger, khatr, is all hard edges and guttural sounds made in the back of the throat. This car is khatr, too, with its sharp steel edges, its shattered screens, its eviscerated machinery. The women in the cave have crashed into their lives the same way a mudslide or a flood comes, treacherously, bringing devastation in its trail. And khatr, for her and her child.

On the mountain trail, a larger panic eats at Alia now, growing bigger the closer she gets back to the village. What, exactly, is she supposed to do with these women? "Noor-baba, listen to me."

The child is doing an impatient dance, jumping from

one rock to another, while Alia catches her breath. At the sound of her voice, he spins around to pay her attention. "Yes?"

"Go and get your brothers. Come here, tell no one else. Do you understand me?"

He nods solemnly.

"Bring them here. I'll wait."

Alia stands at the lip of the cliff, hands on her sides to ease the sharp pain under her ribs. In the sky an eagle wheels on a downdraft, sending a distant scream into the thin air. The wind lays a cold knife's edge across her cheek. As far as her eye can see, scrub brush and scraggy trees dot the mountain's crags, breaking up the earth with splashes of dark green and sandy yellow. She tastes dryness in her mouth. The pulse in her stomach hammers right under her skin; she felt like this when she was pregnant with Noor. As if everything is drenched in meaning, even the smallest fallen leaf on the ground.

She breaks off a small twig from an arak tree and chews on it to clean her teeth, then plucks off a few leaves and tucks them into her pocket. The leaves work well for winter coughs. Her stock is running low and the trees nearer the village aren't as healthy and flush as this one. The pungent mustard taste of the bark spreads across her tongue as she works on the twig with her teeth, thinking carefully about the women. Should she tell the elders of the village about them? It would cause a furor. They are all used to the absence of other women—in these parts, one woman to every twenty men; it's been like this for two or three generations. Now things have started to change, but the Collectors don't know. The villages at the farthest reaches of the mountain don't dare reveal their newborn daughters to anyone. The

Husbands go along with it, having long grown accustomed to the extra help an army of boys provides them with.

If four beautiful, young women, higher in value than the women of the village, appear overnight, the hated Collectors will surely come sniffing around again to claim them. They'll find out about it somehow, maybe even from the elders themselves: a cache of women such as these would means rich rewards for the village. The villagers might petition to have them stay as Wives for their men, many of whom are still unwed.

But these are choice women for city men, rich and influential. Chances are the Agency will find out about them, and then they'll be carted back to Green City for punishment and reeducation. There will be so much attention on the village, no matter what happens, that their own hidden daughters might be found out.

Alia hears high-pitched voices carrying on the wind, calling to one another, laughing and shrieking. Led by Noor, running, tumbling pell-mell, they climb over the clifftop and descend toward her. Alia doesn't flinch as they race one another down the slope. The older ones are like mountain goats: If they fall, they pick themselves back up like acrobats, ignoring the scratches and cuts from the rocks and branches on their arms and legs.

Within minutes they've encircled her. "Mama, Mama!" they cry, clasping her legs, hugging her. Despite her annoyance, she laughs and cuffs one, ruffles the cropped hair of another. She'll make them obey her every word. As she protects her children, she'll do her best for the women of the Panah, too.

She claps her hands and they line up, giggling. "Now listen to me. This is a dangerous job. You have to do it quickly, and you have to swear to me you'll tell no one about this. Not your fathers, not your friends."

"We promise!"

"Do you see that black thing down there?"

They lean over the edge in a pack, pushing at one another, arms around one another. They do everything together, her children.

"What!" Astonished cries and gasps rain from their mouths; they've never seen a car in real life before. Their impressions of fast-moving cars, trains, or planes come from quickly watching videos on old devices they snatch from their fathers.

They pepper her with a thousand questions: "What is it?" "Where did it come from?" "Why is it there?"

"Just do as I say; I'll tell you everything later. Did you bring your knives?"

The sun breaks free from a heavy cloud cover and sweeps across the valley like a piercing searchlight. The children brandish their daggers to show her, small blades glinting in the sudden brightness, no bigger than toys for the youngest, proper ones for the oldest. They dissect insects and small rodents, just for fun, or threaten one another in mock fights, but they never draw blood against one another.

"Good. Now go down there. You're faster than I could ever be. Cut off as many of the branches as you can, as you go. The more leaves, the better. Cover up the car with them. I don't want to be able to see anything from here."

"What do we get for it?" says Mehran, her eldest son, his wiry limbs not quite matching a chubby, red-cheeked face splashed with so many freckles, it looks like a brown birth stain across his nose and under his eyes. "Will you pay us?"

She raises her hand threateningly. "Ask what you'll get if you don't do it."

Mehran ducks, then waves the others on. "Let's go!"

She watches the child army scampering down the trail,

hacking down tough branches and low-hanging limbs of trees as they go. She takes out her lightphone and checks its signal: full strength, meaning the Spectrum works well here. In the village, the network transmits through cells embedded in the LEDs of their light bulbs. But how will her message go through from this spot, where there is no electricity, no houses, no bulbs? The mountain walls sometimes bounce the signals strangely, concentrating them in one area and fading out in others. This must be one of those spots where the signal pools into the best strength she's ever seen anywhere on the mountain.

Alia types out a message: *Come quickly, Katy Azadeh. I need you.*

The children now surround the wreck, branches and leaves in their hands. Noor clambers up onto the car roof and reaches out a hand to his brothers. The others give him their branches and he lays them on the top of the car, carpeting its twisted roof in a careful arrangement of leaves and twigs. The older ones weave the branches into the rippled metal on the hood and trunk, standing up the bigger branches so that from above the car looks like a clump of ordinary bushes growing jaggedly in the cleft of the mountain.

Mehran gives Alia a thumbs-up sign, which she flashes back to him. They cheer and climb their way up to her.

There's no response to her message yet. But no matter: Katy Azadeh will send word when she's on her way. The Hamiyat are always out on patrol, or attending training sessions on first aid or advanced martial arts. Sometimes they have lectures or talks about women's science and the philosophy of the liberation movement. When she comes, Katy Azadeh will decide what's to be done with the women. The women of the Panah belong in nobody's hands but the Hamiyat, the Protectors. They are the only ones who can be trusted to do the right thing.

Nobody in the village, not her Husbands or her children, knows that Alia is an Ababeel, a secret spy and helper of the Hamiyat. She took the vow of allegiance to the Hamiyat two years ago; they've gone by so fast, Alia herself can hardly believe it.

All the villagers had ancestors who fought for the independence of Dhofar at the tail end of the Final War. The Final War gave Green City the perfect excuse to subsume Dhofar into the bigger country of Mazun. The insurgents wanted a return to the arrangement of the pre-War years, when the people of the mountain lived under their own rule. The Dhofaris fought for years, but their small skirmishes hardly won them a few feet of territory at a time. At the same time, the female insurgents were fighting a battle against the rape gangs that marauded the mountain in search of women and girls to rape and kidnap among the upheaval and chaos of the War. These female fighters called themselves the Hamiyat, the Protectors.

Most people dismissed the Hamiyat as an old legend. Then one day, through the whisper-network that existed among the women of the mountain, Alia learned that the Hamiyat were still secretly active. They'd gotten rid of the rape gangs, but found another enemy: the Collectors, who acted as pimps for Green City's Perpetuation Scheme, stealing the most beautiful women and girls of Dhofar and sending them as brides to different parts of Mazun.

Alia became obsessed with the idea of finding out more about the Hamiyat. She put her ear to the ground, paid bribes to learn where the nearest Hamiyat camp was, and told her Husbands she had to visit a cousin recovering from typhoid on the other side of Sun Mountain.

After a half-day's walk, she reached the camp, a small

brick hut in a dusty compound. A giant bougainvillea tree dropped pink and white flowers onto the ground in the strong breeze. Alia hesitated at the entrance, then skulked in, eyes down. By chance, it was conscription day for new recruits. Alia stood apart from the teenagers who milled around in groups, chattering and laughing. A few of them linked arms and danced to a radio precariously balanced on a low wall that spat out rousing songs celebrating the Hamiyat.

Some talked loudly, telling anyone who would listen why they'd come to the camp, why they'd left their homes—to join the Hamiyat. One young girl said she'd heard about the exciting lives the Hamiyat fighters led. "I hear they sing and dance, they have weapons, it's like a party." Another said her mother beat her too much and she wanted to escape. Many girls were bored with their lives; they didn't want to get married. They'd much rather spend their lives in the company of other women instead of serving ancient Husbands. One or two clamped their mouths shut tight and refused to say why they'd left; Alia suspected they'd suffered abuse at a father's hands, not a mother's.

Waiting among the girls from the hamlets and villages dotting Sun Mountain, Star Mountain, Lion Mountain, Water Mountain and the Three Brides, Alia almost lost her nerve. But then one of the women organizing the conscripts into a line noticed her and approached, smiling.

"You, sister, come here and introduce yourself." The organizer took down her name and the village she came from. "You're a little older than the others. Are you married? Do you have children?"

Alia silently nodded yes to both questions.

The organizer told her to wait. Alia began to feel panicky. What was she doing here exactly? She was too old to be a foot soldier. She couldn't leave her Husbands and children for extended periods of time, not while Noor was still so small. Yet she couldn't make herself leave. She squatted on her haunches and waited, ignoring her pounding heart and jangling nerves.

A commotion spread among the recruits at the arrival of Fatima Kara, the commander of Sun Mountain's Dawn Battalion. Kara was a battle-hardened woman in her forties, a scarf wrapped around her head to tie up her hair. Her thickset waist and full breasts, not quite hidden under her battle fatigues, indicated that she, too, was a mother. Alia stared at Fatima Kara as she inspected the new recruits, accompanied by her lieutenant, a tall woman called Lateefa.

As Fatima Kara came to Alia, she drew out a cigarette from her pocket and lit it, drawing in deeply. "And why are you here?"

Alia choked out that she knew all sorts of secrets. She was married to a high-status man; at sixty-five, he was the oldest man on Sun Mountain. Everyone in the villages confided in him.

"What else?"

Because of her clever ways with food and supplies, Alia said she did good business as a trader of sorts. "You need food, don't you? I can help." She knew her answers were disjointed, but she hoped the commander could find something redeemable in her jumble of words.

"Food has its importance. But you have more talent than that. You could be an Ababeel," said Kara. Then she lit another cigarette, throwing the old butt on the ground at her feet.

Kara's lieutenant Lateefa explained that the Ababeels were as important to the battle as the warriors. "An Ababeel knows when to talk and when to keep quiet. She knows what to take notice of and what to ignore. And she knows that the battle cannot be won without her contributions, no matter how insignificant she seems. In her insignificance lies her strength. It's a disguise that allows her to do many more things than one who is easily noticed by the enemy."

"Does that sound like you?" Kara said to Alia.

All the teenagers swiveled their heads and stared at Alia, who blushed and couldn't meet anyone's eyes. "I'll still bring you food," she said miserably, hating being the center of attention.

Commander Kara said, "That's a given. I've heard your harees is the best on the mountain."

"How did you—"

Fatima Kara laughed, and Alia understood the Ababeels' effectiveness immediately.

That day, Alia was sworn in as an Ababeel. After the oath-taking, an organizer briefed Alia and the other four Ababeels. "We need to know everything about the Collectors' activities. Everything they do when they come here. Where they stay. Whom they trust. What they eat. Whom they bed."

Alia relished the thought of helping to ambush the Collectors, whom everyone hated for controlling their lives through power, fear, and bureaucracy. She imagined Nayaba's corpse, covered with a blanket, her feet sticking out. The organizer handed out the devices that would keep them all connected through the Spectrum. "Show these to no one."

"When do we start to kill them?" said an Ababeel from Widaa, the village on the highest peak in Dhofar.

"Not yet. Be patient. It's easy to kill; you need to learn how to fight."

Alia nodded and put the device away in her pocket. She didn't bother to ask what the Spectrum was. Silent acceptance, unthinking obedience were as important to the success of their mission as fighting and resistance.

Alia watched all the young women take the Oath of Protection, the Himaya. There were young women of different ages and sizes, some with short hair who swaggered like boys, others with long braids down their back and flowers tucked behind their ears. Not one of them older than twenty, each one of them ready to lay down her life to protect the women of the mountains. Katy Azadeh was among them: Seventeen, thin, and wiry, with intense green eyes and pink splotches like roses on her cheeks, she was to be Alia's personal contact in the Hamiyat. Her voice rang out before all the rest, singsonging the words of the oath, which the other girls repeated after her.

We are the Women Protectors, the Hamiyat; we fear no man.
Every woman and girl is promised shelter under our wings
We swear our allegiance to the liberation movement,
And the principles of fairness
We will fight until all women are free.

When the ceremony was over, and all the women were hugging and kissing one another's cheeks, Katy Azadeh took Alia's hands in her own and clasped them hard. "Remember what our Commander told you. If you need us, we will come. Only if I am dead will you not hear from me when you call. And I assure you, my time is a long way off."

The girl emitted a glow of heartfelt exuberance, her joy at being at the camp, and the path that lay ahead of her. They were off to their military academy, at a base even higher and more secret than this camp. There, they would undergo eight weeks of training: weaponry, the basics of guerrilla warfare, and insurgency tactics, the girls rattling off those terms as if they knew exactly what they meant.

"As God wills," Alia had said, staring at the young woman, trying to read her green eyes, shining with the spirit of many battles yet to be fought.

"No, Alia-jaan," said Katy, laughing as she kissed Alia on both cheeks, then slung the rifle she'd just been assigned over her thin shoulder. "Don't you remember? We protect you, and the Warrior Queen protects us. God forgot about us a long time ago."

# 5.

Alia floats in the upper layers of sleep, lost in a half dream that disappears like mist when her device vibrates under her side of the mattress. Her first Husband barely stirs. They all live in the house his father built fifty years ago; he doesn't mind the idea of sharing it with two other men and five children, three of whom are not his.

They rarely have sex anymore on his allotted nights. Instead, he lies on his back under the covers while she rubs his aching legs. "Will they know if we don't try for more children?" she asked him once. Her Husband only grunted. Over the years, theirs has been a partnership not of active words, but of wordless actions: the massaging of limbs, the making of a cup of tea, her Husband's long gaze on her as he eats a meal that she has concocted out of a stringy chicken and herbs foraged from the mountainside. At his age—sixty-seven to her thirty-five—he is a silent presence, more of an uncle than a Husband to her. In many ways, it's like being married to a benign ghost.

The Hamiyat become most active at night, darkness cloaking their movements. Alia uses the late hours while her Husband snores to send updates to them about the village: the Collector's unexpected arrival to verify the new babies, or news of a fight between two wives over who had the right to draw water from their communal well.

*"It's petty jealousy. They say she's already got two Husbands, what does she need with men that aren't hers?"* Alia messaged to Katy when the fight happened.

Katy told her to keep an eye on the situation. "We'll use it to our advantage somehow."

"How?" wrote Alia.

"The women believe they need to fight one another to retain their Husbands' favor. Once we show them it's not natural, that they've been programmed to think that way, we win them over to our cause."

Katy talks a lot about something she calls "women's science." Alia doesn't understand all the theories Katy is so enthusiastic about: how a society can function without control of women or domination by men, or that full dependence on men hurts women. These are ideas for smarter women than Alia, who's got to cook dinner every night for screaming children and hungry Husbands, and barely has time to feed herself afterward.

But when Katy says the Hamiyat will set up communities where women and men can lead together, where leaders will serve their people, rather than rule over them, and where being a woman or a man doesn't affect your capabilities or your mind, her eyes burn with a light and heat that Alia can't resist. Alia thinks one day she might be worthy of a role at the head of such a community, if she can learn enough about this women-ology. Which, Katy says, is really about freedom.

Every time she hears the word *freedom*, there's a pull in Alia's stomach, almost like a sexual urge. It takes over her head and her heart, and makes her do crazy things: joining the Hamiyat, or being an Ababeel. And helping the women of the Panah avoid detection and capture.

The device vibrates again, and Alia thinks of her children in the next room. They are all asleep on the floor next to her other two Husbands. Mehran, Insaaf and Sami, Hamza and Khatib. And Noor, little Noor. Song of her heart, happiness of her eyes. The freedom she wants is for them. The deception can't go on forever; they need to be free so they can be normal girls, not hiding as boys.

She slides the device out on the floor beside her and opens one eye to look at it. *Come outside*, says the message. She raises her head and glances sideways at her Husband. He sleeps on his stomach with his face pressed into the pillow, violent snores racking his body. She pushes her feet into her worn boots and wraps a shawl around her head and shoulders.

Katy will be at their usual meeting place: across the rope-and-wood bridge on the southeastern path outside the village, in a clump of baobab trees on a plateau shielded by the high walls of a box canyon. The path there is overgrown with scrub bush; Alia always has to make up some excuse when anyone notices the scratches on her arms and her face.

She slips out of the house and scrambles over the low stone wall at the village boundary. She crosses the bridge, biting her lip as it sways under her weight. There are wide gaps between its planks, and she fears plunging down into the river, because she can't swim. As a young girl sent to fetch water from the river, she loved to look down and watch its heady torrents breaking over the stones in the shallow stream bed. Broken flowers and branches of leaves flew down in its waters, the jugular vein of the mountain. But darkness robs her of all sense of direction, of time and distance. She crosses the bridge with her heart in her throat, cursing the Collectors, who promised them a proper bridge of steel and fiberglass, so that the children could cross safely on their way to and from school. But like all their other promises, this one was never kept.

The hill she climbs is as dry as the parched skin of a nomad in the desert. Every year when the khareef comes, six waterfalls cascade down the limestone cliffs into a long vertical opening in the east wall of the canyon. An underground tunnel takes the water to a lake a mile away, its green waters mirroring the sudden vegetation that covers the mountains during the monsoon. Once the khareef ends and the clouds melt away, the waterfalls, too, disappear, and the mountains fade back to dull brown and bleached-bone yellow again for the rest of the year. The yearly magic hasn't happened yet, even though the whole village is impatiently waiting.

At the baobab copse, an owlet flies from one tree branch to another, hooting loudly. Two figures, neither of them Katy, are standing there. Alia stops short, alarmed. She'd just assumed the message was from Katy. Has she walked into a trap?

When the two figures remove their cloaks, Alia recognizes them as Katy's squad mates. Marzi: tall and skinny, with short, close-cropped hair and cheekbones that stick out like the edges of a knife on her angular face. And Laleh: shorter, plumper, her hair tied in a high ponytail under a beret that she never takes off, even when she is asleep. The three of them work together on small missions, Katy and the other two, who have been best friends since joining up. Katy referees their bickering, knocks their heads together when they need it. She calls them Marzipan and Lalehpop, nicknames they hate for belying the sweetness under their tough exteriors. Katy has assured Alia more than once that if something ever happens to her, Laleh and Marzi can be trusted completely.

Alia says now, "Where's Katy?"

Marzi's hand caresses the pistol strapped to her belt as Laleh scans the clifftops with infrared goggles to her eyes.

Laleh's ponytail dances with the motion of her shaking head as she searches the distance. "Can't tell you."

Marzi says tersely, "We have the women."

"What women?" Alia mutters, still wary.

Marzi says, "The women in the cave. They're in our custody now. They're safe. They're lucky we found them first, not the Collectors, or other men. But they won't talk without you."

"You have to come with us," says Laleh. "Commander Kara's waiting for you."

Alia's breath hisses sharply between her teeth. Her only job was to tell the Hamiyat about the women. She'll do no more for those fugitives. "But where's Katy?" If Katy Azadeh were here, Alia would feel completely relieved; she'd hand them off to Katy without hesitation. Marzi and Laleh may still blame her for waiting so long to tell them about the women. And she's frightened, still, because of Noor.

Laleh keeps the goggles firmly pressed to her face, hiding her expression. "She's busy."

"What do you mean, busy?" Alia begins to panic. Has Katy fallen out with her squad mates?

Alia remembers Katy's words: *You can trust them.* She doesn't want to. But trust, like fate, is not always a choice. Sometimes it's a necessity.

Marzi says, "We have to go quickly. Commander Kara said to be back by dawn."

"But I can't . . ." Alia stammers. "I have to go back . . .my children . . ."

"Look, Alia, I'll tell you what happened. We were patrolling a few days ago and we saw their car. When we went back for a closer look, the car had been covered up with bushes. Then Commander Kara heard reports on the Spectrum about a Leader's car stolen by fugitives from Green City. We went looking, but it wasn't hard to find them. We got them out of that cave and took them up to the base. We saw your message to Katy, and Commander Kara realized they were hiding in your area. They said they would only talk if you were there."

Laleh says, "We'd recruit them, but they're no use if they're mute." She reaches into her pocket and offers a cigarette to Marzi, who shakes her head. Then she holds it out to Alia, who stares at it blankly.

Laleh shrugs, then sticks the cigarette into her own mouth, lights a match, and cups her hands around her face to draw in quick little sucks of air. The glowing end of the cigarette is a firefly in the dark, flicking this way and that as Laleh purses her lips to blow out a long column of smoke into the cold night air.

"Shut up, Laleh," says Marzi. "We can't shoot four women just like that."

"Not without a trial first," concedes Laleh.

"Well, they still have to tell us why they are hiding in that cave like a bunch of bears. Remember, ask questions first, shoot later. You can't do it the other way around."

"What if they're spies for Green City?"

Alia says, "They're not spies!" Then she bites her lip, hard.

Laleh makes a noise between a snort and a cough. "You'd better come with us and tell Commander Kara yourself. She's not so picky about things like trials and evidence. If she doesn't like the look of even one of their faces, they'll all be locked in that car and set on fire to hide their bones." At this, Alia scrambles to her feet.

Even in the dark, she sees the look of triumph Laleh flings at Marzi. "I told you she knows more than she's telling us."

*Psychopaths*, Alia thinks angrily to herself. Marching up and down the mountain and telling everyone what to do, they're as bad as the Collectors themselves . . . Then she remembers that Marzi said the crashed car belongs to a Leader, and she shivers. Katy Azadeh can't handle this. The fighters are right; she'd better go to Commander Kara after all.

As the three of them make their way to the mouth of the canyon, Marzi shines a laser flashlight in front of them to show the way. When they reach the wooden bridge, Alia looks longingly at the path sloping downward to the stream, but they tread in the opposite direction on a steeper path up the eastern face of the cliff.

All the way, Alia berates herself. Fatima Kara will band her in with the runaways, then shoot them all. She'll probably never see her children again. She bends over, pretending to massage her ankle so that the tears in her eyes can fall onto the ground.

"It's a tough climb. Are you all right?" Marzi says, not unkindly.

Alia straightens her back and starts to walk again, determined that no more words will cross her lips. Her tongue, and those cursed women, have already betrayed her. Why did she tell her children to hide the car? Noor's involvement is bad enough. It's probably just Alia's fate to be caught up in their mess. Her whole life is only a thin thread woven into the lives of others, creating an odd patchwork carpet in whose design she's never had any say.

This path is almost a vertical climb now, the shrubs becoming denser and taller. More than once Alia has to grab at them to pull herself up a particularly difficult patch. Even Laleh and Marzi are breathing hard, and Alia is drenched in sweat.

The sun rises to the east, over the sea. Alia sees the white thread that separates the darkness of the sky from the horizon. Then, the brightening of the entire sky, heralding the sun's arrival. In the sunrise, the cliffs change color like chameleons, from stone gray to dark red, rich in oxidized iron. Frankincense trees dot the plateaus at the top. The higher they climb, the older the air smells, stippled with the scent of juniper and pine.

Soon they arrive at a small shrine where the figurine of a woman standing in a dancer's pose, her hand on her hip, is carved into the rock wall. Lower than the woman is the bust of an old, bearded man, with a patterned shawl on his shoulder. Around the figure of the woman rest bunches of flowers, strings of beads, handfuls of nuts, and small burned-down candles.

Laleh unshoulders her rifle and lays it on the ground. Then she kneels down in front of the figures and touches her forehead to the base of the female figurine no more than a foot tall, completely naked, the slit between her legs exaggerated to emphasize her sex. Her right arm is bent at the elbow, hand on jutting hip, and on the left arm, carvings of bangles cover her skin from shoulder to wrist. Her hair is tied back in a bun, a necklace of shells hung around her throat.

Marzi touches the statue of the man, then touches her own chest in a salute. The man has holes in his ears, but no earrings; his lips are large, his eyes half-closed, as if he is asleep, or deep in meditation. He looks older, weightier, but it is clear who is more revered by those who come to pay homage.

The Warrior Queen and the Priest King: Alia has heard of the deities, but this is the first time she has seen them worshipped by anyone. She briefly clasps her hands together in front of her chest and bows her head to the Warrior Queen. She herself doesn't believe in them, but it's good to pay respect all the same. Alia thinks she may be the first person outside the Hamiyat to ascend this mountain and see this shrine.

As Laleh, Marzi, and Alia keep climbing, Alia recalls a video clip Katy sent her in which she, Laleh, and Marzi reenacted a Green City girl's wedding night. Katy was the bride and Marzi the groom, while Laleh was a first Husband observing his own state-sanctioned cuckolding. Katy and Marzi writhed on the ground in a clumsily acted deflowering, Katy's legs kicking in the air, Marzi moving on top of her as if having a seizure, while Laleh staggered around with her gun pointing straight out from her hips in imitation of a painful and humiliating erection. The three of them were screaming with laughter.

Alia laughed, too, when she saw the video, even though it made her think uncomfortably of her own wedding night, something these fighters might never experience. Do they ever really get the chance to just be girls? To play, to feel the stirrings of a crush, to be as raunchy as they want? To fall in love with a man, these Hamiyat who have committed themselves to facing death for the sake of women like her?

An hour later, the path turns into a series of white stone slabs, roughly hewn and laid on the ground leading to the summit. Some are broken, the pieces buried into the ground at odd angles. Alia steps carefully, not wanting to break her ankle, or fall down the side of the mountain. They have to drop down onto all fours to make it up the last, steepest part of the stairs, then crawl through a covered tunnel.

Finally, they emerge into the open air at the top of the mountain. Before them lies the ruins of an ancient city, an intricate network of crumbling stone. Walls, buildings, water canals, even a sunken area that looks like a giant bath—this was once a carefully planned settlement on the mountain plateau.

There are traces of rooms, large and small, that might have been living spaces for many families. Every few feet or so, a pitted rock is filled with rainwater, perhaps once used for drinking or washing. Scrub brush the color of straw grows through every gap, and the wind whistles through the holes in the walls. A few goats traipse the margins of the cliff, pulling down berries from the juniper trees, and a kestrel patrols the sky, wingtips pointing to sky and earth.

"Earthquake." Laleh points at the edge of the cliff: A part of the wall has been torn, revealing giant ridges plunging down between the rocks in jagged lines. A thin coating of ridged mineral deposits shimmers in the sunlight. "Happened hundreds of years ago. Maybe thousands. Killed them all, I bet. We wouldn't have to dig far to find their bones."

"Come on," says Marzi impatiently. "They're waiting for us."

Alia then sees a rounded watchtower rising up high in the city's parapets, its slitted windows like eyes observing the haunted, cratered landscape they're now crossing, Marzi striding ahead, Laleh galloping beside her, Alia straggling at the rear. Dizzy with exhaustion, Alia draws cold air into her lungs, thin and sharp as pine needles prickling the insides of her chest. She feels as though she is watching herself from above, walking this wasteland, waiting to see what happens to her next.

# 6.

A woman's voice echoes around them as they enter the watchtower. "What took you so long?" Alia instinctively looks up; sunlight reaches into the darkness through long narrow slits at the top of the column. Dust motes filter the light into a hazy film, giving the hall a smoky, undulating air.

A woman, tall, heavy shouldered, bareheaded, stands above them at an interior balcony: Commander Fatima Kara. It's been two years since Alia last saw the leader of the Hamiyat's Dawn Battalion. A lit cigarette at her mouth makes small bright lines in the gloom as she lifts it up and down, tapping the ash out onto the stone floor.

Marzi and Laleh salute the Commander. "Commander Kara, ma'am. Apologies for the delay," says Marzi.

"She slowed us down," adds Laleh. Alia, standing behind them, looks at the floor, frowning.

Commander Kara brings her cigarette to her lips again. Alia hears her short crisp inhalation, and the low cough that follows. She thinks of an herb that might sooth that bronchial spasm. At least the Commander doesn't smoke anything stronger, like qat or hash. There are few herbs to help curb that addiction on the mountain. But Fatima Kara needs all her wits about her to lead the Dawn Batallion, the most well-known on all the mountains. She carries her own atmosphere with her, heavy with responsibility.

The Commander finishes her cigarette, then climbs down a small stone staircase that hugs the wall. She reaches the three of them in an instant, looking past Marzi and Laleh as if they weren't even there. She's staring directly into Alia's eyes.

Alia flinches, then draws herself up tall, even though her muscles ache and she desperately wants to lie down and sleep. Dirty, sweaty, covered in dust, Alia begins to worry: What if they punish her for not telling them sooner about the women of the Panah?

"Commander," Alia says in a low voice. A salute is not required of an Ababeel. "Please, where is Katy Azadeh?"

There are frown lines on the Commander's face, the number eleven written like an omen between her eyebrows. Alia observes the grim tilt of her mouth, the marionette lines drawn from lips to nose. Women age quickly on the mountain, thanks to the harsh winds, strong sunlight, and the unkindness of life. Alia holds her breath, standing on the balls of her feet, leaning forward to wait for Kara to pronounce judgment on her, or to tell her that Katy Azadeh is dead. Either one is a possibility.

Fatima Kara says, "Katy is not with us. But she's safe, and she's on a mission. I'm sorry, I can't tell you anything more than that."

Alia still holds her breath, waiting for the scolding, the debasement.

"Alia. They're here. The women. In the next room." Then the Commander smiles, and suddenly Alia sees the bold and magnetic aura of a woman in her prime. "Well done, Alia. This is magnificent."

Alia's legs shake with relief. Katy isn't dead, and she's done nothing wrong! The Panah women are here, in this watchtower, under the Hamiyat's protection. And for all her battle-hardened wariness, Fatima Kara is clearly awed by the unexpected treasure brought to her doorstep.

Commander Kara leads the way to a small antechamber

dimly lit by a small lantern set on the floor. Its low ceiling is arched, crossed by wooden beams with hooks for hanging butchered animal carcasses. Grace, Diyah, Rupa, and Mariya sit on the floor in a circle. When they see Alia, their eyes glitter with hope and apprehension. Next to Diyah lies the tiny figure of her youngest, Noor, asleep with his head in Diyah's lap. His thumb is stuck firmly in his mouth; his other hand clasps Diyah's own.

Alia realizes with a jolt that she never actually counted her children when she left the house to come here with Laleh and Marzi. She wants to run forward to snatch her child, but Marzi holds her back. Laleh catches her eye and holds a finger up to her lips. "Don't wake him."

Alia struggles against Marzi's firm hand on her upper arm. Marzi murmurs, almost apologetically, "He was with them when we found them. He wouldn't leave them. He insisted on coming, too. They took turns carrying him up here. Don't worry, he's all right. Tough little shit, your kid."

Alia doesn't believe this for a minute. They could have run the child off, told him to go back home, given him a slap or a warning. No. The women of the Panah have taken her child hostage in order to control Alia and bargain their way to freedom. Or the Hamiyat have brought him up here with the women to make sure that Alia cooperates, hides nothing from them. He's their bargaining chip. Her oath of allegiance to them isn't good enough for them.

Alia stops struggling. The Panah women all rise to their feet as Noor stretches all his limbs like a lion cub and opens his eyes, blinking, confused.

Commander Kara clicks her teeth and with a swift hand movement waves away this minor drama. "Now that you're here, maybe they'll tell us where they're from. And what they're doing here."

Rupa steps forward, her face as beautiful as a poem. If she's frightened by the soldiers' rifles or the Commander's pistol holstered at her hip, she doesn't show it.

She draws close to Alia and embraces her, winding her arms around Alia's waist. The other women envelope her in their hugs, bending their heads down like swans, communing, grieving, breathing. Alia, inhaling the warm perfume of their skins, absorbing the scent of their fear, feels the current of their sorrow. They're saying sorry in this silent way; that they need as many friends as they can find, in this harsh and difficult place.

Alia glances back at Noor; he's playing with some colored rocks that he's collected on his way up here. She prays silently—to the Warrior Queen, the Priest King, anyone who will listen—that he'll somehow steal out of the room and hide himself somewhere far away.

"You came," says Rupa. "Now I can tell them everything."

"So you're runaways from Green City," says Commander Kara.

"We were Illegals, refused to live by their rules."

Kara nods. "That's enough to condemn you, in their eyes. But what exactly was your crime?"

"We hid underground and we were companions to rich men at night. What we did in Green City . . . call us whores, we don't care. What choice do you make when you have no choices? We traded with what we had, in return for survival. It sustained us. But it couldn't last forever . . . Our leader died, and we had to run."

Commander Kara considers this, then shrugs, disinterested. "It doesn't matter. When there aren't enough women, anything female becomes a commodity to buy and sell. It's Green City that made sure you didn't have any other way."

Rupa says, "It's the same for you; you hide here, on this

mountain. We went underground. We aren't that different from you."

"Except we haven't killed anyone," says Mariya defiantly.

Commander Kara crinkles her eyes. Finally she speaks. "We're soldiers. Our fight is long and hard; our aim is to end this regime of enslavement and torture. We women are paying for the mistakes of powerful men. Politicians fighting wars that can't be won. Nuclear bombs that they invented without realizing how many they would kill. Broken countries. Nations destroyed. We don't want it, not on our mountain."

Kara points at Alia. "Look at Alia here. She has three Husbands, six children. She'd have more if her body hadn't given out, miscarriage after miscarriage. Until she stopped getting pregnant. It's no way to live. We protect women like her. We make sure they're safe."

Alia's second Husband is a squat, short man with muscles and a bowlegged stance, who thinks it's funny to throw stones at cats and push his children off the boundary walls they like to sit on, hanging their legs over the sides. He used to beat Alia often, and her first Husband turned a blind eye to the second one's behavior, either too tired or too indifferent to put himself into trouble on her account.

One day Katy Azadeh showed up with Laleh and Marzi and ambushed her second Husband as he was on his way to work laying bricks in the next village. They dragged him off the path to a small glen, where they forced him to dig a shallow grave. Then they made him get down on his knees and Katy Azadeh took out her pistol, undid the safety, and stuck it in his mouth while Marzi held him in place and Laleh filmed the retribution as proof of their actions.

"Consider this a warning. You ever touch her again, and we'll come back for you," said Katy. "And next time, I'll pull the trigger." He stopped beating Alia from that day onward, left her bed, and hardly meets her eyes or the eyes of any other person in the household. He only stays because of the income benefit, and the fear that he'll lose his social credit from Sheba City if he walks out of the arranged marriage.

To Alia's relief, Kara does not go into details about her second Husband. A small warm body presses against her legs; it's Noor, his face upturned, searching for reassurance in the form of a hug or a kiss. Alia runs her hand through his fine hair, short but silky, and holds up a finger to her lips; he nods back at her and imitates her gesture, to show that he understands. Alia knows she will kill anyone for this child. That isn't murder; it's love. Under those terms, maybe even these soft, perfumed women can become soldiers, too.

"How did the men let you fight?" says Rupa.

Kara laughs. "When the men were killed, we picked up their weapons and told them we wanted to fight, too. There weren't that many of us, so why not use everyone who was willing, regardless of what lies between their legs."

"We heard about the insurgents back in Green City," says Rupa. "We learned about you in school. They always told us you were traitors. Why didn't they wipe you all out in the beginning?"

"They can't," says Kara. "Mountain combat is very different from combat in the plains, or the cities. They can't fly their planes up here when the weather is bad. They can cut off our supplies. But the mountain provides, so we never completely starve. But we want more than to just not starve. We want to rule ourselves, free of Collectors, free of Green City. And there are others who might be willing to help us."

"I have to pee," whispers Noor to Alia.

It should be safe enough for Noor to go and come back quickly. "Go outside," Alia tells him.

Noor shook his head, lisping, "I'm too scared. You come with me."

"I'll go with him," says Mariya.

Alia doesn't hear Mariya make this offer, as she tunes back into the conversation between Fatima Kara, Rupa, and Grace. "They call us the Hamiyat, the women who protect," says Kara. "Alia joined us, as an Ababeel, a spy. There are many more of us, all over these mountains." Kara gestures again at Alia, who straightens her back proudly. "Now we're going to free ourselves. But we can't do it one woman at a time, one house at a time, not even one village at a time. We need to go bigger. We need a war. Will you join us?"

"What?"

"Us?"

"You want us to fight?"

"I don't even know how to fire a gun!"

Kara says, "They called me crazy when I put on a uniform. Nobody's laughing at me now. If I could do it, why not you? Laleh, Marzi, all the women in my battalion. You've not even met Lateefa, my second-in-command. They call her Majnuna, the Madwoman. That's what they always say about women who rebel. We deserve as much of the world as the men. But we have to fight for it. They're not just going to give it to us like that."

"We aren't fighters," says Rupa. "We would only hold you back."

Alia finds herself agreeing. A gazelle can run swiftly, but it's the lion that has the fangs and claws needed to kill. The Hamiyat uses their bodies like machines, pushing themselves to the limits of their endurance. They crawl through mud in training exercises, rip their nails off while cleaning their rifles, break their noses and chip their teeth when they fight. They display their scars to one another with pride.

Alia can't picture these pretty Panah women in battle uniform, guns in their hands, attacking a Mazun soldier. They lack the strength to spend days and nights in the cold, driving rain, guarding a village from marauders. The women of the Hamiyat don't let any so-called feminine qualities—pity, softheartedness, mercy—get in the way of dispensing justice in the form of a bullet.

"What is it? Are you afraid to die?" says Kara. "One of you already did. You want it to be for nothing?"

The women are so green, compared to the Hamiyat fighters, and even to Alia, who feels as though she's lived three lifetimes in one. The young still believe life is a game you can play and win; death waits for others, not them. Alia studies the women surreptitiously, letting her mind reach out and take the measure of each woman. Intelligent, well-spoken Rupa; visionary Diyah; Mariya, still an unformed girl; and skeptical, cynical Grace.

Grace is the one who speaks now. "Just a few of you, hiding out here on this mountain, against everything that Green City has? Its army, its weapons? You'll all die."

Laleh and Marzi stiffen, but Kara says, "I agree, it wasn't possible before. But things have changed. In fact, there was never a better time than now."

"If we say no, will we still have your protection?" asks Rupa.

A door bangs in the distance. Laleh and Marzi whirl around and crouched into defensive postures, and Fatima Kara's hand goes to her gun. Noor runs into the room, Mariya following behind. Noor dashes to Alia and wraps his arms tight around her legs, hiding his face against her stomach.

"What? What is it?" says Alia.

Mariya stretches an accusing finger at Alia. "You've been

lying to us!" All the women from the Panah freeze, and the soldiers put their hands on their weapons again.

"What are you talking about?" says Alia.

Mariya pulls the child away from Alia, then turns him around to face the others. "You told us all along this was your son. But Noor isn't a boy. Isn't that right, Noor?"

Noor whimpers, not understanding why everyone is staring at him. Mariya shakes him by the shoulder. "Speak up! Tell them. You're a girl!"

Then she turns to them and says, "I went outside with him. He pulled off his pants and squatted, and that's when I saw. Noor is a girl. She's told him he's a boy, but he's not, he's a girl. You lied."

"But why does it matter?" stutters Alia. "It's none of your business."

"How can we trust you if you can't even be truthful about your own child? It's gender distortion!"

"Why do you care what we do here on our mountain?" says Alia, desperate to make them all stop talking, jabbering, questioning her. "He's my child."

"It's a serious crime," says Diyah gently. "Especially in Green City. They execute women who try to hide their gender. And anyone who helps them."

"You're a bad mother!" says Mariya. Alia's head snaps up, as if the girl has slapped her on the face. Out of the corner of her eye, Alia sees Marzi reach out her hand and signal to Laleh, warning her not to react just yet.

Commander Kara cuts them all off, her voice pushing in above all the rest. "Silence!" All the women obey her immediately, even Noor, who chokes down his sobs as best as he can.

"Alia, tell them why you raise Noor as a boy."

Alia looks at Kara, begging the Commander with her eyes not to force her to speak the secret out loud. Kara's stare is relentless, so Alia parts her lips. The noise that comes out of her is a dry wheeze, until the sound comes back into her throat. "We . . . I . . ."

"Tell us," says Rupa. "Please."

Alia can't understand why they're all so upset. She owes none of these strange women the truth about her children. She puts her hand on Noor's forehead. Noor, her child, whom she held inside her like a secret for the first months of her pregnancy. Alia is small and insignificant, but through this child, she knows immortality. What else does she have to fear in this world?

"Yes, it's true. Noor is a girl. All my children are girls. Half of the children in the village are girls. Green City doesn't know. We never tell the Collectors when a girl is born here."

"How?" says Diyah, stunned. "How do you get away with it?"

Alia's tongue is loosened. "We all do this, here on the mountain. When a new baby is born, we report to the Collector that it's a boy. We make DNA submissions from the bodies of men who died long before Green City took over. They were never registered in the official records. Each family keeps a lock of the hair of their ancestors; it's one of our traditions."

"They don't take samples directly?" asks Grace.

"No, the Collectors don't bother with blood cards. They take the money from the Bureau and pretend they've got the right samples, but they just pocket the money and they tell us that hair is good enough. After a few years they stopped expecting girls from us. They call us the dead villages, where only boys are born."

"You still haven't said why," says Fatima Kara.

Alia says uncomprehendingly, "But you know why."

"I do. They don't."

Alia is suddenly worn out. She wishes she could take Noor

and go back down the mountain and never has to see any of them again. She'll stop being an Ababeel. She'll have nothing more to do with the Hamiyat. She just wants to be left alone with her children and her Husbands and her mountain.

Noor is the one who breaks the silence. "I'm not a girl," he lisps. "I'm a boy. Mama always says if anyone is to ask, I have to tell them: I'm a boy. She says boys do more things; they can go outside and play; they can do what they like. So I want to be a boy, and I am. One day I'll have a Wife and I'll bring home lots of money to her and our children. And I won't mind if I have to share her with my brothers."

Alia gathers Noor into her arms, lifting him up and holding him tight. He settles his arms around her neck and whispers, "Did I say it right, Mama?"

"Yes, Noor-baba. You were perfect."

Fatima Kara says to the Panah women, "Now do you understand why we're fighting? What we're fighting for? It's not for us. It's for them. Our daughters, who deserve to be free."

Rupa lifts her chin, meets Commander Kara's eyes. "We do."

"And will you join us?"

Alia holds her breath. Laleh and Marzi wait. Commander Kara lifts an unlit cigarette to her lips, her head cocked to one side. Noor blows the women a kiss, certain that they love him still, no matter whether he is a girl or a boy. He isn't really sure of the difference, Alia knows. It's that innocence that has kept him safe all this while.

A strange alchemy is at work, making the Panah women start to look stronger, more substantial. Comprehension is dawning across their faces. Rupa says, "Yes. We can't fight, but whatever else we can do, we will."

The wind whips around the watchtower, piercing the room through the small square windows, making the lantern gutter and weaken, bouncing the shadows of all the women onto the walls, the combined shapes of Alia holding tightly to Noor larger than the rest of them. Mother and child, the entity that nobody can break apart, though men have tried, for hundreds, if not thousands, of years.

The hiss becomes a steady downpour. The khareef has come to the mountain at last. Rain, with its ability to purify, to clean out accumulated dirt and to make everything new again. In their parlance, a revelation.

"Excellent." Fatima Kara's eyes gleam in the dark. "It will be a monsoon war."

# PART TWO

## The Fighter

# 7.

"The latest rules from Green City," says Raana Abdallah, the Deputy Foreign Minister of Eastern Semitia. "What will they think of next?" Her voice is weary and cynical, as if Green City never fails to amaze her, or to keep her amused and irritated in equal measure. She leans her back against the screen and stares cagily at the Security Council seated around the table, her eyes narrowed. "So? What are we to make of these amendments? Is Green City showing mercy to its women at last?"

There is a long silence as the members of the Council shift in their seats, confounded. Abdallah lets out a growl of impatience. She turns to the youngest woman in the room. "Katy?"

Katy Azadeh squirms under Abdallah's attention. She's still not used to being at such a low altitude; the light's too soft for her eyes, the air's too dull. Smells, tastes, sounds, sensations, everything muddied and unclear. She is starving for her mountain, its clean, sharp air, its honest light, its familiar rhythms and rituals. And her friends, Laleh and Marzi.

"Everything all right? Not in too much pain, I hope? The doctors said they're pleased with your progress. You're recovering well."

She's on top of everything, Raana Abdallah. Of course she's been keeping track of Katy's medical reports. "I'm fine," says Katy. "No, it doesn't hurt. I feel much better."

"Good," Abdallah says. "We need you as alert as you can be."

Katy touches the scar on her shoulder, the remnants of the

two bullets she'd gotten during the ambush on the mountain, on a night so cold and foggy, they couldn't see their hands out in front of their faces. Katy still doesn't remember anything from when she went down until the moment she woke up in the Semitian hospital. It took her three days to realize she wasn't in Mazun anymore, but in its next-door neighbor; the borders are closed and nobody ever travels between the two countries.

At first, Katy was too afraid to let the medics come near her with their microneedles and nanocameras. They said they had to remove the two bullets lodged near her spinal cord. If they didn't, a bullet could move in her body, killing her in an instant. Katy agreed to let them try.

They wheeled her to a brightly lit room where a doctor was waiting, a Maghribienne with a wide gap between her two front teeth and a tattoo in the shape of a palm leaf on her chin. She was the first woman doctor Katy had ever seen. The doctor snapped on a surgical mask, then leaned close to Katy's head, preparing to make a slight cut just below the nape of Katy's neck. "Relax, relax, think of something else."

"Your tattoo. What does it mean?" asked Katy, her lips trembling. She bit her bottom lip hard to keep them steady.

The kind doctor pretended not to notice Katy's fright. Working quickly, she murmured, "A leftover from the ancient times, in the last century. My people thought it made women more fertile. Don't worry now. Just trust me."

Katy felt the sting of the needle and immediately sent her mind to the Three Brides in Dhofar, serene and mysterious, veiled by low clouds. She imagined herself there, bathing in a waterfall. Before she knew it, the procedure was finished. The doctor laughed and showed Katy the two bullets in a bloodied metal tin. "You can keep them if you want."

Three months later, only a small scar remains, a slight indentation that Katy touches from time to time to remind herself that everything is different now. She's still stuck in this dry, rotting desert. Why haven't they sent her back to her friends, to Laleh and Marzi and the rest of her comrades? They're treating Katy well, but she has no idea when she's going to leave Zarzura, the smartest city in all of Eastern Semitia. They call her their guest, but right now, she feels like a hostage.

Raana Abdallah paces back and forth. She is dramatic, in the style of an old-time actress or a great singer. Strong words with strong gestures to drive home her points, a fist here, an upward twitch of her eyebrows there, the picking up of a tablet to let it drop to the table. The small, sharp clicks of her steel heels punctuate her words like castanets. Katy thinks that nobody in the Hamiyat would ever make so much noise. Noise does not always equal power.

Abdallah says the border skirmishes have been increasing in the last several months, and something happened in Wabiha Valley that got Green City nervous. Katy doesn't know anything about the border skirmishes, but Wabiha Valley, that's another story. She'll keep it to herself, how Laleh, Marzi, and she sneaked into a village, stole a veil hanging from a washing line, and then Marzi climbed a lamppost and strung it up there for a joke. Soon black veils were appearing on hilltops, hanging from the roofs of houses: a signal that something was brewing. Katy and her friends aren't really sure what they've started, so they agree it's best not to talk about it to anyone, especially not Lateefa, one of the most fearsome lieutenants in the entire Hamiyat.

Abdallah and her Council members ask Katy more questions about Sun Mountain: How do the mountain people feel about the Leaders, about Green City? What do other women say about the regime? Do they ever get together to talk about the situation, or is that not allowed? Are the Husbands kind to their Wives, do any of them ever talk about being dissatisfied, or are they happy to maintain the status quo?

Even though Katy mumbles one-word answers, the Semitians listen carefully. The assistants take notes, but Katy feels like she's failing them. She has no Husbands, only two names: Katya, from one grandmother, and Khatija, from the other.

Two generations ago, Katy's grandparents fled the Tehran bombardments of the Final War, but instead of heading east to the Blue City, where most refugees went, they traveled south. The journey took weeks, by truck and horse cart and sometimes on foot, but they finally made it safely to Dhofar and the high land of the mountains. That journey created the spirit of Katy: restless, shiftless, free-willed, and untamable.

Her parents had been born on the mountain, but their mothers, their DNA damaged by the radiation of the bombs, were never able to have more than one child each. Both of those children, Katy's parents, had inherited both their mothers' ill health and the trauma of their expulsion from their homeland. Katy's father died when she was only four, and Katy grew up as a boy, like all the girls of her generation on Sun Mountain. It made things easier for her mother to send a boy out into the village for errands and chores, unlikely to be spotted by the Collectors and marked for early marriage.

Her mother was always anxious, afraid of everything; she rarely ventured out of their house. She could not bear the thought of Katy being sent away to a Girls' Markaz in the lowlands. She hovered over her daughter whenever the girl was in the house, always holding her hand or putting her arm around her neck. Katy shrugged her off, squirming, suffocated by her mother's clinginess. She couldn't understand her mother's fear at things that had happened long ago, or those not even yet come to pass. Despite her father's death, the confidence of youth ran strong in her veins, coupled with a cheery faith that things would always go her way.

Katy took to running away from home and disappearing for hours, romping with the other boys of the village and coming back in the late evening with her clothes ripped and her skin scratched and scraped. Although Katy was expected to turn back into a girl once she reached adolescence, they were already fighting about the future transformation. "Who will marry you if you look like that?" cried her mother.

"What makes you think I want to get married? And who'll look after you if I do?" Katy retorted.

"Don't worry about that; I'll be long gone by then." Katy's mother always grew tearful when she said this, and Katy would sidle up to her mother and put her head in her mother's lap. She loved the feeling of her mother's fingers running through her close-cropped hair; her heart was torn between staying close to her mother, and venturing out into the world.

But Katy's mother turned out to be right: She grew ill and died when Katy was sixteen, leaving Katy all alone in the world. So when Katy turned seventeen, she joined the Hamiyat as Katy Azadeh, her nom de guerre, as Commander Kara told her: Katy the Free. The first time she put on her khaki uniform, her fellow fighters said her eyes turned the color of grapes, the same color as her Iranian grandmother's. But once the uniform is on, tribal affiliations and identities fall away. Katy's battalion is her country; her co-fighters are her compatriots. The only question of any importance is not where they come from, but what they are fighting for.

Katy has heard that Raana Abdallah trained as a scientist, started out in the solar lab here in Zarzura before changing careers and becoming a diplomat. Now she's the Deputy Foreign Minister, but rationality and reason are still her bywords. Raana Abdallah can never understand the passion and spirit that makes young women like Katy join the Hamiyat: fired up by the stories of the women who had vanquished the rape gangs two generations ago, armed only with old rifles and ammunition handed down from their brothers and fathers.

Soon they excelled at fighting, at being snipers, bombers, all types of guerrilla combat. Feared for their skills and their viciousness, the Hamiyat cleared the rapist gangs from Sun Mountain, Star Mountain, Lion Mountain, Water Mountain, and the Three Brides. Even after the first insurgency was defeated, the women fighters stayed in uniform, to keep protecting the women of the mountain.

"How old were you when you joined the Hamiyat?" asks Abdallah.

"I already told you," says Katy. Fifteen when she'd first heard of them, when she was brave enough to run from home and present herself for recruitment. Refused, told to come back when she was older. Finally, at seventeen, she was accepted into Fatima Kara's Dawn Battalion.

"She's answered that before," says an older man, the one they call the General. An unspoken warning to Abdallah is embedded in his stern voice. He is dressed in a military uniform, and his graying hair lines the edge of his scalp, but his face is taut and unwrinkled, making him look old and young at the same time.

"But we need to find out . . ."

"Then you need to listen!" chides the General. "All these questions are repetitive! Unnecessary!"

A murmur goes around the table. They look the same age, Abdallah and the General: in their mid-fifties, with the weight of their lives' experiences starting to bring their features down, carving out lines near their eyes and noses. Both have immaculate posture and hawkish noses, high cheekbones and shadows under their eyes. They could almost be brother and sister.

"I was seventeen," Katy says, to break the tension. A sigh goes around the table and suddenly the energy in the room shifts to something more sympathetic, less clinical.

"So young!" says an assistant to Abdallah.

Katy barely refrains from rolling her eyes. "If you're old enough to marry, you're old enough to fight. That's what I believe anyway."

She doesn't want to share her war stories with Raana Abdallah. She doesn't even want to be in this room, studied and prodded like a specimen in a lab. But as soon Katy had healed from her wounds, she was "invited" to these Security Council meetings to discuss affairs across the border, which have been going on for months, apparently, even before Katy got to Zarzura. What information does she have to give them about Green City? She's a fighter from Dhofar, not a top-level lieutenant with access to the higher channels of the Spectrum. These Semitians are treating her like an asset, though. Maybe this is even a bit of spectacle, to help Raana Abdallah make her case for some policy or the other.

Raana Abdallah points at the screen, reading the words aloud from Perpetuation Bureau's Internal Notification No. 1707. Katy wonders if the previous 1706 notifications are all as ridiculous as this one.

*To All Officers:*

*The Leaders have announced the relaxation of some of the rules outlined in Notification No. 305 (see attached for reference) with immediate effect.*

*Only two Husbands will be assigned to each Wife, except in exceptional circumstances, with appropriate increases in the Family and Childrearers' Allowances.*

*The family unit will now be responsible for drawing up its own schedule of time-sharing and procreation.*

*Schedules will be reported to the local office of the Perpetuation Bureau on a monthly basis, but Officers may make spot checks if suspicions are raised.*

*There will be a continuation of fertility tracking and medication, but with an increase in the number of girl children being born in the last year, a medical advisory will be put into place for women whose health may be endangered by multiple pregnancies.*

"What does this mean to you?" says Abdallah.

*Blah, blah, blah*, thinks Katy. "In the villages lower down, they organize themselves into pretend families so that when the Collector shows up, they seem to be following the rules. The higher up the mountain you get, the fewer and fewer people care for their orders and instructions. They barely show their faces twice a year up there anyway."

"She's tired," says the General.

"Don't worry, General," Abdallah answers back. "She's strong." She looks at Katy, the words *good girl* written all over her face. Does she expect Katy to be won over, to simper at her approving look? Katy wants to tell Raana Abdallah that she stopped being a girl the day she joined the Hamiyat, and she stopped being good the day she killed her first man.

But then, suddenly, Abdallah changes her mind. "You're right, General. I think we've done enough for one day. We'll take a break. And continue next time." She nods curtly at everyone around the room, saving her last acknowledgment for Katy. Her single raised eyebrow says, *Don't disappoint me next time.*

The Council members begin to pack up their things, switch off displays, and turn their chairs to one another, murmuring among themselves.

"Thank you, Miss Katy," says the General gruffly as he passes, giving her a half bow.

"Oh . . . you're welcome, General." Katy stands up quickly; she has to stop herself from saluting him.

"Go and get some rest," says the General.

He smiles in a way that reminds Katy of her father, returns the smart salutes of the Guards as he marches through the door with a slight limp. The room empties, the ministers and deputies chattering like children let out of school at the end of a long afternoon. Some of them nod to Katy; others look away awkwardly. Katy flattens herself against the wall and waits until they've all gone.

The lights shut off one by one as Katy walks down the corridor. The buildings in Zarzura are smarter than the people; they have cameras, sensors, and microphones that track the presence of people and adjust the lights and temperature accordingly.

Katy goes down a spiral-shaped staircase at the end of the hallway, on the outside of the building. Slowly at first, then faster, rushing round and round the steps. When she jumps off the last step, dizzy and red-faced, the sudden realization that she's alone, outside, unobserved and free, makes her fizz with energy.

She leaves the Security Hive and walks the shortest path through downtown Zarzura. The smart tiles underneath her feet light up the streetlamps in the ground. Above her, cool, dark windows are shaded by louvers and screens decorated with intricate latticework and floral patterns. Zarzura's red-colored buildings, made of eco-friendly sand from the Empty Quarter, nestle close, blocking the light from one another and shading most of Zarzura's paths.

The giant white wind tower, the landmark of downtown Zarzura, makes a noise like the continuous rushing of ocean waves as it vacuums the hot breeze from the streets and directs it up and out into the sky. The walls, too, undulate, following a particular wave form that captures the breeze and directs it through the streets, to keep the air cool and circulating.

Residential blocks, schools, parks, and playing fields surround the center like the layers of an onion, protecting its heart, where the scientists toil, in the Knowledge Hive, and in the Incubator Building. Meetings and events are held in the Multi-Use Hall; the Education Hive disseminates news broadcasts and educational programs to all of Semitia.

There's no local government here in Zarzura; major directives come from the capital, the City of Gazelles, in Eastern Semitia. Katy can't comprehend the country's vastness: thousands of miles of desert all the way to the Jordan River. It would take four days to travel by car from one end to the other.

And that's only Eastern Semitia, to the west of Mazun in the Peninsula. Western Semitia goes even farther, all the way to the Red Sea. Its capital is the City of Peace, in the former Levant, and Neom is Zarzura's sister smart city in Western Semitia. The two halves of the entire Semitian nation are conjoined twins, linked together by shared land and common languages. In comparison, the South West Asian Territories, including the country of Mazun, where Katy comes from, are sparse and straggling, beads strewn from a broken necklace, compared to this giant land that is Katy's temporary home.

Mazun and Semitia have never gone to war, but there are no diplomatic relations between the two: something to do with settlements after the Final War. Katy never paid attention in history class, never thinking she'd need to know. Now, sitting in these sessions with Raana Abdallah prizing out information from her, she wishes she had. It might be easier to figure out what exactly the Minister wants to know, and to what end.

At the station Katy climbs into an autonomous pod car, which drives her to her apartment. The sun is sinking into the western horizon, the sky above compressed in layers of pink and purple. Back home in Dhofar, the first stars are already shining in a sky of crushed velvet, strands of the Milky Way shimmering above the heads of the mountains. *Sun Mountain, Star Mountain, Lion Mountain, Water Mountain, and the Three Brides.* Katy says all their names to herself like a prayer, reminding herself that they still exist.

As she looks into the sandy expanse that runs along the periphery of Zarzura, there's a strange thing happening: two large sand twisters are dancing together in the dry, hot breeze. Katy has spotted a few small dust devils before, but never any of them as massive as this. She knows how they're formed: hot air rising quickly through cooler air above, turning into a vortex.

Here in Eastern Semitia, they call it a wedding of the jinns. The name is a throwback to the old days; it's stuck even though superstitions are discouraged in this most scientific of cities. But the Final War changed the climate, turning all kinds of weather phenomena into extremes of almost mythical proportions. The two long columns of dust bouncing toward one another, then parting, fascinate Katy. She follows the sight with her eyes as long as she can, until she's driven past it.

Just as the sun sets, Katy prays to the Warrior Queen, wishing to be pulled like a magnet by the deity in the direction of home. Her heart is an empty suitcase that's strewn its contents all the way along the road from Dhofar to Zarzura. She worries that she'll never see Sun Mountain again, never feel its mists on her cheeks, or hear the welcoming voices of her friends. She has nothing else to do but wait until the morning. That's when she feels hope return.

## 8.

Katy is in the shower, the hiss of the water and the steam taking her far away from Zarzura, back to Sun Mountain during the khareef, when the rain falls, the fog rolls in, and mist covers everything in a damp embrace. Zarzura is hot, dry, dusty; her mouth is always dry, her head aching constantly. She drinks water all the time, but it doesn't help. Sometimes Katy turns the heat down and spends hours in the bathroom like this, eyes closed, breathing deeply, and savoring the cool humidity. In Zarzura, they use recycled water, collected into capsules, filtered, sterilized, and sent back up through the shower pipe, for Katy to enjoy without guilt.

Today, Katy doesn't have the luxury of unlimited time. Soon a car will arrive to take her to an evening gala at the Etoile Museum in the City of Gazelles, the capital of Eastern Semitia. The city is made up of two hundred islands, some of them natural, others man-made, and the only way to the Museum is by boat.

She doesn't know why she's been invited to this gala, but she suspects Raana Abdallah wants to provoke the General, by showing her off to high Semitian society under his nose. She's Raana Abdallah's secret asset, but the General doesn't want too many people to know about her. Katy hates being a pawn in whatever power game is going on between the two of them. She vows not to let herself be used for anything that would go against Dhofar's interests.

Katy is excited about the excursion; she has never been on a boat before. Even though the mountains overlook the sea, the Hamiyat don't exactly have the time to come down for boat rides and pleasure trips from Mirbat, the fishing village on the coast. Women are rarely allowed on boats anyway, especially when they're pregnant; it's considered bad luck, a possible danger to the unborn child. Katy imagines the poor girls of the coast, feeling small and shrunken with envy, watching the tall ships docked in the harbor. They see the boys clambering aboard the boats, laughing and pushing one another, knowing they can never have the same fun.

A soft chime signals the end of the timed shower and the water turns off automatically. Katy squeezes the last droplets of water from her hair and steps out into the bathroom. She turbans her hair in one towel and swathes her body in another. She presses a small silicon patch onto the skin behind her ear: an anti-seasickness device, in case she gets nauseous on the boat.

There's a box on her bed, which Katy found outside her door earlier in the day. Adeefa must have left it there, rung the bell, and disappeared—she's fleet-footed, small-boned, and like a sparrow, she has a habit of vanishing and reappearing. Assigned to help Katy settle in, Adeefa stocked the pantry with food and water and showed her around Zarzura when she had recovered from her surgery. They've become friends of a sort, although Adeefa does most of the talking. She's always glancing at Katy shyly when she thinks Katy isn't looking. Katy suspects Adeefa has a crush on her, even though she wonders what the delicate Semitian sees in a rough mountain dweller like her.

The wrapping paper is beautiful, velvet-soft, the writing on it a delicate snaking calligraphy that Katy traces with her fingertip. The box itself is equally plush; it feels soft and buttery, seductively rich. Katy opens the clasps and lifts off the lid. Inside is a dress, but *what* a dress! Katy holds it up to the light. The long, floating robe shimmers in a color between smoky gray and powdery lavender. The sleeves are threaded with silvery patterns that match the calligraphy on the wrapping paper. The shape of it is irregular, like a triangle with uneven sides, but Katy still thinks it is perfect.

Katy eagerly shimmies into the dress, which falls down in a whisper over her body. The soft woven cloth tightens gradually, adjusting itself to the contours of Katy's body. In moments, it forms the perfect silhouette around her. Its color has changed, too, settling on a shade of violet that suits her skin perfectly. *Magic*, thinks Katy, for her first time in a formal dress as a grown woman. She lifts her arms so the sleeves flutter like sails and the embroidered threads twist and glint all around her.

Suddenly Katy wants to dance, just like they did on the mountain after the night of her squad's first shoot-out, when Laleh killed three men known to be spies. Katy and her comrades had been trained to be efficient killers, but despite the Hamiyat's fearsome reputation, they weren't psychopaths; they were soldiers, defending their homeland, and they knew how to get the job done. Drunk on their first taste of victory, some of the fighters began ululating, the trill bursting out of their throats for the joy of being together, triumphant, alive. It's a long way from there to here, but the feeling is the same.

The doorbell rings. Katy steps into her slippers and rushes out the door. Her face is bare, her hair loose and untidy. She'd wanted to tie it up into a ponytail, but Adeefa told her not to. "Tonight, you're not a soldier, you're a woman."

"I can be both, you know," was Katy's bristly retort, but Adeefa only smiled genially at Katy's irritation.

Adeefa is smiling now as she stands on the street next to the driverless car. She wears a black-and-gold dress, her hair is done up into an elegant twist, light color on her lips and cheeks. Katy moves hesitantly down the stairs, more used to sturdy laced boots than flimsy slippers.

"Well?" says Katy. "Is this all right?"

"You look stunning," Adeefa says. "Like a butterfly."

There's a small gap in the back of the dress, letting cool air touch her bare skin. Katy turns her head, craning to see it. "Are you sure I'm not wearing it backwards?"

"Who'd know? You're beautiful."

Katy's had plenty of hero worship on the mountain, but nobody calls her beautiful. Beauty is something meek and fragile, like gossamer. Katy is a prickly mountain weed, not a fleeting flower that takes ten years to grow, one day to bloom, one hour to die. She isn't sure what to do with the compliment, or what to think of Adeefa's blush.

"You'll have to be careful tonight. There are a lot of men who would love to take that dress off you, if you'll let them." She bundles Katy into the car and runs to the other side to get in, before Katy can tell her not to worry.

The air in the car is cold; the violet dress warms up slightly, sending a tingle down Katy's arms and legs. Adeefa falls quiet, but her hand stays close, and every once in a while, their fingers meet in silent reassurance. As the car glides toward the city, both of them are caught up in the anticipation of something new and unknown.

The driverless car is unexpectedly zippy, and the scenery flies past Katy's window. The road is lined by choppy blue-green water on both sides. Water is an integral part of the archipelago that makes up the City of Gazelles, with a myriad of bridges to cross from one island to the other. Silence contracts time on a journey like this; the forty-five minutes from Zarzura to the Aero Dock seem to take only ten.

Nosing down an off-ramp where the creek meets the open water, the car speaks in a computerized voice: "Arriving at your destination now. Please exit the car carefully and proceed to your left for boarding protocols in the departure lounge. Your craft leaves in thirty minutes."

Sudden panic grips Katy. "How will I manage this dress on the boat? It's too complicated. I shouldn't have come. Should I go back? What should I do?"

"Breathe," says Adeefa, laying her hand on top of Katy's. "I'll be there with you the entire time. Don't be scared."

The car doors have opened, revealing a hubbub outside. Katy's been dreading this all along, from the moment Raana Abdallah's invitation arrived. It'll be like one of the security sessions, only ten times worse. How will she answer the million questions they'll ask her? Katy gulps down her fear, trying to be brave, but it's as if she's on the battlefield for the first time all over again. "What do I say to them?" she croaks.

"Just hello. That's all."

Adeefa squeezes Katy's hand properly, then she plants a quick kiss on Katy's cheek. The pillowy softness of Adeefa's lips distracts Katy. She wants to turn her head toward Adeefa and taste her mouth, just briefly. But Adeefa motions slightly with her head toward the car dashboard: The car isn't just listening, it's watching.

Katy breathes deeply to slow her galloping heart. "All right. I'm ready."

When they're both standing outside, Adeefa cranes her neck at the Aero Deck. "I think that's where they store the boats," she says, pointing up at the gleaming glass structure several stories high, slanting in on itself at one side and projecting out at a sharp angle on the other.

People dressed in glittering thobes and robes, elaborately jeweled and accessorized, are milling around, staring at Katy and Adeefa. Katy clutches Adeefa's hand as they follow the others through the entrance into the Dock, pausing to flash their eyes at the retinal scanners.

Inside the grand marbled hall, guests chat and laugh; some of them send quizzical glances in Katy and Adeefa's direction, then whisper into one another's ears. Katy's identity is supposed to be a secret, but it's obvious these people, so deeply familiar with one another, are curious about the stranger. As Katy and Adeefa join the line for the escalator down to the lower level, a woman in front of them, wearing a ruby red jalabiya with gold loops on the sleeves, pulls on her companion's arm. "I heard there was supposed to be a surprise."

Her companion, a tall man in a black cloak with gold trim that covers his shoulders and surrounds him in silk and a strong, musky perfume, chides her. "The city doesn't *do* surprises."

"You never know!" she trills back. Her voice is melodious, her consonants softer, her vowels stretched so that they sound like she's speaking in exaggerated, courtly tones. "Perhaps the surprise *is* the surprise!"

The woman sounds so hopeful that Katy giggles under her breath. The cloaked man turns to look at Katy. He's wearing a pair of opaque glasses whose lenses turn clear as he gazes at her. Then he blinks, gives a start, and reaches his hand out to her with a warm smile that creases his face and lengthens his patrician nose. "Katy! What a pleasant surprise!"

Katy recognizes the General, his dress uniform covered

partially by the ornate cloak. Instead of a military cap, he wears a rich wine red beret with a gold crest: a gazelle standing on its hind legs.

"Good evening, General." Katy offers him her hand and he clasps it, then bows and brings his lips just above her skin without touching it. The gallant gesture feels odd to Katy; she's unsure of all these Semitian mannerisms and flourishes. She glances at Adeefa, who's hanging back, awestruck.

The General says, "May I present my Wife, Saffiya."

"Madame," Katy says, the word feeling strange in her mouth. Saffiya nods her head graciously. Her hair is swirled in a magnificent mass and dressed with a black veil pinned far enough back to show the front of her bouffant hair, rich, glossy, and brown. Katy hopes the General hasn't fully registered she was laughing at his Wife. Has he told her everything about Katy?

"So you are our young guest," Saffiya coos. "He didn't tell me you were coming! We'll have to look after you this evening." She turns to her Husband, her eyes crinkling. "I told you there would be a surprise." She flutters her hands so the late afternoon light, streaming through the plate glass windows, sets the red and orange jewels in her rings aflame. "You'll have to sit at our table, of course."

She slips her arm around Katy's waist, hugging Katy close. She's soft and curved; the motherliness of her body gives Katy a pang in her chest. Suddenly, Katy feels six years old, her cheek resting against her mother's breast, her breath lifting Katy's head up and down gently. She misses the warmth of her mother's body, the safest port Katy had ever known.

"I'm not sure about the table," says Katy. "Our seats may already be assigned?" She glances at Adeefa for confirmation, then steals a look at the General's uniform. His chest is covered with medals. Each one bears a small moving image of the action that earned him the award. In one, a miniature General can be seen pulling a wounded comrade away from enemy fire; in another, he's commanding troops over a barren, rocky crest. Nobody gets medals in the Hamiyat; everyone who has seen battle carries their histories in their chests, not on it. Katy. Laleh, Marzi, the other girls in the Hamiyat. Commander Kara. Where are their medals? Who will laud their bravery after they're gone? These thoughts nibble around the edges of Katy's mind as they walk to the slipway where the watercraft is anchored and waiting.

Adeefa has dropped her earlier reticence and is now conversing shyly with the General. Saffiya stays close to Katy. "We go to the Islands at least twice a month. For my Husband's job, but also sometimes just for leisure. It's wonderful to get away from the city. We're not completely anonymous out there, because of security, but at least it's not the fishbowl that this place is."

People are staring at Katy still, wondering who she is, why the General and Saffiya have her under their wing. What does she have, in terms of cachet, power, information, knowledge, that earns her the right to be with one of the most important couples in this City, maybe even the country?

The sea breeze lifts Katy's hair, tickles her back, and wafts her shimmering dress around her legs as they walk to a large white boat resting solidly on an aluminum cradle at land level. Five feet below, the water awaits. Passengers are lined up, filing onto the boat, finding their seats, and settling in. Katy had expected a skiff rising and falling on a rough sea; she had hoped to stand in the boat, legs planted firmly apart, riding the waves and laughing. Instead, she's disappointed by this tame sight, as exciting as boarding a bus.

The General nods his approval. "Automated docking was a real revolution in recreational boating. Cleaned up the timetables by a good hour! Although we had to suspend our boat-hailing services the time that shark swam up into the creek."

Saffiya rolls her eyes to the heavens. "He tells that joke every time to visitors. They're the only ones who would believe him even for a minute."

"A dry dock makes it easier for the passengers," the General continues. "Not everyone's got their sea legs around here. I can't believe they let you women wear those sharp-heeled—"

"High-heeled," Saffiya corrects him, turning her own exquisitely shod feet back and forth to show off the jewels on the three-inch heels.

Once all fifty passengers are seated, life jackets and seat belts in place, the cradle lowers the boat smoothly into the water, and then slides away, leaving the boat gently bobbing in the water. The gates to the port slide open, and the boat moves out into the sea. Katy's skin begins to tingle as the boat coasts, slowly at first, then faster. There's a slight lifting and tilting as the hydrofoils open up and raise the boat just above the water's surface. Soon it's cutting a path through the blue, but Katy feels like she's a kite soaring on the breeze.

Sea spray hits her face, the gentle breeze turning into a strong wind. Other women are fastening scarves onto their heads, but Katy wants to feel everything, every salty drop, every chill wind. She could dive right in under the water and feel no fear.

When the boat reaches top speed, a calm descends amid

the hum of the hydrofoil, the babble of conversation. Katy looks back at the city they've left behind, its distant buildings encircled by blue-green water, lending it an air of serenity. Sailboats and old dhows, tourist attractions on the Gulf, dot the ocean like the images in a children's story. Seagulls punctuate layers of thick cloud arching away from the horizon. The sky above struggles to contain all the blue beneath it.

Soon another island comes into view, where spiked thin towers reach up into the sky from low, domed buildings. "Pearl Island!" says Saffiya. "The cultural center. They have a spectacular show, my dear, about the Ancient Regime of the Bedouin, when pearls and oil were Semitia's main exports. Look, can you see the mosque replica? It's the sole place in the city where they exist."

"The westernmost part of our peninsula was the center of the Religious pilgrimage, but that ended after the Final War," the General interrupts. "And because of the Virus, authorities clamped down on travel and borders so much that the pilgrimages dwindled down to almost nothing."

This time, the General's warning glance silences Saffiya. Katy understands, in that moment, that there are things they are not supposed to say, even in a place as seemingly free as Semitia. There is only so far they can go with words and memories.

Saffiya points out the other islands flying past: Gazelle Island, filled with one-story houses all painted white, so that they shimmer in the sunlight; Turtle Island, where the liquid-gas refineries were rebuilt just after the Final War. Founding Fathers Island, where the city's masterminds and planners work in shining towers; Happiness Island, with pristine beaches filled with white sand and recreational grounds, where the people flock to on the weekends to swim and relax.

"Our people made these islands and inlets themselves," Saffiya says proudly. "They didn't want the city to look like—well, like Green City. All steel and glass, not a sign of nature anywhere."

Adeefa says, "You know so much about this place, you should have been a tour guide."

Saffiya laughs. "My Husband would never allow it!"

The General smiles. "Have I ever stopped you from doing anything you wanted to do?" His hand goes up unconsciously to one of his medals and he fingers it, as if it gives him reassurance that he really is a benevolent man.

"No," says Saffiya. Her cheeks color a little. Then she whispers to Katy, "He knows nothing about what I do or don't do. It's a good thing I'm cleverer than he is. This marriage would never have worked otherwise."

Perplexed, Katy leans her head against the cool window and lets her thoughts drift. She thinks of Adeefa's soft lips; mountain flowers all in bloom; water trickling around Katy's ankles, her feet plunged in time's shallow stream. The boat begins to lower as they approach Star Island. Étoile, Saffiya explains, means "star" in some European language. There's the Museum now: a vast, multisided silver-gray building constructed of a myriad of walls and beams intersecting at odd angles. As the hydrofoil fins fold in, they sail right into the Museum through an inlet built into the building's structure, like a river entering a wondrous cave.

The boat lines up perfectly with the cushioned arms of a pier at the bottom of a wide staircase. The gates on both sides slide open to start letting everyone off and up the staircase. Down in the water, Katy sees the twisting bodies of saltwater carp, bred and raised in the city's own fish farms, illuminated by underwater lights.

Pinholes of light in the ceiling form the shapes of constellations that float above this part of the world at night. Everything glimmers as they climb up the stairs, Katy's dress taking on even newer hues in the interplay of light and shadow.

"Hurry, hurry!" says Saffiya, who has beaten them to the top of the stairs.

Inside the Etoile Theater are a hundred round tables laid with fine china, silverware, glass goblets, flowers bursting from the middle of each. And the walls are lined in rose damask, with more folds of damask arranged high up into an ornate tent. Flickering candles emit the rich scents of oudh, jasmine, and roses. In a corner of the room, male and female musicians caress oud and tambura, tap darabukkas gently, and sing soft poetry as the guests walk into the theater.

At the doorway, Katy freezes. She's never been in a theater or a museum, doesn't really know what the difference is between both. Adeefa takes her sweating palm in her cool, firm hand, and coaxes Katy over to the table where the General and his Wife are greeting all their guests.

"Yoo-hoo! I was wondering where you had gotten to!" says Saffiya. "Sit down next to me, Katy." The table is laden with food: olives, bowls of creamy hummus, fragrant moutabel and other appetizers, dates, honey, dried fruits, samovars of coffee and tea, crystal vases of sparkling water. The plates are lined with gold, the napkins the same dusty rose as the drapes—threads and flashes of gold everywhere.

Saffiya heaps Katy's plate with a little of everything, and prods her to eat. Katy pushes the food around, too nervous to eat, then gulps down the whole plateful, while Saffiya is distracted by the throngs of women and men who come to greet her, surreptitiously examining Katy from head to toe.

One wealthy woman after another kisses Saffiya on both cheeks and sends a warm, curious glance in Katy's direction. The men throng. She wonders if she can bolt out of the theater and commandeer one of the boats back to Zarzura when a group of people walk swiftly down a red carpet at the far end of the room. Everyone rises to their feet. Adeefa pokes Katy to stand up, too. Raana Abdallah, resplendent in a bright blue embroidered thobe, walks behind a tight knot of three or four men.

Adeefa whispers, "That's the President." The bearded old man wearing the wine red embroidered cloak over his white robe, the gold dagger in his belt and another gold sword at his side, emits authority, force, prestige. Everyone leans toward him as if he is the nucleus, his entourage surrounding him in a swirl of activity, Raana Abdallah the outlier and the only woman among them. The President stops in his tracks, turns around, beckons Abdallah to walk beside him. She strides proudly to him; the men allow her to enter the inner circle, and one of them takes Abdallah's place at the end of the group.

This man who's fallen behind glances at Katy as the group passes the General's table. He's short and slim, and his hair flies away from his head in a halo of loose salt-and-pepper curls. His glasses magnify his small eyes into wide brown pools, darting this way and that to see who's looking at him. A Pakistani, Katy thinks, from Kolachi or beyond. An outsider. Like her.

Unlike the rest of them in their long white ceremonial dress, he's in a brown tunic and trousers, over which he wears a short chocolate brown jacket cut in a dashing style.

He holds her gaze for a long moment, then goes to sit at the same table as the President and Raana Abdallah.

The chandeliers are dimmed. The musicians stop their performance, strings and drumbeats fading into silence, and a fanfare of trumpets and drums drowns out everyone's chatter. A single beam of light hits the stage; a figure steps out from the darkness, a hologram that is neither merely man nor woman, but a hybrid of both, projected in 3D on the stage. When they speak, it sounds like they are sitting right next to each person, murmuring in everyone's ears.

"Welcome," says the voice. The figure raises their hands up in the air and lights swirl around them—blue, purple, pink—as the entire stage brightens like sunrise. "My name is Hana and I am your host for tonight. On behalf of the President of Eastern Semitia, I welcome you to this event to celebrate the accomplishments of our brightest visionaries, the scientists of Zarzura."

A wave of applause, at which Hana holds up their hands again. "Our scientists work day and night to provide us with the best solutions for living our lives as we were meant to: empowered, intelligently, and responsibly. From the very first days in Zarzura, we worked on solutions for green power, zero carbon emissions, and transport solutions."

As Hana continues to speak, giant screens light up, flashing images to accompany their words: rows and rows of houses with solar panels; a field of sunflower solar panels that turn and follow the sun; green forests; ocean waves with wind turbines turning in the sky.

Then the scenes on the screens change to horrific ones: nuclear explosions, flames, troops in battle, the same peaceful houses turned to rubble. "In the days of the wars that afflicted neighboring countries in the South West Asia Territory and beyond, we provided medical technology and equipment to treat the worst of those afflicted by the radiation." Children with their bodies burned, melted, necks fused to shoulders; men and women with hair and teeth falling out; animals staggering in a daze; miles of fields devastated, turned gray, destroyed utterly.

Saffiya, beside Katy, sobs openly at the table. The General's face is grim as he watches the parade of death go by. Katy thinks about her Hamiyat training, where they studied some of the key battles in this war. The warring armies fought many of their battles on a glacier, where thousands died because of the extreme cold and the dangers of mountain warfare: avalanches, strong winds, extreme temperatures. Many came back missing at least a few fingers or toes, if not whole hands or feet, to the cold.

Laleh and Marzi were most excited by the idea of nuclear weapons that could deliver unequivocal victory, the end stage of the Final War. Laleh was convinced that the Hamiyat could still get hold of a weapon and use it to their advantage today. But none of them had seen what these bombs did to the wider world. Katy feels ashamed to remember that they thought this was the answer to anything.

Hana's presentation continues. "We created solutions to save lives, and to help clean the earth and water that had been decimated by nuclear fallout." Now, here are children in clean hospitals, smiling through their pain; brown fields that turn green again; deformed trees that grow leaves and stand tall once more.

"The world looks to our smart cities, Zarzura in Eastern Semitia, and Neom in Western Semitia, as examples of how humanity can achieve the impossible." A swift pan over a map of the three cities, from one end of Semitia to the other, taking in Zarzura and Neom.

Hana bows toward the table where the President is seated, with Raana Abdallah and the rest of the powerful ones. "May I now call to the stage the Chief Scientist of Eastern Semitia's Ministry of Science and Technology . . . Dr. Zayn Battuta."

A man stands up at the President's table. Of course. It's the short brown-skinned man in the jacket and trousers who had come in with the President's entourage: the one who caught Katy's eyes and stared at her as if she were a creature he'd never seen before and was trying hard to classify.

Adeefa is leaning forward in her chair as Zayn Battuta straightens the back of his jacket, nods to everyone at his table, then climbs up to the stage and stands next to Hana, nodding out at the crowd. Katy observes the tension in Adeefa's body, the softness around her eyes and mouth, the slight parting of her lips. *She does have a crush*, thinks Katy. *But it's not me. It's him.* She feels a little envious, a sour feeling in the middle of her chest that she blames on all the rich food she's stuffed herself with, out of politeness and nerves.

"Dr. Zayn Battuta is Zarzura's top scientific authority," says Hana. "He implements Eastern Semitia's scientific policies, short-term and long-term, as directed by the President's Office. He heads the Forum of Prime Scientists, which brings together global professional bodies and academic institutions. He works closely with the Ministry of Foreign Relations to showcase our scientific advances in other countries. Because of his work, the world's best scientists travel to Zarzura for exchanges of ideas and knowledge. Tonight, Dr. Battuta is going to introduce one of Zarzura's most exciting projects, under development for the last seven years, and now, ready to be unveiled to all of you at last. Dr. Zayn Battuta!"

"Thank you, Hana," says Zayn Battuta. Hana steps aside graciously, giving him the center stage. He tips forward on to the balls of his feet, as if he's about to spring off the stage. The stage lights are reflected in his glasses.

Katy shivers. The people of Dhofar never trust messiahs. She dreads hearing about the visions this one will present, as urgently as if there were only one way to make it safely through this world—his. And the rest must either believe, or die.

# 9.

"Your Excellency," says Battuta, addressing the President. "Distinguished guests. Honorable ministers, dignitaries and diplomats, ladies and gentlemen of the city." His speech is fluent but his accent is strange, foreign. Katy sees his accomplishments scrolling on the screen behind his head: all his degrees, honorary and real, his discoveries, his memberships on scientific councils all over the world. But she finds it hard to reconcile them with the slight, impish man standing on the stage, rubbing his hands together like a boy with a trick up his sleeve.

"Thirty years ago, I came here from Kolachi, a young man wanting to discover the world. We were just recovering from the Final War, and Zarzura took me in and gave me a place to educate myself. After finishing my PhD, I wanted to contribute to the place that made me who I am today. I felt I had a debt to pay to Zarzura. Today, with the fruition of the last twelve years of my work here, I feel that debt has been repaid."

Battuta walks up and down the stage, chopping the air around him with quick hand movements. He draws everyone's eyes to him, with his handsome face and taut, energetic body.

"Algorithms, ladies and gentlemen," says Battuta. "From the Arabic name for Al-Kwarizmi, the ninth-century Persian mathematician Abū Ja'far Muhammad ibn Mūsa. He was the head of the library, the House of Wisdom, in Baghdad." A bearded man's face appears on the screen, then a red statue of the entire man, holding up an astrolabe.

"Algorithms are simply the steps, or a set of rules, that you follow to solve a problem. When we invented computers, we were able to perform thousands of these steps in a short amount of time—a program. We began to depend on them for our communications, our navigation, financial transactions, security systems."

Upbeat music, chirps, chimes, and machinelike sounds pulse in rhythm with Battuta's words; the screen fills with images of numbers arranging and rearranging themselves in calculations that turn into calligraphy. It's beautiful to watch; Katy is mesmerized.

"Algorithms became more and more sophisticated and elegant. Machines began to learn how to create their own algorithms, and to correct their own mistakes. Yet algorithms still dealt with routine tasks, the fundamentals of everyday life. Then, as the problems of the world became more and more complex, scientists concentrated not just on artificial intelligence, but beneficial intelligence.

"Beneficial intelligence concerns itself with questions of ethics and values. That's what I find myself intrigued by today. How can we use beneficial intelligence to help our country align itself with the role we want to play, that of regional and global leadership? Can we design a system that will help us avoid the nuclear war and political disasters that other countries have suffered? We have been lucky in that the Final War stopped at our borders, but in the future, this might not be the case. The winds that kept the fallout away from us might blow in the opposite direction next time. The bombs might come from elsewhere. Are we prepared for that possibility?

"As I began to develop the idea further, it really excited me. I loved the challenge of creating a giant, overarching computer-generated system of governance using input from our best diplomats, philosophers, generals, development specialists, economists. One that would deliver ethical solutions to our problems in ways that benefit our people. One that would truly belong to us, work for us, with us, and capture what we hold dear and value in ourselves. And what we want the world to know about us as a nation. One that is ready to lead the world in peace and harmony."

People nod and murmur as they begin to warm to Battuta's words. Katy feels a little bored now; her shoes are tight and her toes are starting to go numb. She glances around the room: The General looks proud. Raana Abdallah, on the other hand, is a study in suspicion. Her lips are drawn down, and strong marionette lines appear on either side of her nose. She's watching Battuta like a tiger, waiting for him to slip up.

"So I began with a dream. And then, after the dream, I woke up. I began to study the world's disciplines," says Zayn Battuta. "Which ones would apply to this project? Which were most relevant? Philosophy? Economics? Physics? Psychology? Languages? Art? The answer, ladies and gentlemen, is all of them.

"So we compiled the teachings of all the major thinkers, philosophers, economists, scientists, and artists as they are taught in our schools and universities. We turned their thoughts, their teachings, into programs."

Battuta folds his arms over his chest, chuckles self-deprecatingly. "When I first thought of this concept, I can tell you, it even sounded crazy to myself." The audience laughs at this. They're completely charmed by his humility, his modesty.

"I'm an admirer of the Socratic method: a way of asking questions in order to find the truth and question false assumptions. We used the simplest if-then pattern of algorithmic computations to encapsulate the Socratic method in the system.

"So, too, with the philosopher Ibn Sina, and his contemporaries: Al-Farabi, Al-Ghazali, and the other Persian logicians. Inductive reasoning and syllogism strengthened the system's ability to evaluate any condition we might be faced with and return a logical and ethical conclusion."

Katy picks up a gold-plated spoon on the table in front of her and begins to tap it against her plate. One look from Saffiya stops her cold; she puts down the spoon sheepishly.

"We developed a digital neural network that could learn how to be an ethical thinker, how to evaluate choices and options not by efficiency or task completion, but by the more humane qualities of compassion and warmth and goodness that we tend to believe distinguish us from machines."

Katy rolls her eyes, but it's too dark for anyone to see her. "Where are the women philosophers?" Katy whispers to Adeefa, who shushes her. She tries to concentrate on Battuta again.

"All computations are put through a rigorous process of ethical evaluation. We will never use this system to engage in hostilities with another nation, to use nuclear weapons, or to justify repressing our own citizens, even in times of crisis.

"So, we fed it with as much information as we could: Famous court cases and legal rulings that changed the world. Science's most difficult conundrums. The outcomes of the world's major battles. Problems and dilemmas that confounded the world's best thinkers. Questions of art and science and logic and progress. All the dilemmas in Shaykh Zubair's plays, for example: Should Romeo and Juliet have killed themselves? How could their families have settled the matter in a less fatal way? For one of our more challenging experiments, we even tried to make it tell us if God existed." Zayn Battuta smiles. "I am disappointed to say that we did not get an answer to that question. In fact, the system told us to pray about it and we might eventually understand."

Zayn Battuta bows his head and lowers his tone. "We made many mistakes along the way. There were times when I despaired of accomplishing what I'd set out to do. But today I am happy to inform you that we have completed the final testing on our system. We have, I am proud to announce, the world's first ethical computing system. And I am here tonight to show you what it can do."

All the walls of the room light up at the same time, then appear to be blown apart by an explosion that startles everyone. Katy, alarmed, readies herself to take a defensive position under the table. Adeefa leans in to whisper in her ear: "It's 4D, don't worry!" Her lips brush close to Katy's skin. Katy's heart beats fast at the combination of panic and excitement that the moment gives her.

A single word appears in the darkness on the screen, a name that glows as it enlarges until it takes over the entire wall behind Zayn Battuta:

Al-Ruh Al Zakiyah
The SmartSoul

The entire room buzzes with confusion, adrenaline, astonishment. "How clever!" says Saffiya. "A computer with a soul."

"But there is no such thing!" says the General.

"I don't understand," Katy says. "How can a computer have a soul?"

"Of course it can't," says the General. "Even humans don't have souls. Our scientists disproved it beyond a doubt thirty years ago. Souls, God, life after death, it's all nonsense! Why on earth has he chosen this . . . this anachronism?"

"Maybe he's being ironic," says Saffiya.

Beyond their table, the rest of the people seem equally divided about the presentation. The President is deep in conversation with his advisers, some of whom look up worriedly at Zayn Battuta on the stage, Hana by his side. How much money must they have put into Zayn Battuta and his crackpot computer? Katy knows that money and power are the base of any society in the world, once your survival's no longer at stake. On the mountain, people still need their gods. The Semitians and the Mazunians in Green City can afford to kill them and replace them with algorithms.

"Ladies and gentlemen, please," says Hana. Next to them, Zayn Battuta looks worried, as if he can't understand how what he's said is so controversial.

Before coming to Eastern Semitia, Katy had never seen a scientist—Sun Mountain barely has a school, let alone fancy laboratories or science centers. None of the Dhofar women ever dreamed of becoming scientists. But over the last three months in Zarzura, Katy has seen many of them as they stream in and out of the Institute and the Knowledge Center. They come out in twos or threes, engrossed in conversation about their work; they go to the café and talk science over their expensive coffees, which they get for free in Zarzura's eating spots, like all their food.

They're mostly men, a few women, tall, small, Asian, Arab, Indian, white; even the dark ones have an unhealthy pallor, as if they never venture outdoors. They all wear enhanced glasses, the figures and images on the lenses dancing as they thumb their devices for information to support their points.

Adeefa blinks out at the audience, frowning. *She's worried for him*, Katy thinks. She must really be in love. Katy doesn't know what that feels like; she's been trained to avoid men. She took the vow of celibacy when she joined the Hamiyat, which is meant to keep them focused and strong. Love is dangerous, they were taught: it weakens judgment, makes a fighter vulnerable to distraction and betrayal.

Then Raana Abdallah moves toward the stage. Her usual powerful stride is restricted by her rich robe, cinched in at the waist by a jeweled belt. She stands at the edge of the stage and beckons Battuta toward her. He springs forward, bends down to listen as she whispers in his ear. He nods eagerly, bounces back to his place at the center of the stage, and raises his hands imploringly, causing the hubbub to die away.

"Your Excellency, ladies and gentleman, my distinguished colleague, the honorable Deputy Minister for Foreign Affairs, Madame Abdallah, has made an excellent suggestion. She requests that I demonstrate the powers of our system by posing it a question and having it give us a response in real time. Would you indulge me in this little experiment? With your permission, Your Excellency?"

The president glances at his advisers for their confirmation, then waves one hand in the air magnanimously. With his other hand, he brings a date to his mouth and chews on it reflectively. Nobody else dares touch their food, although it's long past dinnertime and everyone's starving.

Battuta clasps his hands behind his back and looks all around him. Raana Abdallah sits back in her seat, leans forward intently. The rest of the audience hold their breath. The lights change ever so subtly, turning a mysterious shade of violet. Pinpoints of light twinkle overhead like the constellations, the first mystery that confronted humans when they were able to lift their heads and look up at the sky.

"SmartSoul," says Zayn Battuta, speaking slowly and clearly. For him, the audience no longer exists. Now it's just him and the system that he has invented. "What is the biggest moral problem facing the world today, and how should we as Semitians address it?"

There's a hush as everyone waits to see what the algorithm says. Katy fantasizes that the computer will tell them to just blow themselves up, like India and Pakistan, and take away the world's biggest burden—human beings. If the computer is a reflection of the heights that humanity can achieve, why not counsel humans to commit collective suicide for the betterment of the planet? Katy is amazed by people who would listen to a machine that cannot possibly know what it means to be dead or alive.

A great light ricochets all around the room: a bright orb above their heads, the energy created by the millions of computations SmartSoul is performing at the same time, working on the challenge that Battuta has given it.

Then SmartSoul speaks for the first time, in a voice that is more like light than sound. The words speak directly in Katy's mind, and the minds of everyone in the hall.

"The world's biggest moral dilemma is what is happening to women in Mazun."

Zayn Battuta says, "Ah . . . could you clarify?"

"They are trapped. Enslaved and oppressed. They must be freed. Green City must be liberated."

SmartSoul projects images on all the walls of the room, of Green City's women, in black veils, with swollen pregnant bodies, accompanied by two and three men on the street, in malls, in parks. Masked men bundle people into cars and drive them away to a large white building with no windows. Multiple babies are pulled out of women's bodies, lined up in group neonatal incubators that warm them like piglets in an oven. Katy recognizes the images from what she's been taught about Green City; she feels shame that she comes from this country, even though she fights against it.

She watches the people around her: Saffiya and the General are both frozen-faced. The President looks enraged; his advisers are trying to calm him down. People are booing the screen, as if they can be heard by those who are trapped in those pictures. Battuta is stunned; he's unleashed something he didn't anticipate. This is not just a program Battuta has invented. It's something more than that. It knows how to make people *feel*, not just think. And feelings are more dangerous than thoughts: They're irrational; they can't always be controlled.

Katy shakes her head. This can't be. Of all the problems in the world, SmartSoul wants Semitia to do something about Mazun? To take on Green City? Katy's mind sparks with the possibilities of help coming from a country as large and powerful as Semitia, East and West.

There's only one person who looks pleased in the midst of this angry commotion: Raana Abdallah, always so tightly controlled, so perfect, never revealing a base emotion or a human desire. But now she looks at Katy like a shark: with dark, sharp eyes that reveal a hunger Katy hasn't seen before.

Raana Abdallah gets up from her seat, walks toward the General's table, says hello to him and Saffiya, who have managed to pull themselves together and nod tightly back at her. She ignores Adeefa, who scrambles out of her seat and dashes off to a far corner. Raana Abdallah sits down in her place, waits a few moments, drinking in the commotion, before she turns to Katy.

She leans in, puts a hand on Katy's forearm. "What did you make of that, Katy? Wasn't it terrible? Amazing that SmartSoul homed in on the one thing that keeps me up at night. Zayn Battuta really is a clever man."

Out of the corner of her eye, Katy sees Zayn Battuta explaining something to the President's advisers, tugging his hand through his hair nervously. Raana Abdallah is smiling, and it terrifies Katy more than anything she's seen here tonight.

"Funny that it took a computer to tell all these men what we women already know. We must do something to help the women of Green City, of Mazun. It's the only honorable thing to do."

"It is?" Katy should be pleased at what SmartSoul has told the people of Semitia to do about Green City. Overthrowing the government would suit the people of Dhofar very well, so she can't understand why she feels so much fear.

But Katy realizes what SmartSoul is really for: It may be made up of a thousand intricate steps, but it leaves the final decision up to human beings. And there's no telling what they might decide upon, while hiding behind a computer program. They would leave the responsibility of choosing between right and wrong to the computer, instead of taking it on themselves. They could use it to justify any number of deaths, even her own. And if it all went wrong, they would blame it on SmartSoul, not themselves. And to Katy, that is the real horror.

"Of course. Your Hamiyat have been fighting for a long time, but a women's protection unit can hardly be expected to make a dent in Green City's power. However, all that's going to change now. We will go to war against Mazun. We will help your Hamiyat start a revolution. And you, Katy Azadeh, will be the one to lead them."

"Me?" Katy's voice is strangled.

"Yes, you, of course. Did you think it was your destiny to spend the rest of your days on that mountain, playing at soldiers with your girlfriends? You are meant for bigger things, Katy Azadeh. As am I. And together, we're going to make them happen. Wait and see."

Something inside Katy snaps. She abruptly stands up, pulls her beautiful dress up above her knees, and runs toward the doorway. There are people surging around her; she twists and turns her body like a knife slipping through their hot, buttery mass. "Katy, come back," shouts someone, calling to her as if in a dream. But she doesn't stop moving until she's gone.

## 10.

Katy bolts down the halls of the Etoile Museum like an animal chased by fire. The Museum is eerily empty, all activity concentrated in the theater where Zayn Battuta has alarmed the crowd with his out-of-control computer. Her first instinct is to head straight for the underground jetty, but she's already forgotten the way back to the boats. So taken with the amazing sights and sounds and the magnificent people around her, she's forgotten to work out how to escape. Raana Abdallah's hand on her arm was not a sign of her affection; it was a shackle around Katy's wrist.

She passes one door, then the next, and the next, rejecting each one. Heart pounding, legs pumping, she stumbles over a set of black marble steps going down, recovers, and keeps on running. She can't outrun Raana Abdallah's words echoing in her ears . . . "Katy Azadeh, you will be the one . . . the one . . . the one . . ."

Katy doesn't want this crown on her head, this mantle on her shoulders. She doesn't want to be at the head of any Semitian wars. She only wants to go back to Sun Mountain, to her friends, her sisters, her comrades-in-arms. She wants to fight for the liberation of Dhofar, not the interests of a foreign power. She wants to never set eyes on Raana Abdallah or Zarzura ever again.

She's running in circles, passing the same doors again and again. Finally, she chooses a doorless chamber at the end of an uncrossed corridor.

Once inside, Katy is bathed in pink light. Rose-colored

tiles are spread upward and outward in swirling patterns, up the walls and across the intricate five-arched domes in the ceilings. Katy leans against a wall that feels surprisingly cool. She sinks down onto a rich red carpet, unable to move any farther. The silken weft is soft on her cheek. Her heartbeat throbs in her ears, and there's a whooshing sound that she's startled to recognize as her own ragged breath.

She looks up at the windows, made of stained-glass panels in all the different colors of the rainbow: deep blue, warm red, joyous green, vibrant yellow, cool violet. The glass panels are arranged in geometric patterns, flowers, rectangular blocks. Lights behind the windows throw colored reflections onto the walls at slanted angles. Katy is astonished to be inside a life-size kaleidoscope.

"Incredible, isn't it?"

A man steps out from behind one of the pillars and Katy's breath catches in her throat. The man comes closer, swimming into focus. Only when he kneels next to her does Katy recognize the scientist Zayn Battuta.

Behind his glasses, his eyes are mild, curious. He glances around, and Katy thinks he might touch his head to the floor the way the Religious used to in the days of belief. But instead, he smiles as if recognizing his own handiwork. "The Pink Mosque in Shiraz. It was destroyed during the Iran bombardments."

Katy knows that mosque now that Battuta has named it. Her grandparents talked of the morning light of Shiraz that woke up the poets, brought its gardens to life, stirred the nightingales in the cypress trees. Her grandmother said that people came from all over the world at the heart of dawn to see that place, not just to worship the Creator but to be awed by his Creation.

But this is just a replica, a pretty jewel box in a museum,

walls behind walls, not light upon light. Even the fake sunlight comes from a powerful lamp that imitates the splendor of the sun.

"We couldn't save the Glass Mosque, which was even more beautiful than this, if you can believe it," says Battuta. "We didn't have the cameras in place to make the 3D scans. Too much got damaged already, before we could do the recording. And it's particularly challenging to replicate all that glass. Such intricate work. Luckily, we had a fantastic digital record for the Pink Mosque. Our printers were able to recreate it in time for the opening of this museum. We've got plans to replicate the Taj Mahal, too, if we get the go-ahead. That would be our biggest triumph yet."

Katy thinks of Dhofar, after the khareef has come and the mountains are carpeted in flowers. As a little girl, she picked peacock flowers the same bright yellow from the Sherboon valley and tied them up in a posy for her mother. The Wife Alia gathers basil flowers of the same cool violet for her soups and stews. The frankincense flowers are the same burning orange staked to the wall of this toy. The mountain is real. Those colors, those flowers, that light can never be replicated by any man-made machine.

"Your computers made this? Or just copied it?"

Battuta says, "That's what I was just telling you. We had the digital records, we only had to reproduce—"

"A poor imitation," Katy says. "And it's cursed, just like your machines are."

Battuta looks at her closely. "You're Katy Azadeh, aren't you? The fighter from Dhofar."

"How do you know about me?" *He* likes to give speeches, Katy thinks. He's in love with himself, or what he thinks he can accomplish, with his computers and machines and scientific principles. He'd replicate the human heart if he could, and command it to love whomever he told it to adore.

"You're Raana Abdallah's secret weapon. But I didn't know you could talk this much. She's actually quite annoyed at how silent you've been all this time."

Katy doesn't like how close he is. But she knows how to defend herself if he crosses the line. She silently orders her muscles and tendons to relax. "Raana Abdallah's secret weapon? I thought that's what your invention was. Your . . . what is it again? Soul Sucker? Super Fool?"

"SmartSoul," he chides Katy, as if she's misnamed his child. She grins, and he half smiles back at her, his eyes warming at her teasing. Then she turns serious again.

"The women of Green City are just Raana Abdallah's excuse to go to war. You don't really care about what's happening to them. You just need a justification to use your computers and bombs, to kill us all so that you can take over."

"Not true."

"Prove me wrong," Katy says. It comes out like a threat.

Battuta's eyes grow wary again. But Katy wants him to know how furious she is at the idea that the Semitians should interfere in her country. The Hamiyat have been fighting the Collectors for nearly five years now. "It's our mountain, it's *our* fight," she says, wishing she had Raana Abdallah's eloquence.

Katy still can't remember how she got from Dhofar to Zarzura, and it frustrates her. Wounded fighters go to a makeshift hospital on the other side of the Three Brides, where there are still medics who lived and worked with the insurgents along the border between Dhofar and the Southern Republic. Captured fighters, if they don't kill themselves first, are taken away to Sheba City, or prisons farther beyond. If Katy was actually captured by the enemy, why isn't she a prisoner in a Green City hospital instead?

Battuta sits cross-legged now and props his elbows on his knees, his chin on his hands. Hunched over like this, he looks like a young boy. He and Katy are almost face-to-face: close up, his face exudes an eager energy, restless and untamed. But his eyes take on a shade of sadness.

"You think I don't know war," he says softly. "You think I spend all my life inside a room, behind a screen, doing calculations that don't mean anything to the real world."

Katy says nothing, watching his lips move as he talks.

"I was born in Kolachi ten years after the Final War had ended. We thought Partition was bad, but it was nothing compared to nuclear war. What you saw up there on the screen? Those were the acceptable images. You don't know what war looks like until you see people eating tree bark, insects, worms. Dead dogs. Dead children."

Battuta continues, "Imagine this, Katy: Farmlands destroyed. Cattle gone. Our rivers poisoned. The factories blown up. Food production finished." He speaks slowly, as if remembering a bad dream. "In the South, we could fish and eat seaweed. In the North, they starved.

"We have more birth defects in the South West Asian Territory than the rest of the world. My older brother couldn't walk, talk, feed himself. Some babies were born without limbs. If they were born at all." He shudders, then gathers himself. "I was lucky. I was born normal. Smart, even. So my parents sent me to Kolachi to study. I never saw them again."

He scoffs under his breath. "War. It's the worst things humans have ever invented." Then he narrows his eyes at Katy, sounding stern. "Do you understand, now, why I would never purposefully create a system that would lead us all down that path again?"

Katy doesn't know what to say. The desire to trust and actual trust are two shores on the opposite ends of a vast ocean. His words are convincing, but Katy doesn't know how to swim from one shore to the other. She glances at the door, wanting to get up and leave Battuta and go somewhere where she can be alone again.

Battuta says, "Don't worry, nobody's going to come here. They're all still in the theater. They'll feast, then watch the entertainment. Although they probably found my presentation more entertaining than they expected."

"But they'll still agree to what your computer said to do?" says Katy.

"Easterners," he laughs softly. "Give them food and wine, that's all they need. They like to leave the thinking to other people. The Westerners are more serious. I like that. I had some wonderful colleagues at the Orb. We did excellent work." His lips twitch, like those of someone who wants to tell a secret. He bends even closer to her. "You aren't the first one from Mazun to end up on this side of the border, you know."

"What do you mean?"

"I'm not supposed to tell you this. But I think it's the only way you'll believe me." Battuta pulls out a device from his pocket and waves his hand over it. An image appears on the screen, which he shows to Katy. He's so near to her now, she can smell his scent: moss, sweat, a sharp tinge of alcohol. She's never been this close to a man before. It feels strange—she wants to lean in and pull back at the same time.

The face of a beautiful woman, with brown hair, brown eyes, and smooth olive skin, appears on the screen. Katy has just enough time to register her loveliness when Battuta flicks his thumb, bringing up the image of a man: blond, thin, glasses, arms folded over a white coat, shy and kind-looking.

Katy says, "Who are they? I don't know them. Are they actors?"

Battuta shakes his head and *tsks*. "Heroes. They came here from Green City. They escaped the regime. He was a doctor there, she was . . . a rebel."

*This woman, with her delicate features, her sad expression, isn't Hamiyat material*, Katy thinks. Heroes are made on a battlefield, not by running away. "How did they get here?"

Battuta says, "They disguised themselves as Virus victims. They hid in coffins to get past the authorities. Sabine herself drove them across the border. In an ambulance!"

Katy has never driven a car before. She only travels on the autonomous vehicle line in Zarzura. "Did she crash?" Katy says. "Did they have to be rescued?"

Battuta doesn't hear her envious tone. "They smashed through the border fence. We took them in, gave them protection and asylum. They sent them to Neom, in Western Semitia."

"The other smart city," Katy says tartly. "I saw your presentation."

"The woman, Sabine, hid underground for years in a place called the Panah, with other women who didn't want to be part of Green City's awful system. But she got sick and almost died. Julien saved her life. While she was recovering in the hospital, the Agency sent one of their most dangerous men after both of them, a man called Reuben Faro. They escaped just in time."

Katy is quiet, digesting all this information. Battuta mistakes her silence for disbelief.

"I met them," Battuta says. "Their story is true."

"Was she wounded?" Katy wants to show Battuta real battle scars, made by bullets tearing into flesh, lodging into bone. A real warrior carries the scars on the outside, not the inside, fragile as a porcelain doll.

"Not all wounds are on the outside, Katy," says Battuta,

as if reading her mind. "She's traumatized from her years in hiding. She's adjusting well, but it will take her a long time to heal."

Katy says, "And the doctor?"

"We have him working on one of our medical projects in Neom. He has a brilliant mind. And we've learned a hell of a lot about how things work in Green City. We put everything they told us into the program for SmartSoul."

Katy asks, "What about what I told Raana Abdallah and the General about Dhofar . . . is that in SmartSoul, too?"

"You don't even realize how much you're going to help your own people," says Battuta softly.

Katy is suddenly aware of Battuta's knee touching hers. He's nudging her gently with his shoulder, too. Is this what men do, try to be near women in any way they can? But as the rosy pink light surrounding them blurs the boundaries of their bodies, she knows that she likes to be touched by this man. She likes how he smells, and she's been watching his mouth when he speaks. What would his lips feel like: rough or smooth, reticent or forceful? She's only ever kissed girls before; this would be something entirely new.

She tells herself not to get distracted by Zayn Battuta as another idea begins to take shape in her mind. How many times has she heard Commander Kara bemoan the early insurgency's lack of equipment, unable to hit the enemy where it truly mattered? How many times have the Hamiyat Commanders dreamed of a march on Sheba City, the capital of Dhofar, and from there to the Red City, even Sana'a, in the subsumed province of Yemen? It would take ten thousand women, transport vehicles, logistics, and as many weapons and ammunition to the city. They would probably all die in the onslaught. But what if the support of the Semitians made it possible after all? What if the Semitians could help them seize Dhofar?

Just then, Battuta murmurs into her ear, "Who do you think created the Spectrum?"

His breath, warm and intimate, makes her shiver. It's not fear, but a frisson of pleasure. "*Our* Spectrum?" Katy says, her mouth suddenly dry. He's leaning against her now. His skin is warm and his fingers, brown and slender, are stroking her arm like a musician gently trying out the strings of an unfamiliar instrument.

"It was one of my earliest projects. A fun little challenge, to make a data network that operated through light, not radio. We sneaked a few transponders here and there, to see who might be listening. One day, someone answered. Someone who called herself a commander of a women's unit. Her name was . . ." His lips are coming closer to hers; she only has to turn her head slightly and they'll meet.

"Katy!"

The cry echoes along the walls, making Katy and Zayn Battuta spring apart. Adeefa is standing in the entrance to the Pink Mosque chamber. Backlit by the brilliant lights in the corridor, her elongated shadow nearly reaches Katy's feet.

Katy stands up slowly, holding Battuta's hand for support. Her knees are weak. She's a little overwhelmed by Battuta's words and his proximity to her, the kiss they almost shared. It would have been her first with a man. From her vantage point, Adeefa can't see Battuta, half-hidden by another pillar. When he rises to his feet, too, Adeefa draws in a quick breath. Battuta shakes himself lightly, slides past the two women, and melts into the bright light of the corridor.

"I've been looking for you everywhere," says Adeefa. "Raana Abdallah sent me to find you."

"I needed some space," Katy says. One foot is askew in its

beautiful shoe. She bends down to grip it, hard, as if trying to twist it back into place, avoiding Adeefa's eyes. "She must be furious with me."

Adeefa shakes her head. "That's what I don't understand. When she saw you run, she laughed."

"Why?"

"'We're on an island,' she said. How far could you have gone?"

Katy lets Adeefa lead her back to the Etoile Theater. There's a reason they put Katy in this dress, these flimsy slippers. These borrowed feathers are exquisite, but too heavy to let her fly away.

# 11.

Raana Abdallah and Katy Azadeh are alone in the Zarzura conference room for the first time. It's always been filled with other people: Security Council members, various personnel, aides and assistants. Today, the morning after the gala, only the two of them are seated at the table. The microphones and screens are switched off. A set of small bright lights illuminates their faces, but the rest of the room stays dark.

A few people discreetly walk up and down the hall at random intervals, letting Katy know that she's being monitored in case she causes any trouble. Their silhouettes cross the opaque glass doors, invisible sentries meant to intimidate her.

In this limited, isolated space, it's difficult to project defiance, or anger, or any of the other emotions that fight inside Katy. Abdallah regards her coolly, daring her to speak first. Never has Katy felt smaller, or weaker, than in this moment, where this woman has her trapped inside a web that others have been weaving for years.

Abdallah's so serene, as if the commotion that broke out when SmartSoul made its pronouncement at the gala last night never happened. She hasn't mentioned anything about that.

After returning to the theater, Adeefa didn't take her eyes off Katy for a second, and Katy was sure other Guards had been instructed to watch her, too, from a distance. The General ignored her, and Saffiya busied herself playing gracious hostess. Katy helped herself to some fish and pretended to eat for politeness' sake, but whatever she put in her mouth tasted like sand.

As Zayn Battuta predicted, after the banquet, there was a show. A series of tall, ethereal models walked onstage wearing outlandish headpieces and garments made entirely of multi-colored flowers, vibrant greenery. Blossoms fell like waterfalls over their heads, branches entwined around their arms, and other finery twisted into shapes and figures that soared high into the air and around their swaying bodies. A woman floated by with an enormous helmet made entirely of pink and white orchids, another wore a face mask that resembled a giant butterfly, a third sported the wings of a giant insect fluttering behind her. The Semitians applauded each creation wildly.

Hana, the androgynous hologram, then announced that not only had the flowers been created by 3D printers, but the models themselves were the most lifelike robotic mannequins Semitia had ever invented.

"Unlike other countries, the Semitian nation believes in giving respect and dignity even to humanoids, whether in male or female form," intoned Hana, their voice melodious and convincing. "Tonight we combine art, science, and nature as a message of harmony among all these elements, and to showcase the highest values of our society."

The Semitians gave this pronouncement a standing ovation. Raana Abdallah, back at the President's table, beckoned Zayn Battuta over to her side to congratulate him. Bewildered, Katy glanced from one face to the next, after the President shook Battuta's hand in front of everyone, wondering if he'd already been absolved. But maybe if you were one of them, you could never truly do anything wrong.

On the way home, Adeefa was silent. Katy had been planning to ask her to come upstairs, maybe even to stay the night, but Adeefa left her at her apartment and didn't even say good-bye. Katy went upstairs, took off the beautiful dress, stuffed it into its beautiful package, and put it in a closet, never wanting to see it again.

"Ask me anything," says Raana Abdallah suddenly, bringing Katy back into the present moment. Her voice is not friendly. "I know you have questions. I promise I'll tell you what I can. And then I'll tell you what you have to do."

Katy says, "I don't want to know anything. I don't want to have anything to do with your plans." For the first time, she dares to say it out loud: "I want to go home, back to Sun Mountain."

"Ah, your mountain." Raana Abdallah stretches her legs, points her heeled shoes at the floor, then sets them down again with a strong clack. "When the insurgency erupted in Dhofar, we wanted to keep an eye on it. The Spectrum, Zayn Battuta's communication channel, allowed us to monitor the fighting."

"Why?" Katy still can't believe that the Spectrum belongs to the Semitians, that the insurgents didn't invent it.

"At first, just to listen. We keep tight controls on our border and didn't want any trouble from the insurgents. Then, one day, they made contact with us through a female fighter. They were looking for urgent support in a battle they were losing badly. We didn't promise much at the time; it wasn't official policy to get involved with Mazun's affairs. It still isn't."

Here, Raana Abdallah looks straight at Katy.

"That's how we learned about the Hamiyat, when they formed, after the main rebellion had been defeated. An insurgency is one thing, but a women's fighting force is quite another. I encouraged them to mobilize and protect themselves even after the main fighting had ended. And I convinced my superiors that we should find a way to be mutually useful to one another."

Katy says, "What do you need with us? We're just an annoyance to Green City. They send the Collectors to harass us, but it's only a game of cat and mouse to them."

Abdallah takes the question seriously. "Katy, do you think I like what has been happening to women in Green City all these years? As a junior diplomat, I learned about what the women were forced into—multiple marriages, multiple pregnancies, procreation schedules—so many injustices, so much inhumanity, it made my blood boil . . . I wanted to do something for them. I am a woman, too. It's just that I was luckier to be born here, in this country, and not in Mazun. We were incredibly lucky: The Virus didn't affect our female population; otherwise we might find ourselves in the same situation."

Katy says, "I always wondered why Semitia wasn't affected the way we were."

"Nobody knows how or why the Virus, which killed off so many women in South West Asia, didn't affect us Semitians. Common knowledge says it's because of our ocean breezes, carrying the fallout away from us, but that can't be the only thing. Our scientists think we may carry a genetic mutation that protected us from it, because we've been inoculating our female children against HPV since the late twentieth century. They never did that in South West Asia, especially in the territories. Too much vaccine hesitancy.

"But if we hadn't had the foresight, and our women had died like they did all across Mazun, would our leaders have protected those of us who survived, or parceled us out like rations to be shared? I can't say for sure.

"I know they call me ruthless, ambitious, power-hungry. But you cannot do anything for anyone else without power. I mean real power, over people's lives. I got to where I am today because I realized that very quickly, but you haven't yet, because you're young, and because you see the world differently than I do."

The familiar dismissal makes Katy snort impatiently: youth, inexperience, lack of exposure to the wider world.

Raana Abdallah waves her hand impatiently, as if pushing away dust in the air. "No, no, don't take that as an insult. I actually respect your opinions. Do you think the others would want me to talk this openly to you? The General? He's been against my plan from the start. He doesn't like you very much. On the other hand, I see potential in you, Katy. You could be like me. You could be the catalyst that changes everything for your people."

The sting of betrayal catches Katy under the breastbone. The General's civility, Saffiya's warmth last night—all a charade? Or is Raana Abdallah trying to keep Katy paranoid and off guard? Katy only allows herself a moment of grief, surprised by how quickly she's become attached to the idea that the General and his Wife might be fond of her.

Abdallah flicks a switch underneath the table, turning on an extra light and opening a small screen that pops up in front of them. The screen glows into life; a map of Dhofar, its mountain ranges, rises up in 4D. The image is so precise, so detailed, there are even little clouds of mist clinging to some of the peaks. Tiny waterfalls move downward, threading their way to the sea that Katy has yet to see with her own eyes.

"We set up a listening post at first, here, on Sun Mountain." Her finger outlines the tallest peak, indicating one of the main camps. "We provided logistics and intelligence to the Hamiyat through the Spectrum. We spied on the Collectors and gave away their positions to the Hamiyat."

*So that was how the Hamiyat could hold off the Collectors from fully taming the mountain*, Katy realized. They'd blocked Collectors' supplies, sabotaged their vehicles, sent them to desolate places where Hamiyat waited to ambush them. But it had all been with Semitian help—the truth is beginning to dawn on Katy like a day she doesn't want to face.

"We like to irritate Green City as much as we can. We started to trust one another, us and your Hamiyat. We expanded from intelligence to supplying equipment. We made drop-offs here, here, and here."

Katy recognizes one of her own camps on Sun Mountain, and two more on Water Mountain. No wonder their weapons were increasingly better-made, more sophisticated, with each passing year.

"We've yet to perfect our stealth drone delivery systems for larger things," says Raana Abdallah. "But we're almost there. And then we'll be able to give you the weapons you really need."

A series of images appears on the screen: adaptive camouflage, hydrodynamic artillery, and precision-guided firearms.

Then the screen ripples, and there sits Fatima Kara, in a beige tunic and trousers, on a couch next to Raana Abdallah in a private antechamber. A low window behind them looks out to a backdrop of carved terraces, interspersed with date palms, a bubbling fountain at the top. No place on the mountain looks like that; it's the carefully landscaped terrain of a Semitian government building. Fatima Kara and Raana Abdallah are laughing, smoking cigarettes. Screens on the table shine in front of them, but they're not paying them any attention. They look as though they've discovered new continents in one another's eyes.

Photographs can be doctored; even a child knows that. Katy stares at the image, trying to recognize the usually hard-bitten, unsmiling Commander in this unexpected camaraderie with the more polished, sleeker Semitian.

"Your Commander, Fatima Kara. These were taken when she came to the Presidential Palace."

"What? When?" Katy's knee begins to jig up and down with nervous energy. She tries to hold still, but can't. She knows nothing about Fatima Kara traveling to Eastern Semitia; nobody else does either.

Raana Abdallah ignores Katy's astonishment. "Three years ago. We'd figured out routes to get a few people out of Dhofar, for deeper training and diplomatic talks. It was a very good meeting, Katy. We realized that we had the same objective: to free the women of Dhofar from the tyranny of Green City. Since then, we've been making plans. And this is where you come in. We need you for a secret mission. Commander Kara handpicked you herself. She has a lot of faith in you, that you'll succeed."

At this, Katy's knee hits the table so hard that the screen wobbles and falls over. Raana Abdallah calmly straightens the screen, then folds her hands and gazes at Katy.

Katy mutters, "And what exactly is my part in this grand scheme?"

Raana Abdallah lays a sympathetic hand on Katy's shoulder, close to her scars. "You got these when you were injured in a skirmish with a group of Collectors, am I correct? And you've been recuperating here as our guest."

"Your prisoner," Katy says. This is too intimate a touch for someone she doesn't consider a friend. "You've been keeping me here all along."

Abdallah taps on the screen, bringing up the image of an X-ray with a name printed neatly in the corner: *Katy A.*

"Forgive us the pretense: You were never as badly injured as we made out, actually. See this?" The two bullets, gray dots in contrast to the white of Katy's bones, are lodged in the fleshy part of her shoulder. "Not quite a skin wound, but nowhere near your spinal cord, as you were originally told."

The Maghribienne doctor had said that if the bullets been a centimeter closer, Katy would have been paralyzed, or dead. She'd praised Katy's quick recovery, her ferocious dedication to the rehab program that Katy had attended every day to regain her strength and the use of her arm again. It had all been . . . what, a lie?

Abdallah says, "It takes skill to shoot someone from such a distance and not cause any real damage. But then, Kara knows her women well. That's what makes her such a good leader. And that's quite a sniper you have on your team. What was her name? Lulu? Lena?"

As Katy strains to look at the X-ray, she slowly realizes that her friends could have taken out these bullets on the mountain, with sterilized pincers and a good amount of qat to keep her from screaming. "Laleh," Katy says dully. Laleh, Katy's friend, the best sniper in the Dawn Battalion. The night of the shooting, Laleh had been seconded to another squad on the heights near the entrance to the box canyon where Katy usually meets Alia the Ababeel. She's the only one who can pull off the kind of marksmanship Abdallah's talking about.

"I was shot by my own squad mate and Fatima Kara sent me here on purpose?" Katy is scornful. "It's not possible. I don't believe you."

Raana Abdallah brings up yet another image on the screen: a drone has filmed Katy's squad in a skirmish with a group of Collectors on the lower part of the mountain. They are trying to stop the collectors from getting to one of the villages to harass them for bribes and scout for minerals in the mountainside. Positioned on a hilltop, Katy and her squad mates, minus Laleh, rain down bullets and shells on their hastily dug-in trench along a dirt road. What Katy remembers of that night is the chill and mist, the moon's corona showing up as an eerie halo between patches of cloud.

The darkness gives them enough cover to come down farther than usual on defensive actions, but the Collectors have brought strong lights with them, which they beam up in the Hamiyat's direction. The lights mark the women out in stark relief against the rocky outcrop on which they are hiding. It's always harder to shoot up than down at a target; wind and gravity affect a bullet's trajectory. But their bullets find Katy nonetheless—or so she was told.

Laleh knows full well how to compensate for shooting down a slope, not just for gravity and wind, but for the weight of her bullets, the humidity in the air. She knows the science behind velocity and force, and she practices her art by intuition and talent. Perched even higher than Katy's squad, lying on her stomach and finding Katy in her sights, she settles the crosshairs on Katy as she crouches in the dirt, shooting at the Agents below. A squeeze on the trigger of her precision weapon, as tender as a kiss, sends two bullets into Katy's shoulder, pushing her sprawling onto her back.

There are shouts and cries from the others in the squad—"Katy's been hit! Save her!" They drag Katy off and signal for help. Katy's unconscious, unknowing, the shock and pain of the bullets sending her to another plane of existence, setting course for a different journey than the one on which her friends still travel. Meanwhile, Laleh dismantles the scope from her weapon and quietly melts away, her job done.

A quadcopter sails over the tops of the pine trees, scattering the birds that scream angrily into the night. It cuts through the clouds clinging to the sides of the dark mountain like gray cotton wool, then lowers down to the uneven ground cautiously, humming like a bee. The women pick Katy up as one and rush her over to the rescue drone. She's quickly co-

cooned in its cabin, lifted into the sky like a comet. Direction: Zarzura.

"You were sedated and flown in through an air corridor with a southern approach, around the border and over Yemen. A little melodramatic, I know, but we had to do it this way; you wouldn't have agreed to come here on your own. At least that's what Fatima Kara told me."

Katy can't stomach the idea that Laleh, her own friend, would agree to shoot her like that. Such a dangerous gamble: She could have easily killed her. Why couldn't Fatima Kara have just ordered her to go to Eastern Semitia? She would have obeyed! She wouldn't have questioned the Commander; nobody ever does. If Raana Abdallah's telling the truth, Commander Kara has collaborated with her to bring Katy to Zarzura in a way that goes against everything the Hamiyat stands for: loyalty, sisterhood, and honor.

Katy rises and pushes her chair away. It tips over and hits the floor with a sharp clang: The sound of betrayal is unleashed in Katy's head.

Raana Abdallah's hair, cut in a short, sleek bob, swings like a curtain, revealing her face as she turns to look at the chair fallen behind her. She gazes up at Katy, unfazed, eyebrows raised.

Katy picks up her chair and sits down again, unexpectedly humiliated, humbled. "What do you want from me?"

"I already told you, Katy. You're going to help us liberate the women of Dhofar."

Time to stop being a fighter, and instead become a listener; Katy is reminded of Alia, the silent Ababeel who listens more than she talks.

Raana Abdallah nods in approval. She has a severe sort of beauty, no softness to mitigate the cold stones of her eyes. "Pay attention, Katy. This is going to be a lot to take in."

All is not well in Green City, explains Raana Abdallah. There is dissent among the Leaders, some of whom disagree with the easing of the Perpetuation system. They argue that this can only lead to disorder and insurrection. So far, the more liberal Leaders have gotten their way. But the stricter ones are pushing back. In the meantime, something has happened to make them uneasy in their beds at night, shaking up the entire establishment's illusion of security and absolute power.

Raana Abdallah brings up a video of an older man, standing at a podium delivering a speech: Tall, broad, bearded, he's welcoming people to a conference on trade and commerce across the South West Territories. "That's Reuben Faro. He's one of the Leaders of Green City."

She switches to the map of Green City, zooming in on a building called the Shifana Hospital. Its sleek glass tower rises up out of the screen, then narrows down on a private room high above the skyline, where the same man, now unconscious, lies in a hospital bed.

"He's recovering from a brutal beating he received at the hands of a group of illegal women."

*Illegal women*. Katy is curious about what this means. Abdallah tells her that very little is known about them: ten or so in number, they were living in hiding in an underground bunker. At night, they performed "intimate" favors for a select few of Green City's elite. This reminds Katy of a woman hiding, then escaping from Green City. But she can't remember it properly; she's concentrating too hard on Raana Abdallah's story.

"Reuben Faro was their patron. He protected them from being caught by the Agency."

"What happened to them?"

"The women ran away after beating him nearly to death."

"Were they caught?" *That would be a pity*, Katy thinks.

They sound brave, in their own way. Their ways may be different from what the Hamiyat do, yet they are still designed to subvert and resist.

The display shimmers, bringing up another image. Katy recognizes the Hamiyat base camp on the top of Sun Mountain, at the Ruined City, high mountains ringing the peak and the sky cloudy with coming rain. Four young, attractive women sit on the ground, Laleh and Marzi stand to one side, Commander Kara to the other. And in the background—you'd almost miss her if you weren't sharp-eyed—is Alia, with her youngest child, Noor. The child is the only one smiling widely in the photograph.

The illegal women are nothing like the women of the mountain: They wear simple shift dresses instead of fatigues or the workworn clothes of the village women. Their faces are smoother, less weathered. The difference between them and the Hamiyat women is like black and white.

"They hid in a cave for weeks on Sun Mountain, until they were discovered and taken in by the Hamiyat."

"And the man, Faro?"

"The authorities in Green City put out an official statement. Reuben Faro had an accident, his autonomous vehicle malfunctioned. His injuries have left him in a near coma for twelve weeks now. He was attacked at almost the same time you were brought to Zarzura. He's being kept under a tight watch, amid strong security. They're waiting for him to recover before they bring him to task for his rebellion, in helping the women of the Panah. But just imagine if he were to die unexpectedly, before coming to trial. It would mean all sorts of trouble for them. They'd be accused of killing him in case more of their corruption comes to light."

Katy understands: The Leadership of Green City would

face uproar with this kind of scandal. Enough pressure, and it could even completely fall apart.

"Now imagine, Katy, if it was a woman who killed Reuben Faro. A fearless, brave woman, who could move without being detected." She looks at Katy. "You, Katy."

Katy feels a tightening in her chest, as all her muscles begin to tense up. "Oh no, no, no. Pay one of your spies to do it."

"Fatima Kara said you were her best fighter from among the young recruits: You have battle skills, but also intelligence and cunning. And you're one of the special ones: the girls who grew up as boys. You know how to be both. They'd never catch you."

Katy is aghast. Fatima Kara has told Raana Abdallah everything, it seems, about how they live on their mountain. Does she really trust Abdallah this much?

"We have technology and surveillance, Katy, but we don't have people on the ground in Green City. We could get you in there. We'd provide the biometric cover: Your DNA would show up as male on the security systems. A quick job, in and out. There would be a clampdown, a pushback. And then a revolt. Maybe even a coup. They would scramble to secure their capital. And then, in the void, the Hamiyat would move to take control of the valleys in Dhofar, some of the smaller towns. Who knows how far a revolution can go once it's started?"

Katy's lip trembles. Raana Abdallah takes Katy into her arms, holding her in a tight, soothing embrace. Katy goes completely stiff as the woman croons in her ear: "Katy Azadeh, I promise: Once you've done your part, you will go back to your mountain again."

It's late afternoon when Katy returns to her apartment. The streets of Zarzura are emptying out, the curved shadows of the louvered walls lengthening underfoot. Darkness and light alternate across Katy's face as she walks to her building, cheerfully named Sunflower 2, even though the desert that surrounds the city is barren of flowers.

Katy looks around at the walls, the table and chair, the bed, the galley kitchen, where she prepares her utilitarian meals. It's all so arbitrary, benevolence that they can provide or take away whenever they want.

The afternoon melts into evening and Katy sits on a chair by the window, watching the sun sink toward the horizon. The airplanes are taking off from the Presidential airport a few miles down the road; the intermittent buzzing of planes and drones interrupts the silence that cloaks the tiny city, and its older sister, the vast desert of the Empty Quarter. Katy's wounded shoulder twinges, aching in sympathy with the conflict in her head.

Unexpectedly, the doorbell chimes, and Katy lifts her head to stare at the door suspiciously. She isn't expecting anyone right now. Sometimes Adeefa drops by, with food or other supplies, and she stays for a little while to chat about inconsequential things. But now she's probably been warned to keep her distance. Katy glances at the door cam: It's a man, looking around nervously. When he glances back into the camera, Katy sees it's Zayn Battuta.

He rings the doorbell again. He wears a tense expression and holds his hands tightly behind his back. Katy debates whether or not to open the door. What does he want from her? Katy isn't afraid. She'd rather find out if Battuta is friend or foe and deal with him accordingly than cower on the safe side of a locked door. She presses a button and the front door slides open, revealing Battuta in the flesh, three-dimensional, dressed all in black.

Katy beckons him in silently, and he quickly crosses the

threshold, standing in the middle of the room, bouncing up and down on his toes and shooting glances all around him.

"What do you want?" Katy says, still in her chair. "Why are you here?" No preamble, no niceties; he is not her friend.

"I had to come," he says. "I know what they've asked you to do." He isn't wasting time on niceties either. His hand moves a little, as if he wants to reach out and touch Katy, but then he pulls it back, still glancing around as if a hundred cameras are capturing him at all angles.

"I tried, I promise you, to get them to call it off. It's too dangerous. I told them it was wrong. They wouldn't listen. They're adamant that you carry out this mission."

"Did SmartSoul come up with my name, or did you put it into the system yourself?"

"Raana Abdallah told me to arrange your biometrics, so that you're shielded from their security when you're in the hospital. She knows I can do it."

Katy shakes her head.

Battuta continues: "Julien used to work in that very hospital. I planted a digital tracker in their system when he first came over to us, so we keep getting their updated security codes. Don't worry. You'll be completely safe."

"I'm not stupid. It's likely I'll never come back." Katy turns to the window again.

"Please don't say that, Katy." Zayn Battuta takes two hesitant steps over to her, and falls at her feet.

"What are you doing? Get up," Katy says. Battuta doesn't listen. He takes her hand in his and squeezes it tight, then presses it to his lips.

"I'm sorry," he says.

Katy feels his breath on the back of her hand. His head is bowed, his neck vulnerably presented, as if to an executioner. Days and weeks of pent-up frustration, of being unable to move, of impatience and impotence, are boiling over in Katy now. For one dangerous moment, she wants to turn her hand into a weapon and bring it down hard on the place where his spine meets his skull. For one dangerous moment, Katy thinks he would let her. Like a lone tree that sways against the shumaal, the desert wind, he's willing to bear the force of Katy's rage and despair.

"Get up," Katy says again. Battuta, rising up, takes Katy's face in his hands. Katy rears back, wanting to push him away, but he leans forward and kisses her hard, as if there's redemption to be found in her mouth. Then he sinks back onto his heels. There are tears in his eyes.

"Why did you do that?" Katy says. Her head is a whirlpool; her heart beats a fast, incoherent rhythm. All the Hamiyat teachings flash in her mind: Men are the enemy, the tempters, and fighters must never be distracted by their wiles. But Katy wants him to kiss her again. The knowledge of that sensation, once learned, can't be forgotten.

He lets out a small, embarrassed laugh. "We planned for an assassination. We had it all worked out, we simulated it several times. It wasn't until you came to Zarzura that Abdallah got it into her head that we should actually go through with it."

He sighs, flexing and unflexing his hands like he wants to discharge a heavy burden from his body. He has prominent knuckles and strong fingers: the hands of a man. His lack of height, his clean-shaven face, make him look younger than his years, but he's not a boy, Katy warns herself. He can hurt her the way only a man can. "The General doesn't want to keep you here, Katy. You're a liability. He's been pressuring her to get rid of you once and for all."

"So take me out back and shoot me."

"Don't talk like that." Battuta tugs at his hair worriedly,

the way he did in the Etoile Theater when his presentation went out of control. "SmartSoul assessed world events that justified hostilities between countries in the past. Assassinations were the answer. It's so clumsy. So twentieth-century. It's a flaw that we yet need to work on, but it suits Abdallah's purposes. She thinks that if this works, and Green City falls, she'll become the Prime Minister."

"Your computer needs help," Katy says. "So does Raana Abdallah. They're both crazy."

Battuta smiles, and Katy feels her muscles untensing. They both know the kiss will happen before it does, and she lets him. There's no audience to judge her; no Hamiyat friends to tell her that she's letting them down. In a few days she'll be gone and that makes this moment a hundred times sharper, more exciting, more desperate.

His arms tighten around her, his lips firm and insistent, his clean, caramel smell. His hands roam Katy's body, holding her close so there's not an inch of space between them. His skin is warm and soft. Katy had expected him to feel as rough as sandpaper. His mouth finds Katy's neck and clings there as he reaches down to her thighs. But when Katy feels him move her dress aside, she freezes.

"Stop," Katy says.

Battuta holds still, giving Katy time to decide. She hesitates at the edge of an invisible cliff. But she doesn't jump. She touches Battuta's cheek with her fingertips, then lays her palm flat against his face, feeling the line of his jaw, before she puts her hand around his throat. He closes his eyes, waiting for her fingers to tighten, but she lets him go.

"You should leave," Katy says softly.

Battuta is breathing hard, from arousal or fear, Katy can't tell. "You're a very strange woman, Katy Azadeh." His hand is at his chest, as if he's feeling some sort of pain in his heart.

"Look, I'll tell Raana Abdallah that I won't do it. It won't work without me."

"They'll make me do it even if you back out," says Katy.

Battuta stares at her, ashamed. "You're right. It's too late. But you'll succeed. I'll make sure of it." He reaches for Katy's hand once more, then leaves her. At the door, he looks out into the corridor, then glances back at Katy. "I promise. You won't be alone. We'll keep track of you all the way."

But when he's gone, Katy feels herself drowning in an overwhelming silence. The truth is so simple: All promises are as empty as windcatchers on a sultry night.

# 12.

The next day, Katy is driven to a secret military sports complex a half hour away from Zarzura, deep in the desert. Raana Abdallah, the General, and Zayn Battuta wait for her in the gym, sitting behind a table as if judging a sports event. Equipment is set up for Katy to demonstrate skills with gun and knife. She hits all the targets with the rifle they give her and throws the knives like spears into a block of wood ten steps away. This is child's play for Katy.

Next is a round of sparring with one of their martial arts trainers. Katy fights off the trainer when he attacks her from behind, escaping his grip and turning around swiftly to deliver a nose-breaking blow to the face. Zayn Battuta winces, the General watches with a stony face, and Raana Abdallah smiles her cold smile just as Katy stops short of driving the trainer's nose bone into his brain.

"She's well trained," says Raana Abdallah.

The General says, "She fights like an animal." Katy doesn't think this is an insult—the snow leopard of Dhofar is one of the world's most efficient killers.

Zayn Battuta is looking down, thumbing through what looks like reams of coded information on his screen. When Abdallah strums her knuckles on the table impatiently, he looks up, startled. They stare at him for a reaction. He gives them one that puzzles them: "She fights like she has nothing to lose."

Returning to Zarzura, Raana Abdallah and Zayn Battuta take Katy to a secret briefing room housed deep in the bowels of an administration block. They walk through long corridors to get to a room with no windows, and it's freezing cold.

"Do you know where we are?" says Raana Abdallah, taking her place in a deep-backed chair with controls on its arms. Zayn Battuta is setting up displays, queueing up maps and photographs. The General has gone on to another function. Katy guesses he will permit the mission to go ahead, but he doesn't want to be involved.

"Underground?" Katy says, feeling more confident now that she's shown them she's dangerous. Fighting, after so many months of being treated like a patient and a prisoner, has stimulated her body and mind. She's still wary: She's proven her worth as a valuable asset, but not a human being.

Abdallah points upward. "The wind tower is right above us." The pipes that cool the floors of Zarzura's buildings run all around the room, which is why it feels so cold here. She reaches for a shawl draped over the back of her chair and wraps herself up in it, then turns to Battuta. "Are we ready?"

Battuta turns a display toward them, where another man's face is waiting on the screen. Katy recognizes him as the doctor who ran away from Green City with Sabine.

"Dr. Asfour," says Battuta. "Thank you for joining us."

"My pleasure," says Julien Asfour. Blond, thin-faced, he nods his head politely at Abdallah. "Greetings, Madame Minister."

"Dr. Asfour," says Abdallah, leaning forward, steepling her fingers and resting her sharp chin on her nails. "I am very eager to hear the plan that you and Dr. Battuta have devised to get Katy into Shifana Hospital."

The doctor looks directly at Katy and smiles. "Hello, Ms. Azadeh." Katy lifts her hand at him in a half-wave, feeling self-conscious at speaking to someone from Green City.

The people are educated and sophisticated; she's just a barbarian from Dhofar in their eyes.

Battuta flicks on an image of Shifana Hospital, right on the coast of Green City, overlooking the Gulf Sea. Katy is to travel two days at sea by boat, then get off just near a construction site for a new shopping mall a kilometer down the road from the hospital. Underground tunnels bring construction materials to the site so that the view aboveground isn't spoiled by debris and workers.

"You'll enter the lowest level of the hospital through one of the tunnels," says Battuta.

"And from there you'll be able to get to the staff entryway," adds Asfour. "You'll go to the lockers where the nurses change into their scrubs."

"But the tunnels," Katy says. "Won't they be full of workers? Won't they stop me?"

"Only if you're careless," says Raana Abdallah.

"Normally yes, but the day you're going in is a holiday in Green City—National Day," says Battuta, ignoring Abdallah. "So the workers will have the day off. The hospital will be operating as normal, but you'll be ID'd as a temporary worker filling in for someone on leave."

"Will I have weapons on me?"

"No," both Zayn Battuta and Julien say at the same time.

"What? You expect me to go in there unarmed?"

Katy stares incredulously at both the men. Raana Abdallah's eyes are narrowed and she gives Battuta a hard look. "Why shouldn't she be allowed a weapon? She'll need it for self-protection."

"It's impossible," says Julien onscreen. "Nobody's allowed in the hospital carrying any sort of weapon, except security."

Battuta adds, "She's going in with so much tech already, we can't afford to give her anything more dangerous."

Katy says, "Let me see the gender gear." The two men look relieved, and Raana Abdallah a little disappointed, that Katy is conceding to their opinion.

Battuta shows Katy an ID tag that validates her as having XY chromosomes when it's scanned by any Green City machine. There's a small chip to press on at the base of her throat; as soon as it's activated, Katy says "Hello" and can't recognize her own voice, because it's become suddenly lower by two pitches. A smart mask filters her facial features and makes them look more masculine to anyone who looks at her.

Finally, Battuta gives Katy a chest binder and directs her to a bathroom in the hallway. The door safely locked behind her, Katy takes off her shirt and slips on the binder, a thin tank top. It's lightweight, made of a mesh material that feels cool and easy on her skin. At the touch of a button, the device flattens her breasts comfortably inside the tightened mesh, without constricting her breathing.

Katy turns on the smart mask and examines herself in the mirror. Her eyes are smaller, her skin looks rougher, and there's even a hint of beard on her cheeks. Anyone looking at her for a long time would be able to tell something was amiss, but for a brief encounter—passing someone in a darkened tunnel or hallway—she looks and sounds, for all intents and purposes, like a young man.

"I'm Katy Azadeh," Katy says to herself, in her new voice. The man in the mirror squints back at her. And then, for good measure, Katy adds, "Reuben Faro, I'm going to kill you."

When Katy returns to the room, gender gear fully activated, the three of them are having an argument. Katy stands just outside the door to listen.

"I don't see why all this is necessary," says Raana Abdallah.

"There are only male nurses and doctors in Shifana. In all of Green City," says Julien.

"We've already been through this," sighs Battuta.

"Ridiculous," says Raana Abdallah. "I find the whole thing insulting. We moved beyond maleface and femaleface a long time ago. Gender's a thing of the past. That's what has kept humanity moving forward. We left those regressive binaries behind here in Semitia. Green City is the dungeon it is because it hasn't."

Julien says, "I agree with you, Madam Minister. But our brains are wired to look at a person's complexion, even the space between eyelids and eyebrows, to judge whether someone is male or female. Our biology has yet to catch up to our political sensibilities."

"Besides, it's for her own protection," says Battuta. "If we're going to send her in there, unarmed, she should at least be able to blend in. Provided you want her to survive, that is, and not be caught at the first checkpoint."

Katy is puzzled by this argument. As a woman, she's been able to become a soldier, to enjoy her freedom, to find companionship and love. But that's only on the mountain. Of course, things are different in Green City. Being disguised as a male will give Katy access to places she needs to get to in the most literal way.

She moves into the doorway and clears her throat. When they see her, Raana Abdallah's mouth is actually agape, while Julien whistles in appreciation.

"Amazing. Well done, Dr. Battuta. Don't you agree, Dr. Asfour?" says Abdallah, as if it were her idea all along.

"Absolutely," says Julien. "Very convincing."

Battuta folds his arms across his chest and grins for the first time today. "You make a very handsome young man, Katy," he says. "You'd have turned my head if I were thirty years younger." A wave of warmth spreads over Katy's cheeks. Is Battuta *flirting* with her as a man? That can't be it. No, he's too high on his own scientific achievement; in his mind, the Katy he was with last night is not the same Katy who he's disguised as a man today.

"I've only got one question," Katy says, in the masculinized voice. "If I haven't got a weapon, how do you expect me to kill Reuben Faro? Or did you think I was just going to walk into his room and strangle him with my bare hands?"

"You'll put a chemical into his IV. It will kill him within six minutes."

"His what?"

"His intraveneous medicine delivery system. It's very easy. A few drops, and boom, you're done. It leaves no trace."

"And how exactly do I get out of there and get back home?"

"Now that we *have* thought of," says Battuta.

Julien says, "Every Friday, there's a scheduled transport of lab-grown organs that goes from Shifana to Salala Hospital. A medevac helicopter will be on the roof, scheduled to go to Sheba City. You'll go with it."

"From Sheba City," Battuta says, "you'll be taken to the Wabiha Valley. From there, you can return to Sun Mountain on your own."

Katy has heard enough. She's a Hamiyat fighter, not a parcel at a children's birthday party. When she and her sisters were boys, back in her village, they swaggered down the streets and walked freely; her body has never forgotten how to take up space and be big in the world. As a member of the

Hamiyat, Katy uses that muscle memory to project strength and confidence to her friends and foes alike. These Semitians will listen to her properly as the fighter she is, not the cowering stranger she's been for all these weeks.

She turns off the projector, the voice filter, and the smart binder. Her face and body become her own again; she's Katy Azadeh, not the strange hybrid they've tried to make out of her.

"I'm not doing anything unless I have a weapon. One that I know how to use, and can rely on. I'm not going to go in there like a sitting duck."

Battuta stops smiling. Julien falls silent, too. Raana Abdallah looks as though she's got a frog in her mouth, pressing every which way against her cheeks. Clearly, her refusal is something they hadn't banked on. But they aren't fighters; they're just petty bureaucrats. They're not even like the Collectors, who at least don't hide behind desks, but come out to face the Hamiyat's bullets in the field. Katy feels no respect for these Semitians with their science, their plots, their need to assert their power over everyone.

"Well, Dr. Battuta?" says Raana Abdallah, when she's managed to contain her own anger. "Didn't I tell you she'd need a weapon? Surely you can come up with something that won't show up on a scanner?" Abdallah sends a glance toward Katy, who realizes that Abdallah knows, after all, the importance of giving arms to women, not just men.

"You know we aren't allowed to print nonmetal guns," snaps Battuta, showing his ire for the first time. "It's one of the strictest prohibitions in Zarzura."

"All you had to do was ask me for permission and I would have gotten it!"

"The blueprint's not even in Eastern Semitia! That's how dangerous it is."

"As if we don't have ways of getting it. Even through backdoor channels."

"It's out of the question, Minister."

Julien says, "Why not give her something that wouldn't be out of place in a hospital?"

"What?" says Battuta, frowning.

"A handheld laser imager. We use them all the time for lab investigations. Nurses are allowed to use them; they're not as powerful as the surgical scalpels. If we can tweak it so it won't kill, but it can incapacitate, would that work for you, Katy?"

What a simple solution, almost elegant. They're all watching Katy now, their breath suspended in their throats, waiting for her to answer, yes or no. Katy stretches the moment out as long as she can, enjoying her power at last. Will she put her life on the line for Raana Abdallah's ambitions, for Zayn Battuta's vanity, for Semitian glory? They cannot do this unless Katy agrees.

Katy closes her eyes and thinks of Sun Mountain, of the waterfalls that cascade over its jagged edges during the monsoon, white froth like the flowers of bougainvillea over the moss green rain that makes its way, eventually, to the sea. She thinks of Laleh and Marzi, of Fatima Kara, of Alia. She sees an expanse of blue sky, brilliant as sapphires. Her mind wanders to her long-dead mother and father, to Tehran, to Uzbekistan. And she imagines Dhofar, freed from the rule of the Collectors, from the long arm of Green City.

"Send me the laser tonight," she says. "Send it with Adeefa; nobody else. And we'll see if I like it."

Adeefa comes to Katy at ten o'clock, letting herself into the apartment with her spare key. Silently, she hands over the laser to Katy, who examines it, turning it around and around. It fits into the palm of her hand like a little white stone.

"It's like a dazzler," says Adeefa, who is wearing a pale pink dress, even though it's too dark outside for such a daytime color. She looks like a trumpet flower that has fallen from the vine in a monsoon rain: delicate, fresh, her body shaped like a bell. There's a soft sweet scent in her hair as she leans toward Katy to show the indentations in the laser that turn it on and increase its strength.

"How does it work?"

"When you fire it, it blinds and deafens the target temporarily. This one will also disable other weapons with sonic waves. Zayn . . . Dr. Battuta put a little extra punch into it. You don't need exact aim for it either; just point it in the direction of a weapon, and squeeze."

They are sitting together side by side on the bed in Katy's room. Even though it's late evening, and the room lights are dimmed, Katy sees Adeefa blush when she utters Battuta's name. She would be upset if she knew Battuta had kissed Katy just last night, wouldn't she?

"Do you like him?" Katy asks her.

Her eyes widen. "Is it that obvious? Oh my god, do you think he knows?" She's only pretending to be embarrassed, though. She wants to confess her love for him, Katy knows. That's why she's mentioned him by his first name.

"Have you told him?"

Adeefa puts her hands over her face. "I couldn't ever tell him. I'm nobody of importance. He's a Minister. He'd never look at me." She's squirming into the side of the bed. Katy wants to tell her she's a grown woman; she's too old for this awkwardness. And that she's beautiful, and Zayn Battuta has definitely looked at her with more than just scientific interest. He'll sleep with her sooner or later; all Katy can do is warn her to look out for herself when he does.

The sudden realization comes to Katy that Zayn Battuta tried to seduce her last night so that she would be more agreeable to the assassination plan. Maybe Raana Abdallah even told him to do it, thinking that the way to Katy's acquiescence lay between her legs, that sex would have eased the deal.

"He might do more than look at you, Adeefa. But he's no good for you," Katy says, thinking how in the end, Battuta didn't even have to sleep with her to get her to agree to go to Green City. But he still might have had her just for his own pleasure. "He only thinks of himself. If you're useful to him in his work, he'll make time for you, but you'll lose your heart and he won't."

"For someone who's spent her whole life on a mountain with only women, you seem to know a lot about men," says Adeefa. There's a little whine in her voice, but she can't look Katy straight in the eyes because of the truth in what Katy says.

Katy puts her hand on Adeefa's shoulder and pulls her so that they're face-to-face. She wants to shake Adeefa, as she might a younger sister. "I don't know men at all," Katy says. "But I know Zayn Battuta's not good enough for you. He would hurt you."

"And you wouldn't?" Adeefa says softly. The look she gives Katy is mischievous and hopeful at the same time: a confession in and of itself. Katy's breath quickens at her tone, innocent yet provocative, as if Adeefa is enjoying walking a tightrope toward her without really grasping how far she could fall. At the same time, the trust in her eyes is too intoxicating for Katy to resist. She touches Adeefa's face lightly with her fingers, then plants a firm kiss on her closed lips.

For a moment Adeefa's lips pucker slightly, and then she's ready to open under Katy's mouth. Their tongues touch. *Yes*, Katy's body says. This is what she does know: a woman's softness, moistness, sweet hesitation. She's been wanting to do this for a long time now; she's only surprised that Adeefa has come out with the truth about her feelings for Katy as well.

As they kiss, Adeefa gives a soft little sigh, like a child before it falls asleep. Katy decides then and there not to ease her down onto the bed. She and Adeefa are the same age, but Adeefa is more innocent than Katy has ever been. She doesn't know yet who she is, whom she really wants—Katy or Zayn Battuta.

Their lips part, and Katy gazes into Adeefa's eyes. Adeefa is a little stunned, as if she can't believe what's just happened. Katy has seen that dazed look before on other girls. She wants to be gentle with Adeefa; out of all the people here in Zarzura, she's someone who has never harmed Katy. Seducing Adeefa and leaving forever—whether by choice or not—would give her more pain than Katy wants to inflict on this sweet girl.

"No," Katy says at last. "I don't want to hurt you, Adeefa. That's why you have to go now."

"Then why did you kiss me?" Tears fill her eyes, but Katy knows she's disappointed and relieved at the same time. Adeefa is incapable of wounding another human being; she's embryonic, not fully formed. She doesn't yet have that tough outer layer of skin that protects women from the pain of being alive.

"On Sun Mountain," Katy lies, "this is how we say goodbye."

# 13.

Katy moves through the chilled air of the hospital like she's swimming in a cloud. She shivers, feeling the sting of goose bumps on her skin. The mountain gets cold, but she's uncomfortable in this artificial, sterile atmosphere, pumped in through vents in the ceiling and smelling sharply of antiseptic. She feels exposed in the fluorescent lights that remove the veils between day and night; you can't tell what time of the day it is because there are no windows. Ever since she left Dhofar, she's been inside so many industrialized buildings that she feels totally out of touch with the rhythms of the natural world.

As she creeps through the hallways, following the map of the hospital Zayn Battuta has loaded onto her device, she keeps her head down to avoid meeting the eyes of passing staff. A few attendants offer her a greeting—"Morning of light"—but instead of returning the customary response, she just nods and scurries farther along down the corridor.

She's reached Green City just as planned, traveling by boat from the port at the City of Gazelles all the way to Mazunian waters. They put her ashore at the mall being built on the outskirts of Green City. There, she was met by a Semitian spy, who led her to the construction tunnels and waved her in the direction of Shifana Hospital. She hesitated at the mouth of the tunnel, but the spy just turned his back on her and walked away.

Katy has never liked rats, but she had to turn into one and do this job with all the stealth and cunning of a rodent. This is not an open battlefield, where there is nothing to hide, where your courage shines five feet in front of you and keeps you going even when you have nothing left to give. Into the tunnel she goes, holding her breath all the way, until she's out on the other side, and moving in the bowels of the hospital. It's empty right now in the middle of this early-morning shift, so she manages to slip into the staff changing room undetected. The gender gear is hardly making any difference to how she is being perceived because there's no one around to perceive her presence.

While she's scrambling into the nurse's outfit left for her in locker number 17, she thinks about the man whose life she's going to end in a matter of minutes. Zayn Battuta has given her the liquid that she is to put into Reuben Faro's intravenous infuser, delivering fourth-generation antibiotics and fluids to him as he lies in his bed. She's gone over it many times in her mind on the way over to Green City: the design of the infusion device, where she has to insert the capsule, what Reuben Faro will look like as he receives the poison directly into his bloodstream. Will he die the way men have when she's done it with a bullet?

Katy knows why she has to kill Faro—to create a little chaos, as Raana Abdallah puts it—but she still can't believe how she was tricked by Fatima Kara into coming to Zarzura. She's compartmentalized the betrayal; she can only think that Raana Abdallah must have forced Fatima Kara to participate in another one of her intellectual games. By now, Katy is familiar with how good Raana Abdallah is at them.

She's heard Raana Abdallah's voice in her head over and

over, in that imagined conversation with Fatima Kara: "Of course we can't send a Semitian assassin, it has to be a woman from Dhofar, so that it looks like an internal conflict. If they find out it was us, it'll be a diplomatic incident. They'll attack us, but we don't want that. We have to be the ones to strike first."

Fatima Kara must have been desperate enough for the outside help to agree to this plan. If she had asked Katy directly, Katy would have never willingly agreed to come. She would not have left her beloved mountain, her friends, in order to perform a cold-blooded killing for another country's benefit. In a way, Katy *had* to be tricked. Once she performs all these mental gymnastics in her head, it makes a twisted sort of sense to her.

Katy moves silently along the last stretch of hallway; the entire floor is empty, devoid of any activity or ornate decor. Katy would never have guessed that an important figure is being held here. She's getting ever closer to Reuben Faro's room, and she feels something growing hard and steely inside her, a resolve that crowds out any doubt. The extraneous drops away; no longer is she hearing anyone else's voice in her head. There is only the sound of her breathing, her footsteps in the hallway. Her eyesight becomes more focused; her heartbeat begins to race; her muscles tense in anticipation of this explosive act she's about to commit.

She has killed men before, but always directly, never in such a duplicitous way. Will he go quietly, unconsciously, without noise or pain, or will he scream and clutch at his throat? Worst of all, will he see her as she ends his life, and beg her for mercy she isn't able to give? At last she approaches the door that has been marked out on the map, feels for the vial in her pocket, takes a deep breath, and pushes her way in.

Reuben Faro is lying unconscious in a single bed. His salt-and-pepper hair is partly visible under a white bandage. The other half of his scalp and half his face are covered in angry red scars: the telltale signs of a burning. Some of the scars glisten with a healing gel, others have already turned into thickened tissue. In photos he'd been a strong, powerful man; how diminished his body appears now under the crisp white sheet. There's no beep of a life support system; he's breathing on his own. A single IV drip behind his bed sends clear droplets into his left arm.

Katy glances around to make sure the room is clear. She expected Guards in the hallway, and at least one Guard in his room, keeping an eye out for intruders. Reuben Faro is such an important man in Green City, but astonishingly there's no one here, and Katy herself feels like a ghost. Her target seems to have been long forgotten by his keepers. She takes in the armchair and the closet, the bathroom—empty—and picture windows that filter the strong sunlight. An angry sea rushes the shoreline hundreds of feet below.

The vial feels heavy in her fingers as she slips it out of her pocket. She steps forward and throws a glance at his face. His eyes are closed, but she can tell he is not peaceful; his eyelids tremble and every once in a while his entire body gives a myoclonic jerk. Katy feels nothing for him, not pity, not sorrow, not anger. He is simply a man whose time is up, and the lives of many people depend on Katy's ability to send him into oblivion, if he isn't there already.

There may be cameras in the room, but she's not worried about being detected; she looks just like a Shifana nurse, checking on a patient's status. It occus to Katy there is no honor in assassination, as she moves quietly to the IV infuser and finds the chamber where she has to put in the capsule. She's about to open the vial, when her fingers stop moving.

She glances again at the door, at the window, then back at Reuben Faro, lying still. His lips are drawn into a grimace; it makes him look like he's smiling and in pain at the same time.

She can't do it. She, Katy Azadeh, whose reputation for being fearless in combat is known to all, hesitates. The seconds of this crucial moment are ticking away, but Katy can't bring herself to kill this man, no matter how ruthless he's been in the past. Right now he can't defend himself against anyone.

She backs away from Reuben Faro even though a voice in her head is urging her on. *Do it, do it*. But Katy doesn't want to kill him in this cold-blooded, ugly way. She's a soldier, not an assassin. Yes, she's celebrated death with Laleh and Marzi, danced when the enemy have died. But the rules are different on a battlefield. This man is someone else's fight, not hers.

Suddenly, her hackles raise. A sixth sense she's always had tells her that someone is moving close to the door, and she quickly ducks into the closet. Two orderlies enter the room, talking cheerfully to one another. "Good morning, Mr. Faro!" they intone. Katy's heart is pounding so fast and erratically that she's astonished the men can't hear it.

"Mr. Faro, can you hear us? Can you open your eyes?" They're busy now, performing ministrations Katy can't see, and talking about how they've been growing back his skin in the hospital lab; the surgeons are waiting in the operating theater to graft it back onto his ruined body. "You'll be fine after that, won't you, sir?" says one.

"Don't get his hopes up," says the other.

"Shut up," says the first, "he can hear you. Did you learn nothing in nursing school?"

Nevertheless, they start to discuss the fire in which he was wounded, in an underground brothel of some sort.

"What was he doing there?" "What do you think?" They handle him deftly, detaching him from the IV infuser and putting him onto some other sort of machine, which whirs and bleeps. Katy hears them calling out to Faro again. "Mr. Faro, can you hear us? Do you know where you are?" But Faro remains as silent as a cold night on the mountain.

They wheel him out of the door and away. When she's sure they're gone, Katy comes out of the closet and stands in the empty space where Faro's bed was. Now what does she do, wait around for them to bring him back? It could take hours. She can't stay here; every moment increases her chances of getting caught. If that happens, she doubts Raana Abdallah would come to her rescue. She won't spend the rest of her life rotting away in a Green City jail, or tortured and executed for rebellion. But what happens if she doesn't complete the mission: Will her failure to assassinate Reuben Faro endanger the Hamiyat? She's kicking herself for stopping herself earlier, but it's done now and there's only one thing to do: survive.

Every breath she takes is like fire in her lungs. Every sense screams at her to run, to escape. But she doesn't want to go to the rooftop and meet the Medivac helicopter as planned. She's had enough of these Semitians pushing her around. With a greyhound's swiftness, she bolts for the door, dashes down the hallway, ignores the elevator. She takes the stairs, jumping them two and three at at a time, until she's made it to the bottom floor. She leaves the hospital the same way she came in: through the half-constructed underground tunnel, still wearing the male nurse's uniform.

She finds her way to a small pier not far from the entrance to the tunnel. There, a small fishing trawler is about to make its way into the ocean, and she bribes the crew to take her all the way south to the fishing village of Mirbat, on the southern coast of Dhofar.

Once she's out at sea, the shore of Green City receding behind her, she checks the hand laser Zayn Battuta gave her, which serves another purpose as a communication device. The laser lights up with a coded warning from Adeefa: *Raana Abdallah has been detained by the General.*

*What do I do?* Katy asks Adeefa. They're talking in a simple binary code Katy learned in her communications training in the Hamiyat. She told it to Zayn Battuta, whose minions worked out a key for the Semitians to use it with her.

*Warn your Commander.*

It takes a day and a half to reach Dhofari waters. Adeefa pinpoints the Hamiyat's location at the Khor Rori inlet. The troops are massing there before moving on to Sheba City. They'll cross the water in barges that Raana Abdallah has prearranged for the transport of troops and equipment.

At Khor Rori, Katy slips onto one of the Semitian barges and mingles among the soldiers without revealing her identity. She's long shed her Shifana nurse uniform; she's wearing the simple clothes of a fisherman, and she steals some fatigues from the supply barge. The women on the barge assume she's a soldier from some other battalion, displaced from her original group. Katy drifts from one squad to the next as they cross Khor Rori, then joins in on the march to the forest camp where they will wait for the assault on Sheba City.

Katy tries to think of the right words to tell her story to Commander Kara, everything that's happened from Zarzura to Green City and back to Dhofar. She prays to the Warrior Queen that when the time comes to speak, her own tongue will show its constancy, her mind clear and sharp enough to explain the unexplainable.

# PART THREE

## The Commander

# 14.

Fatima Kara was born in a mountain village where her parents barely made a living thanks to a flock of goats and some meager crops for part of the year. When she turned sixteen, they arranged to marry her off in the illegal, old-fashioned way, trading her for cash and livestock; the deal was more lucrative because they promised her exclusively to one man, an old farmer with no children to inherit his land. The arrangement was made directly between families, without the Bureau's oversight.

But Fatima had other plans: The day before her marriage, she slipped away from her parents' house, ran to the nearest rebel base, and joined the second Dhofar insurgency. It was not a mixed force, but if women could hold their own in battle, they were accepted in the militia. So many men had already been killed fighting the Green City regime, which wanted to extend its rule to the fiercely independent southern province of Dhofar.

Fatima Kara did more than just keep up with the men. She enjoyed the authority a rifle gave her over men and women. She carried a fifty-pound pack and the rifle through treks up and down the mountains, took part in ambushes and raids along with the men of her squad. She learned discipline, punctuality, obedience. Her body physically transformed from a girl's slight physique into a solid machine, able to endure discomfort and pain. There was still harassment and abuse at the hands of those men who didn't think women belonged in the fighting units. At twenty, she married another fighter, who promised to castrate anyone who laid a hand on her.

On their wedding night, she took out her dagger and placed it on the bed between their pillows. "Remember," she told him, "you have to sleep sometime, too."

She was shocked by the weight of her newborn twin babies when they were placed on her chest: impossible not to love, impossible to give up. But the two girls died as toddlers. Even though the Virus had mutated greatly since the Final War, years before she was born, it lingered in Fatima Kara's DNA and stole away her children before either of them turned five years old.

The night she lost them, Fatima Kara staggered to her feet and watched as her Husband buried them in shallow graves dug into the sides of the mountain. Later, her Husband was killed when peace negotiations with Green City were sabotaged by a rival faction, who bombed the camp where the talks were taking place, eliminating much of the rebel leadership. Eventually the insurgents were overtaken by the need to earn a living and feed their families. They renounced violence and were allowed to tend to small farms and keep livestock.

Green City held a tenuous rule over Dhofar after the fighting ended. The central government gave more powers to the local government in Queen of Sheba City, known as Sheba City for short. Collectors were dispatched from the capital to oversee affairs in the various regions of the province, including the mountainous areas of Fatima Kara's home.

The women fighters from the insurgency morphed into the Hamiyat, small battalions of fifty or so women. They patrolled the mountains and protected the women of the villages from domestic violence, resolved conflicts, provided women with safe places to stay when they needed to flee their homes. The village men were surprisingly unresisting to their activities; they were too tired, too battered, to fight against the women who laughed at death, as they were colloquially known.

The Collectors turned a blind eye to them, as long as they didn't interfere with government business. Fatima Kara became a lieutenant, then a captain, then a commander in the Hamiyat. She convinced the other commanders to become more aggressive toward the Collectors when they came to collect taxes and count babies.

Now, Fatima Kara thinks they've reached a tipping point where overthrowing them altogether could become a reality, under the right circumstances.

Reaching out to Eastern Semitia is Fatima Kara's idea, but it happens almost by chance. Fatima Kara remembers how communications with the Eastern Semitians were the norm during the second insurgency. So one day, she sends out an innocuous request over the Deep Web for weather reports of the border areas.

The Semitians respond to her over the Deep Web, and for a few weeks they exchange innocuous information about wind speed and rainfall measurements. Then they announce that they want to speak over a more secure channel. They'll smuggle a dozen specially marked boxes of light bulbs in a shipment of goods headed for the Collectors in Akoub village. Her Ababeels in Akoub tell her when the shipment is on its way. She sends a Hamiyat squad to intercept it before it reaches the Collector depot at the halfway point up Sun Mountain.

When Fatima Kara opens the first box, she finds a device nestled underneath the packed-in bottom layer of bulbs. She switches it on, and information fills the screen:

*Install these light bulbs in as many houses in as many villages as you can on Sun Mountain. This will guarantee you an uninterruptable communication channel between us and your network.*

Fatima Kara gives the light bulbs to Lateefa, and tells her to distribute them to the Ababeels. The Ababeels will do what needs to be done. Soon, an LED bulb is fixed in every house in every village and Sun Mountain is connected to the Spectrum. The Spectrum is transmitted through Li-Fi, light fidelity, using different types of light—visible, ultraviolet, infrared. The bulbs, LEDs that flicker faster than the human eye can notice, send data signals that can't be hacked. Unlike electromagnetic waves, they can reflect data anywhere that light can bounce off a surface: mirrors, windows, even bodies of water.

Now the Hamiyat and the Ababeels can talk to one another, and Fatima Kara can talk directly to the Eastern Semitians, without fear of being intercepted by the Collectors, or worse, the Agency in Green City. Some years after the Spectrum is installed on the mountain, Fatima Kara's contacts reveal that a very important official of Eastern Semitia has taken a personal interest in her. Will she come to the City of Gazelles to meet with the individual?

*I am sure you'll find the weather conditions favorable*, says the message. *We are in a position to be very helpful to you.*

Fatima Kara is flown from Sun Mountain to the City of Gazelles by night, her passenger drone weaving through the mountains and skimming the border to dodge the Sheba City radars. She meets Raana Abdallah in person for the first time at the Presidential Palace. Although they're the same age, Abdallah looks younger than Kara. The Semitian Deputy Foreign Minister is more polished, impeccably dressed in an eggshell blue silk shirt and skirt. Kara wears a loose tunic and loose pants in matching beige, as well as her waistcoat and shawl. The fatigues are for the mountain, and besides, Fatima Kara has grown heftier over the years, though she wears the weight as authority. Raana Abdallah is trim, well-kept; her skin smooth and jawline sharp. Fatima Kara's face is weatherworn, with deep wrinkles at her eyebrows and the bridge of her nose.

The two women sit on a plush velvet couch, sipping tea served by uniformed Palace butlers. Back on the mountain, Fatima Kara has a batwoman called Pireh, who keeps her uniforms clean and runs messages for her; the young girl is awestruck by Fatima Kara and efficient in her duties. These Palace servants show no excitement at being given the honor to serve the Commander of the Hamiyat's Dawn Battalion. Stern-faced and silent, they proffer tea and plates of dried fruit, dates, and nuts, then leave the women alone.

Raana Abdallah says, "I apologize for shrouding this entire exercise in so much secrecy. But it's quite necessary, as you'll soon see."

Fatima Kara says, "Secrecy is my preference, too."

"I've spent quite some time learning about you, Commander. Much of my job is to know about what's happening in the world, especially with our neighbors. When I heard about you and the Hamiyat, I insisted on finding out everything I could. You tend a beautiful crop of roses."

They are both speaking the formal, standard language of the peninsula, which Fatima Kara has learned in school, full of metaphor and poetry. She is not embarrassed by her Dhofari accent, or her serviceable clothes. The antechamber, with its exquisite silk rugs and rich draperies, does not intimidate her. She settles herself more comfortably into the sofa, chewing on the cardamom pod infused into her tea.

"I'm proud of them, my fighters. They defend themselves with their thorns, but without giving up an ounce of their womanhood, or their femininity."

"Your life has been hard, but you are free, on your mountain. Very unlike the rest of the women in Mazun."

"We've earned it."

"Yes," says Abdallah, leaning forward. "But what about the rest of Mazun? Do you think they deserve freedom, too?"

"Freedom's like a rose, the most beautiful one on the bush. Everyone wants to pluck it. But sometimes it dies, too."

"Not if it has the right gardener. And the right soil."

Later, they share a meal at an ornately carved wooden dining table set in an alcove that overlooks a lush garden. The servers lay plates of delicately grilled sea bass, rice, roasted vegetables in front of them. The aromas of lemon, sumac, cumin, and garlic waft in the air. As they eat, Kara observes Raana Abdallah through her most critical of lenses. She knows what Abdallah is getting at, even if she speaks more obliquely than people on the mountain.

Just before the dinner ends, over pastries and warm rose tea, Raana Abdallah spells it out: She proposes revolution in Dhofar. And Fatima Kara must be the one to lead it. "Tell me what it would take to turn the Hamiyat from a women's militia into a serious fighting force, one that can prevail over any army."

Fatima Kara, a little wary of Abdallah's enthusiasm, explains that although they have fewer fighters, better information, weapons, supplies, and training would improve their chances.

Raana Abdallah says she can provide everything the Hamiyat need in terms of material goods. "But once the fighting is over, you need a plan. Revolutions fail not because they are outgunned, but because they have no way to create real change after the guns are laid down. A revolution that will win freedom for the women of Dhofar, and beyond, must show them how to safeguard it for generations to come."

"Hmm," says Fatima Kara, who knows that Abdallah's offer isn't mere altruism; Abdallah is looking for a way to exert her influence beyond Semitian borders.

"You teach your Hamiyat fighters about women's emancipation, women's science, women's dignity. Isn't that a message that should spread far and wide? You need to get it out to all the women, so that when you march into a village or a town, you already have conspirators and allies. Sympathizers and collaborators."

Fatima Kara feels a little breathless. Raana Abdallah is seven steps ahead of her. Kara doesn't even know if the other Commanders would agree to the plan. They protect the mountain women, fight the Collectors where they can. But full-scale revolution is a giant risk. It could destroy them all.

Raana Abdallah shifts the conversation suddenly. "This is top secret, but I'll share it with you: We have a woman who escaped from Green City."

Fatima Kara's eyes widen. She's never heard of anyone fleeing Green City and surviving to tell the tale. Agents in Green City, unlike the Collectors in Dhofar, operate with impunity and deadly efficiency.

"Her name is Sabine," continues Raana Abdallah. "She lives in White City now, in Western Semitia. We debriefed her extensively when she came to us for asylum. We have learned a great deal about Green City's soft underbelly."

"How did she escape from the Agency?" says Fatima Kara, incredulous.

"Cunning, and a lot of luck. Her escape shook the highest echelons of Green City. They're nervous now. They can feel their grip on power is slipping. A shove, and they'll topple."

"And then what?"

"First, let's concentrate on creating a little chaos in Green City. And in the meantime, we'll work on getting the message out to the women of Dhofar: to be ready."

"And you'll do that how?"

Raana Abdallah says, "Through your Ababeels. I hear they're very good at keeping secrets. I'm willing to gamble they're good at spreading them, too."

"They're versatile, the Ababeels."

"Do you have children, Commander?"

Fatima Kara shakes her head. "I gave birth twice, but my children weren't lucky enough to live long. Both girls."

"I'm sorry."

"An old wound."

"Old wounds ache still, when the weather's bad. I never had children either. Didn't get married. Well, I am married, but to my job. And I suppose the Hamiyat are your children."

"I don't think of them that way. They're fighters; I'm their leader. It's my job to keep them safe, but I don't fret over them as a mother would. After all, it *is* my job, sometimes, to send them where they could be killed."

They speak a little more, exchanging personal anecdotes. Fatima Kara tells Raana Abdallah about how she climbed the ranks through the second Dhofar insurgency, which failed, just like the first a century ago, to become the Commander of Sun Mountain. In turn, Raana Abdallah tells her about her career: A girl from an upper-class family in the City of Gazelles, she excelled in school, then started out as a scientist in Zarzura. Her twin brother, Rami, meanwhile, was training to be a diplomat in the Eastern Semitian foreign service.

When they were both in their late twenties, Rami was killed in a car accident. She speaks calmly about the tragedy her family suffered twenty years ago. It compelled her to switch careers, leaving the laboratory for the place in diplomatic service that Rami had left vacant. The government offered it to her, and Raana Abdallah decided, in memory of Rami, to give it a try.

She served as Ambassador to several different countries before being summoned back to Eastern Semitia and fast-tracked in the civil service, the government having discovered her talent for communication and analytical thinking, as well as her scientific training. And now here she is, Deputy Minister for Foreign Affairs; one day she might even become First Minister.

But civil servants are essentially bureaucrats, she tells Fatima Kara, enacting policies formulated by cabals above their ranks. Raana Abdallah doesn't want to join those cabals. She hungers for a role in which her decisions, powered by her own brilliance, serve and uplift millions. "I want to be like you," she says. "Like a Commander, with women who I can trust with my life, and who trust me with theirs, working together to change everything."

Then Raana Abdallah looks at Fatima Kara keenly. "Tell me, Commander, who is your best fighter? Someone who you could trust with a mission that requires strength, stealth, secrecy, and skill?"

Fatima Kara closes her eyes, pictures her fighters in her mind. A face begins to swim into clearer view: a young woman with short brown hair and piercing green eyes. Rosy cheeks, a jaunty grin. She's younger than the more experienced fighters, but she's cunning, spirited, and can think on her feet. In a midnight raid on the Collector depot near Wadi Hamdan, she sneaked up on the guard from behind, stole his gun, and fought him in hand-to-hand combat. While she kept him busy, her squad mates entered the depot and made off with some weapons and ammunition. Reporting back to Lateefa, the fighter related her satisfaction at hearing the bone crunch when she broke his jaw and knocked him out cold on the floor. "I know just the person. Do you want me to get her here now?"

But Raana Abdallah says that Fatima Kara must trick the chosen fighter into coming to Eastern Semitia without knowing why she's been summoned, or telling her what she's going to do in Green City.

Fatima Kara grows wary. "But why all the secrecy? Why can't I just tell her what this is all about?" She doesn't like the idea of lying to one of her women: The Hamiyat survive on trust and transparency, and lying and tricking one another isn't their modus operandi.

"If you want my help," says Raana Abdallah, "we have to do it this way." At Fatima Kara's stern look, she adds, "It's very complicated here. You must understand, I have enemies who would love to see a woman fail at something this momentous. I need your fighter, but by virtue of being an outsider, she's vulnerable to other influences, to others convincing her that what we're trying to do is a pointless quest to serve my greed for personal power. Believe me, that's what they say about me: I'm power-hungry; I'm too ambitious. They even accuse me of having slept with the General—my colleague, the head of Security here in Eastern Semitia—to get to where I am today."

Fatima Kara nods. She understands Raana Abdallah's situation. Outside of the Hamiyat, all women in power face similar accusations, whether voiced directly or whispered about behind closed doors. She decides, then and there, to take the risk. "Katy Azadeh. She's the one you want. But only as long as you guarantee her safety here."

"As long as she's here in my country, she's not just my guest, she's my responsibility."

Fatima Kara falls into bed in her chambers at three in the morning, her mind filled with the seeds that Raana Abdallah has planted in her head. She doesn't dwell on the subterfuge that Raana Abdallah proposes, to bring Katy here so that she can be used for the mission in Green City. It seems less and less outrageous, a small injustice that will serve the revolution.

The next day, when the Commander departs for Dhofar, Raana Abdallah holds her close, like a sister, and whispers, "Thank you," and then kisses Fatima Kara's cheeks, left and right and left again, Semitian-style. "We treat our guests very well, but we treat our friends even better, Commander. You have nothing to fear."

The security entourage salutes the Commander as she climbs into the drone and straps herself in. A few moments later she is airborne, and on her way home in the quadcopter drone that flies like a mosquito through the mountain passes. All along the journey back to Dhofar, Fatima thinks not about Raana Abdallah's promises, but about what Fatima Kara now has to deliver. And Katy Azadeh is the first on the list.

Fatima Kara takes the other Commanders into confidence about Raana Abdallah's proposal. She travels to each mountain and meets with each Commander individually for war talks.

There are five other Commanders in the Hamiyat at her level: Commander Leila Ortabi of Star Mountain; Commanders Khulud and Zayna Al-Maliki, sisters in charge of the Three Brides; Commander Hind Qassemi of Lion Mountain; and Commander Soraya of Water Mountain. Star Mountain has the fewest fighters, a hundred and fifty; Lion and Sun Mountains have three hundred each; Water Mountain two hundred; and the Three Brides is the biggest division, with nearly seven hundred women in the ranks.

Commander Qassemi opposes the proposal outright, but Ortabi and Soraya agree to commit their fighters. Fatima Kara doesn't give up yet; she goes to see the Al-Maliki sisters last.

Zayna Al-Maliki is the younger of the two sisters, and the

more beautiful. She carries two pistols, one in a side holster, the other at her ankle. Khulud, the elder, does not display her weapons, but her body is thickened by a bulletproof vest; as a young soldier, she was wounded in a skirmish with a band of rapists, and nearly died. A bullet to her face has cut the muscles in her cheek, and she can move only one side of her mouth; the other falls down, giving her a lopsided appearance.

The sisters sit together, cross-legged, on the ground. Kara kneels in front of them, explaining her plans for the battle: which routes they can use to descend from the mountains into the valley, where they will set up camp, how many women to send ahead for sorties, and when.

Khulud says, "But the Collectors will never show their faces in full force. It's always just one or two at a time, heavily protected. How would you lure them out of their base, and up into our territory, without their security?"

"I've got a secret weapon," says Kara. "But it's going to be disguised so it looks like prey. Vulnerable, wounded prey. If the Collectors are like jackals, they'll like to hunt alone. One by one, we'll pick them off. Capture or kill. If alive, we'll use them as hostages for later negotiations."

"We'll help you get the Collectors off the mountain. More than that, we can't promise," says Zayna. Fatima Kara nods; it's enough for now.

Meanwhile, Raana Abdallah sends drones that drop off weapons and ammunition in the mountains every week, at various Hamiyat bases, on Fatima Kara's instruction. They fly out over the sea to elude the radars, then cut a straight line into the mountains and back again; they haven't yet been spotted or stopped by Dhofar's air defenses, which are, by all accounts, not very strong. The Al-Maliki sisters, impressed by the weapons, agree to join the fight. Fatima Kara thinks it won't be long until Hind Qassemi changes her mind and pledges her troops to the battle, too.

The final stages, the takeover of Queen of Sheba City, known as Sheba City for short, is still being worked out by Raana Abdallah's strategists in Eastern Semitia. Semitian satellites hover far above the city, mapping out safe streets, neighborhoods where sympathizers live, where a siege could last.

The Ababeels have been spreading the messages throughout the villages up and down the mountains, whispering them into the ears of other women. The Spectrum has been expanded; there are houses now in the outskirts of Sheba City where the light bulbs transmit the messages to the women living there. To show sympathy for the Hamiyat, women are instructed to hang a black veil from the highest point in their home, their street, their neighborhood.

*We, the Protectors, will know where to find you.*

Three weeks into the campaign, Raana Abdallah and Fatima Kara are conferring via video link over the Spectrum. A map of Dhofar flashes on Fatima Kara's screen, showing black flags marked in different areas: the fishing village of Mirbat, villages up and down the mountain, small enclaves along the coast, and even in the hearts of Sheba City's northern and eastern neighborhoods.

"That's more than I anticipated," says Fatima Kara. "Word's spread fast."

"We're piecing all the information together: who's willing to join you, provide a safe house, or give you food and supplies, or pass on information."

"How do you put it all together?"

Raana Abdallah smiles. "A supercomputer. It calculates risks. It'll tell us everything we need to know."

Fatima Kara shakes her head, disbelieving. "Did it say

we were going to be this popular?" She enjoys their talks; the conversations satisfy a loneliness she's long felt, one she can't reveal to anyone, not even the other Commanders. With them it's camaraderie and competition and grudging respect, but it's never easy, always hard-won. Raana Abdallah has become the only woman whom Fatima Kara considers a friend.

When she switches off the screen, she sits in silence, contemplating. The uprising is gathering pace, just like the khareef, when the clouds mass in the sky like hammerhead sharks. The air pressure drops, and dragonflies suddenly appear, darting everywhere to devour insects. But this is a storm she and Raana Abdallah are stirring up together. They will direct its intensity onto the representatives of a regime whose hour has come at last.

She knows that her fighters see her as the ideal woman, femininity in its most empowered form. To them she's an avatar of the Warrior Queen, the deity whose shrine the Hamiyat visit to pray for success in battle. But will the Warrior Queen favor them now that they're taking the fight right to Sheba City's doorstep?

She calls for Lateefa, and when her second-in-command appears in the doorway, she says, "Who's the best sniper in the Dawn Batallion?"

"Laleh," says Lateefa without hesitation. "Katy Azadeh's squad mate, the one I told you about. She's so good, she can put a bullet in someone who hasn't even been born yet."

"Bring her here at once," says Fatima Kara. She hopes the Warrior Queen understands she has to do this to Katy Azadeh, in order to advance the greater cause. And she hopes the Warrior Queen will forgive her for her sin.

# 15.

The women of the Panah move into a small white house that stands in the shadow of a slope in the grassy upland. Fatima Kara has decided to house them a safe distance from the village, so that the Hamiyat can keep an eye on them during their routine patrols of the mountainside.

The house needs a little work: Grace paints the door of the house, Diyah washes the windows, Mariya runs the taps, making sure the kitchen is in working order. They've been given Spectrum light bulbs to install, as well as devices for each of them. In the garden, Rupa clears out weeds and prepares raised beds for growing vegetables.

Slowly, life on the mountain resurrects them all. Breathing the thin air, walking up and down the slopes, sitting on a ledge staring out into a valley of pine trees, erases their pale, wan looks, and color starts to bloom on their faces. Their eyes are finally beginning to adjust to the sun, to colors seen in the clarity of morning light. Sunrise amazes them still.

Some of the Hamiyat fighters have befriended the Panah women after Fatima Kara's declaration in their favor at the Ruined City. They come around to the house at night to play cards and take them for walks on misty mornings. They laugh at the way the Panah women wrap themselves in woolen shawls, a gift from the Ababeels, to keep the damp fog out of their bones.

Marzi catches rabbits in traps and Grace cooks them with mushrooms and herbs that Alia's child Noor brings up from Alia's pantry. Once in a while Alia joins them for a meal, then slips away back to her home as quietly as she came in, like a ghost. Grace and Lateefa, Commander Kara's second-in-command, are often spotted talking companionably together, Lateefa leaning against the gate of the house, her rifle propped up against its low boundary wall.

The Hamiyat are curious about every aspect of the Panah women's lives: what they ate, how they dressed, what the men of Green City were like in bed, whether the buildings were taller than their mountains, what Lin had taught them about sex. Diyah tries to explain the nature of their assignations, but the Hamiyat women pooh-pooh them and refuse to believe there was no sex involved. Which only makes them insist that they're telling the truth.

During these conversations, Rupa catches Laleh, the squad mate and best friend of the missing Katy Azadeh, looking at her with narrowed eyes. Rupa knows how to keep her face wiped clean of incriminating expressions and stares back at her innocently. Laleh makes a crude gesture with her fingers—a finger going back and forth through a circle made with the thumb and forefinger of her other hand. Rupa stuffs her knuckles into her mouth to stop the laughter from spilling out.

Early one evening, the off-duty Hamiyat fighters hanging around the house see Fatima Kara and Lateefa coming up the rise toward the house. They all stand straight and salute. Lateefa barks at them to be on their way. They salute her and march up the slope behind the house, disappearing at the top of the path. The women of the Panah come outside and wish Fatima Kara and Lateefa a good day.

Fatima Kara says, "The house looks good."

"It's very comfortable," says Diyah. "Thank you."

"You've worked hard on it."

Grace says, "We're used to hard work. Contrary to the

rumors." Mariya giggles, but Diyah silences her with a sharp glance, while Lateefa stares ahead, expressionless. Decorum has to be maintained in front of the Commander at all times.

Fatima Kara examines the Panah women with a keen eye. They're far from the luxuries of Green City, the perfumes and lotions that softened their skins and the subterranean existence that gave them their languid, colorless air. Here they're exposed to harsh sunlight and cold wind, thin air and toil. But they're still exotic and strange, an unstable element that can set an entire village on fire.

"We're grateful for your hospitality, and your protection," says Rupa.

"I'm glad," says Fatima Kara. "Think of it as your new Panah." Then she explains to them, quickly, precisely, what she needs them to do: help the Hamiyat to trap and capture the Collectors, using all the powers of seduction they've brought with them from Green City.

Lateefa already knows the plan; she watches the women's faces as the Commander speaks. Rupa, the Indian one with the nosepin, the loveliest; the silver-eyed woman, Diyah, who the others say can see the future. Mariya, coltishly tall and thin as a reed.

Lateefa likes Grace best, her cool manner contrasting with her sharp tongue in a way that Lateefa finds intriguing, compelling. Lateefa wants to see as much of her as she can, stealing moments out of her free time to visit with her at the new Panah. Lateefa doesn't care whether they are prostitutes or not; her own ancestors were the slave-concubines of rich men. Grace is the only one she's told this to. Whatever the women of the Panah have done for the rich men of Green City, Lateefa doesn't want to know. But in the uprising, they will all have to play their part, or else they will just be a hindrance.

The women confer among themselves, while Commander Kara waits. Lateefa begins to count under her breath: *one, two, three . . .* If they protest, Lateefa will remind them that they're lucky Commander Kara has taken them under her protection. If they'd been caught and trafficked to Sheba City, where women are passed between the sailors and the police, they'd have learned what whoring was really all about.

When Lateefa reaches twenty, Rupa says, "We'll do it. We can't refuse you now."

Commander Kara nods. "Very good."

"But I want to fight," says Mariya.

"Don't be ridiculous," says Lateefa. "You're untrained. We don't have the time to get you up to speed. You don't even know how to fire a gun."

"Yes, I do," says Mariya. "Marzi's been teaching me."

"What? I didn't authorize that," says Lateefa, her scalp prickling. Fatima Kara glances at her. She's the Commander's most trusted woman, but the anger is always there, lurking underneath the surface of her stern, disciplined exterior.

It's been a long hard battle for Lateefa to conquer her temper and her impatience. She killed another woman once, in a fight, before joining the Hamiyat; it was why she'd had to run away from her village. They'd fought because the other woman objected to Lateefa drinking water from her well; she didn't want a black woman dirtying their water source. Lateefa became enraged and next thing the woman was dead on the ground in front of her. Lateefa ran away and didn't stop running until she was standing in front of the famed Commander of the Dawn Batallion, ready to confess her sin and take her punishment from the Hamiyat. No one else could be the judge of her.

Fatima Kara told Lateefa that cold-blooded murder was never justified, but that atonement was possible, if she channeled her rage to serve a higher purpose. Then she offered Lateefa a place in the Hamiyat. Since then, Lateefa has worshipped Fatima Kara, the woman who, she likes to believe, has absolved her of her worst crime. Being near her quells Lateefa's anger, her restless spirit; Lateefa will take a bullet for Fatima Kara and never betray her to another soul.

The Commander says, "Show us what you can do. Lateefa, give her your pistol."

Lateefa slowly unclips the pistol and unlocks it with her fingerprint, then hands it over to Mariya.

"Do you see that pomegranate tree over there?" says Fatima Kara. "Aim at the one that's hanging there, to the left. And don't use the optimizer."

No visual optimizer? The pomegranate tree is at least thirty yards away from them, beyond the low wall that surrounds the house and its small yard. Nobody can shoot like that, except Laleh, thinks Lateefa. She begins to count again. One, two, three . . .

Gently leaning her head to the right, Mariya sights the red globe hanging from the lowest branch on the left side of the tree. At the end of an exhalation, she squeezes the trigger. The pomegranate explodes like a man's head, a blur of red guts and pulp flying in all directions. Lateefa whistles; the Panah women cheer.

Mariya lowers the gun and turns around, wide-eyed. Lateefa knows well the adrenaline coursing through Mariya's body, the bloodrush of hitting a difficult target, the spine-tingling pull in the pit of your stomach that makes you want to do it again and again. This is the power to kill: stronger than sex, better than love.

"Well done," Fatima Kara says. "There's a Collector coming to Akoub. The Ababeels have reported he's a day away. You'll bring him here." Commander Kara sweeps out of the gate, and Laleh and Marzi materialize out of nowhere and accompany her up the hill.

"So you can shoot," says Lateefa. "You'll protect your new Panah. It'll free up the real fighters for the real battle. This is your job from now on. Is that understood?"

Mariya nods, her plain face alight with purpose. She hands back the pistol to Lateefa, who takes it from her and holsters it silently. Lateefa faces the Panah women. "So. The child will fight. And the rest of you will fuck." She says it on purpose, to unsettle them; this, too, is part of being a fighter, becoming mentally toughened, impervious to insults and provocations. Learning how to shoot a gun is the easiest part. Then she catches Grace's flirtatious gaze on her, and her body grows hot. A spark passes between the two women as Grace bites her lower lip.

Music begins to play from someone's device: a mountain folk song, popular with lovers. Lateefa sets down her rifle on the ground, Grace faces her, and the two of them slide into an energetic dance, moving and stomping their feet. Grace claps high and low, while Lateefa turns slowly around her, their eyes locked into an intense stare. The others cheer them on, calling encouragement in high, excited cries. A few more Hamiyat soldiers gather around, whistling and trilling, while Grace and Lateefa execute faster, trickier footsteps, until they both stop, chests heaving, cheeks flushed.

Lateefa wonders, *Is this what they call fate?*

The next night, Alia stands outside a small bar in Akoub, shrouded in a black veil. In the street a dog lets out a long, melancholy wail, echoed by other howls, coming from different directions, joining in the chorus of nighttime despair. *Even the dogs here are desperate*, thinks Alia, wanting to be in her bed. She doesn't come to the tavern often. A few lamps glowing here and there mark the path that slopes steeply downhill. Doors are shut and windows closed, blinds pulled down, giving the appearance of an entire village as one body, deeply asleep.

The door to the bar opens and out comes the Collector. Alia has given the bartender, a sympathizer, a special flower from Yemen to grind and drop into the Collector's drink. It seems to have worked: He veers down the path a little drunkenly, aiming in the general direction of his quarters. Then he sees a black cloth hanging from the far corner of the tavern, flapping softly in the wind. He flinches, stares up at it, rubs his face, then stumbles down the street again.

Alia follows him surreptitiously as the Collector takes one wrong turn, and then another, and then instead of walking downhill, he's headed uphill, the village behind him, a starry sky above him, a rising cliff on his right and a forest on his left. Disoriented, he stands still and tries to figure out where he is.

A fog has rolled in, and Alia can't see more than a few feet in front of her. The air is cottony thick against her skin, wet with humidity, damp and cold. She walks up to the Collector and whispers his name. Anas . . . Anas . . . He whirls around and sees her standing off the path, against the trunk of a baobab tree. The moon has come out from behind a cloud to illuminate both of them and the tree with a glowing, pulsing light. The leaves on the tree shimmer like silver.

"Anas . . . come a little closer, so I can see you . . ."

The Collector hesitates, so Alia lifts the veil off her head slightly, showing him her face. "You're lost," she whispers. "I have a house not far from here. Would you like to come see it?"

"Is it the brothel I heard about back in the bar?"

Alia smiles. She has told the bartender to tell him there are women on the mountain, women from Green City, who might be whores. No man can resist investigating whether such a thing is true. "It's called the Panah," she says. "Come see it for yourself." She reaches out for his hand, and he gives it to her unsteadily. Raindrops begin to spatter on their faces. Alia looks up at the clouds and laughs sweetly. "The khareef. Come on. Let us give you shelter."

She knows he doesn't want to be alone in the monsoon rain, which can be long and relentless, making mountain paths slippery and treacherous at night. She walks close to him, warming him with her presence. She hears the hiss of rain in treetops, the Collector's footsteps crunching in the wet gravel on the path, his strained breathing, her heartbeat drumming in her ears. The air has changed pressure, becoming close and thick; petrichor, rich and loamy, rises from the earth and fills her nose. They come to a house, brightly lit windows glinting in the darkness. Its windows are like eyes and its door is a smile underneath. The raindrops falling all around them are confetti, celebrating his return home.

Alia glides to the door and beckons the Collector inside. He hesitates, looking back over his shoulder, but there is nothing behind him save for a few ghostly-looking trees, the shadows of low hills, and rows of bushes, pale flowers bobbing under the weight of the rain. He sticks his head cautiously through the door of the house, looking for men waiting with guns, while Alia scurries into the kitchen and disappears. But there's just an empty hallway, stone walls freshly whitewashed, a worn carpet thrown on the floor as a welcome mat. A light on the wall gives off a warm yellow glow.

"Come, come," calls another woman's voice. The Collector follows the voice down the corridor to a room, a space small but inviting: a low sofa set against a far wall, on which two women are sitting. They lean back, long limbs relaxed, hair loose and flowing down their backs. The brunette is in a red dress and the blonde in a green shift. He has never seen women offering themselves to him like a gift.

The dark-haired woman pats the sofa; the Collector joins them hesitantly. The blood is turning to sludge in his veins, thickening in his legs, weighing him down to the point of near paralysis. At the same time, he's filled with need; the desire to be fully accepted, not to be hated for being the Collector. He wants to be loved.

As if he's said this out loud, the two women put their hands on his thighs and rest them there lightly, in a gesture of affection and compassion. The Collector can barely breathe. They apply the slightest pressure of their fingers on his flesh. The dark-haired woman puts her hands on his face, and his hands encircle her waist.

Alia watches from the doorway as he leans forward and begins to tighten his arms around Rupa in a python's embrace. The slightest moan escapes her lips. Their kiss is deep and lush. Alia is sure Rupa's mouth tastes like honey.

Marzi rises from behind the sofa, her gun in her hand. She brings the butt down onto the base of his skull in a blow so hard that he howls out loud. He releases Rupa from his embrace and slumps forward into her lap. A trickle of blood snakes its way down his neck. Diyah puts her hand on his shoulder and shakes him; he falls off Rupa's lap and onto the floor with a loud thump.

"Is he dead?" Marzi is ready to hit the man again if he moves. Lateefa and Laleh appear in the doorway, their guns aimed at the Collector prone on the ground.

"I don't think so," says Diyah. "Look, he's still breathing."

"Well done," says Lateefa. "We'll take it from here. Grab his device," she says to Laleh. Then the three of them drag him by his arms and legs outside the house. Alia and the rest of the Panah women come into the room with Diyah and Rupa. They wait for the single gunshot that cracks out just as a flash of lightning brightens the windows and the khareef pours down on the mountain.

# 16.

On Sun Mountain, Star Mountain, Lion Mountain, Water Mountain, and the Three Brides, the Hamiyat begin to move down from the peaks and into the villages, clearing them of Collectors and Guards, street by street, alley by alley. At this stage, with the advantage of surprise, there are no Hamiyat deaths and only a few wounded troops in minor skirmishes. At every village the women are ready with food and water for the fighters.

Some villages are already theirs by the time they arrive. When the Hamiyat fighters walk into the smaller hamlets, they're met with celebration: singing, ululations, children following them, rioting and saluting, black veils fluttering from windows and rooftops. Everyone thrills at the sight of the fighters, dressed in camouflage, colorful headscarves and checked cloths slung around their necks, boots stamping in unison, rifles at the ready.

Raana Abdallah's technologists cut off communications between Sheba City and the Collector's Houses by crashing their network, which is not as invulnerable as the Spectrum. Now the local government is blocked from gaining any accurate information about the Hamiyat's movements. Any official resistance to the uprising is isolated and uncoordinated, quickly overcome by the Hamiyat fighters and their conspirators living up and down the mountains.

Now they've come down to Haffa, now they're at Aqwad, now they've taken over the land between the three branches of the Mughsil River. It won't be long before they're ready to leave the mountains for the plains below.

At her base in the Ruined City at the top of Sun Mountain, Fatima Kara talks daily to her co-commanders over the Spectrum, planning the next part of the uprising in detail. Commander Leila Ortabi and the Al-Maliki sisters will bring their troops down with Fatima Kara's women; Soraya's troops will stay higher to protect the mountains. Although Hind Qassemi, Commander of Lion Mountain, has still not pledged her troops, some of the villages are rising up of their own accord and throwing out the Collectors where they can.

"We'll have two thousand fighters. But will it be enough?" Kara asks.

"Once we establish ourselves in the safe houses, as long as we use the terrain to our advantage, we will prevail," says Soraya, the Commander of Water Mountain. She's an enthusiast of military strategy, spends all her time studying famous battles in history. They call her the Professor; it's her code name for their communications over the Spectrum.

"How?"

"Look, Sheba City is not a mountain. It's buildings and concrete. Concrete is our friend: It can stop enemy bullets, limit their navigation and radio signals. Every piece of concrete is a place to hide behind, a bunker to defend. We establish sniper perches, gun positions, pill boxes. We clear, seize, secure the area, then we defend. We'll still work in small teams, quicker, easier to move in constricted spaces. Then we regroup as larger squads to take over the next street, and the next, and the next."

Although they've been largely successful so far, everyone looks thinner and more pinched in the face than before. Fatima Kara is smoking more than ever, staying up nights, unable to sleep for more than a few fitful hours at a time. A harsh cough afflicts her, but she ignores it like most of the complaints of her body.

"Abdallah's promised us whatever we need, when we get to Khor Rori," says Fatima Kara. This is the water inlet that the Hamiyat will cross before making the final push to Sheba City.

So far, the Semitians have provided training modules for city fighting: virtual reality headsets and combat simulators designed by Semitian scientists, with enclosed cabins with screens for vehicle simulators. A fighter can stand, turn around, maneuver, shoot at a computerized enemy in an apartment complex or on a busy market street. In the simulation pods, the Hamiyat fighters encounter the nausea and claustrophobia of tight spaces, the smoke and heat of a city gunfight, drills where they drop down beneath walls or take cover behind doorways, instead of trees or rocks.

"Do you trust her?" says Hind Qassemi, the only naysayer of the group. She is in her forties, strikingly beautiful, with a long sweep of auburn hair that she ties up in a scarf emphasizing her aristocratic bone structure and the fineness of her skin. She is rumored to have royal lineage to the old rulers of Mazun. She usually speaks with stiff formality; her directness now underscores how close to life and death things have become.

Fatima Kara pushes her hands deep into her pockets to warm them. The khareef brings chilly temperatures, as well as the fog and the damp. Sometimes when she wakes up, she can't move her fingers due to stiffness. Her rooms in the Ruined City are freezing cold in the early hours.

She chooses her words carefully, speaks with calm. "I have no reason not to. She's come through on everything else so far."

The others nod. "So our next objective," says Leila Ortabi, "is to get down to the Darbat Valley."

"And on to Khor Rori," adds Zayna Al-Maliki.

Fatima Kara's skin tingles with relief. These are hardened, tough women, excellent soldiers, inspired commanders; each has risen, as she has, through the ranks of the second insurgency and then the Hamiyat. Fatima Kara never expected an easy time, even after they had agreed to participate in the mission. But they're still with her, for now.

After the meeting, Fatima Kara loosens her belt and places her attached holster and pistol onto her desk. She lifts her boots up onto her desk, lights a cigarette, and gazes at the far-off sea. A sheet of shimmering silver pulses underneath a red sinking sun, caught halfway between thick cloud and horizon, as raindrops pockmark the gray surface of the waves closer to shore. Breathing in deeply, taking in the scent of the khareef, Fatima Kara closes her eyes and pictures the recruitment camps, the faces of those raw, excited girls who lined up and took the Hamiyat oath.

She and her lieutenants have trained them in military tactics: how to advance across open ground, to mount guard or take cover, to handle light and medium weapons. They've spent hours learning combat techniques: hand-to-hand fighting, using knives and pistols at close range, martial arts, and self-defense. Through countless foot drills, field training exercises, rifles lifted up and down until shoulders ache and muscle memory makes the movements automatic. Changing from girls into women, from women into fighters, the roses have grown thorns to defend themselves.

Now the roses will become grenades, hurled into alleys and streets, onto rooftops and into rooms full of enemies. Thorns will become shrapnel, ready to dig into flesh and bone.

The color red blooming wherever a bullet bites into tender skin.

Fatima Kara throws her cigarette butt into a corner of the room. Her young batwoman, Pireh, named after the dawn, cleans them up faithfully every morning and night: In the last month there have been mounds of them to sweep away. Fatima Kara wonders if this is why Pireh joined the Hamiyat: for the chance to clean up the Commander's cigarette ends? But every act for the resistance is an act of honor, the girls tell themselves, even the lowliest. Fatima Kara hopes that history will be as kind to her when this is all over.

Two days before Kara leads her troops off Sun Mountain and down toward the Darbat Valley, there's a shoot-out between the Hamiyat and the Collector's Guards in their village. The Hamiyat and the Guards exchange gunfire, three or four fighters taking position in a safe house and another two on a rooftop nearby, while the Collector's Guards crouch behind a low wall, outgunned and outnumbered.

After four hours, the guards are all dead. Some of the villagers are wounded, too, though they had all been warned to stay in their houses. Stray bullets find them anyway. One pierced the wall of Alia's house and struck her eldest Husband in the chest. The bullet did not kill him instantly, but the ensuing heart attack did.

Kara's fighters melt away as the villagers drag the enemy's bodies in the pouring rain and throw them down into the ravine where the Panah women's car had crashed. Alia's Husband is the only civilian casualty in that skirmish, but all up and down the mountains there are more scenes like this one, more bodies to bury, more families left stunned and uncertain, awash in grief and loss.

It's still raining when Lateefa comes to Alia's village that evening to offer condolences for the death of the Ababeel's Husband. She enters Alia's house, her overcoat heavy and sodden; she doesn't like dripping water onto Alia's floor, but the Ababeel doesn't seem to notice. Lateefa says a few words of commiseration to Alia, who nods. Then she says, "I want to come with you when you go to Sheba City."

"Absolutely not," Lateefa replies, crossing her arms and shaking her head.

Thunder rumbles overhead, as if punctuating Lateefa's refusal, but Alia stands there mulishly. She closes her eyes, remembering the moment her Husband was shot: how he dropped to his knees while her children ran to him, screaming, as more bullets zinged by their house. How she stood by in the tiny village cemetery as her other two Husbands etched the gap of his grave into the earth. She recalls the sound of Noor clutching her hand and sobbing, like a kitten who has lost its mother. It wakes up a desire in her, like a slow angry burn, to exact revenge for her Husband's death. She doesn't know how she'll accomplish this, but neither can she imagine staying back in the village while the Hamiyat go to battle in Sheba City.

"I can be of use to you all. I'll manage your food supplies, your cooking," says Alia. "And keep the women strong for the fight ahead."

"You will?" says Lateefa, her resolve weakening. She loves Alia's food; they all do. It would be a comfort to have good food while they're on the march.

"Yes. And I know herbs and local medicines. You'll need poultices, teas, all sorts of things. I can make tisanes that increase a woman's strength, or help her sleep before a dangerous day. If a woman is pregnant, I know how to get rid of it."

"No chance of that," snorts Lateefa.

"You never know what happens in war," says Alia ominously.

"Fine. I'll tell Commander Kara. The last word is hers."

"Fair enough," says Alia. "I'll wait."

"What, you want me to ask her now?"

Alia crosses her arms in imitation of Lateefa. The lieutenant, sighing, quickly sends the message across to Commander Kara. "You're wasting my time, you know—"

The device flashes with an almost immediate reply from Commander Kara: *Tell her to be here in two days. The Panah women, too. We need everyone we can get.*

*The Panah women*, Lateefa thinks to herself. How will they manage this entire circus? But secretly, she's a little glad. After that time that she and Grace danced together when the women had painted the new Panah, Lateefa began to visit the new Panah after patrol. Grace waited for her with a hot cup of tea, a smile, smoothing the tension out of Lateefa's shoulders with her strong fingers. Grace listened to Lateefa talk about the veiled whisperings when she passed a group of women who liked to mutter under their breaths, *Habshi*. Grace tightened her lips in a grimace of recognition of the word for "slave"—the only word needed to articulate their shared burden as black women of Mazun.

One night, Lateefa fell asleep with her boots still on in Grace's bed at the Panah, finding it warmer than her own lonely cot back at the base. Grace slipped into the bed and lay there all night by her side. In the morning, when Lateefa awoke, her boots standing at the foot of the bed and Grace's arms around her, she wondered if she was still dreaming.

The two instincts, to draw close and to kick away, are always fighting inside Lateefa, but in the space between them, somehow Grace has slipped in. Lateefa knows there's no way they will be parted now.

She glowers at Alia, still feeling she's lost a battle to a less worthy opponent. "All right then. Get your things in order. And come alone. Your Husbands can look after your children while you're gone."

After Lateefa leaves, Alia goes to her pantry and lies down on the cold stone floor, pressing her face into it as penance for still being alive. She thinks of the village after the gun battle: bullet holes riddled the walls of the houses, debris littered the street—spent bullets, pieces of stone dislodged by gunfire, shreds of cloth. A single shoe. The ground stained red with blood, mixing into the dirt. *Funny how men and women bleed the same color*, she thinks abstractedly.

All her bottles have been hit by stray bullets in the pantry, an addition to the house that her oldest Husband built for her in the early days of their marriage. The scents of vinegar and onion find her, and she lies there, eyes streaming, until she finds the strength to get up off the floor and start to clean up.

But Alia intends to disobey Lateefa's last command. Noor will come with Alia, hidden in the folds of her skirt. And nobody will notice until they are already down the mountain, and it's too late to send either Alia or the child back.

# 17.

In a lookout post in a hill high above the Hamiyat camp at Khor Rori, a steady rain beats down on Laleh and Marzi as they watch for enemies coming their way. The fog rolling in from the sea hides them from visual surveillance. Far below, the Dawn Battalion prepares for the push toward Sheba City.

Ensconced along the rocky outcrops, natural shelter that confounds the enemy's thermal cameras mounted on drone patrols, the Hamiyat fighters move everywhere. They drag camouflage nets over tents, clean weapons, sort through equipment packs, count ammunition.

Two soldiers prepare a meal over smokeless coals under an Ababeel's direction at a cooking station, where women line up to gulp down a quick meal of eggs and flatbread. Latrines are established in a makeshift shelter, although nobody will bathe or wash their clothes in case the scent of soap carries on the wind to enemy noses.

They've trekked three hours from Sun Mountain to Jebal Samhan, the Mountain of Mercy, the last major peak in the Dhofar range. Then four hours to Darbat Wadi through an empty riverbed that cuts across the plateau, and a straight march all the way to the camp, a mere mile from Khor Rori. It's four in the morning now; troops from the other mountains will arrive over the next six hours.

Two hundred women of the Dawn Battalion have traveled with Fatima Kara, the soldiers all trained to move stealthily, communications equipment silenced, backpacks, vests, and weapons carried carefully. They speak to one another only in hand signals or low voices. The Commander and her lieutenants wear Infrared goggles to see in the dark; they lead the women through terrain covered by foliage, in small groups of four or five, but no more than eight. They wear ponchos and caps that keep them dry but also break up the shapes of their bodies, disguising their shadows as they creep down the mountainside and across the coastal plain.

With them are some of the Ababeels who have decided to leave their homes and help set up camp. And the Panah women: Grace, Rupa, Diyah, and Mariya. The youngest woman still wants to fight, while Grace has deemed herself Lateefa's personal companion, promising to find ways to be helpful, unobtrusive to Lateefa. "I'll polish your boots. Make your bed. Mend your uniform. Nothing's too small. I just want to be near you."

"It's dangerous, Grace," Lateefa protests. She doesn't want to ask, *Why?* The answer is too dangerous to know, more dangerous than a bullet or a bomb.

"So what?" laughs Grace. "Fate checkmates us all in the end. Wouldn't you say?"

Before leaving the mountain, the Panah women have seduced at least a dozen Collectors and their Guards for the Hamiyat. Their bodies are spread out over miles of the mountainside. Now, the villages are mostly clear and Hind Qassemi's Lionness Brigade, deputed with protecting the mountains, move around in plain sight.

Next week in Sheba City is the Khareef Festival; the people will feast and dance to celebrate the arrival of the rain. Free food and drink, trading markets and sports competitions, mostly men attracted by the rumor of brothels with imported prostitutes from Kolachi, capital of the South West Territories. Wives have stayed at home to look after children and those too old to travel. The Hamiyat have chosen this time to amass their troops; the security radars unable to tell the difference between civilians and fighters moving toward the city.

Inspecting the camp, Fatima Kara strides past a medical tent. Its flap is pulled open to let in the dim light of predawn; Alia is inside, squatting on her haunches and wrapping bandages. The Commander stops abruptly in front of the tent. "Alia, greetings, my dear."

The child Noor is beside her, stacking the rolls into neat pyramids, small hands quick as birds. He lifts a white tube from the top of the pile and pushes it into the air, turning it into an airplane, a drone, a falling bomb. When he sees Fatima Kara, he jumps to his feet and salutes her. Alia looks up to acknowledge the Commander mutely.

Fatima Kara has heard about the death of Alia's eldest Husband. "My condolences," says Fatima Kara, putting her hand to her heart. Alia repeats the gesture and mumbles something under her breath. Fatima Kara considers saying more, but what really is there to say? The uprising is taking them all up in its current and dragging some of them under in a riptide of uncertainty and chaos. Husbands are beginning to question whether their Wives are secret sympathizers; Wives wonder if their Husbands are reporting the Hamiyat's sweep through the mountains to the Collectors. Some say the uprising should never have started at all. Lateefa reports the unrest to Fatima Kara; the Commander shrugs her shoulders.

The Commander leaves Alia and her child and walks on. The rain drifts down in a fine mist, beading her face. She adjusts her coat, pulling it tighter around her body. Her mind is on too many things at once.

On the march from Darbat Wadi, the Hamiyat used abandoned buildings they came across for urban combat practice drills. They rehearsed in small fire teams of four women, kicking in doors, clearing out rooms, establishing captured territory and holding it while moving on to the next area.

Fatima Kara recalls observing the drills: The women performed well, but being on the ground in the middle of a firefight is a completely different beast. The only way to win the city is to outflank the enemy and overpower them with quick bursts of fighting, street to street, house to house. Will her women hold their mettle when trapped in the heat and smoke and claustrophobia of the assault? Most, she thinks, will stay, some will run, and many will die. How many can they sacrifice before they'd have to give up?

Fatima Kara heads for her quarters. They've been marching all night; she's going to get a quick nap before the meeting of the Commanders. Inside, her batwoman, Pireh, polishes Fatima Kara's boots, humming a war song popular with the younger soldiers. Every few moments, she spits on the boot in her hand and rubs the cloth even harder to bring up a more vigorous shine.

Kara walks in. "You can go, Pireh. Get some rest."

Pireh lines up the boots by the cot, salutes, and dashes out of the tent. She'll stand guard outside while Kara is still awake, then prepare her kit while Kara sleeps. Anticipation jumps from one woman to the next, like a current, setting them all humming. They all have too many thoughts racing through their minds, regrets about the past, anxieties about the future. Later in the day, all the Commanders will meet for the first time in person: an occasion that racks up tension, anticipation, and excitement among all the fighters.

Fatima Kara is one of the constantly sleepless. Instead of lying down, she sits in her chair, staring at the screen of her display. For some reason the live video link isn't working tonight, perhaps because of Fatima Kara's location, her tent well hidden among the heavy rocks and boulders. There's a static image of Raana Abdallah on the screen when Kara checks in with her.

"Was it a success, the mission to Green City?"

"Reuben Faro is dead. Your fighter was very effective." Raana Abdallah's voice, warm and smooth as honey, pours into Fatima Kara's headset.

"Where is Katy Azadeh now?"

"We've got her back with us here. She's perfectly safe. We'll get her back to you after this is all over. She's earned her rest now."

"Oh, well done, Katy," says Fatima Kara under her breath. The niggle of doubt she's felt all evening evaporates like mist; Katy's triumph is a good omen, too, for their own success. She says with confidence, "We move forward tomorrow then."

"Tomorrow. The reconnaissance team, the advance guard, then the rest. Don't worry about the air support. The drones are ready."

"To Sheba City, then."

"To Sheba City," says Raana Abdallah. They exchange the security codes and counter-codes, as they do at the beginning and end of every communication stream, to make sure each is truly who they say they are. The screen fades to black.

Kara settles down on her cot and thinks of her soldiers, bundled on the ground in their sleeping bags. They don't rest easily, one hand on a knife or a gun, always ready for an attack or a call to duty in the darkest hours of night. She knows all their faces—Ahlam from Al-Ashkarah, Naima from Bani Awf, Zeinab from Shaat, Duaa of Batinah, Gamila, Sofiya . . .

As she's nearly drifting off to sleep, she has a terrible vision of her fighters, not asleep, but dead—bodies strewn on the battlefield: an open desert, sand covering their limbs, their torsos blown apart and exposing the meat and bones inside. Fatima Kara sits up, lights a cigarette, silently sends an entreaty to the Warrior Queen. Not a prayer, exactly, but an offer for negotiation: *Let my women live, and I'll worship you for life.* The smoke in her lungs, the damp chill of the tent, the sea, and the desert march ahead of her lulls her back into a disquieted sleep.

Pireh, sneaking back into the tent, plucks the lit cigarette from Fatima Kara's loosened fingers, a deep furrow between her eyebrows and her lips slightly parted. Her breath rattles hoarsely in her lungs. Pireh wishes her Commander would stop smoking so many cigarettes. But whenever Pireh says so, Kara always laughs that a bullet will kill her long before the cigarettes ever will. And the laugh turns into a prolonged cough that sounds to Pireh like disdain for death as much as for the pain of being alive.

By midday, all the troops have settled in at the camps surrounding Khor Rori, a sea inlet that fills up every year during the khareef. As the sun struggles to assert itself through the thick clouds, the inlet is now in full flood, a vein of blue bisecting the sandy banks, pulsing steadily in and out with the strength of the sea tide.

Under the gray sky, their camp is a riot of moss green, almost electric in intensity; over plateaus farther away, little waterfalls cascade down the rocks and into the main river. Acacia trees stud the terrain, leaves trembling with the weight of rain. Not far from the camp, a large pool of green water beckons invitingly, but there's no time for a dip, as much as they long to clean themselves after the night's long journey. They're only allowed to fill their jerry cans for drinking water.

At the appointed hour, all the Commanders of the Mountains, save for Hind Qassemi, stride to the Command tent. Commander Kara waits for them outside in the chilly dawn, her breath a misty plume in front of her face. Lateefa stands straight-backed at her side. The Dawn Batallion is lined up in two rows and the Commanders march between them. At a shout from one of the sergeants, an honor guard presents their rifles and fires a quick round of celebratory shots into the air, sending a nearby flock of birds hurtling out of the trees and into the sky. Fatima Kara salutes Leila Ortabi, Khulud and Zayna Al-Maliki, and Soraya. Then they kiss and embrace one another, and the fighters all ululate in triumph and joy.

Mariya, Diyah and Rupa, Grace, Alia and Noor stand to the side. When the aerial firing begins, Noor puts his hands over his ears and buries his face in Alia's legs. The Panah women join in with the ululations, but Alia watches impassively, her face a pane of glass that lets nothing in or out. Grace smiles at Lateefa, but Lateefa's eyes are flat and small under her cap. She glances at Grace, then quickly away. Grace still smiles, pretending it doesn't hurt to be snubbed.

Inside the tent, the Commanders are all smoking cigarettes and sipping cups of hot tea. They put their heads together and begin to discuss the last phase of the advance, the details of the troop movements and the crossing of Khor Rori. Maps of the area flick onto the display—the different battalions are depicted in four colors: green for the Star Mountain battalions, yellow for Sun, blue for Water, and red for the Three Brides. Over Sheba City, black spots blink on and off: the locations of the Zaalims, the wandering munition drones that are the city's primary defense system.

The Zaalims are feared by everyone because of their dual treachery: They don't just deliver surveillance; they can drop explosives, too, using built-in algorithms to discern, without an operator, enemy territory, or installations or even a single hostile individual. Raana Abdallah claims that her technology specialists can track the Zaalims and blow them up in the air. She promises Fatima Kara that the Semitians will disable as many of the munitions as they can to protect the Hamiyat during the siege

When the black lights show up on the screen, a sheen of sweat rises in the curve of Fatima Kara's back. Her heart is a drumbeat marking off the time they have left until the irreversible move toward the city. The women gathered in this tent know that some of them will not survive the assault. Unlike other Commanders and Generals who stay back at base while the soldiers fight and die, the Commanders of the Hamiyat will fight alongside their women at the front line.

After the Commanders' meeting, the message goes out to all of Fatima Kara's fighters: *Dawn Battalion, Squad 32—Depart Khor Rori at 3:30 a.m.*

Laleh and Marzi, relieved from guard duty, receive the message on their devices at the same time as everyone else. "That's it, then," says Marzi. "We cross tonight."

Laleh grins in excitement. Ever since they left the mountain, Laleh dreams of riding in on the S-ATVs entering Sheba City at lightning speed, waving her rifle in the air, cheers of the grateful city-dwellers ringing in her ears. But their devices ping again with their orders, assigning them both to the body of ordinary troops, not the advance guard.

Marzi accepts the order with a resigned shrug. But Laleh is furious; she stomps back to Lateefa, Marzi tugging on her arm the whole time, and pleads with Lateefa to reassign her to the advance guard, made up mostly of fighters from the Water and Star Mountain battalions. Lateefa will not change the orders; once plans are made, they won't be undone for the whims of an ordinary soldier.

Laleh then demands to see Commander Kara.

Lateefa gets close to Laleh's face, opens her mouth, and lets out a roar that makes every fighter within a twenty-foot radius snap her head and stare. "You'll follow the orders you've received, or I'll boot you all the way back to Jebal Samhan. Is that clear?"

Fists balled and eyes burning, Laleh refuses to salute Lateefa. Marzi hisses at her to salute her superior or she'll be sent to the lockup. Defeated, Laleh stalks away, not wanting to be charged with insubordination. Then she disappears inside herself, her eyes dark and glassy, and refuses to speak another word for the rest of the day.

It's now one a.m. and Laleh is still muttering angrily under her breath, with hardly an hour left until they have to assemble for the Khor Rori crossing.

"Shut up, Laleh," hisses Marzi for the hundredth time. "You haven't let me sleep all night."

But Laleh is unable to lie still. "You know that Panah woman with the silver eyes? She says we're all going to die."

"She doesn't know anything. Go to sleep."

But Laleh cannot sleep. Only when she is squinting down the barrel of her rifle scope, concentrating on the body her bullet will penetrate, does she know anything close to peace.

The Hamiyat have been Laleh's mother and father since she was twelve years old, when she'd run away from a looming marriage to two brothers, both of them over forty years old. She'd come from one of the dead villages at the forgotten reaches of Star Mountain. In those lost places, the young girls sometimes did not even survive their wedding night.

The Hamiyat took Laleh in and raised her, and in Laleh grew an unbreakable loyalty to the Hamiyat. Whatever the Hamiyat demands of Laleh, she obeys, unsmiling, dispassionate, which the other soldiers mistake for a criminal bent of mind. She can't face the alternative to disobeying the Hamiyat: expulsion, homelessness, orphanhood, statelessness.

So back on the mountain, when she read the top secret message on her device ordering her to shoot Katy Azadeh,

Laleh pulled the trigger and sent the bullet crashing into Katy Azadeh's shoulder, wounding but not killing her. Then Laleh threw the deed out of her mind like the discarded bullet casings that littered the ground around her.

Yet the shooting still haunts her; Katy's absence gnaws away at her like an ulcer. Now that the final battle is nearly on them, Laleh is afraid she will die before she's able to confess what she did to Katy the night of their last action together. She knows the Warrior Queen will damn her for betraying a comrade, ensuring she doesn't survive the battle in Sheba City. *Perhaps*, thinks Laleh, *death will actually be a refuge.*

At two a.m, Laleh, Marzi, and the rest of the Dawn Batallion file down to the water. Wearing ponchos and thermal blankets to fool the cameras, they've tucked tree branches into their headscarves and caps. Their faces are darkened with mud and soot.

Small barges wait to ferry the soldiers quickly across the mouth of the inlet that opens onto the sea, from the eastern promontory. Semitian barges loaded with heavier weapons, artillery, light vehicles, and provisions are standing by, in the waters just off the western promontory. They're manned by pilots dressed as ordinary fishermen. The pieces of the disassembled camp—tents, other light equipment and mo-bikes—are being loaded onto the barges, as the troops clamber on to lighter transport rafts, twenty women at a time.

It takes fifteen minutes to cross the calm waters of the inlet. Once the women disembark, the rafts go back to ferry over more fighters, while the arrivals get into formation for the quick march to their temporary bivouac at the caves of Ayn Razat, before going to Sheba City.

Standing on the rocks of the western promontory, her poncho pulled over her head, Fatima Kara watches the Hamiyat troops climb off the barges and splash through the shallow waters of the inlet. The crossing will continue all night. And in the darkness, Katy Azadeh, who has been waiting on one of the Semitian barges, gets off with the 12th squad of the Water Mountain battalion and melts into the formation. She takes up her place within it as if her absence is already a long-forgotten dream.

# 18.

Raana Abdallah, in her cell in the basement of the Security Hive in Zarzura City, tries to calculate frantically where the Hamiyat are supposed to be, hour by hour. She's memorized the maps showing the routes the Hamiyat have taken from the mountains all the way to Khor Rori, the caves, and to the forests north of Sheba City. She can picture the roads that the Hamiyat will concentrate on capturing; aerial reconnaissance has ensured the route isn't littered with land mines.

She's not a military woman by training, but she has learned throughout her career the language and rhythms of peace and war. She has put everything on the line to ensure the Hamiyat succeed, because she believes in the necessity of their resistance. Now that the General has betrayed her, she has learned the limits of her own power.

At midnight last night, she was still at her desk examining the positions of the Hamiyat on the moving map, so absorbed in her work that she felt the cold nose of a pistol pressed into her back only after some time. The shock surged through her but she held still, knowing that to react badly was to die then and there. Slowly she put her hands up, and they allowed her to rise from her chair, her legs and back stiff from the hours of sitting there with her neck craned forward, her body racked with tension.

The armed Guards led her down the back stairs of the building, holding her in a tight grip above the elbow. Occasionally they pressed the gun into her to remind her that she was no longer in control of anything. Round and round they marched down the spiral staircase, while Raana Abdallah looked out frantically for someone, anyone—her aides, Zayn Battuta, even the girl Adeefa—to help her. Then the Guards pushed her head down so that she could only see her shoes on the steps.

"You're lucky we aren't putting a bag over your head," said one of them, and Raana Abdallah shivered at the woman's cold voice. Hardly half an hour ago, nobody would have dared touch her, let alone take her prisoner.

And now this cell is the entirety of her world.

The same cold-voiced Guard tells her to continue to lend her voice to the communications with the Hamiyat, repeating exactly what she's told to say, or she will be executed then and there. If she diverts from the script, tries to give anyone a warning in code, she'll take a bullet to the head. The decision is hers; the General is a generous man.

Raana Abdallah agrees to continue sending Fatima Kara updates and instructions as they're fed to her by the General and his team.

When he comes to see her in the middle of the night, she's sitting on her bed, unable to sleep, her head in her hands. She sees his boots, then lifts her eyes to take in the rest of him: the uniform, the dancing medals on his chest, the cragginess of his face. His eyes, not cold and cruel, but warm and alive with adrenaline, the joy of being in charge. His clothes are clean and crisp, hers crumpled and stained. He has minions standing behind him; she is completely alone.

He sighs. "Please don't take it personally, Raana."

She rises, approaches him like a leopard stalking prey, her muscles tense, eyes slits. "How else am I supposed to take it?"

He waves off the minions who leave them alone in the cell. "You forget your place in the chain of command. Did you consult me before you hatched this plan with the insurgents?"

"They're not insurgents. They're—"

"Resistance fighters? Bandit queens? Freedom fighters? Oh, please, Raana. You never received approval from the Leaders to foment an insurgency in another country."

"You knew about it."

"I knew nothing about it. Until that girl showed up here, Katy Azadeh. And that's when I was informed about your plot. You had no authorization to send the equipment that you did. You overstep your bounds. Military affairs, that's *my* domain."

"SmartSoul—"

"The ravings of a mad scientist. A cliché. But our Leaders were never going to agree to the invasion of a sovereign country, on the advice of a computer. A *game*. I thought you knew that. But after that debacle at the gala, I knew you'd gone too far, and I had to step in."

She holds back from hurling herself at him. Bullets have a way of finding themselves in the bodies of people who insult the General. "The women will die."

"They won't be the first," says the General calmly. "And then we'll have real reason to go to Green City. If you behave yourself, we might even let you come along."

Raana Abdallah says, "You would never have done this to Rami."

"Rami would never have gone behind my back like you have. After everything I've done for you, plucking you out of an obscure little laboratory and bringing you here to blossom under my eye. You should be grateful Rami was such a loyalist. I spared your life only in his memory."

As he leaves, Raana Abdallah can control herself no longer, and runs after him, but they've shut the door to her cell. She flings herself at it with all her strength, then collapses to the floor, the wind knocked out of her. She stays there for an hour, counting the tiles on the ceiling to calm herself. It doesn't work.

All night, she paces the floor of her cell, underneath the very building where she used to run the entire Ministry. She's been stripped of her device, her security passes, all the tools of her authority. She racks her brains, trying to think of a way out. Whom can she bribe, whom can she cajole or threaten?

Rami, when he was still a young diplomat in training, shared everything with her, telling her about life among the civil servants of Eastern Semitia. He had disliked their politicking, the ease with which they backstabbed one another. "Sister," he told her once, "remember this: When you're in power, friends appear out of every corner and crack in the wall, ready to help you enjoy the perks of your position and benefit from your good fortune. But when you lose that power, those friends disappear, steadily taking one step and then another in the opposite direction. When they are gone, you're on your own."

If only Rami were alive now, to tell her how to escape this trap . . . Raana Abdallah has missed her twin every day since he died, a private grief she has locked away from everyone else. She always imagined his spirit guiding her as she climbed the ladder of Semitian leadership. She closes her eyes and imagines him talking to her now, but he has nothing to say. She has to get herself out of this one by herself.

Nothing that happens in Zarzura is a secret, she reasons. There's too much technology and surveillance for that. Zayn Battuta will find out that she's disappeared, and he'll be suspicious. Or he won't; he'll hear her voice on the Spectrum channels and think all is proceeding as normal. They don't run into one another every day in Zarzura; the Science Center is self-contained, on the other side of the city.

When the Guards aren't looking, she turns her face to

the wall and weeps. The General doesn't care if everyone in the Hamiyat dies, as long as he gets to accomplish his goal of taking over Green City. The fate of Fatima Kara is her burden now, and she cries as she thinks of what's to befall the Hamiyat. Her fault, for trusting the General; despite all their differences of opinion, she thought they were allies. She should have realized they were never actually on the same side. Would Rami have made the same mistake, or did she rely on the General because she thought she saw some of Rami in him?

Sheba City is relatively small, with a population of only one hundred thousand and a radius of eight miles. The police force is about two thousand; Sheba City Guards are roughly twelve hundred in number. Without her help, Raana Abdallah knows that by the time the battle is over, every inch of those eight miles will have been painted in Hamiyat blood.

Marzi tries to calm Laleh down, after the ill-advised confrontation with Lateefa, but it's now three a.m., and Laleh is still muttering angrily under her breath. They've been demoted to staying back with the rear guard, and in a particularly sadistic twist, Lateefa has commanded them to keep an eye on the Panah women. So they're lying down now, with hardly an hour to go until the departure, which they won't be part of, thanks to Laleh's tantrum.

"Shut up, Laleh," hisses Marzi for the hundredth time. "You haven't let me sleep all night."

"Yes, shut up, Laleh," says another voice. "You've become awfully noisy for a sniper."

Both Laleh and Marzi sit bolt upright. "It's a ghost!" says Laleh, her mind still loopy from all her brooding. "A jinn!"

Marzi reaches for her gun but it isn't where she's left it. She feels down inside her boot for the knife she always carries, but a whisper of laughter stops her from brandishing it. She knows that voice. It's one she hasn't heard in a long time.

"Who are you?" she says. "Identify yourself immediately!" Perspiration beads on her forehead and back, the chill of the coastal fog adding to the eeriness.

"It's me, Marzi-pan." The darknesss coalesces into the shape of a woman crouching by their side, Marzi's gun in her hand. "Laleh, don't you recognize me? Have I changed that much?"

Laleh moans in fear, but Marzi feels a burst of joy. "Katy!"

"Shhh!" says Katy. The gun is on the ground and the three women are hugging, crying and laughing together, breathless. The sounds of their names in one anothers' mouths after all this time is like the tart-sweet taste of pomegranates, bringing tears to their eyes.

"I had to take your gun; I didn't want to get shot. Again." Katy speaks in a low, hot whisper, and they draw their heads closer together. Katy hands Marzi's gun back to her and settles onto her knees. Even in the dark, the relief is palpable in every line of her body.

"Katy? Is it really you?" gulps Laleh.

"Yes. Why are you still here? Aren't you supposed to be on the way?"

"How did you get here?" Laleh reaches out and touches Katy again. "Are you sure you aren't a jinn?"

"Do you want me to slap you to prove I'm real?" says Katy.

Marzi puts an arm around Laleh and squeezes her hard. She's shivering; she's had a genuine shock. The monsoon's low cloud cover reflects whatever light emanates from the ground. This trick of the light turns the night's usual darkness into a misty white, washing them all in tones of silver-gray. Katy has on a cap Marzi doesn't recognize, and someone else's uniform with a camoflauge scarf wrapped around her neck. She looks thinner; a scar runs down her neck and disappears into her shirt. Her hair is longer than before, but it's still Katy, the missing third of their trio.

"If you ask a jinn whether it's a jinn, it has to say yes. And if you ask it to leave, then it has to," says Laleh.

"I'm not going anywhere; it took me long enough to get back," says Katy, taking Laleh's hand and kissing it.

"Stop your blabber and tell us where you've been all this time," says Marzi gruffly.

"I've been in Eastern Semitia." Katy holds up a hand to stop their questions. "I can't tell you about it just yet. I have to report to Commander Kara. Do you know where she is?"

"We don't," says Marzi. "There's a temporary base, but we don't know where it is. All the Commanders have gone off the grid now."

"Any safe words, for the sentries?"

Marzi whispers it into her ear. "But wait, you can't go now; you haven't told us anything . . ."

"I have to. But I promise I'll be back." Katy rises to all fours, then crawls out from between Laleh and Marzi. She kisses them both once more, Marzi on the forehead, Laleh on the back of her head. With her lips still pressed to Laleh's hair, she says, "I missed you, you idiots. Wait for me."

She slinks off, head down, body crouched, lithe as a fox. Marzi wants to call after her, to tell her to be careful. Then she stops herself; Katy's survived all these months on her own, outside their circle of protection. It's clear she has her own destiny to fulfill, and Marzi is not fool enough to try and get in the way.

# PART FOUR

## The Warrior Queen

# 19.

The evening before the assault on Sheba City, some of the Hamiyat shoot a deer, and Alia cooks the women of the Dawn Batallion a spectacular predawn meal: a venison stew flavored with potatoes, harissa, and onions, and seasoned with herbs and vegetables and mushrooms she's foraged all the way from the mountain. Afterward, she and little Noor hand them all hot peppers to carry in their pockets, to mask their smell in case there are military dogs that track their scent on the breeze.

The women of the advance guard check their rifles, count their ammunition, and test their devices. Some joke that they're so full of venison, their protective gear doesn't fit them anymore. The Panah women wonder how they can laugh at a time like this, when death is closer to touching them than any lover, real or imagined. But the Dawn Battalion have faith in the Warrior Queen, and in Fatima Kara.

At Ayn Razat, the resting fighters sleep in turns on thin mats, in uniform and still wearing their boots. Their blankets are made of special adaptive camouflage that scrambles their infrared signature so the thermal cameras are fooled. The night sounds of crickets and frogs, a hooting owl, the hiss of soft rain fill their ears as they lie in the darkness, flat and silent as lizards.

It's hard to truly sleep; the bounty from Semitia has got them all excited and overstimulated. The fighters are all talking about the new vehicles, hidden nearby under their camouflage nets and tree branches. Piles of heavier weapons, machine guns, grenade launchers, and automatic weapons have already been loaded onto ATVs and MTRs, ready for the assault. They've had a day and a half to learn the new technology, but they've adapted quickly, and the urban combat drills have all got them thinking in new ways about battle.

The women have already said their good-byes to one another. There's no more time to write farewell notes to family in the villages that they've left behind. The night before battle is for unspoken endearments and promises, felt by every woman in the Hamiyat. For remembering a teenage crush, or acting on one, telling a girl in another unit that you've longed to kiss her for months now. The night before a battle ends more quickly than any other night in existence.

In the middle of the night, from the caves between the springs of Ayn Razat and Salahout, the Hamiyat begin to move. Women in twos, threes, and fours slip down the hills, veering away from the known roads and trodden paths. They creep through the jungle that miraculously appears once a year on the outskirts of Sheba City, thanks to the khareef, when usually barren desert turns overnight into lush rainforest, dense and moist. It is the perfect cover, with fog so thick that seeing two feet ahead of you becomes impossible.

The Ghaziyahs and the squad leaders never raise their voices; this is a silent advance that requires hand signals, eye signals, the synchronization of footsteps and breath and heartbeats, the choreographed movements of an entire army.

The women keep their eyes on their leaders at all times for instructions. At last, after the hours of waiting, the boredom and the mind-numbing inertia, they are coming closer to what they have trained for all these weeks and months. They flatten themselves against rocks, bend down low under branches, become as still as stone to avoid detection. They melt into underbrush, coil themselves behind tree trunks and boulders, their rifles strapped to their backs. Gone are their colored headscarves and bare faces; now they wear dark caps and black cloth wrapped over their mouths and noses. They move with one purpose, between the black thread of the night and the white thread of dawn.

At the gathering point in the forest on the outskirts of Sheba City, they assemble into columns, the reconnaissance teams first, the advance guard next, the foot-soldiers not far behind. Using a network of hidden trails, combat drivers transport the weapons and munitions on the Semitian ATVs, snipers and gunners riding in the back.

As the Hamiyat advance, Fatima Kara feels reassured that Raana Abdallah is continuing to send them intelligence about troops and safe houses and Guards in Sheba City. Their aim is to capture the city, but not to destroy it; to win the people over, not make enemies of them. There are already enemies to kill, the police and the Sheba City Guards, who protect the city's important buildings downtown: the Governorate, the treasury and bank, the police stations, and the telecommunications center. Once the enemy are overcome and the buildings captured, the Hamiyat can dictate their terms to Sheba City.

The Commanders move behind the women in separate mine-proof vehicles, passing messages to one another via their devices, while their lieutenants monitor the intelligence relayed by the advance guard, the progress of the main troops, and the location of the rear guard. They'll direct the Hamiyat to the highway north of Sheba City.

There are two vulnerable checkpoints on the road to Sheba City, each a mile apart, on which the advance guard will mount their first attack. They'll cut Sheba City off from the rest of Dhofar as efficiently as amputating a limb. Nobody will be able to enter or exit Sheba City without the Hamiyat's permission. They'll trap the Guards and drive them south toward the coast, then either shoot them or drown them in the ocean, like rats.

The soldiers at the first checkpoint on the northern highway watch the crowds on their way to the Khareef Festival. Most travelers are on foot, using the overhead pedestrian ramps, but a good many come in vehicles from the neighboring villages. They're prosperous farmers, many of them former nomads who gave up their wandering ways for a stabler life. They've put down roots, built houses, cultivated farmland. The Khareef Festival is a way for them to reconnect to some of the old traditions.

Today the soldiers expect to let through hundreds of men, fewer women. Thermal scanners monitor the men for body temperature, to ensure nobody is ill, and for illegal weapons and drugs, which make crowds unruly and harder to control. Cheerful music plays at the checkpoints, and colorful flags flutter overhead. The gray skies and soft rain add to the festive atmosphere; everyone prefers the cooler temperatures and misty weather to the pulsating heat and punishing sun of the rest of the year.

A young man whose beard has grown in during the months he's served in the Guards, brings a tray with teacups for his seniors; it's eight a.m., and they need the hot mixed brew to wake up. They've been at the checkpoint since five in the morning, waving through the happy revelers. The Guards decide to close down the checkpoint for fifteen minutes, while they drink their tea. Some use the toilet, in a small portable container behind the post.

The sign goes up that the checkpoint will be closed until a quarter after eight. The travelers move off the road to enjoy the snacks from roadside stalls that eager hawkers have prepared all week long in anticipation of their hungry stomachs: spicy grilled meat sticks with tamarind sauce, fresh fruit—apricots, grapes, pomegranates, peaches—and fruit drinks, toasted nuts and roasted corn, flatbreads and crispbreads and cakes and sweets of all sorts.

The young soldier with the patchy beard has just finished serving the tea and sits down to lift his cup to his lips when the explosion comes: a whistle, a silence, and then a devastating wave of force and heat that knocks them off their chairs and kills some of them outright. The men in the crowds scream and run for cover.

At the checkpoint, behind sandbags and blocks of cement, the Guards who are not dead or injured shake themselves to make sure, and then begin to shout. "We're being attacked!"

Someone lunges for a communications headset, but the explosive—an e-bomb—has knocked out their network with a strong electromagnetic pulse. They realize they've been cut off from their fellow Guards at the other checkpoint just as the bullets start to hit the sandbags. Soon they are all dead.

The women of the Hamiyat swarm up the sides of the embankment and check for survivors among the dead bodies and the rubble. Their boots make dirty red prints in the soot and the men's blood, marking the checkpoint in a grotesque swath of oxidizing mud.

The Hamiyat signal back to the snipers on the pedestrian bridge that the strike has been a success; they've secured the checkpoint. The Commanders give the go-ahead for the second checkpoint to be attacked in the same way before the Guards there realize they've lost contact with the first.

The crowds see the women emerging from the forest

like spirits. The witnesses don't notice the uniforms—they see only the black cloth hiding the faces of the attackers—but they instinctively know these are women, not men. The Hamiyat are silent, so it's not their voices that give them away; it's the way they move, their physiques, powerful but still feminine. The men flee, screaming about female demons and jinns as they run pell-mell from the checkpoint.

The screen in Commander Kara's tent shows the two checkpoints, the tollbooth, and the empty road between all three positions, beamed down from drone cameras the Hamiyat are controlling from the base.

The infiltrators have already gone ahead. They're dressed as ordinary citizens, in black veils, hiding rifles underneath the folds of cloth that waft around their bodies. These women who will enter the city on foot and move quickly to the safe houses. Once there, they'll take up sniper posts on rooftops, at windows, bore holes in the walls to aim their guns at the Guards outside. They'll blow larger holes in the walls between houses so they can move from house to house undetected. That way, the Guard will already be under pressure by the time the troops come. Then the drones will attack from overhead, disabling the Zaalims and taking out as many of the Guards' installations as possible.

The timing of the drones is essential: too soon, and the firepower will be wasted before the ground troops can consolidate the advantage. Fatima Kara has to give Raana Abdallah the go-ahead based on the information she receives from the Ghaziyahs in the battle, in real time. It's not enough to depend on satellite imagery; Fatima Kara's had to explain this carefully to Raana Abdallah, who thinks that fighting runs on a schedule. Fatima Kara has to keep reminding her that a battle is as fluid as water. Something unexpected can change the entire scenario, upend plans, cause crisis after crisis. Disorder is the only thing they can count on: Her women will make mistakes, misinterpret intelligence, receive bad information. They have to be ready for it, and keep going through the chaos to claim the biggest prize: the command and control center of the Guards, deep in the heart of Sheba City.

The display now shows the second checkpoint: an explosion, shots fired, men running in all directions. The Hamiyat fighters enter the installation and claim it for their own. The bodies of the murdered Guards show up on the screen as gray lumps, lifeless and broken. Fatima Kara does not allow herself to feel remorse for these men, who would just as easily have killed her women and left them lying on the ground.

The rear guard are busy securing the highway: Some vehicles have ground to a halt, including a convoy of self-driving trucks carrying shipping containers. Hamiyat combat drivers climb into the trucks, override the digital dashboards and unload the containers onto the road, then nose them into place using the trucks' built-in cranes.

Now that the road is blocked completely, the vehicular troops drive their S-ATVs from the forest onto the protected road between the blockage and the checkpoint, with the Hamiyat snipers atop the pedestrian walkways ready to shoot anyone who tries to pass or stop them. The advance guard ride on the S-ATVs, while the ground troops quickly get into formation to follow on foot, columns of women streaming out from the cover of the forest and onto the highway into Sheba City.

Back at the camp, Mariya, overwhelmed by the noise and chaos of the departure, decides she's not cut out for fighting after all. She separates herself from her companions in the camp and sets off for the highway amid the Hamiyat fighters. She'll look for an abandoned car that she can drive in the opposite direction of Sheba City; she'll go back to the mountain, or maybe farther than that. She's sure she can do it; Grace drove Reuben Faro's car easily all the way from Green City, and anything Grace can do, Mariya can do better.

Noor spots Mariya as she leaves the camp. Thinking they're playing another game of hide-and-seek, he decides to follow her. He glances up at his mother, who's busy organizing the food supplies, and gets up, quietly as a cat.

Alia, sensing movement, looks up just in time to see Noor slipping away; she lets out a piercing scream that brings Grace running over. Both of them chase after Noor, pushing their way through the lines of women, but the fighters' bodies make a moving sea of uniforms and rifles and equipment that is impossible to navigate. Fighters carry heavy packs on their shoulders, creating an obstacle course that the women try to weave and duck through.

Finally, Grace and Alia reach the highway, where they see Mariya sitting in an abandoned car on the highway, Noor standing happily on the seat next to her.

Grace pounds on the window. "Mariya! Where are you going?"

Mariya lowers the window. "Back to Green City. I've had enough." The car's engine switches on. Alia and Grace look at one another, aghast. Alia dashes to Noor's side and tries to open the door, but it's locked.

"Are you out of your mind?" shouts Grace. "Don't you dare move!"

Noor beckons to his mother. "Come with us, Mama! This car goes really fast. Come on!" He sits down as the seat belt clamps him into place.

"What are you doing?" screams Alia. "Noor! Get out!"

But Noor just shakes his head. "Come on, Mama!" Alia

desperately tries all the doors, and the back door behind Noor opens at last. Alia dives into the back seat, grabbing at Noor. She takes Noor by the shoulders and shakes him hard, scolding him, trying to yank him out. But he's strapped into the seat and Alia can't find the seat belt button to release him. Mariya revs the car; she's in no mood to stop for anyone now.

It's not safe to stand on the road arguing with Mariya; bullets could start flying again at any minute. So Grace, too, dives into the back seat and unleashes a storm of invective on Mariya. "You little bitch! How could you be so selfish? You're abandoning all of us! You're only thinking of yourself, but look how much danger you're putting us all in!"

"I'm sorry, Grace," says Mariya. "But nobody asked me if I wanted to come here. No, not to the battle. I meant to the Dhofar. We didn't all want to leave the Panah. I want to go home."

Grace tries to land a slap on Mariya from the back seat as the younger woman searches the dashboard for the controls, fingers scrabbling over all the buttons and trying them one by one. The vehicle suddenly speaks aloud. "Commencing journey in three . . . two . . . one . . ." The back door closes and locks automatically. The car speedily reverses, sensors beeping. The dashboard screen shows the roadblocks getting farther away. In moments, the car swerves onto the other side of the road and begins to head toward Sheba City.

Alia and Noor are thrown from one side of the car to the other as it increases its velocity, weaving in and out between the troops that are marching in the same direction. "Make it stop!" yells Grace. Mariya is sweating, but the car has already heard her command to "go home."

"Destination: Sheba City," says the car. "Estimated arrival time: forty-five minutes."

* * *

Katy slips along with the fighters, her cap pulled down low over her face, muttering the safe word—*rojava*—to the sentries. Once she's reached the assembly point, she lurks around the different squads, pretending to be from one, then another. Her laser device hasn't glowed with a message from Zayn Battuta or Adeefa since she reached Dhofar. She wishes she could talk to Raana Abdallah. She misses the Deputy Foreign Minister's rigid determination, cold and bright as the air on a winter's day.

Suddenly, the pressure drops and a thunderstorm sweeps in, with streaks of lightning and a heavy burst of rain. Raindrops pelt hard on the vegetation around them, a driving, droning sound that gives the Ghaziyahs enough noise cover to switch on their devices briefly and check for updates to their orders.

She shifts her weight from one leg to the other. The movement of her thigh forces the laser from Zarzura out of her pocket. It thumps on the wet ground, pulling Katy out of her whirling thoughts and the search for her squad mates.

Katy quickly picks it up, wipes the mud and water off it. Its lights flash gently in standby mode. They're talking in a simple binary code Katy learned in her communications training in the Hamiyat. She told it to Zayn Battuta, whose minions worked out a key for the Semitians to use it with her. Katy presses the laser's activation key, and its lights spit out the last message that Adeefa sent Katy, while Katy was getting on to the barge at Khor Rori. She must have missed it in the melee; she strains to understand the code now: *Raana Abdallah arrested. Operation Sheba in danger. Abort mission.*

There will be no help for the Hamiyat from Easterm Semitia. For her treason in cooking up a plot with foreign insurgents, Raana Abdallah will either be executed or rot in a jail cell for the rest of her life.

In that moment, Katy knows what it feels like for her heart to stop beating. It kickstarts a few seconds later, as she stares up at the tops of the trees swaying in the monsoon breeze, trying to absorb this new information. It's suddenly all too much; she sinks down onto her haunches and holds her head in her hands. The departure is already underway; the operation can't be called off now! How is she going to explain any of this to Fatima Kara?

Then Katy rises again, knowing she has to find Fatima Kara's tent and tell her what's happened. Maybe it can still be stopped, before it's too late.

She speaks quietly to a few Ghaziyahs, and finds out that the Commanders have taken up a secret position in the forest, from where they will direct the women before joining the columns themselves. Then she runs into a lieutenant from another company who is the aide-de-camp to Leila Ortabi. Katy Azadeh tells the lieutenant she's carrying an urgent message for the Commanders, and the woman, seeing the desperation on Katy's face, points her in the right direction.

Katy runs until she's out of breath, and there looming in front of her is the Commander's olive tent, a square vinyl structure inside which Fatima Kara has sequestered herself. The window cutouts in the tent's walls are zipped closed, blue light emanating from within. All the other Commanders of the various mountain battalions have tents like these, equipped with telecommunications screens, a cot, vent pipes for heating and cooking. They can be set up or struck down in fifteen minutes by three people working quickly.

Standing guard right in front of the tent flap is Commander Kara's batwoman, Pireh, trying to hold herself erect but unable to stop yawning. Katy lurks in the shadows; Pireh will recognize Katy for sure. She doesn't want everyone to know she's back just yet. She can't deal with questions, embraces, welcoming faces. The only person Katy wants to see right now is Fatima Kara, to tell her that it's all a trap, the whole operation planned by Raana Abdallah doomed to failure.

Pireh glances up just as Katy is sprinting toward her, and her mouth drops open. "Who are you? What do you want?" Katy remembers her face is covered with a black scarf, like the other fighters, although she doesn't have their protective gear.

Katy grabs Pireh's hand, presses the laser into the girl's open palm. "Give this . . . to Fatima Kara . . . Tell her . . . I gave it to you." Pireh's hand shakes. She almost drops the laser, but Katy clamps her fingers hard over Pireh's. "Now."

Pireh nods and disappears into the tent. Katy bends over, puts her hands on her knees, gulping down ragged, torn breaths of air. A minute later, Pireh reemerges, beckoning Katy inside. "The Commander wants to speak to you."

Pireh holds open the tent flap for Katy. Fatima Kara is standing in front of a large display; its blue light shines at Katy like the underwater portholes of the boat she rode to Dhofar, cutting through marbled seawater, past fish swimming by in schools, kelp flying in streams. She who'd never been near the ocean in her life has ridden in a boat twice this month. Katy remembers this as she pulls the black cloth down from her face and salutes Fatima Kara. "Commander."

"Katy Azadeh," says the Commander. "Welcome back."

Katy is nervous; she's never faced the Commander alone. These months of absence have dulled her shine, taken away some of the swagger and confidence she had when she was roaming around the mountain with her batallion. "Reporting for duty, ma'am. But I have bad news first."

Lateefa materializes by the Commander's side, but she won't speak until the Commander allows her to, so instead, she glowers at Katy. It's her default expression; the fighters are all used to her ferocious looks. Fatima Kara instructs her lieutenant and batwoman to wait outside, while she briefs Comrade Azadeh.

When they're gone, the Commander holds up the laser dazzler in front of her. Its lights are still pulsing in code. "Is this saying what I think it's saying?"

"Yes, ma'am," says Katy. She's taking in the Commander: the solidity of her body, the cool confidence with which she holds herself, even in these circumstances. The plan that she's worked on for months with Raana Abdallah is in utter danger, and the fighters have already departed for Sheba City. But Fatima Kara betrays no sign that any of this is troubling her just yet. Katy admires her composure, wishing she had some of it for herself.

"I know about your time in Zarzura," says the Commander. "So let's skip that part. What happened when you got to Green City?"

Katy begins to tell her about the hospital room, and her plan to kill Reuben Faro. "It was a deal," she says. "If I did it, Raana Abdallah promised I'd come back to Dhofar." Fatima Kara purses her lips as Katy describes the way she disguised herself as a male nurse, went into the hospital, found the target, only to be thwarted at the last moment.

"I just can't understand how Raana Abdallah got the timing wrong."

Fatima Kara's face is grim. "The General. He must have given her the wrong intelligence."

"But why?"

"A double cross," says Kara. "While we keep them distracted in Sheba City, the General will invade in the north. Our troops will bear the brunt, while his waltz to victory."

Katy says, "The General told Rana Abdallah in front of me that she'd forgotten which one of them was the soldier."

Now Fatima Kara grows pale and Katy quickly calls Lateefa and Pireh back into the tent. "Get her some water," Katy says to Pireh. A muscle in Fatima Kara's cheek is twitching as Pireh helps her sit down and hands her the water. She takes a sip, then pushes it away, and begins to interrogate Lateefa on the positions of the troops.

Katy listens as Lateefa spits out the names of lieutenants and squads in the advance guard, with the batallions from other mountains not far behind. But by now, a good two hundred women have surrounded the first checkpoint on the Sheba City highway, and the assault is already well underway. The fighters of Sun Mountain will enter the city first.

Fatima Kara is silent. Only her eyes move back and forth as she calculates timing and coordinates in her head. Katy doesn't dare breathe for fear of disturbing her. Then Fatima Kara looks up.

"Get the other Commanders here now. Then get my transport ready."

"Yes, ma'am," says Lateefa. She lifts her device to her ear and begins to issue orders. Pireh gathers up Fatima Kara's weapons and ammunition, while Fatima Kara takes her combat uniform off its rack and begins to put it on.

"Thank you for this, Katy Azadeh. We may be able to abort the mission in time. You stay here; get some rest and then fall in with the rear guard. You're exhausted, and an exhausted fighter is a dead fighter. That's an order."

Katy opens her mouth to object, but Fatima Kara has already stopped listening to her. She doesn't have to ask where the Commander is going: She's getting ready to move to the front, with the fighters of Sun Mountain. Whatever happens, Fatima Kara will not let her women die alone.

# 20.

On this drizzly morning, Sheba City is buzzing with activity, the preparations for the Khareef Festival coming to a head. Schools and offices are closed to let the people enjoy the rain and the first day of the festival. When they wake up and open their windows to the new day, they call out in excitement to their neighbors across the houses. The city has been cleaned, beautified, decorated until it shines. Even at a distance, Sheba shimmers like a pearl seen underwater.

In the North Square, workers staple pink bunting to the edges of the canopies and hang strands of pink roses threaded on ribbons to the backdrop of the stage. Loudspeakers churn out cheerful music, traditional folk songs given a modern twist with techno drums. A thumping bass beat booms through the sleepy square, waking up anyone who thought they might sleep late on this public holiday.

The light rain and gray clouds temper the usual hot sun and blue sky. To counter the monsoon heat and humidity, the North Square wind tower stands tall in the middle of the open space between the buildings. It pulls down cool air from higher up and spreads it across the expanse of the Square, sending a soft moist breeze down the streets and lanes. In Sheba City, they call this "romantic weather." The khareef is marriage season, and today's festival will see many weddings, with first, second, third Husbands pledging to support and honor their Wives and raise families together. Most of the province's babies are born nine months later; the children take the middle name *Khareef*, boy or girl, considered particularly lucky.

Children, mostly boys, a few girls, have come down from the apartment blocks surrounding the Square in this area, a less well-to-do neighborhood than the others. Boys shout and romp among the construction blocks, the girls clutching their fathers' hands and oohing and aahing at all the pink roses everywhere. Women, married and unmarried, watch from above, perched like lines of hawks all along the open-air balconies that give relief from stifling, cramped apartments.

The festival is spread out across the city, each venue assigned a different theme: The South Square is for the harvest, featuring food, produce, and livestock. The East Square showcases Dhofari culture, with music, plays, poetry readings going on around the clock. The West Square commemorates the history of Dhofar, while the North Square is dedicated to the Dhofari woman over the last hundred years: her origin from women of the desert tribes, her sacrifices and her resilience throughout the difficult decades.

They've all been given Mazunian flags to fly from rooftops and balconies, banners to put up in their windows. Later, there will be special Family Hours for the women to visit the festival exclusively. They can venture out among the other women of Sheba City, a rare time when not in the tow of their Husbands. The women generally like to stick to the Family Hours; it's a system that has worked every year, guaranteeing the women of Sheba City safety and security in public spaces. There will be no bother given to the women by roaming groups of single, excitable young men.

Looking up from his work, one of the laborers notices that there are already some women, six or seven, standing around in the Square, wearing black veils. Alone, not with Husbands or children. Where are the Guards anyway? He spots a few milling about, their sand-colored uniforms and red berets making them easy to spot in the crowds. They're supposed to keep an eye out for trouble, but they usually just end up chatting with the workers and munching on free snacks.

The worker sidles up to one of the lone women and stands beside her. Instead of shifting away from him, as most women do when a solitary man approaches, she stands her ground. He doesn't dare look her in the face, but he steals glances at her body, checking to make sure it's enveloped correctly in folds of black cloth.

"You aren't supposed to be here," he mutters. "Where's your Husband?"

The woman answers him matter-of-factly, as if he's merely asked her for the time. "I'm looking for my sister's house. I was just getting my bearings. In fact, I think I see her now." She lifts her arm to wave at a balcony, then steps briskly away from the man and moves toward a white apartment block. He only lifts his head when she walks away, his mouth open to shout something at her back. Quickly, the other women in the Square follow her, some seeping into the same building, others heading elsewhere.

The workers are looking forward to their tea break when the explosions begin. The children look up excitedly. *Pap-pap-pap-pap*, like the sounds of small crackers exploding. "Fireworks!" cries a small boy. Suddenly everyone is craning their necks to look up at the sky, searching for the colored smoke—rainbow, gold and silver, eerie black against the blue sky—that forms itself into patterns, flowers, birds, the national flag. They see only small plumes of gray rising from some of the windows on the highest stories of the apartment blocks.

And then the screams begin, as the women on the balconies point at the bodies of the felled Guards in the streets surrounding the Square. Men grab their children and run into the apartment blocks, but the workers, two dozen of them, have nowhere to go. They look around frantically for cover, then duck under the stage, pushing themselves underneath the platform until they're hidden from view.

The women's screams continue, violin wails punctuated by more gunshots. Heat and smoke begin to fill the air, and the metallic scent of blood reaches the nostrils of the men trapped underneath the stage. Poor men from Kolachi, from Gwadar, from beyond in India, some of them have already seen war and know what it looks like. They know they'll be the first civilians to die, their bodies fragile and expendable, valued only as long as they can labor for the government. None of them expected their lives to end on this day, in this manner.

There's a break in the firing, then a woman's voice crackling on a loudspeaker, speaking in an accent that comes from the mountains of Dhofar.

*Civilians! You have ten minutes to leave this place and go into your houses. We will not harm you. Take your children and seek shelter. Go!*

Her words echo around the Square, bouncing off the walls and straight into the men's hearts, setting them beating at a rapid hammer pace. Do they dare believe it? Is this really a cease-fire, or a trick designed to draw them out into the open, so they can be gunned down by these attackers—these women? In this moment which has come so suddenly upon them, there is trust and there is death. Does one lead to the other or do they lead in opposite directions?

Suddenly, louder explosions rock the Square: mortars fired against sturdy walls, making the ground shudder. The worker thinks of his daughter, waiting for him, already wearing her red dress since dawn. He says a prayer to the Priest King, and the Warrior Queen, too, for good measure. Then he slides out from under the platform. He steps over the corpses like hurdles in an obstacle course. He nearly trips over a black snake twisting around his feet. He stumbles, catches his balance, and frees himself from the discarded veil. He flees as though dogs were chasing him to the death.

In a darkened apartment above the North Square, Fatima Kara lowers her long-distance goggles. Two women crouch next to her, snipers from the Dawn Battalion. The noses of their rifles are slotted into the holes they've drilled into the walls. The drawn curtains block out any light that might reveal the Hamiyat's position to the Zaalims, the wandering munitions that fly around the city, spying on the rooftops.

The advance fighter unit sent to the North Square in the early part of the assault had set up operations in a small unguarded library. It's a good spot for a rudimentary outpost; the fighters were fortifying its walls against attack when Fatima Kara and Lateefa arrived in the Square. But there were too many Guards firing at the Hamiyat, and instead of joining the unit, the Commander and her lieutenant sought cover in this apartment building opposite the library.

They climbed up the stairs, higher and higher, until they found a sympathizer's apartment. The sympathizer, a City Wife, let them in and led them to the bedroom, where the snipers immediately took up positions and began shooting at the Sheba City Guards. Meanwhile, Fatima Kara has been trying to make contact with the team in the library.

Lateefa signals the snipers to fall back, and they sit on their heels, alert and watchful, waiting for her next command. "Eight Guards down. Well done."

One says, "Thank you, comrade." A look of grim satisfaction crosses Fatima Kara's face. They've worked fast, sighting the Guards one by one, squeezing the trigger, then moving to the next target. The Guards don't have a chance to return fire.

Fatima Kara has insisted on coming into Sheba City herself, to oversee the evacuation of the advance guard, including her own women from Sun Mountain. The other Commanders objected, but she refused to stay back while her fighters faced the Guards of Sheba City without the air cover that Raana Abdallah had promised. Fatima Kara believes it's better to die with her women, if only to atone for the vast error she's made in trusting the Semitians. She says this to the other Commanders when she leaves the camp; they bow their heads and don't try to stop her. Their crisp salutes serve as their last farewell to Fatima Kara as she clambers into the transport vehicle, Lateefa at the driver's seat.

The ground troops are waiting just outside the city limits, amassed like storm clouds ready to unleash driving rain and thunder. They're firing mortars on some of the police posts, the source of one of the big explosions, a foretaste of what is to come: the fight for the city, street by street, area by area. But they've held off on entering the city per the Commanders' updated orders. Back at the base, the remaining Commanders wait until Kara tells them whether she's been successful in her attempt to evacuate the advance troops. Only then can they carry out a full-scale retreat back to the mountains.

This battle was not supposed to be a linear event, but a series of assaults, one layered on top of the other, in order to keep the enemy fearful and off guard. Fatima Kara goes over the timelines in her head, trying to figure out whether the assault can be salvaged at all.

Lateefa keeps an eye out for more Guards, for Zaalims, for anything that might bring them all to ruin. She feels safe enough in this apartment, their temporary base, chosen for its proximity to the Square, and the sympathetic Wife who believes in the Hamiyat and their mission.

There is a part of Lateefa that had to get away from Grace, from her warmth and her constancy and her unspoken expectations. Lateefa is a soldier who can't make her own heart follow a steady path of peace and love, even when offered it freely by someone who wants nothing more than to make her happy. Maybe it's because she's seen too much fighting and death, the worst of humanity. Happiness is not Lateefa's birthright; Grace's open arms make her want to run the other way.

So here she is, in this apartment in Sheba City, taking a sip of air between these fraught moments, as Fatima Kara calculates how many women there are in the Square, and how they can escape.

One of the snipers says, "Lieutenant, look at this." Fatima Kara waves Lateefa to her side, and crouches under the window, her goggles raised to her eyes. The music has stopped and the people have disappeared from the Square, but there's movement from the stage. Lateefa watches, eyes narrowed, as a man in a workman's uniform crawls out from underneath the platform. He waits there on hands and knees, looking around wildly, then wobbles to his feet and begins to run. The sniper's finger is on the trigger, ready to shoot, but Lateefa shakes her head. "Civilian." After a few moments, another man emerges, and runs off in another direction.

*How many more are underneath the stage?* Fatima Kara thinks to herself. "Do you think there's a bomb there?"

"Do you want me to check it out?" says Lateefa.

"Be careful, comrade," says Kara.

Lateefa spits to the snipers: "Cover me." They get back into position while Lateefa pulls out her handgun and opens the door of the room. The family is huddled there, the City Wife keeping her children away from the windows, the Husbands drugged and asleep on the living room floor, blissfully unaware of what's going on in their own home. The Wife reaches out her hand to try to touch Lateefa as she passes.

In two strides, Lateefa's into the hallway and out the door, moving fast down the stairs, out into the vestibule. There's no one else around; they're all hiding in their apartments, terrified of what's coming next. She has no time to feel sorry for any of them. Her mind is solely focused on her immediate task: to check underneath the stage for a bomb, or for Guards hiding underneath.

Lateefa pauses in the doorway, then darts out into the Square. The snipers will make sure no Guards pop out of unexpected recesses in the walls or around corners to ambush her. If they do, they'll have bullets in their heads before they can do any harm.

She ducks behind a concrete staircase and ramp that leads down to the Square, shielding herself from view behind its low walls and crouch-walking the last few feet into the public area. At the ramp's end, she kneels down to peek underneath the stage. Her thermal goggles reveal a mass of human bodies, wavering red and orange blobs. She can't tell whether these are civilians or combatants. It could be a booby trap, the civilians' bodies bunched around an explosive, hiding it from view.

Lateefa wipes the rain off her forehead. Should she start firing underneath the stage, or lure them out and dispatch them once they're out in the open? For a minute, she regrets banishing Laleh, whose sniping skills are on another level—the woman can sense movement before it even happens, it's almost supernatural—but it's too late now to unmake that choice. Two reliable snipers are better than one gifted, unpredictable one.

A car screeches around the corner and careens into the Square. Lateefa clocks the vehicle: It's not one of the L-ATVs that the Hamiyat have gotten from the Semitians at Khor Rori. As the car suddenly jerks to a stop, Lateefa sees it's an ordinary one, filled with women that she recognizes. But it can't be . . .

The car doors open automatically and out tumble Alia, Noor, and Mariya from the front seats, Grace from the back. Lateefa cannot believe her eyes. Her mind reels. What in the name of the Warrior Queen are they doing here? The Panah women and the Ababeel and her little son, here, in Sheba City? But she'd left them behind at the base at dawn. The question of a bomb under the stage suddenly becomes a white-hot alarm flaring behind her eyes.

Grace stares, stunned, at the pink tent and the decorations, the apartment blocks surrounding them on all sides. Noor tugs at his mother's hand and points at the stage with the lights flashing pink and red. Mariya looks down at the dead Guards, and the blood. Her face contorts, a scream about to escape from her mouth.

Lateefa abandons her hiding space, jumps up, and runs, handgun at the ready, straight toward the car, the women frozen in place. She barrels down on them and it's such a short distance that she's almost on top of them within seconds. Lateefa pushes Mariya to the ground, then she yanks at Alia's robes, bringing her down like a lassoed cow, Noor clutched tight in her arms. As Grace turns around, shock telegraphs from her widened eyes straight to Lateefa's heart.

"Get down!" roars Lateefa.

Grace drops down to her knees. The car acts as a shield for all of them. Lateefa aims her gun underneath the platform and fires, once, twice, three times. She doesn't know what she's hitting, but all she can think about is protecting Grace and the others from harm. She can hear the men screaming from under the stage. At least she's disabled them, if not killed them outright, and there is no bomb blowing them all away.

In one fluid motion Lateefa whirls around and pulls the

women all to their feet again, pointing toward the apartment building. "Go, go, go!" Now they're all running, legs pumping, arms flailing: Grace, Mariya, Alia pulling Noor by the hand. The Wife, who has come out to the balcony, shouts and waves her arms. "Over here, over here!" Lateefa picks Noor up in her arms and runs as hard as she can to the doorway, propped open for them by the sympathizers in the building. As soon as they're all safe, the door slams closed, shutting out the Square and the world outside.

The Wife beckons them to the top of the stairs. Pure adrenaline gets the women all the way up to the apartment, where they tumble into the living room. Mariya is crying hysterically. Alia grabs Noor and crouches over him, trembling, hiding her face in his shoulder.

"Water, please," says Grace to the City Wife, who snaps her fingers at her oldest child, a daughter. Two of the girls run back and forth to the kitchen, bringing tin cups of cold, delicious, and lifesaving water for all of them. Grace pours a little of it into her hand and splashes it onto Lateefa's head and cheeks. "Are you all right?"

When Lateefa has caught her breath, she nods tersely at Grace. "Thanks." Then she straightens up and snaps, "Tell them all to shut up," and walks back to the other room, where Fatima Kara and the snipers are waiting. Grace hesitates, then follows Lateefa to the bedroom.

The fighters are picking their rifles up from the bed, getting ready to resume their sniping. Fatima Kara's on her device, trying to catch the Spectrum signal. From below comes the angry buzzing sound of more vehicles driving into the Square. Grace tries to go to the window to look, but Lateefa yanks her back, hissing, "Stay away from there." Grace pushes herself into a corner of the room and stands still, commanding her body to melt into the shadows.

Fatima Kara looks up. "I saw what happened."

"I don't understand why they're here," says Lateefa, as if it's somehow her fault.

"Never mind that now. Let's concentrate on joining up with the others at the outpost. Then we can work on getting out of here."

But something is blocking the signal; Fatima Kara's device shows a dead screen when she tries to get onto the Spectrum. Kara paces back and forth in the room, waving her device this way and that. The snipers are on the lookout for more Guards, but from this vantage point, they can't see the library. "It's no good, ma'am," says Lateefa. "Not from this angle."

"We have to move," says Fatima Kara.

"Where?"

"Follow me."

The snipers grab their rifles as Fatima Kara exits the bedroom, runs through the living room, out the door of the apartment, and into the hallway again. Lateefa runs behind them, shouting at Grace, "Stay with the others!"

"Where are you going? Don't leave us!" says Mariya, but she's ignored in the commotion.

Fatima Kara mounts the narrow staircase and climbs up to the top floor of the building, Lateefa and the snipers following her close behind. There's a locked door at the top of the stairs. Lateefa kicks it open and then they're on the rooftop, in the rain, crouching against the low wall surrounding the building's perimeter. Fatima Kara signals them to follow her to the corner of the roof. Cautiously, she raises her head and spots the library: a small one-story white building with arched doorways and wooden latticed windows. Some twenty Hamiyat fighters are swarming inside, while others face the Square, firing on the Sheba Guards. The wind tower in the middle of the Square is a sentinel watching dispassionately over all. *It could be the tower that's blocking the Spectrum signal,* Fatima Kara realizes.

Kara turns her head in the other direction; the city's spread out like a carpet: low buildings, white and tan, being washed clean of a year's dust by the rain. Farther beyond, rolling green plains, rising gradually toward the low mountains where the Ayn Razat spring originates. The Square's emptied out, but a few miles away, there's normal activity: cars, pedestrians, markets open for the Khareef Festival. A glance back at the library reveals that the Hamiyat are almost all inside, their vehicles safely stationed in a half-constructed parking garage just on the opposite side of the Square.

Beads of sweat on Fatima Kara's upper lip mix with the steady raindrops falling from above. She checks her device, and to her relief, the signal's back, weakly. She connects with the team leader down in the library below, a senior Ghaziyah with whom she'd planned this part of the assault. "Are you there, comrade? It's Commander Kara."

A second later, the response. "Commander Kara? I can hear you, ma'am. We are in the library, praise the Queen." The noise of the fighters crackles in the background: marching feet, furniture being shifted around, the *click-click* of rifles being loaded, ammunition being stacked into piles for quick access.

"Change in plan, comrade. I'm close by, but we have to evacuate the Square. There's been a problem."

"What?" The voice of the Ghaziyah is incredulous.

Fatima Kara calculates the pros and cons of the current situation. More Guards will be sent in to see what's going on in the deserted square, but then the Hamiyat will have to waste valuable ammunition fighting them off. By now, they were supposed to be pushing forward to gain more territory outside of the Square and heading for the downtown buildings, the most precious territory of all. And if there's a Zaalim in this area, it may spot them as they evacuate.

"I'm afraid so. Hold your position, and wait for my orders." Fatima Kara clicks off from the Ghaziyah. She notices the Panah woman Grace standing in the doorway to the rooftop, half-hidden behind the doorframe.

"What are you doing here?" Lateefa hisses. "I told you to stay inside!" She can see Grace's arms and legs shaking from here, even though her face wears a look of stubborn determination. The door, kicked off its hinges, lies on its side against the perimeter wall, like the boats they used to cross Khor Rori. But this slick rooftop is no ocean, and Grace cannot cross over to her. Not now.

"I'm not leaving you," whispers Grace.

"You have to go back. Get back downstairs. Now!"

Grace shakes her head. Fatima Kara knows Lateefa won't be able to convince Grace to go back down to the safety of the apartment with the others. "Stay there," she calls out to the Panah woman. "Do not come out here, no matter what."

The rain starts to pelt down, and Fatima Kara draws her hood over her head so the water doesn't get into her eyes. Her mind's on the next step of the evacuation, but she takes note of the way Grace's eyes burned when she looked at Lateefa. A force passes between the two women, a warmth that comes from someone who will not look away, who sees you and still won't leave. It doesn't protect you from death, but it makes death seem impossible, when love can burn this bright.

# 21.

As Katy makes her way back to her friends, she already feels Fatima Kara's absence from the camp. Now that the advance guard have gone to Sheba City and the main body of troops wait at the line of departure, just outside the city checkpoints, only the rear guard and the medics remain in the forest, along with the other Commanders in their tents. But for Katy Azadeh, now that Fatima Kara has left, the camp feels cold and soulless. It's as if a flame has been extinguished, depriving them all of its vital warmth.

Katy finds Laleh and Marzi among the soldiers left to consolidate the area after the capture of the northern highway. *Why have they been left behind? They're better fighters than that,* she thinks. What use are they sitting around here, far from the action? The advance guard needs the best snipers. Then Katy remembers anew that the advance guard is in a dire situation, and she feels glad and relieved that her friends are still here.

When she runs up to them, she can see they're in a state of crisis that has nothing to do with the battle. "What's wrong?"

Laleh is too angry to speak, but Marzi mutters, in a low voice, "It's those women."

"What women?"

"The runaways from Green City. We didn't get a chance to tell you about them."

Laleh and Marzi quickly explain to Katy who the Panah women are. Something about the story of women who sleep with the rich men of Green City at night rings a bell in Katy's mind, and then she remembers Sabine, the woman from Green City whom Zayn Battuta was so entranced with. "There was one who escaped to Semitia. You're saying there are more?"

"Yup," says Laleh, between clenched teeth. "Bitches." She's only able to spit out monosyllables. Two crimson splotches burnish her cheeks as if someone had slapped her hard on the face.

"They showed up in Dhofar, on the mountain. It's a long story. They came down here with us, on the march. They were left in our charge," says Marzi, glancing around. "But they seem to have disappeared on us. Which makes us very bad soldiers. What about you, did you find Fatima Kara?"

"Yes," Katy says glumly. "I had to give her bad news. Worse than I thought." She explains to Laleh and Marzi as briefly as she can that the operation is in danger. She tells them about Raana Abdallah and what she had planned with Fatima Kara. She explains how the laser dazzler gave news of the General's betrayal, and what it means for the Hamiyat's attack on Sheba City. And that the advance guard is now trapped in Sheba City without the help that was promised from Eastern Semitia.

She's talking quickly, garbling her words in haste, but it's such a long story to tell and there's no time to give detailed explanations. And she doesn't reveal that she knows Laleh wounded her on purpose, all part of Fatima Kara's plan to have her sent to Eastern Semitia and then Green City on a mission that has been entirely futile. Raana Abdallah's in jail now for her trouble, and Fatima Kara's trapped with the Hamiyat fighters in Sheba City. Katy can't understand how it's all come to this.

When she's finished, she's panting for breath. Marzi's gaping at her, mouth working soundlessly. But Laleh has grasped the most vital part out of all the information they've been bombarded with. "The Hamiyat have to get out of Sheba City! Now!"

"Yes, that's why Fatima Kara's gone to the front, to coordinate the evacuation," says Katy.

"What about the other Commanders?" Marzi finally croaks. "Have they got a plan?"

"They'll have to come up with something. There's nothing we can do about it, so we might as well try to find the women you're looking for."

Laleh and Marzi tell Katy that there were four Panah women, Diyah, Rupa, Mariya, and Grace, but only two have come with them. Lateefa and Grace have become close over the last several weeks, but Lateefa isn't happy about her presence in the camp.

"What do you mean, 'close'?" says Katy.

Marzi, distracted from her worry for a moment, grins. "You know. *Close.*" Laleh rolls her eyes, and Katy, understanding them, chuckles. Who would have thought there was a person alive that could soften Lateefa's heart?

The three of them get to their feet and move quickly, Katy's return giving them renewed energy. Rainwater falls on the leaves and branches of trees in a steady hiss as Katy, Laleh, and Marzi race around the camp in the frantic search for the missing Panah women. The clouds bunch over their heads, the forest canopy enclosing the forest in white, dreamlike fog. Katy feels the chill on her cheeks and thinks, just for a moment, that they're looking for ghosts. And it seems to be true, because when they ask around, nobody knows where the Panah women are. At the medical tent, the other Ababeels and the Hamiyat medics tell them that Alia hasn't been seen for hours. Laleh punches at the tent's central support pole, cursing loudly when her knuckles strike metal.

"Save your hand, Laleh, you'll need it later," scolds Marzi. They're all tense and bad-tempered, unsure of what to do next. They stand in a little grove of coconut palms growing in clumps at the edge of the camp. They're all longing for a cigarette, but with the rain drumming a staccato beat onto the leaves of the palm trees, it's hard to light a match.

Marzi says, "We can't tell everyone we let them disappear on our watch."

"Who cares what happens to them?" says Laleh. "If I see them again, I'll shoot them myself."

"Don't you dare. They're valuable assets. Look how many Collectors they helped us catch . . ."

They're about to dissolve into pointless bickering when another fighter, who's taking a break from standing guard over the ammunition trucks, strolls over to them and offers them an electronic lighter. Soon, all four of them are sharing a cigarette, sucking in the short sharp relief of the nicotine and tobacco, which has always soothed soldiers' nerves through battle and boredom.

"Who are you looking for, comrades?" says the fighter curiously. "I've been watching you go around in circles for the last hour."

Laleh clams up, but Marzi answers the fighter coolly. "There are some women from Green City, who came with us from the mountain." She flashes Katy a glance that seems to say, *No point in keeping the women a secret now*, and Katy nods in agreement. There are more important things at stake.

"And an Ababeel called Alia," says Katy. "Do you know them?"

"I've seen a tall one with Lateefa around the camp. But I didn't know she was from Green City." The fighter glances around to make sure nobody else is listening. "I saw them. They ran away."

"*What?*" gasps Marzi.

"Yes," says the woman, throwing her own cigarette to the ground and trodding it into the mud with her boot. "To Sheba City."

"Those *bitches*," says Laleh.

"It was strange," says the fighter. They're in a huddle, their hoods forming a tent over their heads, the cigarette finished and tossed onto the muddy ground. The fighter introduces herself as Hamda, of Star Mountain. "After we captured the first checkpost, a lot of people abandoned their cars on the road. We were clearing the blockages when we saw some women come out of the forest, cross the road, and get into one of thc cars."

"Oh no," groans Marzi.

"They were arguing with one another," says the fighter. "But then the car took off with them into the city."

"Hold on," says Katy. "Tell me this again. You saw them arguing."

"It looked like some wanted to go, some wanted to stay back." The fighter shakes her head. "They headed in the wrong direction. We could see them shouting to us through the windows. We tried to help. But once the program takes over, you can only stop it from inside the car. They looked terrified. A battle's no place for a kid either . . ."

"Alia's child," says Marzi.

"Like I said, we tried to stop them, but they nearly mowed us down. We had to jump out of the way. Anyway, good luck getting them back."

"Here, thanks for your lighter," says Marzi.

"Keep it. I have another. May it light a thousand cigarettes for you all."

Laleh stares down at the ground, Marzi fiddles with her rifle, Katy turns her face up to the sky and lets the raindrops cover her, seep into her hair, run down her neck.

"How are we supposed to find them now?" says Marzi, sitting down beside Katy, looking equally defeated.

"Let's go to Sheba City," says Laleh.

Both Marzi and Katy stare at Laleh. "To Sheba City now, are you crazy?" Katy says. "I just told you, the operation's being called off. It's a complete mess."

Marzi adds, "Once they realize the city is under siege, most people will be frantic to get out. We'd never find them."

Katy's mind jumps from one scenario to the next. In the distance, she can hear the boom of mortars. The fighters at Sheba City were supposed to split up: half to stay north, while the other half would march south, making two inroads into the city. Has Fatima Kara gotten to them yet? And how will she get the advance guard out safely? It's anyone's guess who's sending rockets into the western wall right now. Worst of all, the Khareef Festival complicates everything. It makes national news every year, but that just means all of Mazun will find out fast that Sheba City is being attacked by the Hamiyat. The General's plan will come to fruition, and the women of the mountains will be slaughtered by the reinforcements Green City's sure to send to quell them.

Laleh's eyes are beginning to shine; she's starting to perk up like a plant receiving water. It's her madwoman look, the one she gets when she's spotted a target through the sights of her rifle scope. "Forget the women, they're already lost. Let's find Commander Kara and Lateefa and help with the evacuation."

"How do we get into Sheba City?" says Marzi. "If we start walking, we'll get there this evening."

"We take a vehicle."

"They're all gone."

"Not all of them," says Laleh, thumbing backward at the ammunition trucks.

"You want us to steal an MTVR," scoffs Marzi. "And ride it all the way to Sheba City."

"They're delivering munitions to the troops," says Laleh, "all day today and tonight and tomorrow. We'll just hitch a ride with one of the transport teams. We were supposed to be at the line of departure anyway. We'll tell them we got separated from our team and we're catching up with them."

"I just told you, the whole thing's been called off," protests Katy.

"Doesn't look like it," says Laleh. "Kara didn't say anything about retreat orders. Not yet anyway. Come on! We're Hamiyat fighters! I'm not going to stand back while our comrades fight for their lives over there!" Laleh pauses, then dashes off toward the trucks, not waiting for Marzi and Katy. Or perhaps she's so confident they'll follow, she doesn't need to look back at them.

The two women glance at one another. Katy takes in Marzi's fearful eyes, but something is growing there, too: a steely determination that outweighs the uncertainty. Marzi's voice is low, urgent, when she asks, "What about it, Katy?" She rests her hand lightly on her rifle, but Katy can see she's ready to hoist it over her shoulder and follow Laleh. She, too, doesn't expect Katy to refuse.

Katy rolls her eyes, thinking, *Typical Laleh.* "She hasn't left us much choice." Both of them know that Laleh's said what's uppermost in their minds, foremost in their hearts: They can't sit on the sidelines while their sisters, their comrades, are facing death. They'd rather run toward death than hang back, like cowards, in safety. This is why they joined the Hamiyat, and now that the vital hour is upon them, they can't resist its siren call. Death and love, after all, are what they've been born for.

Laleh is waiting for them at the tactical assembly point

right next to the MTVRs. Katy thought there'd be more logistics staff milling around, preparing the trucks for deployment, but the area is quiet. Laleh is talking animatedly to two women, one of them Hamda, the fighter who gave them her lighter. As Katy approaches, the women break off from the conversation and greet her with quick, firm handshakes.

"Comrade," says Hamda to Katy. "Your friend here told us you got left behind?"

"Very careless of you," says the other, her smile revealing a charming gap between her two front teeth.

"Arsheen and Hamda have agreed to take us to the LOD," says Laleh. "Maybe Commander Kara—"

"Thanks, comrades," says Katy, interrupting Laleh. No one else should know about the message to Fatima Kara; rumors would spread and the fighters would quickly become confused and demoralized. "But how will we fit?" The MTVR has space in the front for only two people, the driver and the gunner.

"You'll have to ride in the ammo compartment," says Arsheen, the sweet-faced, gap-toothed fighter. "Sorry about that."

"It'll be a tight fit," says Hamda. "Good thing you're all so thin. Not like me—if I were in there, I'd squash you all." She gives herself a shake, jiggling her body, and emits a loud cackle. "Are we ready to go? ETD is now."

Arsheen climbs into the driver's seat. Hamda peers at the retina scanner on the compartment door, which unlocks and swings open, revealing a treasure chest of weapons attached to the walls of the small compartment: bullets for rifles and pistols, boxes of shells and grenades. "Climb aboard."

Laleh lifts herself up into the compartment first, settling in among the boxes on the floor; Marzi's next, and Katy throws her rifle inside and pushes herself up last.

Hamda says, "All set? It'll be dark, comrades, but there is enough ventilation to last till we get there. Hopefully we won't be long."

She shuts the door on them, and already, it feels stiflingly close. A moment later, the engine rumbles angrily underneath them. Their bodies vibrate and jostle as they begin to move out of the forest on uneven terrain. A steep forward slant throws them all backward, then upright again, as the vehicle climbs up the incline and onto the paved highway. Some of the boxes fall over, and Laleh lets out a yelp as one of them lands on some part of her body that Katy can't see in the dark.

She wants to ask Laleh and Marzi for a clearer plan as they grind forward toward the troop line, but instead, a whisper slips out of her mouth: "You shot me."

Marzi is silent. Katy braces herself for Laleh's angry declaration that she's never done a thing to harm any of her friends. Or she might just smack Katy in the face. Laleh's temper is legendary; other women don't dare meet her eye when she's in one of her moods.

Over the shifting of their bodies, the rattling of the bullets inside their boxes, the roar of the MTVR's powerful engine, Katy strains to hear Laleh's answer. Marzi breathes in with a nervous hiccup. The sweat pools under their arms, at the curves of their lower backs, even on their thighs, making their clothes stick to their skin. The rain has stopped, but the pressure is building again in preparation for the next downpour, the compartment growing hotter and more humid with every passing minute.

At last, Laleh speaks in a hoarse whisper: "Yes, it was me."

Katy closes her eyes, a soothing feeling, even in the dark. Before she dies, she wants nothing unsaid or unknown among the three of them.

"What? Why?" says Marzi, horrified. She was there that

night, helping carry Katy to the passenger drone, tears streaking her face as she took off her headscarf and pressed it to Katy's wounds, to soak up the blood. Katy can hear those tears in Marzi's voice now.

"I had no choice," says Laleh, her voice strangled. "They made me."

"Who?" Marzi is so upset that she's shivering, her teeth rattling in the gloom. Katy answers for Laleh. "It was Fatima Kara's order, Raana Abdallah's plan, to get me out of Dhofar and take me to Eastern Semitia. It hasn't worked. But it's not Laleh's fault. She was just obeying orders."

"Why did you go along with them?" shouts Marzi, struggling to understand this betrayal that Katy's already been living with for months. Katy isn't fooled by Laleh's flat tone either; she knows Laleh is as upset at losing Marzi's trust as she is at her own sin of shooting one of her own Hamiyat comrades.

They're all breathing hard, trying to suck the thick heavy air into their lungs. Katy's pronouncement means absolution for Laleh, accusation for their Commander, whom they all trust without question. *How terrifying it must be for them*, Katy thinks. She knows the details, the reasons, and it's hard enough for her to see everything she's trusted in turned upside down.

Suddenly Laleh lunges forward and throws her arms around Katy's neck. She clings to Katy like a whimpering child. "I'm sorry. I'm sorry. I'm sorry. I haven't been able to live with myself since I did it. I wanted to refuse, but I just couldn't." She's hiccuping through her words, her tears wetting Katy's skin.

"It's all right." Katy pats Laleh's head, after poking her fingers by mistake into Laleh's streaming eyes. "I forgive you.

Thank you for aiming so true, Laleh. You're the only one who could have done it and not killed me outright."

Then Marzi is crying and they're all holding one another. "Don't cry, Laleh," says Marzi. "Your eyes will swell up and you won't be able to shoot anyone."

"Shut up," sniffles Laleh.

Finally, the MTVR grinds to a halt. There's a slamming on the side of the compartment: Hamda and Arsheen are calling them to come out. The door clicks open, and the three of them throw their arms up to shield their reddened eyes from the cloudy daylight, sudden and intense and burning after all that time in the dark.

Outside is the great roar of dozens of fighters in idling vehicles and yet more women on foot, their boots stamping on the ground.

But when Laleh, Marzi, and Katy clamber out of the compartment, they realize they're not at the line of departure; they're *in* Sheba City itself. They've ended up at what seems like a site for the Khareef Festival: just off the North Square. But there are no onlookers, just an empty stage, abandoned snack stalls, speakers fallen silent after being blown up by flying bullets. Sheba City Guards fire relentlessly at a small building—a library or a post office, Katy can't tell. Return fire rings out from the building back at the Guards—Hamiyat fighters fighting back. And Katy and her friends have landed right in the middle of this melee.

Katy sees everything happen in front of her in slow motion; time slows down while everything in her body tightens and accelerates: heartbeat, breathing, reflexes. The fighters are jumping from their vehicles, forming their squads, firing their small guns and assault rifles at anyone who looks like a Sheba City Guard. Now Katy notices fleeing civilians, some of them hit by bullets, caught in the crossfire. As they roll on the ground, waves of screaming reach Katy's ears.

The Hamiyat fighters run for cover in the surrounding buildings—apartment blocks on two sides of the Square, shops and a library on a third, a low government building with Mazunian and Dhofari flags on the fourth. Some drag light artillery and ammunition with them.

"Get down! Get down!" screams Katy as the bullets whine past and the roar of battle fills the air. She can't understand how the Dawn Battalion are on the offensive; they weren't supposed to enter the city until the Semitian drones showed up. But Fatima Kara knows the drones aren't coming, so why hasn't she called her fighters off; why are they at the front line?

The five of them crawl underneath the MTVR. Laleh and Marzi get their rifles out and take aim at the Guards, their eyes squinted in concentration. "Got one!" says Marzi, her teeth clenched. Hamda and Arsheen follow their example, and soon they're all firing at the enemy, grunting with satisfaction every time they hit another man.

When they're out on patrol, Katy usually assumes the role of captain; it's easy to just fall back into that familiar formation, and Arsheen and Hamda follow her lead. Katy cranes her neck to scan the tops of buildings; Hamiyat snipers are shooting at the Guards in the Square, and the Guards, around thirty in number, return fire both at the snipers and at the fighters on the ground. But the Hamiyat have them outnumbered, and one by one, the Guards begin to fall. The ground troops are supposed to consolidate the territory the advance team has staked out, but everything has gone so wrong that Katy doesn't know if they're still even following battle orders, or just trying to stay alive.

She looks at her watch, makes a calculation. "We need to

get out from here and get into one of the buildings, join the others. We'll look for a CO there, figure out what we're doing. In two minutes, are you with me?"

"Yes."

"Got it."

"We're with you, Katy."

Katy counts the time off in ten-second increments, punctuated by the reports of the women's rifles as they keep firing at the Guards. But just as she reaches the one-minute mark, there's an ominous rumble overhead. A mechanical buzz, a humming that comes from no natural source.

It's a Zaalim.

The shadow it casts covers the ground around them. Zayn Battuta has told her about the Zaalims, the most dreaded of drones, capable of identifying targets and deciding what to fire at without waiting for a command from the center. It's a combination of camera, artificial intelligence, and weapon—the bane of any battlefield. It can't be taken down by ordinary bullets. The Hamiyat fighters would have to drag an artillery gun up to a rooftop and fire shells at it, but even that way, they're hard to hit. By the time they've managed to set up, the Zaalim will already have done its work and gone.

The Zaalim is scanning the area, but it doesn't fire yet. There are too many civilians in the apartment buildings, a few stragglers on the ground screaming and running and pushing past the Hamiyat women. It holds steady in the monsoon wind, bobbing and wafting, gliding and turning. It's looking for something big and solid, something without any sign of life in it. Something exactly like the ammunition compartment.

"Go!" screams Katy. She pushes herself out and across the Square, dodging the wind tower, feeling its cold air like a whip across her face. She sprints toward the low government building, its flags fluttering in the strong monsoon breeze. Marzi is close behind. Hamda and Arsheen scramble to follow. But Laleh keeps firing at the Guards with grim-faced determination as if she hasn't heard anything, as if she's in a trance.

Katy and Marzi are the first to reach the safety of the yellow sandstone edifice. Its locked turnstiles block them from entering. They stand in its portico, lungs burning, eyes streaming, calling out to the others in desperation. "Laleh, come on!" howls Marzi. The tumult in the Square is too loud for Laleh to hear. Katy feels like she's standing on the shore, watching them drown.

Hamda makes it out and stumbles toward them, but a bullet hits her and she falls to her knees, then crumples face-first to the ground. Arsheen is just emerging, like a baby coming out of the womb, head and a shoulder visible, when the drone fires at the compartment. There's a blinding flash a nanosecond before an explosion so strong that Katy and Marzi are knocked over. The rockets and shells inside the now destroyed compartment are set off by the explosion; they fly around the Square, whizzing and banging, hitting buildings and flying up toward the sky, destruction in their wake.

When Katy comes to, there's a raging fire in the middle of the Square. The heat and smoke drive the surviving animals and people to scream and bleat in fright and pain. Most of the Hamiyat fighters are ensconced in the buildings, but some of them are broken, their bodies scattered among those of the Sheba Guards and the civilians caught in the blast. The Zaalim has blown the ammunition compartment to pieces; there isn't anything left of it but a smoking square on the ground.

# 22.

They're holed up in the government building, Katy, Marzi, and an entire platoon of Sun Mountain fighters, twenty women led by a second lieutenant. They've been here all night. Outside, the people are coming out of the buildings, picking through the rubble for the remains of their loved ones. The sound of their weeping floats in through the windows, a keening chorus behind Marzi's sharp sobs as she rocks back and forth, mourning Laleh. Katy tries to get her to stop, to drink water, to go to sleep, but Marzi is locked too deep in her grief to move.

The empty building has been secured, Hamiyat fighters posted at windows and on the rooftop to defend it from the Sheba City Guards. They're communicating through the Spectrum with other fighters similarly situated all around the North Square. Fatima Kara and Lateefa have been located on the roof of an apartment building facing the Square. Kara is in touch with the Commanders back at the base, coordinating efforts to get the Hamiyat fighters out of Sheba City.

Everyone's been apprised of the situation now, but Fatima Kara's delay in accessing the Spectrum has meant that three hundred fighters from Sun Mountain have already entered Sheba City and spread out to the South, East, and West Squares. There are one or two Zaalims floating over each Square, with Sheba City Guards looking for the Hamiyat fighters in entrenchment or hiding. It's hard to tell how many women have been lost, but there are casualties and wounded fighters on both sides in all the Squares.

Earlier that morning, the fighters arriving in the North Square jumped from their vehicles, ran to the building, and managed to unlock the turnstile, pouring in to seek shelter from the Guards and the Zaalim. When Marzi and Katy sought refuge from the drone that destroyed most of the Square, the fighters let them in, then relocked it after them.

Inside the building, Katy and Marzi identify themselves as fighters from the Dawn Battalion to the platoon's leader, a lieutenant called Suzan. She tells them what has happened: Two hours ago, the ground troops received an order from the forward operating base, where the Commanders are, to enter the city.

"But without air cover?"

"I know," says Suzan, chewing on a protein bar and downing gulps of water from her flask. Luckily the building still has a clean water supply, but if the Guards cut it off, the Hamiyat fighters will have to surrender or die of thirst. Fighters run to and from bathrooms, filling up flasks and jerry cans and janitor's buckets with as much water as they can. "We were told that we would have it, but it never came. I don't know if the Commanders decided to press ahead anyway, or if it was some sort of miscommunication. So half of us are in and the other half are still outside the city."

Outside, ambulances arrive in the Square to take away the dead and wounded. The snipers keep their rifles trained on the moving figures in the Square, but they're not going to shoot medics. That the ambulances took so long to arrive means activity in the city has been badly disrupted. The ambulances take away the Guards and the civilians but leave the bodies of the Hamiyat behind: thirteen women dead in the Zaalim strike. The Zaalim itself waits for them to reemerge, menacing them from two hundred feet above their heads, humming with a buzz that Katy feels next to her eardrums, as if the drone has gotten right into her brain.

Slowly the reports filter in through Suzan's device: The Hamiyat fighters are well established in the West and East Squares; they've blocked key roads that connect those areas to the center and are in active combat with the Guards.

Katy's sitting with her back against the wall in an area with counters and glass partitions, long low benches, digital screens on the walls. But the screens are dimmed, the lights are out, and the large room is plunged in darkness and shadow. The fighters' nervous tension pervades its cavernous space.

Her mind shuffles through the possibilities like a deck of cards. Maybe Fatima Kara tried to stop the assault, but the other Commanders overrode her; or she received information from another source that air cover was on the way but there was a mix-up with the timing. Or the order is a malicious communiqué meant to get the Hamiyat into Sheba City, where they can face the wrath of the Zaalims, and be annihilated. What if the General has somehow managed to infiltrate the Spectrum and is sending fake commands to confuse the fighters? Anything is possible with the Semitians. They use their superior technology to cheat their way through to victory, overcome their enemies, betray their allies. Anxiety and anger wrack Katy, thinking of Fatima Kara trapped in the apartment. How could she get herself into such an impossible situation when her battalion—Katy and Marzi included—need her the most?

"What are our chances?" she asks Suzan.

The lieutenant, in her late twenties, with short black hair and the faint remnants of acne scars mapped across her cheeks, considers. "With air support? Fifty percent. Without them? And that bastard up there?" She jabs her thumb in the direction of the sky. "Not good."

"The Guards? Do they outnumber us?"

"No, there are actually fewer of them than us. In a fair fight, we'd have a decent chance. Sheba City relies on the Zaalims more than it should—that's their weakness, so we were hoping for the Semitian drones to bring them down. That's not an option now." She's speaking openly, treating Katy as an equal. Hierarchy is strictly for the sake of discipline, but the Hamiyat share battle strategy with the juniors; it's how they train them to take the place of the seniors in the chain of command.

"Can't we take them out with our own weapons?"

"It would be a waste of our ammunition, comrade. We don't have anti-drone missiles, just regular shells, and those are no good against a smart drone like this one. We might use communication disruptors, but those only work on regular drones, too. These bastards don't even need operators, so that's futile." Suzan coughs and clears her throat, then spits on the ground. "Curse them and their mothers. I've never seen anything as evil as this."

Katy ponders this. "How many of them are there?"

"Hard to say. I'd guess no more than five, for the whole city. Maybe less, three or four. It's not a big town. Not like Green City."

"And ours. What if it just blows us up in here?"

"It will, once it's identified us as a target. For now it still thinks this is government-controlled space. Until it figures out that we're inside, we're okay. But we have, I would say, fifteen hours at most. And the more Sheba City Guards we kill from here, the sooner the Zaalim will update its maps and line up this building as a target."

"Lieutenant!" calls another fighter from behind the

counter, which serves as a makeshift medical triage area. "Loujain's awake. She's calling for you. Hurry, she's weak. She's lost a lot of blood."

"I'm coming. Sorry, comrade, I've got to go. Take care of your friend." Suzan jumps to her feet, shaking off her exhaustion like a discarded blanket.

Katy turns back to Marzi, who has stretched out on the floor. Her large dark eyes are open; the tears seep out slowly, making her eyes even more luminous than before. Katy reaches up and blots them with the palm of her hand. At her touch, Marzi begins to sob again, her entire body convulsing. Katy tries to shush her, but Marzi refuses all attempts to calm her down.

"I should have died with her . . . I shouldn't have left her . . . Why didn't she listen to us, Katy?" Marzi moans.

Katy shakes her head. "I don't know, Marzi-pan."

"Why did she stay there? She could have made it out; she would be here with us right now. If only she wasn't so stubborn!"

"Here, have some water, please. For my sake? Laleh wouldn't want you to be like this; she would want you to be brave."

"How do you know what Laleh would have wanted?" says Marzi. "Laleh is dead. She's dead. Damn her." She repeats it as if trying to make herself believe it. "And now I wish I were dead, too."

"Nonsense," says Katy, trying to channel Lateefa's sharp swordlike tongue, her complete lack of self-pity. Lateefa would spur the surviving fighters on to victory, telling them that Laleh's sacrifice must not be in vain. "Look, we're miserable enough as it is. Don't make it worse. We've got a big battle ahead of us."

She pats Marzi's hair and rubs her shoulders, lulling her

into a half sleep. At some point, Katy and Marzi will be expected to relieve some of the fighters and take up defensive positions at the windows, too. Luckily, the night has given them extra cover; no Guard's bullets have found their mark. The only wounded Hamiyat fighters are the ones dragged in from the Square. The Zaalim struck with precision, but fighters and Guards and civilians were wounded and killed indiscriminately because of the shells and rockets that were set off by the first explosion. The Zaalim probably wasn't expecting that to happen.

Marzi has finally given in to Morpheus and is sleeping fitfully beside Katy, who keeps vigil, even though she knows she, too, needs her rest. Her mind begins to drift with fatigue and tension. She wonders what Adeefa is doing. Has Adeefa ever seen the monsoon? She doesn't think so. In Semitia, the desert still prevails, reclaiming green spaces inch by inch with envelopes of sand brought forth every time the wind coughs.

And then out of the recesses of her exhausted mind, Katy imagines SmartSoul taking on the Zaalim. Not in an aerial dogfight . . . SmartSoul isn't a physical entity, but its algorithm might have an answer for how to bring the Zaalim down . . . Surely Zayn Battuta's invention is smarter than the Zaalim?

Hands trembling, Katy digs out her borrowed device, the one given to her when she returned to the Hamiyat at Khor Rori. It's connected to the Spectrum, just like all the others still are. Is it possible the General doesn't know how to disable the Spectrum, that Zayn Battuta designed a communications network that can't be shut down once it's up and running?

Katy punches in the code for Adeefa's device. But it's not her own device, and she doesn't know whose identification code will appear on Adeefa's screen. Adeefa might not even answer an unrecognizable call. After several long minutes of no response, Katy sighs, lies down beside Marzi, and closes her eyes.

Sleep is no comfort. Her mind is as active as if she's awake. She dreams of Raana Abdallah's gimlet stare, the taste of Zayn Battuta's skin, the softness of Adeefa's lips. She dreams of her mother and father, calling out to her, as she stumbles toward them, learning how to walk. Then she's in a vast ocean, learning to swim; fish surround her, squirming along her body, which feels light and nimble in the water. Suddenly there's a loud boom and all the fish scatter away. Katy reaches her hands out to catch them but only touches Marzi, startled awake beside her.

"What was that? Laleh, where are you?"

Katy presses her hand between her breasts and feels her heart thundering against her ribs. The pain of remembering Laleh is dead is a tearing inside her chest. Marzi sits up and rubs her eyes, swollen and heavy-lidded from all her crying.

Suzan and the other fighters are scrambling back to the windows to see what the Zaalim has hit now. It's taken aim at some of the vehicles left behind by the fighters. There wasn't time to stow them safely in any of the garages or basement tunnels as they'd planned, not when the Zaalim showed up and began its sweep of the Square. The smell of burning tires, thick and rubbery, rises up in the ugly black smoke. Pieces of metal that flew up in the impact are floating back down to earth, ablaze. The whole Square is lit by tiny fires, people hiding in their homes, too afraid to try to put them out.

"This is going to be a bad way to go," says one of the fighters.

Katy's as wide-eyed as the rest of them at the Zaalim's

unmitigated power. It'll only be a matter of time before they run out of ammunition. Then food. Water last of all. Surely Suzan has radioed back to Fatima Kara to ask for help? Katy still has faith in the Commander; her anger has given way to a dogged belief in Fatima Kara's ability to effect a miracle.

Katy picks up her device to reassure herself it's still connected to the Spectrum. Her throat tightens when she sees that Adeefa has responded to her with a quick callback, while Katy was sleeping. Again she attempts to call Adeefa, and this time, the Semitian appears on Katy's screen.

"Katy, are you—where are you, Katy? Are you in Dhofar?" Worry creases form around Adeefa's eyes as she squints at the camera. It's late in Zarzura; in Sheba City, it's not yet dawn. Adeefa looks half-awake, dark shadows under her eyes telling Katy that she hasn't been sleeping well for a while now.

For a minute Katy is unable to speak and can only stare at Adeefa. Her face, appearing on the screen, is as lovely and familiar as Katy remembers it: liquid eyes, swept-back hair and a widow's peak at her high forehead, those soft rounded features that evoke a sunburst of different feelings in Katy. Right now, relief. Adeefa is a safe harbor.

Katy crouches forward and cups her hand around the screen. She wants to keep Adeefa away from Marzi, from the other fighters. The Semitians are not their allies anymore, but she wants to protect Adeefa from anyone else's judgment or censure. "I'm in Sheba City," she whispers. "The operation's already started. We have no air cover from your drones." Katy runs her hand through her hair. "We're trapped in a building, a government building, in the North Square. Can you find me on the map?"

Adeefa's picture pauses as she searches for Katy on the locator. Then she comes back. "There you are. I found you!"

They're the three sweetest words in the world to Katy right now.

Adeefa tells her the building is the Directorate for Finance, that the city center which houses the other government buildings—the Treasury, the Governorate—is not far away. The coastline is a short distance from their location. She sends Katy a map that shows up in an instant on Katy's screen. There are the buildings, there are the roads, there's the wind tower. The map even shows the position of the Zaalim: It's turning in stationary circles on the map, like an airplane in a holding pattern waiting to land.

Katy tells Adeefa, "There's about twenty, twenty-five of us in here. Hamiyat fighters. Some of them wounded. Our Commander is in another building not far from us, but there's nothing she can do. There's Sheba City Guards; they're firing at us. But it's worse than that. There's a Zaalim. Right above us. It hit a mobile ammunitions storage box. The munitions exploded. Killed and wounded a lot of people."

Adeefa's eyes widen. "Are you hurt?"

"No. But my friend Laleh is dead."

"Oh, Katy . . . I'm so sorry."

Katy doesn't know what upsets her more, the fact that Laleh has been killed or that they can't take her body back to the mountain, give her a proper burial. Laleh was always so frightened of spirits and jinns, of hauntings. What if she's now one of them, wandering forever? "We need to get out of here, but we can't while that Zaalim is above us. Look, we need Zayn Battuta to disable it. It's our only way out. Maybe he can ask SmartSoul how to do it."

Adeefa bites her lip. "He can't. He's disappeared. He went into hiding, after Raana Abdallah was arrested."

Katy feels hope drain away. "And SmartSoul? Is it still running?"

"I think so, but there are Guards outside his office, so I can't really go in there."

"Can't you access it from somewhere else?"

"I'm not authorized, but let me try something." Adeefa moves, goes to a larger screen in her room, types something in. She shakes her head, looking mournful. "No, I can't do it."

The desperation makes Katy's muscles tighten, her teeth clench. *There has got to be a way, there has got to be a way*, she thinks to herself.

"Can't you just blow it out of the sky?" says Adeefa. "You have weapons. Plenty of them. We sent them to you."

A graphic animation of a Zaalim appears on her screen. There it is, a five-meter silver-gray bird, with wings, propellers, a snub nose, and a long narrow body. The graphic comes to life, demonstrating its technical capabilities. Its missiles, at least six, are housed inside that body; they slip down into the delivery system and fire at whatever its computer mind tells it to strike. The graphic shows enemy missiles being fired at the Zaalim, which dodges and weaves like a bird on a draft.

"Not the kind that would destroy this thing. Besides, it's raining, the wind is blowing like crazy, and it isn't even fazed," says Katy. Her eyes are tired and strained, seared from the heat of the explosion that she turned back to look at, even though she shouldn't have. Her voice shakes. "The murdering bastard . . ."

"It has stabilizers, so the weather doesn't affect it as much as other drones," says Adeefa. "Where is it right now?"

"It's just hanging around the wind tower. It's not moving from there."

"Oh yes. I see it on the map. Well, the wind tower is transmitting navigation signals. If there's an attack, it sends a signal and the Zaalims are summoned there; it's the most central location, and they can survey all parts of the city most effectively." She's reading the Zaalim's capabilities from her screen. Katy feels sorry for Adeefa, clearly trying not to show that she's upset about Zayn Battuta's disappearance. *I did warn you*, Katy thinks to herself.

But then Adeefa speaks up again. "I found out about what they did to you. Making you go to Green City, to assassinate someone who wasn't even there in the end."

Katy wasn't expecting this; she's put the whole episode out of her mind, because it's been so incomprehensible to her. "It's true. But how did you find out?"

"Actually, it was Zayn Battuta. I saw him the night the General had Raana Abdallah arrested. I went to his office; he was trying to hide files, wipe his computers. He told me that the whole plan was a decoy, and that I should warn you. That's when I sent you the message on the dazzler."

"But why? Why would you both want to help me? Battuta's life is probably in danger. And you could lose your job."

"Not all of us are like Raana Abdallah, or the General," says Adeefa. "We have some principles. You were a guest, and they used you. It's wrong. I want to help."

Katy realizes she's misjudged Zayn Battuta: He's not spineless, he's just a civilian, caught up in something that science can't help him with. His first instinct was to run, because he's been running all his life, from Kolachi, from war, from loss and trauma. Adeefa, brought up in the security of Eastern Semitia, is steadier than he. Her instincts run not toward self-preservation, but to aid others. Katy senses, too, what Adeefa's not saying: that she's doing this out of love for Katy, and a need to soothe her own bruised heart. Katy remembers what it's like to be so young and open to the world. She's seized by a tender feeling, halfway between protectiveness and fear for Adeefa, and she turns away from the screen for a moment so Adeefa won't notice the tears brimming in her eyes.

When she's more composed, Katy says, "What if we knock out the signals from the wind tower, so it gets confused and flies away? Could *you* do it?" She's always had a hunch that Adeefa is more highly placed in Zarzura's network than she's ever let on. She probably has access to all the Semitian intelligence, which is what she's tapping into right now. But Adeefa also has a quick mind; she was always wasted as a mere assistant.

Adeefa flashes her eyes to Katy's, gives a small, self-assured nod. No matter what Zayn Battuta has done to her heart, she's still fully capable of doing her job. "I could try to override the signals, yes. I don't need SmartSoul to do that. We were already primed to knock out the city water supply; we'd just have to redirect the attack. But that doesn't mean the Zaalim will go anywhere. And even if it's cut off from the tower, it'll still run on its own intelligence."

Katy says, "Tell me more about this wind tower. I saw one like it in Zarzura, in the main square."

"Yes, they're common all over the peninsula. It's a simple design."

"There's no turbine in it?"

"No. It's long and tall, so it creates a convection current that can run either way, up or down. There are louvers at the top. Angle them down, it draws cool air from the sky and sends it down. Angle them up, it sucks hot air out of the streets and sends it up. They're automated, so they operate on weather inputs from the tower. It doesn't work that well when you don't get so much wind. But with a constant breeze, like you have during the khareef, it works beautifully."

Katy whistles, impressed. The strength of nature, harnessed, is still a surprise to her. She remembers the noise the Zarzura wind tower made, the absolute chill of the underground rooms directly beneath it. But there's something Katy's missing, a connection her mind isn't able to make. She shakes her head, frustrated. "Well, all right, then go for it, Adeefa. Let's see what happens."

"I'll need a little time . . ."

"How long?"

"Half an hour."

Marzi is tugging at Katy's sleeve. Katy realizes that Marzi has been listening to the conversation all along. "What is it?"

"It's Suzan. She wants to tell you something. I think it's important."

Katy nods. "Adeefa, I have to go. I don't know when I'll be able to call you back. Keep tracking my device, though, and you'll know where I am."

"All right. Watch the tower. There are green and red lights along its sides. When they switch off, that's it, it's done."

"Thanks. And forget about that bastard. Not the Zaalim. I mean the other one. Zayn Battuta. He's not worth it. He never was. He even tried to seduce me, in the Museum. I never told you."

Adeefa mumbles, "I saw. I was there, but you didn't notice me. You were too busy telling him to get lost."

Katy says, "I wish it had been you." Adeefa turns scarlet with embarrassment and Katy turns off the device quickly, not wanting to get distracted now.

Marzi is staring at Katy. "You didn't tell me you had a girlfriend over there."

"Shut up," Katy says, jumping up and pulling Marzi to her feet. They pad through the hallway to the far end, where a few Hamiyat women are being tended to by a lone medic. The lieutenant is sitting next to a fighter lying on the ground. Loujain, the wounded fighter, is pale but alert, talking to Suzan.

"It's only a cracked rib," Loujain says. "I can go out there. Put a gun in my hands, I can still fight."

The medic shows Suzan the bandages around Loujain's chest, the skin purple and blue from the insult of the wound. "Falling debris from the explosion," she explains. "Two broken ribs. She's lucky her lung wasn't punctured."

"Nobody's going anywhere for now," says Suzan. "Sit tight and try to rest, Loujain. Ah, comrades." She spots Katy and Marzi, stands up, and holds out her hand for them both to shake. "Come with me."

They follow her to an alcove away from the wounded. There are marble benches fitted into the walls, so the three of them sit down. The lieutenant wastes no time in getting to the point. "We have to get our wounded out of here, back to the base. I'm going to put some of them on the vehicles, but we need a driver and a gunner. Would you be willing to do it?"

Katy and Marzi glance at one another. "What about the Zaalim?"

"We'll keep it busy while you get away. What do you say?"

"That's suicide," says Katy.

"I know." Suzan grins.

"You'll all be killed. We saw what that thing did to our friend."

"Comrade, if we have to die, we have to die. Just think about it. I'll be over there."

Marzi and Katy are left in the alcove while Suzan goes away. "Are you all right, Marzi?" says Katy. She still can't get used to the sight of Marzi alone. Laleh was always with her, like a twin. Never has Katy seen the tall, confident Marzi look so shrunken, the light gone from her eyes, as if grief had reached in a hand and rearranged all the bones of her body.

"I don't know," says Marzi. "I don't know what I'm feeling. It's just hollow here," she says and touches her chest. "Katy, she knew she was going to die. She had a premonition. She told me. I wish I'd listened to her. I wish we'd never left the mountain."

Katy averts her eyes from Marzi's naked anguish. She has nothing to offer Marzi by way of comfort. She doesn't believe in premonitions, or jinns, or any of the spiritualisms that comfort the women in times like these. She doesn't know if consciousness continues on the other side of the black veil that comes down when this life ends. "I miss her, too. But now, what do you want to do?"

Marzi says, eyes downcast, "I don't want to leave here. Not while she's still out there."

Katy looks out the small window above the alcove. She can make out the shops with their shutters down, broken glass from shattered storefronts littering the street in front. The fires have been extinguished in the rain, but the wreckage still smokes everywhere. Wet, blackened ashes turn to sludge in the road. "There's nothing left of her." Katy sees Marzi wince. "I'm sorry. But you know it as well as I do, Marzi-pan."

"Don't ever call me that again." Marzi's hands curl into fists. *Good*, thinks Katy. Let rage fill her up, power her to action: Marzi's better as an angry woman than a husk. If they accept the mission to transport the wounded women back to the base, they'll both need the sharp edge of their fury to stay focused and alert.

Suzan returns. "Comrades. I've made contact with your CO. Good news, she's still holding out."

She shows them her device, where Lateefa's image flickers and her voice comes out in a tinny whistle.

Lateefa is saying, "We were on the rooftop, but when the Zaalim attacked, we had to go back inside. We're trapped, we can't get out of here." Lateefa turns her device around, showing the Panah women, Alia, and Noor sitting on the floor.

"We came looking for them! How did they end up with you?" exclaims Marzi.

Lateefa says, "What? But Marzi, I told you and Laleh to stay in the camp. Why didn't you obey your orders?"

"Too late now," says Marzi.

"Laleh's dead, Lieutenant," says Katy. "The Zaalim got her."

"Laleh? Damn."

"But Lieutenant, listen. I've been speaking to a . . . a friend, back in Zarzura. She thinks the Zaalim's connected to the signals coming from the wind tower. She's going to try to switch them off, and maybe the Zaalim will go away."

There's a tumult in the background: Someone's saying something to Lateefa, but the connection wavers, the sound crackles, and Lateefa's image disappears for a moment. When it comes back, it's not Lateefa, it's Fatima Kara. Her face is strained, but there's relief written there, too.

"You're alive." Fatima Kara's voice is warm, and Katy smiles to hear it.

"Alive and well, for now," says Katy. "But Laleh is gone."

"I heard," says Fatima Kara. "I'm sorry. May the Warrior Queen receive her."

"She was a fighter. She died the way she wanted to, with a gun in her hands."

"The Zaalim . . . it surely is a jinn's invention," says Alia in the background.

"I doubt any of us will escape it alive," says Fatima Kara. "Unless we can destroy it."

"Only a bigger jinn can do that," says Alia somberly.

"Blow it away!" screams Noor. "Huff and puff and blow it down!" Alia hushes her child, clamping her hand over his mouth. "Noor, *quiet!*"

Katy glances out the window again: Just as Adeefa promised, the lights on the wind tower have gone out. The Zaalim floats in the air above it, riding the monsoon wind, but now it's unmoored from its homing signal. Katy draws a sharp inward breath. She's done it! Not even half an hour, less than twenty minutes. "Oh, Adeefa, you clever girl!" But the Zaalim isn't budging from its spot in the sky. Katy knows, there's more to be done to defeat it.

Alia's pronouncement and Noor's squeals spark a memory in her mind, of one jinn against another. Two jinns dancing together in a wild breeze, dust twisting in a funnel. What did they call that, back in Semitia? A wedding of the jinns. Her thoughts gather speed: hot air meeting cold air, making a vortex. A convection current, the wind tower's secret. And one they can control, if they're smart enough.

She points out the darkened tower to Fatima Kara on the device. "I think we can try to get rid of the Zaalim. If you permit me, Commander, the first thing we have to do is start a fire."

# 23.

At dawn, the fighters in the North Square reach Fatima Kara, Lateefa, and the rest of the stranded women. In this area of Sheba City, less prosperous than the other neighborhoods, ramshackle buildings are packed tightly together in rows with party walls between. The Hamiyat first break through the wall of the building that abuts the library, then keep breaking through the next wall and the next. The Hamiyat can now move with ease across these internal tunnels, the Zaalim and Sheba City Guards unable to spot them.

When they get to the apartment block, they knock a hole into the side lobby. A fire team of four women moves in, charges up the stairs to the sympathizer's apartment, and recovers the Commander, Lateefa, the two snipers, and the Panah women. The Wife wants to come with them, but she's told to stay put and keep her family out of danger. "I can't thank you enough for what you've done," Fatima Kara says, grasping her hands briefly, before they evacuate.

The Wife's eyes shine. "You are the bravest of the brave. I wish I could pick up a rifle and fight with you."

"When this is over," says Fatima Kara, "and we've won, that's when we'll need women like you. Be ready."

As they emerge into the darkened hallway, the Commander is at the head, with the fire team, pistols drawn, leading the way. Mariya weeps with relief as they're led down the stairs. Grace picks up Noor and carries him in her arms, and Alia floats down the steps, ghostlike and calm, carrying bundles of food the Wife has given them. The snipers bring up the rear, rifles up and ready. But they encounter no resistance. The people who live in the apartment building hide behind their doors, too afraid to stick their heads out and see what the commotion is all about. By now, word has spread that there's a siege underway; the entire City knows what's going on.

The women head back through the tunnels, from one building to the next until they're back in the library. The snipers are reunited with their division, and the Hamiyat set up with their weapons and ammunition among stacks and stacks of books lined up in rows on shelves. The fighters have pushed some of the shelves against the doors and windows of the library as fortification against the Sheba City Guards.

The Panah women, the Ababeel, and the child are sent to the basement of the library, to wait out the operation. Katy has told Fatima Kara her plan for ridding them of the Zaalim that waits for them above their heads. Fatima Kara is highly skeptical that the plan will work, but their Semitian benefactor, Adeefa, says she's checked out the technical aspects and thinks there's a chance they can succeed. Fatima Kara has no faith in the promises of the Semitians now. She finds the privacy of the library's office to sit down for a moment and take stock of what has happened and what needs to happen now.

But before she makes the decision to allow Katy to take on the Zaalim, she tries one more time to connect with the other Commanders at the base. When Zayna Al-Maliki's device accepts the connection, Fatima Kara exhales a long, shaky breath. Soraya, Leila Ortabi, and the Al-Maliki sisters are all sitting together at the command tent, but Fatima addresses Leila Ortabi as their de facto chief. "Thank the Warrior Queen, Commander, I thought there'd been an attack on the base." She quickly sums up the troop positions, the half-in-half-out situation, and the presence of the Zaalims. "Where are the Semitian drones? Can you locate them on the maps? They're the only hope we have against those bastards." The popular epithet for the Zaalims is grimly satisfying to spit out from her mouth.

Ortabi says, "No, comrade, we have a problem."

"Commander?"

"The Semitians . . . we've lost contact with them. I can't get in touch with them."

"I don't understand. You can't reach them at all?"

"All communications went dead last night. We've tried every channel. It's no use. The drones aren't coming."

It's the news Fatima Kara was bracing herself against, not accepting it until Ortabi speaks it into truth. She still doesn't even know whether the botched assault happened by chance or design. It would appear that the Semitians have withdrawn their support for the Hamiyat, but the Spectrum is still operational, even if the drones haven't shown up, and they have Semitian weapons in their hands. Fatima Kara stacks all the facts up in her head, but in the end, one fact overshadows them all: Her job is to lead her women, and get as many of them out of Sheba City as safely as possible. For that, destruction of the Zaalim is a must.

The other Commanders don't know that there's still one channel back to Semitia: Katy's mysterious friend Adeefa. But instinct tells Fatima Kara to keep quiet about it, just in case those who've turned against the Hamiyat find out. They need to protect this benefactor, squeeze as much help out of her as they can. "Very well, comrade. We'll have to take our chances when we withdraw. I'm planning our retreat from the North Square right now; you'll have to coordinate the others."

"We're in council right now, and talking to Commander Qassemi to try to figure out how to get you all back home safely. We'll have a final decision in a few hours, I give you my word."

"Comrade!" says Fatima Kara. "In a few hours it'll be too late. The Zaalims are recalibrating targets all the time. It won't be long before they calculate our positions at every square."

"You'll wait for our signal," interrupts Leila Ortabi. Fatima Kara bites back the protest. Zayna Al-Maliki is grim; her sister, Khulud, looks unwell. These aren't the Commanders she'd left behind at the base. The Semitian betrayal, whatever's caused it, has eaten away at them all.

Over the others' devices, Fatima Kara can hear snippets of news streaming in: the Hamiyat are holding off the Guards in the East Square, but in the West Square, the Guards are squeezing the fighters into a corner. There's talk that reinforcements are being called up from the surrounding towns. More Guards are being mobilized. The city's in chaos, the festival in disarray, the crowds running amok.

Fatima Kara knows the drones aren't coming, but she still has to keep hope alive. As well as encouraging her women, Fatima Kara must persuade Leila Ortabi and the others not to give up. This was all her doing anyway, so she bears the greater responsibility for everything that's gone wrong. They have given her their loyalty. Now she has to give them confidence, even if she feels none herself. But that, too, is her burden. She's led them here and now she has to lead them out again.

She decides to let them in on the plan, but she won't tell them about Adeefa; she'll just say it was an idea they all came up with together. "Comrades, the fighters in this square are going to try something."

"What?" says Soraya. Her voice is tired, a little broken. "What are they going to do?"

"Attack the bastards head on?" Zayna Al-Maliki sits up straighter, rubs at her eyes with two fingers, takes a cup in her hand, and gulps its contents down. "How?" The others crowd in on the screen, demanding answers. Fatima Kara suddenly feels there's new life in her, as if she's a plant that's been strengthened by fresh water.

"It's a stupid plan, Katy, it's never going to work," says Marzi as they wait in the alcove for the Hamiyat fighters to return with what Katy's asked them to find.

"Adeefa says it might."

"Adeefa, Adeefa! I'm sick of that name already!"

"Well, you'll be hearing a lot more of it, so simmer down."

Marzi glares at Katy, who realizes that she's stepping into Laleh's role as Marzi's foil and sparring partner. She'll do what it takes to keep Marzi energized, only for a short while, she promises herself, until they get back to the mountain. She doesn't allow herself to think of any other possibility but return.

Hamiyat fighters materialize next to Katy and Marzi in the alcove, holding out two sets of clothing: uniforms of Sheba City Guards, including the characteristic red berets. "We got them, comrades," says the first fighter, shaking out the uniform and holding it proudly in front of her. It's torn and bloodstained; the second is giant-sized, also in tatters. "Had to pull them off some dead Guards. Hope they'll do."

"They'll do," says Katy grimly, stripping off her clothes. She and Marzi climb into the uniforms, then put the red berets on their heads, tucking their hair into the caps. They rub dirt on their faces so that their skin looks marred by five o'clock shadows. Then they change their posture, throw out their chests, and are transformed into two young men. "There. Now the Zaalims will identify us as Guards, and we'll fool most people, too. As long as they don't look too closely."

The Hamiyat fighters suck in their cheeks, impressed. "You'll have to teach us how to do that," says the second fighter.

"We will," says Marzi, satisfied with her disguise, patting herself down. She glares at Katy. "I still don't think it's going to work."

"Well, either it will or we'll die trying," says Katy with false bravado. But now, she's ready to make her last stand, to sacrifice her life for the Hamiyat if it means the rest of them will live to fight another day. She's made her peace, in this long night, with the inevitable. She's lived a good life, if a short one; she's fought, she's loved, she's been loved. By Laleh and Marzi, by all her comrades, by Alia and little Noor. The times she and the child wandered up and down the mountain paths, picking flowers, his warm moist hand holding hers, gave her one of the best feelings she's ever known.

Marzi, Katy, and the two Hamiyat fighters move from the alcove to an emergency exit on the west side of the building. Suzan and a few of the other fighters are already there to see them off. Suzan holds out her device to Katy and Marzi. Fatima Kara is on the screen, with Lateefa at her side. Other fighters are lined up behind them, and Katy thinks she can see Alia and Noor, but she isn't sure. Perhaps it's just a trick of the light.

"Katy Azadeh," says Fatima Kara. "Are you sure you want to do this?" She has dark circles under her eyes, as if she hasn't slept all night. They all look like that, though, keeping vigil as the Zaalim watches over them, as if they can repel it by force of will alone. They've held it off until this morning, but they don't expect their luck to last any longer than this.

"Yes, Commander," replies Katy.

"And Marzi?"

"I'm ready, Commander," says Marzi. Her voice is strong,

her stance resolute. Every step that Marzi takes from now on is for Laleh.

"Then go," says Fatima Kara, "and Queenspeed."

The two fighters who brought them the uniforms fall back, and two others, also dressed in Sheba City Guard uniforms, take their places, rifles at the ready. Despite their ragged appearance, their floppy uniforms, and too-big berets, an energy emanates from them, dazzling everyone who is watching. "Good luck, comrades," says Suzan, saluting them.

The four women return the salute, then pull down their goggles, breathing hard, readying themselves. A last glance around the room, a prayer to the Warrior Queen, and then Katy kicks the exit door open, letting the air and the streaming rain and wind into the sealed building. The women burst out from the emergency exit, crouch-run along the wall. The Hamiyat snipers at the windows fire steadily at the five Sheba City Guards who have emerged from a shop front and are heading straight for Katy and her team. Within minutes, the Guards are on the ground, all of them dead.

When they reach the front of the building overlooking the wind tower, they drop down onto their stomachs on the open ground of the Square, out of range of the snipers' cover, all firing from a prone position, then two women move forward as two fire from the ground. The two at the front drop back down and begin to fire their weapons, while the back two move forward.

Guards rounding the corner are brought down, falling to their knees before flopping to the ground. Katy crawls by one of them: His body, still bleeding out, doesn't look human. It's a dummy, a bad prop, ripped apart by the high-caliber bullets that the Hamiyat snipers have dispatched.

In this agonizing game of leapfrog, they crawl, inexorably, toward the wind tower. They're spread out in a horizontal line, so that if the enemy throws a grenade, they won't all be hit at once. The Zaalim circles overhead, its cameras whirring. It's recognizing the sound of gunfire, but it can't distinguish between the Hamiyat and the Sheba City Guards. It wheels around from one direction to the other, buffeted by the cool monsoon breezes and riding them like a boat on the waves of the ocean.

When it's her turn to advance, Katy keeps repeating an internal singsong: *I'm up, he sees me, I'm down.* It keeps her oriented toward forward movement, in sync with her teammates, but it also helps to drown out the low hum of the Zaalim that settles itself somewhere between Katy's eyeballs and eardrums. The Zaalim is as much a mindgame as it is a real entity; intimidation is its calling card, imbuing it with a low-level humanlike malevolence even though it's a machine. This is the trap Katy needs to avoid, thinking that it's smarter than she is.

As they come within the shadow of the three-legged wind tower, Katy signals to her teammates. The backup fighters continue to cover Marzi and Katy as they veer toward the pens where the unfortunate festival animals are still imprisoned. The bleats of goats and sheep, the lowing of cows, and the hissing of the lone camel come from all sides; Katy feels desperately sorry for the dumb creatures, but there's nothing she can do for them right now. Instead, she and Marzi gather up as much of their fodder from the feedboxes as they can—straw, grass, tree branches—and run like mad toward the west side of the wind tower.

In a few moments the two remaining fighters join them. No Sheba City Guards are visible for now. That gives the women enough time to drop fodder underneath the tower's shaft, making a base of small twigs, the driest straw to feed a fire. Marzi shapes the tree branches into a tripod that rises up toward the shaft, ten feet above.

"Start the fire," says Katy. "Hurry up."

A Hamiyat fighter takes out a small bottle of liquid and pours it onto the straw. Marzi holds up Hamda's electronic lighter she's had from back at the base in the forest. Anything that Laleh touched in her last days has become precious to Marzi. Even the spark that jumps out as she flicks its button possesses Laleh's spirit.

Luckily the straw and grass aren't too wet; a little flame licks the bottom of the pile, catches the liquid fuel, then grows in size and volume as all four of them fan it, shielding it from the rain pelting in sideways between the tower's legs. They feel the heat on their faces almost immediately. Once it catches the larger kindling, the fire burns strong and bright, even in the humidity; the tree branches are acacia, resinous, sticky enough to maintain the fire without turning into acrid smoke.

"Pray," says Katy, suddenly feeling the urge to call upon the Warrior Queen to help them. "Pray now." She hopes that Adeefa is still with them; turning off the homing signal on the wind tower was only one part of the plan. Now Adeefa has to override the weather signals that keep the louvers pointing downward, bringing cool air into the Square. When the louvers turn upward, the convection current will take the heat of the fire into the air above the tower.

Katy strains to see the top of the tower through the rain: the louvers are still in the down position. The cool air streams down the tower shaft and blows into the middle of the fire, making the flames gutter. "Come on, come on," Katy says. She takes out her device, sends Adeefa a frantic message. *Turn them up!*

"Come on!" screams Marzi. The other two fighters glance

upward, eyes wide. The Zaalim is picking up the fire that burns underneath the wind tower, but it thinks this is the remnants of its own explosion, Katy guesses. She tries to observe everything through its eyes, to think like it's thinking, all the while willing the louvers to swing slowly upward on Adeefa's command. But they don't. They have to keep feeding the fire with fuel or it'll soon burn out. There's no time to waste.

Katy eyeballs the metal frame of the tower, its long vertical slats spaced like the rungs of a ladder. It's forty-five meters to the top, according to Adeefa's diagram, the one she sent when they were talking about the plan. The Zaalim might fire at her, but she'll have to take the risk. The louvers are on opposing sides of the tower.

"Marzi! Follow me!" she shouts. She tosses her rifle to the other fighters. It's like telepathy: The other two women realize what she wants to do and quickly give her a leg up onto the side of the tower. Katy begins to inch her way up the wind tower, Marzi following on the opposite side. The Hamiyat on the ground scream encouragement. People cautiously put their heads near their windows and wonder if they're imagining the two Sheba City Guards climbing to the top of the wind tower, ants crawling up the exoskeleton of a giant standing beast, a fire burning hungrily at its base. The Zaalim, a baleful bird in the sky.

Katy and Marzi are used to mountain climbing; they're nimble and quick at negotiating rocks and cliffs. The strong wind buffets them as the rain hammers at their faces. Their fingers cramp with the strain of clinging on to the metal slats. The treads of their sturdy boots barely find purchase against the thin rungs. Half-blinded by rain, Katy sees Marzi swaying in the wind on the other side of the tower. "Keep going, Marzi, don't stop!"

"I'm trying . . ." Marzi's voice is faint, carried away by the wind, which is now blowing in circles around the tower. There's a huge gust and Marzi's feet slip: She dangles from the tower, holding on with both hands while she scrabbles to gain a toehold. Katy's stomach is in her mouth as Marzi falls.

Katy looks down, trying to ignore the nausea rising in her throat; she's higher than she realized. Marzi is lying thirty feet below on the ground, her leg bent underneath her. She's alive, but groaning, the sounds of her pain coming up faintly to Katy on the breeze. The backup fighters rush to Marzi, drag her out of the way of the Zaalim's roving eye. They're huddled behind one of the wind tower's legs.

Suddenly, a veiled figure bursts out from the library door, running across the Square. Katy hears faint shouting from the library: "Come back! Don't go out there! Are you crazy?" She looks down, sees the drop, retches once or twice.

The running figure comes to the wind tower, shots ringing out all around her. She throws her arms up around her head to protect herself, stumbles, but keeps running. As she approaches, Katy tries to figure out who it is, and whether or not it's a new danger she'll have to neutralize. The Hamiyat women guarding Marzi can take down the woman easily, but Katy's more vulnerable than ever, dangling from the tower like fruit hanging from a tree.

As the figure approaches the Hamiyat, she throws off her veil. Katy gasps; it's Alia, jumping up toward the bottom rung of the tower, lifting herself up without anyone's help. *What is she doing here?* Katy wants to scream, but she lacks the energy to shout down in Alia's direction.

"Come on, Katy!" Alia calls up to her. "I'll help you! Tell me what to do!"

"Alia . . ." manages Katy. "Go back!"

Alia holds on to the slats like a gecko on the underside of

a mountain bolder. The Hamiyat fighters at the bottom of the tower scream encouragement, urging her onward. In minutes, she's made her way up the tower and is now at Katy's level.

"Go back," screams Katy again. "It's too dangerous!"

Alia shouts, "You can't do this alone!" Her face is twisted with exertion, she's panting, and veins bulge out on her neck, but there's no fear in her.

Katy wants to protest, but is prevented by the wind and rain and dark clouds overhead, the sounds of her labored breathing, and the pain of her hands, feet, and body slamming against the metal frame. Alia calls out, "I know what you're trying to do. I heard you and Fatima Kara. Then I saw Marzi fall."

"What about Noor?" Katy manages to say.

"What about her? I want my daughter to see me here, with you. Not hiding in a corner like a coward. Now stop wasting time!" Alia's voice has taken on the shrill pitch of an eagle; Katy's never heard her make so much noise. "Move, Katy!"

Katy starts to climb again. She tries to force her arms and legs to move quicker, but the bulky bulletproof vest drags her downward, like she's crawling through mud, gravity exerting its force on her. They can't do without the vests; any Guards who escape the sniper fire will shoot them down, unless the Hamiyat women can keep them occupied below. But Alia is moving steadily beside her, and together, they find their rhythm and begin to make progress again.

Ten minutes, fifteen, twenty minutes pass in this excruciating manner. Finally they reach the top, the powerful wind from the monsoon storm whipping their clothes around their bodies. The louvers are just overhead; if Katy stretches her hand up, she can just grab the bottom of the louver, shaped like giant open drawers. She hefts herself so that she's draped diagonally across the highest rungs of the tower, distributing her weight across her body. She puts her hand onto the louver and pushes hard. The louver doesn't budge. Katy strains harder. Alia pushes from the other side, grunting. Their teeth are gritted, their eyes streaming.

The louver begins to give way, and then, with a smooth motion, it glides upward. Katy and Alia crawl sideways to the second louver and manage to get it pushed up. The sound it makes as it shifts and clicks into place makes Katy want to weep with relief.

"We did it!" hollers Alia. The Zaalim hears her voice, and its cameras turn in their direction. It's fifty feet in the air above them; Katy has on a Guard's uniform but Alia is wearing normal clothes. A streak of lightning makes Katy think that the Zaalim's already fired on them.

Katy motions downward. Alia, her face red, nods frantically. They're about to start again, but Katy spots a maintenance ladder that snakes all the way up the far side of the tower. She and Alia inch their way, crab-like, to the ladder and begin to climb down, Alia first, Katy above her.

Something in the air shifts around them. Katy glances down; the Hamiyat fighters are feeding more fuel to the fire, and it's growing bigger. Heat emanates from the center of the tower, as if it's a furnace.

Katy whispers under her breath, "It's working . . ."

The heat builds, moves upward through the inner sock. The metal underneath Katy and Alia's hands is warming up. Katy feels a mixture of eagerness and dread.

"Jump!" calls one of the fighters on the ground.

Alia bounces her way down, swinging from one rung to the next. When she reaches the last rung, she hangs in the air, then drops down to the ground, falling heavily to one side to avoid landing in the fire. Katy lands on top of Alia, who lets out a groan.

The flames crackle loudly, the heat an intense wave washing over them as they sprawl on the ground, drenched in sweat. The convection current formed by the upward-facing louvers draws the hot air to the top of the tower and sends it up into the atmosphere. There, it meets the cold air of the khareef, and forms a vortex.

The Zaalim had been holding steady, despite the gusts of wind and the rainfall. But now, instead of floating up and down on the wind currents, it wobbles from side to side, buffeted by the uneven movement of the vortex's spin.

As the Zaalim begins to lose its equilibrium, it starts to shake violently. Its propellers whirl uselessly, then stop altogether. The vortex, now a monster unleashed, throws it back and forth like a child's toy. The drone rises twenty feet in the air, then drops, rises again, drawing gasps from everyone below. Katy, Alia, Marzi, the women all watch, openmouthed. The Hamiyat fighters in the government building and on the rooftops, the Sheba City Guards they've been fighting, all hold their fire, everyone's eyes trained in the same direction.

Another gust from the wind flips the Zaalim over. Robbed of its thrust, the drone loses power. The humming stops. In silence, the Zaalim plummets to the ground. People cheer when it makes impact with the road, smashes into pieces, sending debris flying, shrapnel sharp. Some of the Guards catch pieces of it in their arms and legs, and they fall to the ground, screaming.

"We got the bastard," says Katy. "I don't believe it." She throws her arms around Alia, and they embrace. Katy's shaking, with exhaustion and relief. Alia soothes her as she would soothe one of her own children. Tears mingle with sweat on

Katy's face; she leans her cheek against Alia's shoulder, and sobs.

"For you, Laleh," says Marzi, lying on the ground. Her trouser has been cut off at the knee, and the bone of her broken leg pokes through her torn skin. "We did it for you."

# 24.

The fight for Sheba City lasts for three days after the Zaalim is destroyed in the North Square. In the South and East Squares, Adeefa turns the wind tower louvers up before disconnecting the tower's signals to the Zaalim. Her mistake in the North Square was to cut the signal irreversibly, causing her to lose control over the structure's electronic system. The second and third times she gets it right.

With Adeefa's help, the Hamiyat build a fire at the base of each wind tower, creating the choppy air that upends the Zaalims and sends them plummeting to the ground. Once the Hamiyat have destroyed the Zaalim's munitions in controlled explosions, the people emerge slowly from the buildings to stare and murmur at the wreckage; the deadly machines are now nothing but trails of melted debris scattered across the burnt ground.

When the Zaalims have fallen, Fatima Kara signals to the Commanders back at the base: The invasion is back on, and the Hamiyat troops enter the city in full strength. In far-lying neighborhoods away from the town squares, the fighting rages on until the women overwhelm the Guards. But in other areas, the Sheba City Guards either run away or surrender to the Hamiyat. The capitulation is unexpected; the unfair advantage of the Zaalims until now masked the fact that the Sheba City Guards are simply not very good soldiers, but nobody dared challenge their authority. Most of them are young men recruited from the surrounding villages and towns, slapped into smart uniforms with minimal training and little incentive to sacrifice their lives to protect the city.

Just when the city's about to fall to the Hamiyat, they remove their berets, place their weapons on the ground, and kneel with their hands behind their bare heads. As they're marched off to the prisoner trucks, the children dart into the street and snatch up most of the berets for future games of Soldiers and Hamiyat, boys against girls.

Lateefa is in charge of rounding up the prisoners and dispatching them to a hastily erected jail camp at the line of departure outside the city. There's a spark of hatred in some of their eyes, so she orders them to be blindfolded. The people of Sheba City watch silently as the prisoners are transported on the Hamiyat's L-ATVs, their hands tied and their eyes blinkered.

Lateefa still remembers the sting of being told by the laborer in the North Square that she could not be there without a Husband. Since no man has ever spoken to her like that, his arrogant entitlement still sticks in her craw.

But Lateefa does not allow her anger to rise; her job is to stay cool, to organize the transfer of the prisoners, not to harm them even though she longs to give one or two of them a beating to teach them who's in charge now. She lets herself sink into professional detachment, but first, she swears to herself that the men of Sheba City will never again tell a woman where she should or should not be, what space her body is allowed to occupy.

When the trucks leave the Square, Lateefa's muscles untense. She watches the Hamiyat troops on patrol, among buildings and streets instead of on mountain paths and through forests. She flicks open her device with her thumb, bringing up a picture of herself and Grace, arms around each other. Grace is smiling. Lateefa's face is serious. She looks at the picture for a long, long time. She can't wait to go home.

Once the city has been secured, Commanders Leila Ortabi, the Al-Maliki sisters, and Soraya drive in from the base to survey the territory that now belongs to the Hamiyat. At the city limits, the prisoner trucks pass the armored car carrying the four leaders to the command and control center that the Hamiyat have established downtown in the city government building.

Waiting at the center for her co-commanders, Fatima Kara thinks of the young men in the trucks and shudders. It was all so close to going the other way; the Hamiyat would have been the ones in the trucks, and it wouldn't be a prison camp they'd be taken to, but a reeducation camp for the young women, an execution ground for the officers and the Commanders.

She still can't forgive herself for the debacle, the Semitian drones that never showed up, the garbled command to send her troops into Sheba City without air cover. She doesn't know what to think of Raana Abdallah: Was she really betrayed, or was she the one who betrayed Fatima Kara and the Hamiyat? Despite everything, the gamble has paid off; they've won control of Sheba City. Her co-commanders are quivering and taut with victory, but they don't allow themselves time to gloat or to celebrate. The city belongs to them now; they must take charge quickly, reassure the citizens, implement a rudimentary form of governance. Each Commander will take charge of a square and its surrounding areas, ensuring that all the spaces are cleared of enemy soldiers, that the cease fire holds, that the citizens feel safe under their new rulers.

Hind Qassemi, back on the mountain, is thrilled when they radio back to tell her the siege is over, that the battle has been won. "We're holding steady here, too," she says. "Congratulations, comrades." Behind her voice, Fatima Kara can hear the bursts of automatic gunfire ringing out as the news is relayed from woman to woman, fighter to fighter. In a flash of prescience, she realizes the Monsoon War has really only just begun.

The small towns and villages in the province will soon hear of the victory of the Hamiyat. They'll be eager to establish loyalty to the women, to send negotiators for peace talks. The Commanders have already discussed the structure of the new rule: committees in each town and village, a man and woman at the head, women's concerns and issues to have equal weight for every decision made, every coin spent. There's so much work ahead to establish the new administration. It is opportunity and loss in equal measure: People will need time to grieve their loved ones—those soldiers who died in battle; Hamiyat and enemy are all somebody's sons and daughters.

And even getting rid of the yoke of occupation comes with loss, uncertainty, instability. It will take time for everyone to adjust to the new leadership. The stakes are high. But Fatima Kara feels better that they've won without the overt help of the Semitians. Better to start the new era without being beholden to an outside force: The decisive, solo victory gives the Hamiyat real legitimacy.

When the Commanders have finished their inspections of the battle sites, and taken stock of their troops' numbers and equipment, they return to the government center. Fatima Kara sits down with her colleagues and tells them about the false promises of the Semitians, the arrest of Raana Abdallah. If she had to guess who was behind it, she would assign that responsibility to a high-up in the Semitian Army. Raana Abdallah had said to her, in an offhand way, that they had shown great reluctance to participate in her plan. "But the General is indulging me," she confided in Fatima Kara, on her trip to Eastern Semitia. "To be honest, he always showed favor on my brother, so perhaps that's why he has a soft spot for me."

"Please forgive me, comrades," says Fatima Kara, turning her empty hands palms-up and putting them on the table in front of her. "I'm willing to step down for my mistakes." She braces herself for their recriminations, closing her eyes and waiting for their judgment. Instead, there's only silence. She opens her eyes again to see the four women staring at her.

"What are you talking about?"

"Step down? Now? When there's so much to be done?"

"Stop this nonsense at once, Kara," says Leila Ortabi irritably. "Tell us your plan for the villages. It's one thing to win a battle, it's another to make them like us."

The women all burst into laughter. Fatima Kara lets a smile play across her lips. "We'll tell them that as long as they do nothing to actively oppose our fighters, we'll spare their lives. If they actively help to provide shelter, intelligence, medicine, they'll be allowed to retain their homes and livelihoods, although the women can choose whether or not they want their Husbands to stay with them."

"And everyone's children will belong to their mothers, not the state," says Zayna Al-Maliki. Khulud nods in agreement.

Cups of tea and cigarettes are passed around as the women continue talking late into the night. Women and men will work together to set up a new system of governance in every village, one that addresses the needs and rights of women and men equally.

"They won't like that," says Soraya, clicking her tongue. They've all removed their boots, loosened their collars, and are sitting on the floor on a white cloth spread like a table all around them. Simple food, bread and olives, dates and fruit, can't tempt them away from their plans for the future.

"Let them protest," says Fatima Kara. "They'll see this way is better for everyone, not just the women." She thinks of Lateefa, how the lieutenant stands next to her Commander the whole time. Whenever there's any sort of problem, she never says a word, just shifts her weight from one foot to the other and very deliberately takes the safety catch off her pistol. Any man in Dhofar who doesn't like how things are going to go will catch sight of Lateefa's finger resting above the trigger, and calm down soon enough.

As Kara continues discussing plans for the future with the Commanders, her device rings. She glances at the screen, silences it, excuses herself from the discussions, and walks out of the building and leans against the wall. She lights a cigarette and inhales deeply. There's something about the air here in Sheba City: Thick, humid, it weighs her down, slows her mind. She has to think carefully now; life here isn't the same as it is on the mountain. She's the leader of an entire province, not just a division of the Hamiyat.

She takes out the device and calls back the number saved on the screen. A few rings, and the screen brightens with the face of someone she's never seen before.

"Commander Kara?"

"Yes. Who are you?"

"Allow me to introduce myself. I'm Zayn Battuta. A colleague of Raana Abdallah's."

Fatima Kara stiffens at the mention of Abdallah's name. "Who are you? How did you know where to contact me?"

"I was the Minister for Science in Eastern Semitia. I'm the one who set up the Spectrum; I have all the databases for your devices, so I know which one you carry. And I'm the reason everything went wrong in Sheba City."

Fatima Kara remembers Raana Abdallah talking about this man and his SmartSoul computer. "Where is the Deputy Foreign Minister? Where are you calling me from?"

"She's still in jail, as far as my information goes. I had to flee; I can't tell you where I am right now. But I wanted you to know that it wasn't Raana Abdallah's fault. She was sincere in her efforts to help you. If anything, it was my fault for what SmartSoul told us to do."

"We very nearly got slaughtered here, thanks to all of you. Where were the drones you promised us?"

Zayn Battuta hangs his head. "I'm very sorry. It was out of my hands. Everything happened too fast. It was already happening when Katy was here with us. Is she all right?"

"She survived. We very nearly didn't. No thanks to you."

"Please forgive me. I'll do everything I can to help you succeed in Dhofar, if you want my help."

"We'll see," says Fatima Kara, taking in a long breath and letting it out slowly. "What are they going to do to her? To Raana?"

"I don't know. I don't think they'll kill her. That's not how the General works. But she'll be in that cell for a very long time, if I know him well. I was thinking: We could work together, to get her out of there. It would take some time, but . . . we can't just let her rot there."

There's a part of her that wants nothing more to do with the Semitians, especially since there's been no word of any Semitian advance into Green City. The Leaders in Green City have been watching the Hamiyat takeover of Dhofar, but things are quiet for now. There's been no wholesale slaughter of the women's forces, no pouring of troops from Green City into the south. Everyone's eyes are on Sheba City and what the Hamiyat are going to do next, Fatima Kara realizes.

"I'll think about it," she says, and then she shuts off the call. She's had enough of Semitian game-playing. She'll think about Raana Abdallah and the General later. Right now, she has an entire province waiting for her to become the leader they need.

From her room in the Sheba City hospital, where she lies on her back with her leg in traction, Marzi looks out the window at the newly blue sky. She broke her leg in her fall from the wind tower, but a broken leg will heal; a broken heart takes much longer.

They don't talk about Laleh; she's a presence with them in the room, sitting in a chair in the corner, surveying them with her glittering eyes and dangerous half smile.

This khareef was the last monsoon Laleh ever saw; in their minds she'll forever stay twenty-one years old, young, fiery, flawed. Katy and Marzi have decided that when they get back to the mountain, they'll take an offering to the Warrior Queen's shrine, in place of Laleh's ashes. The Warrior Queen, they agree, will understand.

The Sun Battalion is to go back to the mountain; reinforcements from Water Mountain are on the way. Alia and Noor are to return with them. The Ababeel misses her children, her two Husbands, especially Noor's father, whom she knows now she loves the most, and that he loves her back. She misses most of all her kitchen, where there are jars of torshi to be made and a monsoon bounty to be gathered.

Fatima Kara has told Alia that there is a position for her at the head of the village committee, if she wants it. She makes this announcement in front of the Dawn Batallion, gathered at the North Square, the scene of their decisive victory. The women are lined up in rows, wearing their uniforms. Instead of their guns, though, they hold roses in their hands, given to them by the children of the Square.

"What do you say, Alia?" asks Fatima Kara. "You've been very courageous." Kara is looking much better now; with the strain and tension of the last few weeks easing up, she's almost back to her vital, authoritative self. Alia, standing in front of Fatima Kara with Noor at her side, blushes, but manages to return Fatima Kara's gaze. The fierce warrior who emerged to take down the Zaalim has given way again to her normal, self-effacing demeanor, but she no longer looks like a woman who sees danger at every turn. Noor tugs at her hand. "Say yes, Mama. Say yes."

"Yes," says Alia. She smiles at last, a brilliant, sunlit smile.

And the Hamiyat cheer for her again, tossing their roses up into the air.

Katy fills Marzi in on the news at the hospital after the ceremony at the North Square. In a few days, Grace is to return to the mountain, where she'll wait for Lateefa to finish her tour in Sheba City. Mariya is still trying to decide if she wants to stay on as part of the Hamiyat, or take her chances in Sheba City. Fatima Kara has promoted Katy Azadeh to the rank of lieutenant in the Dawn Batallion. Marzi, too, has been offered the chance to become a Ghaziyah. And Laleh has been given a posthumous award for bravery. Katy and Marzi have been given a choice: They can stay in Sheba City and become part of the Commanding Corps, or they can go back to the mountain.

"What about us?" says Katy. "What should we do? Until your leg heals, that is. For now, you're not going anywhere. At least that's what the doctors say. But if you want, I can get you out of here. And we can go back home."

"I'm going to rest," says Marzi. She lays her head back on her pillow and closes her eyes. The painkilling drugs are already taking effect, sending her into a dreamless sleep, but before she passes out, she says, "You should find your girlfriend. Tell her to come with us."

Katy says nothing. Like the night they spent in the North Square when Laleh was killed, she strokes Marzi's arm, whispering gentle, soothing nonsense phrases to her friend. When Marzi is finally asleep, Katy imagines taking Adeefa to Dhofar, to the mountain. She'd like to show her the waterfalls and springs, green everywhere, cool to the eye. They'll climb to the Ruined City, hold hands, and watch the vista of the sea that stretches all the way to Gwadar and beyond, to Kolachi, to Mumbai, to the Andaman Islands, the only place untouched by the ravages of the Final War. To infinity or heaven, whichever comes first.

# EPILOGUE

## The White Thread

In the public square of a small town in Dhofar, three days' drive away from Green City, there are no more black veils hanging from the balconies. They've been replaced by posters of young women in uniform, their hair in braids, tied back by flowered headscarves, clipped into ponytails. Some of them wear full camouflage, others are in simple tunics, but they're unmistakably soldiers. The various captions underneath the posters read: *The Brave Women of the Hamiyat*; *The Women Who Laughed at Death*; *The Sacrifice of the Protectors*.

On one of the posters is a picture of Laleh, with her beloved rifle, holding it proudly aloft. The caption on her poster reads, *Beloved Martyr of the Monsoon War*.

Three girls stand in front of the poster, eyes wide, taking in Laleh's military gear, her weapon, and most of all, her wicked, fearless smile. "When I grow up," says one of them, nudging the others, "I want to be like her."

# ACKNOWLEDGMENTS

Thank you to: Jessica Woollard, Joseph Olshan, Lori Milken, Molly Crabapple, Shandana Minhas, Amir Qalbani, Phil Klay, Claire Chambers, Aamer Hussein, Lucy Ellmann, Sam Boyce, Nour Hage, Dania Wright.

*The Monsoon War* was informed by the writings of Shawn Gorman, Dilar Dirik, Gayle Tzehmach Lemmon (*The Daughters of Kobani*), and, most especially, Jenny Nordberg (*The Underground Girls of Kabul*). There are many many more writers and journalists who reported on the women of the YPJ in Iraq and Syria, the women of Afghanistan, the women of the FARC in Colombia, to whom I owe a debt of gratitude.

I have even more gratitude for the many women—politicians and leaders, activists, lawyers, journalists, healthcare workers, NGO workers, and ordinary women—in Syria, Afghanistan, Iran, Iraq, Yemen, Palestine, Pakistan, Saudi Arabia, and elsewhere who are still fighting for their freedom.

# ABOUT THE AUTHOR

BINA SHAH is a writer of English fiction and a journalist who grew up in Charlottesville, Virginia, and Karachi, Pakistan, and now lives in Karachi, Pakistan. She is the author of five novels and two collections of short stories, including *Slum Child*, which was a bestseller in Italy. She was a regular contributor to the *International New York Times* from 2015–2018, and she is a provocative and bold commentator for the international press on Pakistan's society, culture, and women's rights. Her most recent novel, *Before She Sleeps*, originally published by Delphinium in 2018, was published in Germany, Turkey, and India. She is a graduate of Wellesley College and the Harvard Graduate School of Education, and an alum of the International Writers Program at the University of Iowa. In 2021, she was awarded the rank of Chevalier in the Order of Arts and Letters by the French government.

*By the same author*

A THIN BODY OF WORK
SUNFLOWERS
LET IT BE A DANCE
SPEAKING POEMS
HIS & HERS
THE VOICE OF THE HIVE

stark naked

stark
naked
in '69 and '79

ric masten

SUNFLOWER INK
Palo Colorado Canyon
Carmel, Calif. 93923

(hardcover) 9 8 7 6 5 4 3 2 1
(paperback) 9 8 7 6 5 4 3 2 1



Library of Congress Catalogue Card No. 80-51980

ISBN 931104-04-1

*for my father*
RICHARD L. MASTEN
*"I Love You"*

## ACKNOWLEDGMENTS

Many of the poems **in '69** first appeared in A THIN BODY OF WORK (1970) published by the Unitarian Universalist Association and then in a revised edition entitled WHO'S WAVIN (1975) re-issued by Sunflower Ink. The poems *On This Bus* and *Looking Out/Looking In* appeared in the textbook LOOKING OUT/LOOKING IN by Adler and Towne (Holt, Rinehart and Winston). *Who's Wavin'* was in FRIENDS by Jerry Gillies (Coward, McCann & Geoghegan, Inc.), *Demian's Mirror* in CENTERING A LOPSIDED EGG by Ed Rintye (Allyn and Bacon, Inc.), The song *What Am I Doing Here?* first appeared in SURVIVAL SONGBOOK (The Sierra Club). *The Walking Voice, The Dirty Word Song, Peace Parade* and *A Hundred Million Miles* all appeared in the songbook MIRRORS (UUA, Boston).

**In '79** the poems *Nude in 1954, The Deserted Rooster* and *A Poet's Lament* first appeared in the journal SEPARATE DOORS and *Fly* in FRESH TRACKS. *The Chef* appeared first in POETS & OTHER LOVES. *The Friends* appeared under the title *Wailing Wall* in SUNFLOWERS (Palo Colorado Press).

The book was produced by NICHOLS & DIMES, 1025 West 15th Street, Odessa, Texas. 79763. It was printed by Cromwells, Inc. Enid, Oklahoma. 73701

The music notation was done by Peter Evans.

The photographs *Nude in 1954, Surf and Headlands* and *Coast Near Bixby Creek* were taken by Cole Weston. *The Chambered Nautilus* by Edward Weston, and *The Friends* by Kim Weston

The songs are all published by MASTENSVILLE MUSIC PUBLISHING, licensed through Broadcast Music, Inc.

Cover painting by Donna Stoner.

# Contents

## the SONGS

*(Sheet Music)*

# Preface

## RIC MASTEN AND "THE HIDDEN HUMAN IMAGE"

Maurice Friedman

My friend, Ric Masten, calls himself "a professional authentic person." At first that label put me off. What has being authentic got to do with being professional or amateur or any other social role? How can one sell authenticity? Whatever else the word "authentic" may mean, it implies something that one is, not something that one can put on or take off for professional purposes. But then I reflected that it is perhaps this very designation that gives us an approach to Ric Masten's significance for us — a significance which has impelled me to write this preface to STARK NAKED, his book of poems from 1969 and 1979. Recently, Ric and Billie Barbara were my guests for a couple of days at my home in Solana Beach. Two days later in the same living room in which we had talked, I watched them on television. I found them absolutely identical on TV, as in the privacy of my home, as I had found Ric the same person when he spoke to my class, as when he spoke with me at a weekend conference for three hundred Lutheran pastors.

Ric Masten is not a "poet" in the detached sense of someone who writes poems for publication, poems which stand fully independent of him as a person. Nor is he really a wandering troubador, much as he may resemble that. He perhaps comes nearest to resembling my one-time father-in-law, Vachel Lindsay, an American poet of the early decades of this century who, like Ric, went from place to place reading and singing his poems and accompanying himself on the guitar. When I say that Ric is not a "poet," I do not mean that there is no value in reading his poems without his being present. What I mean, rather, is that he is a *speaking* poet and that once you have heard him speak his poems or sing them, you can never again read one of them without hearing his voice in them.

All reading of poetry, even when the poet is not present and one has never heard him or her, even on recordings, is a "frozen speaking," a semi-articulation of words and sounds which are meant to be *heard* and not just *seen*. But there are some poets who are meant to be heard, literally heard, much more than others. Even this does not capture Ric Masten's uniqueness. What makes him unique is that it takes not just his voice, but his person, his presence, to give his poems the fullness they require. He authenticates his poems with his own existence, and this is what is communicated to all the many people around the country who have the good fortune to hear him read and sing his poetry. This is not just a question of being "sincere." It is a matter of a deep human concern which reaches beyond the sphere of poetry and aesthetics to the quality of life in our day. Ric Masten stands for something, for a quality of life that is lost and found and lost again. He helps to manifest in our time the hidden, and all too often obscured and eclipsed, image of the human.

I asked Ric what unites the poems of 1969 and the poems of 1979 that he has grouped together in STARK NAKED. He answered, "Myself." At first this answer did not satisfy me since what prompted my question was the feeling, which Ric himself shares, of the enormous changes in our outlook since the poems of 1969 and the concerns about blacks, women's liberation, hippies, and rebellion which they express. But again, I reflected that it is, indeed, Ric that unites them — not just in the sense of happening to be the author of both sets of poems, but of holding the tension in his person and in his living of those two contrasting periods. This led me to think about myself, my own relationship to these two periods, and of the fact that it was in 1974, exactly half-way between the two groups of poems, that I published my book *THE HIDDEN HUMAN IMAGE.**

Many of the concerns that I express in that book — social welfare and social change, new politics, civil disobedience, non-violence, integration, women's liberation, anxiety, existentialism, encounter groups, radical education — seemed quickly to be "dated" as the decade of rebellion and social causes fell away into a new decade of conformity and social apathy. But I, too, must hold the tension in my being of these two eras. In 1968 I entitled my Charles W. Gilkey lecture at the University of Chicago, "The Modern Promethean: A Dialogue with Today's Youth." In it, I remarked that as one who had walked the lonely path of being a conscientious objector during the second world war, it was gratifying to see so many young people who had joined with me in their opposition to the war in Vietnam. I added that I was also ready to stand alone again, if necessary, if this period, too, should pass. Twelve years later I would not say that I stand alone. But the vast ranks of youth who once shared my social witness have shrunk once again to a small and not too well heard minority in a world moving steadily in directions that seem ever more frightening.

These concerns have not diminished because the human image has come out of its eclipse but because the eclipse has deepened. For this reason, it is important that someone like Ric Masten still goes up and down the country holding the tension in his being and in his poetry of 1969 and 1979. It is important that STARK NAKED be read by those who need to discover that we too are "stark naked" underneath our clothes. As in the fairy tale "The Emperor's New Clothes," if an honest child or poet should look at us, he will see that we have no clothes on at all! It is for this reason that I want to point out the connections between Ric Masten and THE

---

*New York: Delacorte Press and Delta Books (paperback).

HIDDEN HUMAN IMAGE — a book in which I applied to a wide spectrum of human concerns the conclusions of my first two books on the human image —PROBLEMATIC REBEL and TO DENY OUR NOTHINGNESS.*

The human image, as I use the term, is not only an image of what man *is*, but also an image of authentic personal existence that helps him discover, in each age anew, what he may and can become, an image that helps him rediscover his humanity."Image", in this context, means not a static picture but a meaningful, personal direction, a response from within to what one meets in each new situation, standing one's ground and meeting the world with the attitude that is rooted in this ground. The human image embodies a way of responding. Because it is faithful response and not objective content that is central to the human image, each individual stands in a unique personal relation to his image of man even when it happens to be shared by a society as a whole. One becomes oneself in dialogue with other selves and in response to one's image, one's images of the human. Yet the more genuine the dialogue, the more unique the relationship, and the more truly is the one who is becoming, becoming himself. The fruit of such response is not that bolstering of the ego that comes from comparing oneself favorably with another or modeling oneself on an ideal, but the confirmation of one's unique personal existence, of the ground on which one stands.

The human image does not mean some fully formed, conscious model of what one should become — certainly not anything simply imposed on us by the culture, or any mere conformity with society through identification with its goals. The paradox of the human image is that it is at once unique and universal, but universal only through the unique.

---

*Maurice Friedman, PROBLEMATIC REBEL: *Melville, Dostoievsky, Kafka, Camus,* 2nd rev., enlarged & radically reorganized ed. (Chicago: The University of Chicago Press and Phoenix Books [paperback], 1970); Maurice Friedman, TO DENY OUR NOTHINGNESS *Contemporary Images of Man,* 3rd ed. with a new Appendix (Chicago: The University of Chicago Press Phoenix Books [paperback], 1976).

For each one of us, the human image is made up of many images and half-formed images, and it is itself constantly changing and evolving. In contrast to any static ideal whatsoever, it always has to do only with the unique response to the concrete moment, a response which cannot be foreseen and cannot be repeated, objectified, or imitated.

The hidden ground of the human image needs to be made manifest even while remaining hidden. The depth of the human, like the original meaning of person, or *persona* —the mask — finds its true meaning and wholeness in at once being revealed and concealed. Our basic attitudes may be totally masked; they can never be totally laid bare; but they *may* express themselves without losing their depth — in our response to the situations that evoke us, in our dialogue with one another. The image of the human can never be a conscious end nor can it be a means to an end. It enters into our deepest attitudes and emerges in our responses to new persons and new situations. Our care and our love are not for the human image but for men and women, for the creatures with whom we live and in relationship to whom we find such genuine humanity and personal uniqueness as are open to us.

"The nineteenth century was the century of the death of God," Erich Fromm once remarked, "the twentieth that of the death of man." In our day, it is the human and not the divine that has become questionable and problematic. This is the second, truly terrible sense in which we must speak of the "hidden human image." Auschwitz, Hiroshima, Vietnam, the assassination of Gandhi, of John F. Kennedy, of Martin Luther King — these have meant in our age the destruction of existential trust and with it of the human image. In our day, as never before in human history, the human image has been injured to the point of eclipse, of obliteration, of possible total destruction.

In the eighteenth century, Thomas Jefferson could confidently declare: "We hold these truths to be self-evident, that all men are created equal." Today it is not self-evident to anyone that all men are created equal because the *inequal-*

*ity* of men has been made a fact of history, and the existence of that fact makes it all too probable that other such "facts" will occur. It is in the teeth of that, if at all, that we must affirm the equality of men — in the teeth of the monstrous consequence with which the Nazis declared some races inferior to others, exterminating six million Jews and a million Gypsies and, by less direct methods, four million Russian prisoners of war, in the teeth of the atomic bomb being dropped by the United States not on Germany but on Japan, in the teeth of men's readiness to turn some human beings into cakes of soap and condemn others to a horrible, fast or slow, death by radiation.

Is the hidden human image in our day so "hidden" that it can no longer be revealed? The basic crisis in modern history is that of existential mistrust — the crisis that comes when man no longer knows what it means to be human and becomes aware that he does not know this. Can we live without that existential trust that would enable us to reaffirm the human, to reaffirm the meaning of words, the meaning of actions? The human image cannot, by its very nature, emerge from its hiddenness. Yet that eclipse which obscures and obstructs its double movement of concealing and revealing can in some measure be overcome — despite and even because of what makes it so difficult to witness for the human in our time. Through our faithful dialogue in and with the crisis, we may discover a way of remaining true to the human image in the midst of its hiddenness so that in the darkness itself, the features of a truly human face can be dimly discerned. A person who in our time is contending with the problematic of modern man and helping to shape it into a way forward is Ric Masten. He is one of those who has taken upon himself the task of molding the resistant clay of contradiction and absurdity into a figure of genuine humanity. For this reason, in STARK NAKED I am joining my voice to his.

MAURICE FRIEDMAN is a Professor of Religious Studies, Philosophy and Comparative Literature at San Diego State University and is also on the faculties of International College, the University for Humanistic Studies, and the Fielding Institute.

# Author's Note

*I do not speak like my poems. They are a bit affected like mother's telephone voice. I, too, prefer to meet the world as someone else. . . . .nor do I behave in public as I do alone with a mirror, leaning over the sink, close to that other face, waiting for it to initiate a wink or give some small sign that didn't begin with me.*

*The upstairs TV, the radio in the kitchen, might as well be off. No one is here.*

*In the final year of his life, there was only one entry in my father's journal, dated July 24, 1940. "Tinker Bell is dead." . . . .and to think the man drove me back and forth to school daily, and I never knew him. . . . .nor do my children know me.*

*But here now, if I get too personal, you would never recognize yourself.*

*Much of what was good enough ten years ago seems awkward and embarrassing when reexamined in the cold light of today. I can't tell you how many times I winced over these songs and poems, appalled, asking myself:*

*"Could I have written this?"*

*I'm aware that the past belongs to the present, that yesterday is mine to prune and reshape, but I also know that a revised yesterday does not represent yesterday at all. So, red-faced and covering my nudity with fluttering hands, I resist the temptation to dicker with this material and concentrate on those few lines good enough to have me asking myself:*

*"Could I have written this?"*

*Here it is then, the way it was — 1969*

# ON THIS BUS

my god
it just occurred to me
underneath
our clothes
everyone on this bus
is stark naked

## THE WALKING VOICE

*(Song poem. Music on page 75)*

There's a walking voice that's talking,
Putting pictures into our head.
If you're hung on the words,
In the nouns and the verbs,
Then you've never heard what it said.

a pearl
i've found a pearl
the plumber cried

and he held it in his leather hand
and rubbed it on his soul
and tucked it safely away
in the deep pocket of his bib overalls
and he could whistle softly
working in the sewer all that day

it was a white marble
a chinese checker
but i couldn't tell him
so i told my mother instead
my mother
who rules the world from an oyster bed

And the walking voice keeps talking,
Putting pictures into our head.
If you're hung on the words,
In the nouns and the verbs,
Then you never heard what it said.

closets used to frighten me
standing up against the wall like undertakers
i feared them most of all in evening twilight
or just before the dawn

my father once came with a candle
his dancing light
chasing off the shadows

see
he said
there's nothing to fear
there's nothing in here gonna get ya
and carry you away

but papa
that was just why i was afraid.

And the walking voice keeps talking,
Putting pictures into our head.
If you're hung on the words,
In the nouns and the verbs,
Then you never heard what it said.

it seemed a very thin line of friends
who climbed the hill that day
to stand in her immaculate garden
holding tight to each other

a celebrated poet was to come
and say some words
but he had other things to do
and now i see that lovely as his poems are
they're not very big

because it was a closing
a time to come and take a flower home
and remember one
bright pebble that skipped across the pond
sending circles out
till tears shine in the eyes
of strangers

And the walking voice keeps talking,
Putting pictures into our head.
If you're hung on the words,
In the nouns and the verbs,
Then you never heard what it said.

isabella
he says it isn't flat

and i do want to believe him
but how does a rube from kansas
know when he has met a sailor?

i mean
all he knows for sure is corn
and this flatlander won't believe in god
until he sees him
and after all what is god
compared to the sea?

we take a sailor at his word
that's what we do

and then one evening
he leads us through the trees and says
look!
and there it is
the whole fucking* upside down sky

wow!

And the walking voice keeps talking,
Putting pictures into our head.
If you're hung on the words,
In the nouns and the verbs
Then you never heard
That it said:

*shining.

## THE DIRTY WORD SONG

*(Childrens song. Music on page 75)*

It's only fair to warn ya 'bout the next song you hear,
It gets a little nasty and it could offend your ear.
You're gonna find the language a trifle strong
'Cause I'm about to sing ya my dirty word song.
Dirty words, dirty words, I'm gonna say a few
Real dirty words like ............ doggy pooh!

Ya give a boy a pencil and put him in the hall,
Turn your back and dirty words appear on every wall.
But force him to talk naughty for an hour each day
And you'll take all the fun of the dirty words away
Dirty words, dirty words, boys talk naughty
They say dirty words like ............... potty!

When your second grader starts sayin' dirty stuff,
Swearin' like a trooper, well it's time to call her bluff.
She likes to think she's bein' real obscene
And she don't even know what the dirty words mean.
Dirty words, dirty words, she swears like a trooper
Saying real dirty words like ............. pooper!

Wouldn't it be awful if people didn't swear,
And when ya bang your finger ya jes' give a silent prayer
If suddenly the dirty words all were clean
Would the poetry improve in the men's latrine?
Dirty words, dirty words, be glad we got 'em
Real dirty words like ............... bottom!

I wonder what would happen if no one were profane,
If no one could remember a single dirty name.
I wonder if they'd scribble on the bathroom door
Filthy dirty things like hate and war.
Dirty words, dirty words, there's no excuse for
Filthy dirty things like hate and war.

## THIS IS A NIGHT

this is a night of little nagging things
that keep me half awake
a night where blankets creep
and a sheet that is torn
just a little bit
keeps tearing
every time i roll over

this is a night full of tiny scamperings
in the wall
with great hunks of silence on either side
to listen through

a night when in the dark
a moth danced on my pillow touching my cheek
and now
i don't know where he is
except for the feeling
of something crawling on my body

this is a night of small nuisances
in which i teeter on the ragged edge of sleep
dying of exhaustion
not quite bothered enough to get up
and do something about it
until the whole roof caves in

wake up america

# PEACE PARADE

*(Song poem. Music on page 77)*

I ain't afraid to step in your bitter streets
And walk away from war.
I ain't afraid tho the boulevard's full of heat
And hate — an open sore.
I ain't afraid, I ain't afraid
Ain't afraid of the hate I see
But when I see all the hate in me
I'm afraid.

I ain't afraid to face the red-neck wrath
And meet their savage need.
I won't run, let em come an' block the path
I ain't afraid to bleed.
I ain't afraid, I ain't afraid
Ain't afraid and that's a fact
But when I find I wanta hit em back
I'm afraid.

I ain't afraid of your hard mean-eyed fuzz
With his hand carved billy-stick.
Ain't afraid when the bull-horns start to buzz
"Peaceniks, now don't cha try no tricks!"
I ain't afraid, I ain't afraid,
Ain't afraid of none of this
But when I feel my hand become a fist
I'm afraid.

I ain't afraid to march to a public park
With peace symbols over my head.
And join with a few to protest the dark,
Call me yella, call me red.
I ain't afraid, I ain't afraid
Ain't afraid of the hate in you
But when I find that I can hate too
I AM AFRAID.

## THE CASTE SYSTEM

at the wheel
of this battered old 1953 GMC
obtained from a holyman for a dollar
painted orange
a shade obscene
and decorated by my own hand
and foolishness

rich is what i feel
and good
to come and go
in such style and splendor
sitting there behind wrinkled fenders
and a quarter mile of dented hood
smiling out
through spiderwebs of fractured glass

hey
this is my idea
of how to get around in class
but because i've noticed
that only the well-off wave
when they see me pass
i find that i am guilty
of the sin of pride
and must remind myself
when those less fortunate than i
go winding by
in a brand new super deluxe XK whatever it was
that

    like it or not
    unfair as it may seem
    the poor
    will always be among us

## A ROADSIDE WOODSTOCK

stop here
i'd like to sing for you now
yes — i'd like to share my visions with you now

> i pulled off onto the shoulder of the road
> and watched him in the rear-view mirror
> undressing his guitar with thin hands
>
> it began
> out on the horizon
> he drew a line between sky and earth
> i waited listening for the sun
> and when it came
> the sound was a golden band of pigeons
> rising in the dawn
> lifting me to the place
> where every eye is blinded
> and then
> on the other side of this
> he lowered his voice
> until even the afterimage
> was gone

you see
it's really not so bad he called
as i left him standing on the curb
outside the monterey bus station

> i looked in the evening paper for a review
> and could find none
> nor were there any photographs
> and the man in the music store was certain
> that it had not been recorded
>
> so i guess it never happened
> huh?

# PISTACHIO NUTS

i'm embarrassed to think
that i was eleven years old
before some skinny kid
brought santa claus down in flames
right in the middle of the noon recess
how i remained
among the faithful all those years
i'll never know
the playing fields of grammar school
are swarming with doubting thomases
shooting marbles for keeps
anyway
i went home mad as hell
demanding the truth from my mother

i think you're old enough to handle it
she said
and then in one fell swoop
wiped out not only santa
but the easter bunny as well

however twenty nine years later
i'm really kind of glad
some bearded dirty old man
doesn't slide down my chimney
every twenty fifth of december
and eat up forty-nine cents
worth of pistachio nuts

like the evening i'm driving home
after putting in
eight hours on a cement crew
feeling tired and dry and dusty
and sorry for myself
so i stop for a treat
a cold can of beer
to hold between my knees

on the road home
and the aforementioned forty-nine cents
worth of pistachio nuts

well i guess i've been so worried
about the conservative faces
in the pontiacs and cadillacs
with stars and stripes stuck to everything
that i just naturally give a lift
to every long-haired freaky kid i see
and these two were beautiful
in their costumes
on their way to big sur
my kind of people
peace brother
peace brother
i was twice blessed
friar tuck and robin are alive and well
on the highways of america

have a pistachio nut
said the sheriff of nottingham
and the cellophane bag
did make a happy crinkling sound
as it emptied
in my brothers hands

they are right you know
i am not to be trusted
i do grow tired of carrying you twelve miles
and paying forty-nine cents
worth of pistachio nuts for this privilege
so
this is as far as i go
i think you're old enough to handle it
there
ain't
no
santa claus

## A HUNDRED MILLION MILES

*(Song poem. Music on page 78)*

He sat down at my table,
Poured me out a drink of guilt,
Laughed his golden laughter
As he watched the lily wilt.
Said: Baby don't look now
But there's a black man in this chair
And it's a hundred million miles
Across the table that we share.

He sat inside a shadow
Lookin' out through yellow eyes,
An' the crown of thorns I'm wearin'
Becomes a string of lies.
He struck me with his kisses
When I told him that I care.
It was a hundred million miles
Across the table that we shared.

I held my hand out to him,
And God it looked so pale,
But I wanted him to notice
Where the soldiers drove the nails.
An' he filled the room with laughter
Not a drop of blood was there
It was a hundred million miles
Across the table that we shared.

He said: I ain't a cripple,
Jack, I ain't an armless man
And I don't trust no "honky"
With such a bushy-tailed hand.
Man, I bet you'd hug the devil
If he put on kinky hair.
It was a hundred million miles
Across the table that we shared.

I told him I was sorry,
And he burned me with a grin.
Said: It's time to watch the pink snake
Struggle with his skin.
An' I cursed the faceless army
That had come to put us there
With a hundred million miles
Across the table that we shared.

A black bird an' a white bird
An' a hundred million miles.
There's a riddle for a liberal
To wrestle for awhile.
Ya better go back to the cupboard
And pray it isn't bare,
'Cause it's a hundred million miles
Across the table that we share.

# PEELING THE ONION

hey columbus
did you hear how flash
got himself a dashiki
and an afro wig
i could dig it
if he weren't scotch-irish
poor old flash
tried to break the mirror
and cut himself on the glass

put me through a trick tho
cause i never went uptight
when old black joe
burnt himself
putting lye in his hair
trying to be white

the onion is all skins columbus
and i am an onion
and as i keep discovering
and you keep pointing out
i am also a white racist
so what do we do now

well
i don't know about you
but being as how i've got nothing
better to do
i'll just pass the time
peeling the onion
laughing at the tears

hey columbus
do you think that you and i
black and white
will ever learn how to sit down
and really relate to a dwarf

# TAP ROOTS

hunkered down back there in the half light
before the dawn when i couldn't see so good
looking out from under a shelf-like brow
i would watch her
        with the child
        with the life
        SHE had created

now this was before the word
and because i knew not the why of it
nor the how
i was filled with envy and rage
and i hated her
for try as i might
strain as i would
i the male
could create nothing more impressive
        than a turd

wasn't i bigger'n her
and stronger
and so to cover my chagrin and disgrace
i gave her a cuff across the face
took up a spear
and walked out into the morning

be patient with me woman
i'm working on it
but when the tap root
goes down that deep into history
the tree is not easily moved

and now that you do have your sperm bank
and have mastered karate
        have i become irrelevant again?
        or just plain paranoid

# CIRCUS MAXIMUS

reaching for a mile she is
hoping for an inch she was
burning her bra
while the cameras pan the crooked smile
on the face of a nervous man
probably henpecked most of his life
the entire spectacle
making good copy i guess
in the chauvinist press

but aside from the rhetoric
and the upraised fist
the central theme of the feminist
was best expressed in a speech
delivered from a double bed
when after twenty years of marriage
my wife said

> the economics of the ERA
> will allow me
> to stay with you
> not because i have to
> but because
> and only because i want to

and this power play more than any other
has the gladiators huddled
beneath the colosseum floor
clinging to the urinal
in much the same way early christians
clung to their cross

but in the words of one true believer
waiting to be flung
to the lions

> brother
> you must admit
> these are sure exciting times

## TO NUKE
## OR NOT TO

is it not disturbing
to consider
that everything in and about
a nuclear power plant
will be furnished
by the lowest bidder

# WHAT AM I DOIN' HERE?

*(Song poem. Music on page 79)*

When you're takin' that vacation
Out in the countryside,
Don't stay too long there in the wilderness.
'Cause a man seems kinda small
And a mountain awful tall.
It could make ya look inside yourself and ask. . .
        Where did I come from?
        Where am I goin'?
        And what am I doin' here?

When you're drivin' in the country
Keep a-steppin' on the gas.
Hurry, hurry, hurry on your way.
If ya slow down to a walk
Ya might hear the country talk,
Ya might hear the country laugh at you and say . . .
        Where did ya come from?
        Where are ya goin'?
        And what are ya doin' here?

Keep the radio playin',
And turn the volume up.
Keep your transistor plugged into your ear.
If ya listen and you're still
In the silence of the hills
Ya might hear things ya wouldn't want to hear . . .
        Like: where did ya come from?
        Where are ya goin'?
        And what are ya doin' here?

Leave your litter in the forest
And scattered by the road
So we can feel a little more at home.
The telltale signs of man,
His papers and his cans,
We see 'em and we think we're not alone . . .

But where did we come from?
Where are we goin'?
And what are we doin' here?

Are we gonna keep a-runnin'
From the questions that we fear
Until we bring the whole thing crashin' down?
And on the day we disappear
There'll be no one left to hear
The burnin' sky ask the barren ground

Where did they come from?
And where were they goin'?
And what . . .
Were they doin' here?

# FALSE PROPHETS

all this talk of false prophets
must be true
for the creator turns out to be
a clever chemist
who has me making a fool of myself
in restaurants and other public places
feeling the foliage
but then one likes to know
what is and isn't real
and these days
to face a caesar salad in a plastic jungle
does test one's faith

and i must admit
these laboratory specimens do look good
seeming sunshine fresh and meadow born
here is loveliness
guaranteed
to hold up in a greasy smoky world
unchanging
always the same
an eternal garden that must only be dusted
from time to time
beauty that will wipe clean
and never die

so you want to live forever do you?
well
then let us now
freeze the sunset and bore ourselves
to death

# MOON SHOT

so it cost billions — so what
money is meaningless
after you've spent ten bucks

maybe we could have fed a hungry world
hotdogs for a week
but you know i am much more worried
about the twenty pounds of fat
around my girth than starving masses
so don't bother me about the cost
it was worth every penny
that photograph
taken from the moon
of a tiny little blue and white marble
hanging in space

it sounds like i'm about ready
to drop reverse gear in my jeep
i hear that five hundred american boys
died in the jungle last week

equally unimportant
from the point of view of the universe

the real wonder is
that i
an infinitesimal piece of star dust
have come to realize this
                              and choose
                              life

# SCHWEITZER

i have noticed that i have a tendency
to bump into flying insects
when i drive my car
and kill them dead

this has been of no small concern to me
and i would gladly give up driving
except that it is such a distance
from here to there
and also
if i walked the ants
would take an awful pounding

i guess it all comes down
to where we draw the line albert
and even you
spray your operating room

# THE WAR GOES ON

The war goes on and once again nearly a decade later I'm called upon to sing some songs and say some things at yet another peace demonstration in another city park on another ice cream afternoon and this time i hesitate.

Not because I've nothing to say about the pointless slaughter of innocent children, but because the very ring and rhythm of that catch phrase has me in the state of deja vu. The years of rhetoric sticking in my throat, a cracked record caught in the same groove. Somehow I feel as though I've been here a thousand times before, talking to myself and the war goes on.

And I hesitate, not because I think a witness against the war accomplishes nothing but because I grow weary of throwing rocks at schoolboy cartoons of slobbery-teeth monsters whose names, faces and politics change every four years. And whose legions are as frightened of me as I am of them, and yet we wear each other's spittle like a crown and the war goes on.

And I hesitate, not because I grow insensitive to the suffering of others but because I begin to wonder how much the mere adventure and excitement of my being here, making this noise is not just busy work. A kind of throwing dust in the air to screen out the sight and sound of my own loneliness and despair. In the sand of social concern behold the ostrich and the war goes on.

And I hesitate, not because I have become a war lover, fond of my eye teeth, but because I have recently discovered that I also have the seed of Eichmann in my soul, ready and waiting. To deny it, to pretend it isn't there is to give it room to grow. How can I accuse when I know that given the right climate and circumstance I am Eichmann also. I must watch myself carefully and the war goes on.

And I hesitate not because I have given up hope of seeing some new kind of dawn, but because yin comes with yang, dark with light, day with night, death with life. And if opposites help to define each other then the peace sign standing alone is only a half truth.

And so
blinded by the pain
i am tempted to retire
from this battlefield of clarity
to meditate
and contemplate my own sad end

but the war goes on
and on
and on
and i find that i cannot remain
in this gethsemane of mine
so i come to keep the vigil once again

this time though
the motivating impulse
is not very easy to explain
it has something to do with the fact
that a human being bothers to come in
out of a freezing rain

and so i came
and will keep coming
just as long as the war goes on

# SILENCE

it began with idle conversation
the exchanging of different points of view
two chinese brain-washers
using chop sticks
deftly
speaking loudly softly

and then the wind died
and we hung like tattered flags
full of word holes
resting now
in the beauty which was the silence
smiling into space

listening to the thunder which was the silence
wondering
who would speak first

listening to the screaming which was the silence
listening to the laughter
of this brutal thing

listening to eternity

trapped
gathering dust
wrinkling
we
will
sit here
forever

# ON A BANKED TRACK

does it surprise you to learn
that the suicide rate is highest
among psychiatrists?

it shouldn't
everyone knows you can't keep a curious kid
from taking a clock apart
to find out why it has that nervous
tick

trouble is it's hard to know where to stop
and if you're not careful you could wind up
with nothing left
but a box full of little pieces rattling
and the philosophic question
of whether you should see another jeweler
    kill yourself
    or go crazy

sometimes when i'm extra low
i can't help wondering if life wouldn't be
a whole lot easier if i could go back
and really get caught up
in something like roller derby

but then in the end
is it not all just roller derby?
thundering around on a banked track
enjoying the action

what ever we choose we do seem to choose
the kind of attraction that gives us a place
to show off our tricks and fall on our face
pretending it's not
but knowing the ending is fixed

## WHO'S WAVIN'

*(Song poem. Music on page* 80*)*

I ain't wavin' babe, I'm drownin'.
Goin' down in a cold lonely sea.
I ain't wavin' babe, I'm drownin'.
So babe quit wavin' at me.

I ain't laughin' babe, I'm cryin'.
I'm cryin', oh why can't you see?
I ain't foolin' babe, I ain't foolin',
So babe quit foolin' with me.

This ain't singin' babe, it's screamin'.
I'm screamin' that I'm gonna drown.
And you're smiling babe, and you're wavin',
Just like you don't hear a sound.

I ain't wavin' babe, I'm drownin'.
Goin' down right here in front of you.
And you're wavin' babe, you keep wavin',
Hey babe, are you drownin' too?

Oh.

## DEMIAN'S MIRROR

*(Song poem. Music on page* 81*)*

At a corner table, alone and afraid
Holding a book upside down
Like a bird come from nowhere in a dead tree
I'm sitting there looking around.

I spied a stranger gazing at me
Through glasses with gold at the rim
I saw my reflection looking at me
As I sat there looking at him.

Look in the mirror, Demian's Mirror
Consider yourself as I pass.
Look in the mirror, Demian's Mirror
Come see yourself in my glass.

The face it was ageless, a boy in his teens,
And old man a hundred and three.
The face of a woman or was it a man
Whose eyes were fastened on me.

I beckoned the stranger come over to me
Somehow I felt we had met.
I asked: Do I know you? He smiled to himself
Said: My how quick they forget.

Look in the mirror, Demian's Mirror
Consider yourself as I pass.
Look in the mirror, Demian's Mirror
Come see yourself in my glass.

We studied each other in that dim cafe
And I tried to guess at his race.
What does it matter he said with a shrug.
His spectacles flashed in my face.

I asked his religion. Christian, he said,
But I am an atheist too.
Sometimes a Buddhist, sometimes a Jew

But right now I'm looking at you.

> Look in the mirror, my face is a mirror
> Consider yourself as I pass.
> Look in the mirror, my face is a mirror
> Come see yourself in my glass.

He told me his story. He talked of his life
His words made me laugh, made me cry.
It was so funny, it was so sad
His life was exactly like mine.

We sat there together till I fell asleep
And when I awoke he was gone.
And all of the mirrors were smiling at me
And out in the street
it was dawn.

# LOOKING OUT/LOOKING IN

he stripped the dark circles of mystery off
revealed his eyes
and thus he waited
exposed

    and i did sing the song around
    until i found the chorus
    that speaks of windows

    looking out
    means looking in my friend
    and i'm all right now
    i'm fine
    i have seen the beauty that is mine

you can watch the sky for signals
but look to the eyes for signs

*On an outing in 1954 my friend, the photographer Cole Weston, persuaded me to pose nude for a photograph he wanted to take.* Ric On a Stick *I have always called it.*

*I remember now how Cole nearly had me falling out of the tree trying to get my arm and knee at exactly the right angle. He was concerned with the entire composition while I was aware only of myself being uncomfortable, stark naked and out on a limb.*

*I look at the work I produced in 1979 as this same kind of self-conscious posing. Exposing myself, but doing it in order to get a better perspective on a much larger picture.*

NUDE 1954: *Cole Weston*

aside from baby pictures
it was the only time i ever posed nude
so i suppose
because the flesh was mine

i blow the whole thing out of proportion

but every time
i see my pale young body
held in the arms of that splintered tree
i cannot help but draw the parallel

it was all there that day
the threatening sky
hanging
like the blunted blade of a guillotine
the hill
black as the one at golgotha
the tree
electric and waiting

we both saw it
but you were older and owned the camera
and so it was
that i
stripped of everything
climbed into the wooden harness
and made the moment work

and now. . . . . .
centuries later
i'm told that what i did for art
has made my backside
the butt of smutty remarks

that in the city of new york
undesirable women
look and leer
licking their lips
calling me "stud"

that i who have stepped to the thud
of norman mailor's drum
have been framed and hung
in homosexual bathrooms

that i so shy i turned my face
have come to see my body bought and sold
in the marketplace

as
al-
ways
the
real crucifixion
comes
long
after
the
orig-
inal
event

SURF AND HEADLANDS: *Cole Weston*

"Never before
have I seen a sea like that.
Giant waves advancing
like great plumed knights
storming ashore
to rage against the blue-black wall
of the continent!"

fairly dancing
you told the story —

described the scene
with all the eloquence
of richard burton on stage
playing arthur

but then you knew

you'd caught a glimpse
of sweeping glory
knew
that in your magic box
you had a view
of something grand enough
to be
        a dream of kings

and history
did mark your shot at immortality

but i have wondered
in the dim light of your darkroom
working there alone
did you ever ask yourself

        "How many times
        can a man
        pull a sword
        from a stone?"

COAST NEAR BIXBY CREEK: *Cole Weston*

there was a moment
when the farmer had finished with his field
and summer had come to the crest of the santa lucia
like a pride of lions
                    a moment
where in the distance
a bridge
looked like the edge of a concrete spider web
and the sky was pale
having just given the pacific a transfusion

but my attention was on the road
racing a station wagon full of post picnic chaos
north toward carmel

yelling at the kids to quit whining
and keep their hands to themselves

telling a wet dog to stay in the back and lie down
trying desperately not to listen
to the sound of a tired cranky wife
as she said
                    "You don't listen,
                    you never do!"
and as anyone knows
there is only one possible solution
to this impossible situation
home — a hot bath — a stiff drink
and a bed
                    but you
right behind me
at the wheel of a vehicle full of the same
pull over to take a photograph
and only a fool would do this
                                        a fool
or perhaps someone
who cared enough to give the rest of us
a second look
                    at what we'd missed that day

CHAMBERED NAUTILUS: *Edward Weston*

inside
    on the title page of a book
    that included your work
    the contributing photographers were listed
    in the democracy of alphabetical order
    but on the cover
        where it counts
you were lost
    in an argosy that began with your father
        edward's name

    seeing this
    i come up with an image of a sailing ship
    caught in the wind shadow of
        an island

dead in the water
    at other times
    helplessly tacking back and forth
    in the wake of
        a father's fame

    it is difficult enough to be
    an author looking for stories
    in steinbeck country
    a poet searching for something to say
    along a shore jeffers picked over

    but how much more difficult to always be
compared
    with a print of something
    as perfect and complete as
        the chambered nautilus

and now your sons
    behind you
    nails stained with amidol
    sailing those same dangerous waters

blessed and cursed with a family name
    indelible as the mark of cain

THE FRIENDS: *Kim Weston*

*(For Cole)*

i will be your wailing wall man friend
lean on me and rail against the insanity
of life / death

we have lost one of our sons old soldier
hold on tight — hammer your fist — shout your curses
shit!

tell me how it was when last you saw him
your golden boy
wild hair flying — king of his mountain

beat on me — weep on me
old fighter
i will hold you up as you would me

later i will stack these words one upon the other
like stones lifted from my chest
and then fall sobbing against this wall of work

## TERMINAL COOL

in the final stages of this cruel affliction
the diseased are often the last to know
how disfigured their demeanor has become

with me
it was not until friends bégan talking through the door
and wore flu masks
not until i began receiving mail addressed to Rex Reed
promotional material — color brochures pouring in
from leper colonies
not until then
did i bother to consult a mirror and see the result
of an unchecked case of skepticism

> the face
> once eager and receptive
> had lost all expression
> every trace of wonder and delight
> had sloughed off
> constant analysis had narrowed the eyes
> paralysis had folded the arms
> and there
> at the corner of my mouth — a hand
> horribly grafted in place

the ghastly sight shot me with a chill
there was no doubt about it
i was critically ill

infected i suspect
by an english professor i once knew
or by ingesting too many clever book
and movie reviews
but the question is academic
you simply don't care when you are the lump
slumping down in the chair

*(to be concluded)*

## FLY

damned fly!
offspring of waste — buzz off!

away from my face
you aerobatic barnstorming
waldo pepper of refuse
you red baron of filth — split!
this is my show
and there are people here
trying to get into my work
and they can't do it with you
trying to work into my ear!

so quit bugging me
mother of maggots — mountain climber of dumps
and don't you dare put your feet
on my cheek or chin
god only knows
what you've been out there steppin' in

oh i get it
landing on my poem like that
as if it were garbage — i'll bet you're a critic
in your next life — being punished
well i've got news for you
you annoying little muckraker
you may think i'm dying up here
but i can tell you i'm not dead yet

fly
philosophically you and i are experiencing
the root cause of all earthly misunderstandings
all holy wars
the basic unanswerable question

are you in my space
or am i in yours?

fly
tiny snowflake of soot
please go — but know it isn't you that bothers me
it's just that when the program is over
and the curtains close
i want to be remembered as "the poet"
not as the guy with the fly on his nose

i mean
how would you like to be known
by your phylum and species
only
as the fly with a guy on his toes

# THE WASP NEST

it held my attention
like the ash on the end of grandfather's cigar
taking shape slowly the way some poems do
the mind flying to and from it
unable to leave it alone

it hung in the eves
on the northeast corner of the house
a small grey planet
inhabited
industrious
a papier-mâché world parallel to mine
benign
        until the child was stung

        coexistence is no longer possible
hissed the canister
breathing violence
into the cells of this geodesic dome
and from deep within the abbey
a choir of small voices swelled
in a final
angry
        ommmmmmmmmmmmmmmmmmm a sound
that clutched the evening air
like a hand sinking in a pool of silence

next morning i took a broom
and once again
the hindenberg came down
like a cardboard head spilling it's beaded brains
then sweeping up and burning the remains
i had intended to put the incident away

and would have
were it not for that tiny starship
coming in from a distant exploration

returning to the place where earth had·been

and i could do nothing but sit at my window
my god's eye
watching the lone survivor cling to the moorings
        having only himself now
        as proof of something more
hanging on somehow
till the darkness took him

        the wasp
        who knew what it was to be human

# JOB DESCRIPTION

*"Assembly line people are mostly bored. The inventive and artistic, forced to work for someone else are usually frustrated and those lucky enough to be at the top, live with anxiety. Take your pick sucker."* A COCKTAIL LOUNGE PHILOSOPHER

never mind the anxiety
just give me poems built like houses
livable
drafted by a batty architect
who is continually
falling down in the road
like st. paul
coming up with visions
wild blue lines
                    given over
to a grim craftsman
who uses his hammer and saw
tirelessly
until he has something
you can close a door on
and walk away from

and never mind the frustration
when you find you are working
with a dull typewriter
a journeyman
does not blame the tools

if the boards split
if the nails keep bending
you can always take
a twelve-year coffee break

or quit
and return to a lower form
of construction
                    where time counts
                    and wages are paid

and never mind the boredom

# ECONOMIC INDICATORS FOR THE NINETEEN EIGHTIES

part time yard work
inquire after dark

waitress wanted
for interview
call the naked lunch

have you ever applied for work
you didn't want
and would never take
just to find out
if you really had an ace in the hole

operating
out of some knee-jerk
sense of self preservation
showing your stuff
throwing your best sunday punch
into the phone
only to be told
you weren't right for the job

have you ever let yourself
get caught short like this?
winding up
wiped out

well i have

and now
a few words
about the great depression

## STRESS

i have just hung up the telephone
but the bad news will have to wait

right now
i must deal with the lump of tension
that has just been thrust into my body
like a frankfurter into a sliced roll

stuffed with stress
my own intestine
swells like a boiled sausage
till it gets all the mustard and relish
leaving the leavened bread
the staff of life
stuck with a red-hot

as a creative person
i try to be thankful
for the sudden presence
of this annoying intruder
knowing that a gut full of anxiety
can be a useful motivator
and knowing also
a bun all by itself
would never make it at coney island

and certainly
i want to make it
i'd love to be an oscar meyer weiner
singing and dancing
a real hot-dog!

but that doesn't mean
i enjoy being eaten

## THE WINE

the vintners speak lovingly
of the compatible enzyme
in a fine table burgandy
and how it works
with candlelight and crystal
to keep an evening gracious

and
then there are those
two-dollar-a-gallon
straight-from-the-bottle
dago red times
when i'm never sure
who's talking
you or the wine

and
it's not that i minded
sorting through all the junk you dumped
i probably deserved it
but in that last minute
if i hadn't caught your coat
do you think
you really would have jumped?

## THE DESERTED ROOSTER

if this were a documentary
lorne green would narrate
describing in his big male-animal-world way
the migration
as one by one the fledglings flew the coop
followed by the hen
liberated and running off to join the sisters
cloistered in the halls of a community college
singing
        gloria
        gloria
        steinem — till it becomes catholic

so far nothing new
children leaving home
a woman's victory over the empty nest syndrome
themes done to death

but the deserted rooster is a subject
that has not yet been addressed
we know him
only as that laughable old strutter
preening and parading up and down
involved in his sexual prowess
and the sound of his own voice
up
at an ungodly hour to start the day
it was all part of the job

        and there wasn't a problem
        when there wasn't a choice

but picture him now
after the exodus
all alone
scratching around in his abandoned domain
looking for a good reason to get up tomorrow

and crow

if this were a documentary
it would end
focused on a stereotype weather vane
rusted on the turning point

        in a changing wind

# COMING HOME

the continuing story of a traveling salesman
continues
        this time
        we find him running
        out of an airport
        giftshop
        with a cap pistol
        and a doll
        a surprise for the kids
        but like oxfords
        hastily bought
                a size too small
(the kids i remembered
were not kids at all)

"i think i've been gone longer than i thought"
        cried
        old saint nick
        as ever ho-ho-hoing
        as ever coming and going
        giving the children puppies for christmas
        never there when the dog died

but it's okay dad
it's all right
they say
        there is no such thing
        as a bad parent
they say
        even people who batter their offspring
        are doing the best
        they know how to do

and you can tell that
to the boxes that were never opened

you can tell that to the shoes that pinch

# WITH A FRIEND DYING OF CANCER

forty-nine and waiting
and what for
the bottom line

back in act one — scene one
it was obvious
we were waiting to see what would happen
but deeper into the drama
we recognize the antagonist
and realize there will be no "surprise" ending
which would seem to make it a farce

so i'll go with that awhile
and tell about a comic
who built a career around a rickety ladder
and he was funny enough
to make us smile and forget

being silly is a noble occupation
so i fashioned some tom foolery of my own
i really didn't know what i was doing
but i loved watching you go for it
coming by
gawking like a tourist
slowing down for a better view
then — WHAM!
i'd be there with a slapstick
clowning around in the death scene
doing pratfalls
waiting for the laughs
that's it!
that's what we're all waiting for
the end is always there
you can count on it
but the laughs
are few and far between

## A MISNOMER

burn-out
you've seen the results
in the shop on the shelf
row after row of grey empty faces
with nothing happening in the glassy eyes
except
a little surface reflection

burn-out
you know the symptoms. . .
a history of dependable service
then suddenly for no reason things go dark
and you're a dead piece of furniture
waiting
to be removed from the living room

burn-out
the psychological repairman said
and shrugged and shook his head
having checked everything
except the cord
which of course
                    was disconnected

in a word unplugged

and to think
i nearly went to the dump myself
because someone less than a poet
trying to describe a condition
came up with a misleading term
clearly
a case of burn-out demands a second opinion
and this is mine
                    find an outlet
                    and if the cord doesn't reach
                    move the set

# FOR THOSE WHO TALK TOO MUCH

(Once Again Gary Cooper
Breaks the Vow of Silence)

if you feel
that you've just been run down
by a thundering herd
that your side of the conversation
has been butted
            battered
            trampled and gored

if you feel
you've been left in the dust
with your thoughts scattered
and your participles
            dangling

            take it
            as a compliment

my mouth
gets away from me like this
only
in the company of folks
i truly care about
with anyone else it's:
            yep
            and nope

so partner
if you're still with me
and not too sore
let's have a look at
            that prize bull of yours

and after this
perhaps a spell of peace and quiet
can settle between us

# HARD LOVE

to understand this you must first understand
that marvin doesn't come to visit
his shoes bring him
so when he says

you will explain won't you
the way you always do
about the revelation
and how i'm not to blame
for the stations of the cross

i could have said something poetic
like: pilate washed his hands 2000 years ago
but instead
i just said: "no"

well — if not you then who
will tell them
to enjoy the scrambled eggs
and ignore what goes on
in the kitchen

i could have said
julia child peels her own potatoes
but instead
i just said: "you"

but without
your good housekeeping seal
they might not understand
about a man who keeps
a skylark in his mouth

i could have said
a lot of things
but instead i just said nothing
and nothing again
when he pretended to be

a tunafish sandwich reciting poetry

hell — he said to the silence
there isn't enough blood
in this conversation
to keep me alive till dinner

and bored with my sanity
he went outside
to see where his car would take him
and it took him back to bedlam
i heard later

but this time
without
my assistance
permission
or help

# THE PARADOX AS HANDLED BY A PHILOSOPHER FROM A SAFE DISTANCE WITH MECHANICAL HANDS

there are those who say
some cases of schizophrenia
may be nothing more than a chemical disorder
and given a day
on something like a dialysis machine
what had appeared to be the cauterized remains
of a dead animal
can now be seen as leg of lamb

at long last
napoleon can take off that silly hat
and go to work in a savings and loan
van gogh can clerk in a shoe store
but what will happen to the poetry
when we are disconnected
from the dream that drives us mad?

some siamese twins are attached in such a way
they can't be separated
and so along with our compulsive drive
toward mental health
let's not forget
that jesus
                    managed somehow
knowing he was lord
and at the same time not believing it
an honest to god
flesh and blood
bread and wine
gemini

## A POET'S LAMENT

the wine i offer up
for communion
was drawn from my own blue vein
        i am that kind of martyr

and when i cough on lillies
the speck of blood is precious
as the hurt of which a child complains
        i am that sorry for myself

at midnight my typewriter
makes the sound
of a blindman's cane
        i am that much in the dark

i speak my poems
with a hand at my brow like olivier
playing the melancholy dane
        i am that despairing

god grant me a storm
that i may once again
walk by your window in the rain
        being that pitiful

you must admit
i cut a tragic figure
but can i say i suffer
        when i so enjoy the pain

# OLD MEN

the one from colorado
stares from faded denim eyes
and lets the sound of a taxi
lift
and carry him back
to a mountain
larger than life

the one from missouri
keeps a seed in his pocket
after the rain
his fingers
crawl on the pavement
earthworms
searching for cracks

i
am a californian
and when it is my turn
i will take off my coat
sit in the sun
and dream
of the foothills
the sleeping lions

# THE HANDYMAN

it's autumn
i feel it in my bones
and other places

it's autumn
i can no longer afford
to own a cricket lighter
having thrown too much away
already

it's autumn
time to maintain
a not-very-
exciting prospect
for those who remain
in a springtime/summertime
frame of mind
but there is more to maintenance
than a drop of oil
        a dab of glue
a thing gathers value
and interest
as you rub off the new
so go to work
on what you've got

it's autumn
and according to my wife
an old chest
becomes a priceless antique
only
if it gets a good going over
at least twice a week

# THE CHEF

*Slice and boil*

the one that got away
the one that would play the lead
in THE SQUASH THAT ATE CHICAGO
the monster
that always has the crowd wild eyed
and screaming

My god! Is that really

*A zucchini.*
*Strain off the water*
*Adding one bouillion cube (any kind)*
*and two tablespoons of olive oil*
*to every quart of cooked squash*
*Puree and serve hot and steaming*
*with a slug of cold sour cream*
*dumped into the center of each portion.*
*Top with a sprinkle of dill seed,*
*salt and season to taste.*

and now let us praise the chef
the only artist whose creative work
must speak to every sense

the literary labors of shakespeare are immense
feeding and filling the soul
but a steady diet of language
leaves the stomach growling

and although it would garnish your life
and delight your eye
a garden salad by picasso
would be as tasty as old canvas and varnish

and whatever the sculpture rodin
might put out on the table
would be a masterpiece for sure
but nothing you could get your teeth into

no doubt
the sound of a string quartet is more uplifting
than the sizzle of bacon in a pan
but by intermission a sweaty musician
doesn't smell as good

the fine art of cookery demands the heart
hand and eye of a complete renaissance man

and as always
muttering into her napkin counterpoint to this
my wife
    why is it when a woman cooks a meal
    it's just a meal
    but when a man cooks a meal
    it's such a big big deal

# THE PROPER PERSPECTIVE

i am moved
by the golden mask of tutankhamun
but in the opposite direction

where i imagine
some buck rogers anthropologist
breaking through a wall

and like the sun
striking the windshield of a car
we catch his eye for an instant

the flash that was america

a footnote
to a footnote

# THE DAY A GREAT NATION BECAME PEDESTRIAN

wouldn't you like to have been there?
the night
the sheik in his tiny sheikdom
came bolt upright in bed
and said:
　　　　fatima!
　　　　it just came to me
　　　　we have america over the barrel

and wouldn't you like to have been there?
the following day
when the gulf islands went high and dry
and grass came up on the freeway
when the highway patrol
had nothing to do but pick its nose
and winnebagos were born
that would never get out of iowa

the day
robbers ruled the intersections
and motorists grew ill at ease
without easy access to the facilities
the day christians lost their christian veneer
and the sign of the times said: the line ends here.

and wouldn't you like to have been there?
for only on days difficult as these
can the man in the street emerge triumphant
and come trooping away from the pumps
a full jerry can at his side
his fist in the air — delirious — whooping
with glee:
　　　　alice!
　　　　get in the car
　　　　we're going for a ride.
and if not here
then where would you like to be?

# NOT EXACTLY A COMMAND PERFORMANCE

have you ever sat back
and looked at the life you were living
and saw that it was playing
like a really bad B movie?

appalled and taken back
by the inane lines you were saying
and the unrestrained way you were weeping
and waving your arms about
over acting

but what really burns
is the knowledge
that someone of your reputed good taste
would sit through such silly hogwash
unable to leave till you learn
how the damn thing comes out

## TERMINAL COOL

*(Continued from page 45)*

recently
i have experienced the miracle of remission

at a sophisticated new york cocktail party
suddenly and for no reason the feeling came back
and i heard myself blurting out
publicly
    that i secretly enjoyed THE SOUND OF MUSIC
    and watch LITTLE HOUSE ON THE PRAIRIE

    that i have been moved to tears
    by a McDonalds ad

    even
    that i can think of at least one
    poem by Rod McKuen
    that's not bad

the next time Peter Pan throws pixie dust
asking the audience to stand
and applaud Tinker Bell back to life
the next time
if my luck holds
i'll be able to do it

the
Songs

# THE WALKING VOICE

*(Poem read against chord changes.)*

# THE DIRTY WORD SONG

2. Ya give a boy a pencil and put him in the hall,
Turn your back and dirty words appear on every wall.
But force him to talk naughty for an hour each day
And you'll take all the fun of the dirty words away
Dirty words, dirty words, boys talk naughty
They say dirty words like.................potty!

3. When your second grader starts sayin' dirty stuff,
Swearin' like a trooper, well it's time to call her bluff.
She likes to think she's bein' real obscene
And she don't even know what the dirty words mean.
Dirty words, dirty words, she swears like a trooper
Saying real dirty words like ........... pooper!

4. Wouldn't it be awful if people didn't swear,
And when ya bang your finger ya jes' give a silent prayer.
If suddenly the dirty words all were clean
Would the poetry improve in the men's latrine?
Dirty words, dirty words, be glad we got 'em
Real dirty words like................bottom!

# PEACE PARADE

# A HUNDRED MILLION MILES

C G7

1. He sat down at my tab-le, poured me out a drink a guilt,
2. sat in-side a shad - ow look - in' out through yel-low eyes, and the
3. held my hand out to him and God it looked so pale. But I
4. said: I ain't a crip - ple, I ain't an arm—less man. And

F C

laughed his gold—en laugh — ter as he watched the lil - ly wilt. Said:
crown of thorns I'm wear - in' be-comes a string of lies. He
wanted him to notice where the soldiers drove the nails. And he
I don't trust no hon—ky with such a bush-y tailed hand. Man,

F C

Ba-by don't look now but there's a black man in this chair and it's a
struk me with his kiss — es when I told him that I care. It was a
filled the room with laugh — ter not a drop of blood was there, it was a
I bet you'd hug the dev-il if he put on kink-y hair. It was a

G7 F

hund — red mil — lion miles a - cross the tab-le that we
hund — red mil — lion miles a - cross the tab-le that we
hund — red mil — lion miles a - cross the tab-le that we
hund — red mil — lion miles a - cross the tab-le that we

C

share.
shared. He
shared. I
shared. He

5. I told him I was sorry,
And he burned me with a grin.
Said: It's time to watch the pink snake
Struggle with his skin.
An' I cursed the faceless army
That had come to put us there
With a hundred million miles
Across the table that we shared.

6. A black bird an' a white bird
An' a hundred million miles.
There's a riddle for the liberal
To wrestle for awhile.
Ya better go back to the cupboard
And pray it isn't bare,
'Cause it's a hundred million miles
Across the table that we share.

# WHAT AM I DOING HERE?

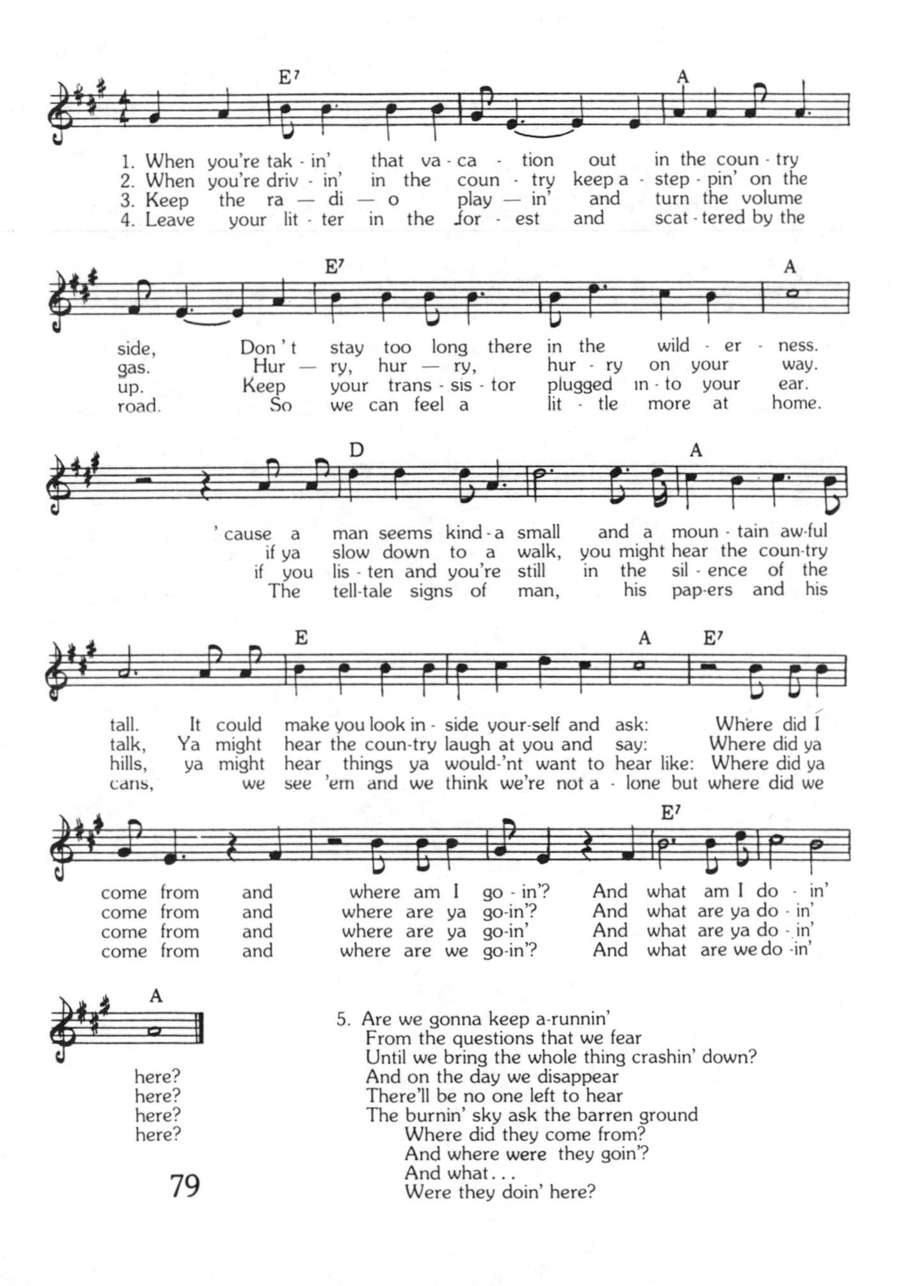


5. Are we gonna keep a-runnin'
From the questions that we fear
Until we bring the whole thing crashin' down?
And on the day we disappear
There'll be no one left to hear
The burnin' sky ask the barren ground
Where did they come from?
And where were they goin'?
And what. . .
Were they doin' here?

# WHO'S WAVIN'

A G E7
1. I ain't wav — in' babe, I'm drown - in'. go - in'
2. I ain't laugh-in' babe, I'm cry - in'. I'm cry-in',
3. This ain't sing-in' babe, its scream-in'. I'm scream-in'
4. I ain't wav - in' babe, I'm drown - in' go - in'
A E7 A
down in a cold lone — ly sea. I ain't wav — in'
oh why can't you see? I ain't fool — in'
that I'm gonna drown. And you're smil — in'
down right here in front of you. And you're wav — in'
D A E7
babe, I'm drown — in' so babe quit wav - in' at
babe, I ain't fool — in' so babe quit fool - in with
babe, and you're wavin - in', just like you don't hear a
babe, you keep wav - in', hey babe, are you drown-in'
A
me.
me.
sound.
too? Oh.

# DEMIAN'S MIRROR